THE RELICANT CHRONICLES, BOOK 2

TRAILS OF BONE

I0563147

AARON ROSENBERG

CRAZY 8 PRESS

Hibitiksu had enjoyed these last few days, riding with Diritan and Nioko and the others, camping with them at night, sharing the same stew and hardbread, passing around the same skins of rice wine, sleeping on the same ground. For that brief time, he had been able to lie to himself and pretend he was just another man, just another soldier.

Now that temporary escape was over. It was time for Hibikitsu, Emperor of Rimbaku, to return.

Dismounting and handing Shisi's reins to Diritan, he retreated to a nearby rock and, setting the bundle down upon that rough natural table, untied it. Within were deo and kazure, haidoto and hanketo and suneoto, karute and menatu and modato. Everything that declared him to be the ruler of this land.

And who was I while someone else wore this? he couldn't help wondering as he began removing the simple aiashe's gear he had grown accustomed to. *If this is all that is required to distinguish an emperor from a foot soldier, was the man who wore this at my behest truly the emperor for that time? Is it so easy to trade roles that a simple change in garb can suffice?*

He hoped that was not the case. His ancestry had entitled him to the throne but he liked to believe he was slowly proving himself worthy of sitting it, worthy of being responsible for this great nation and all its peoples.

Though, as he glanced back at his guards and at the little girl who sat before Diritan on his massive charger, clutching a simple rag doll in one hand and sucking the thumb of the other, Hibikitsu had to admit that he still had a long way to go in that regard.

Crazy 8 Press is an imprint of Clockworks

© 2025 by Aaron Rosenberg

Design by Aaron Rosenberg
Cover art by Lilly Repine
ISBN: 978-1-892544-28-5

To Jenifer, Adara, and Arthur—the greatest magic of all

Fyushu

KITINI

TABICHI

KORITO

IWIKARU

Yatamoro

TATSUMA

SHITIMI

YUNIGIRI

OBANARI

CHIBIRI

SARUTO

HOCHIRO

BEZENKAI

MINIRI

Higinasi

NARIYARI

RIMBAKU

Scale 10 Miles

CAST OF CHARACTERS

Kagiri: the older brother of Noniki. Also known as "Giri."

Noniki: the younger brother of Kagiri. Also known as "Niki."

Seikoku: a graverobber in Ginzai

Hibikitsu: the young emperor of Rimbaku. Descended from the First Emperor, Taido Segei.

Misataki Shizumi: a gunso (sergeant) in the Honjofu, Rimbaku's elite warriors

Chimehara: a young woman living and working in Awaihinshi.

Maniko Kohori: Taikoro (Lord Commander) of the Honteno, Hibikitsu's household guard.

Rilani: Empress of Fyushu

Yanatai Lai: Dogenriku (field marshal) of the Fyushan army

Ito Oicha: A Taisho (general) in the Fyushan army

Dendai En: Another Fyushan taisho

Taemon Ritei: Another Fyushan taisho

Aioi Kazuko: A Fyushan Issa (colonel or commander)

Zeryai Ninbaru: Karo (governor) of Korito

The Hakara Ikibanichi: Brothers of Many Spirits: an order of warrior-monks who don't follow the ways of aitachi

Brother Yamaki: the Hakara Ikibanichi most versed in healing

Brother Pilaru: another Hakara Ikibanichi, in charge of their crops

Brother Nagira: a female Hakara Ikibanichi, in charge of physical fitness

Brother Kalout: another Hakara Ikibanichi, in charge of education

Eldest Brother Taharo: the senior Hakara Ikibanichi

Kishin Narai: leader of a merchant cabal.

Shizu Yokori: Narai's second in the group.

Jiro Masute: Another member of the cabal.

Eien Kawatai: Another member of the cabal.

Fujiko Oritano: Final member of the cabal.

Joshi: Narai's man at arms, in charge of his guards.

Gento: the largest of Joshi's guards

Surito: Another guard

Shisino sukudo: Hikibitsu's horse, "Speed of Thought." Nicknamed Shisi.

Diritan: a Honjofu

Nioko: another Honjofu

Anitu: Formerly Tagami Anitu, one of the emperor's Dojo Kuge

Hintaro: a grocer in Ginzei, friends with Seikoku

The Jogoturi: "Lords of the Street," a gang in Ginzai

Master Eijiri: a wealthy merchant, minor noble, and the head of house Chohu, a merchant house specializing in gems

Master Nagoi: a young trader with House Chohu

Yuni: a cleaning lady in House Chohu

Ritaru: another cleaning lady in House Chohu

Madam Ponsoi: the senior housekeeper of House Chohu

Mistress Oisare: a trader for House Chohu

Mistress Limini: another trader for House Chohu, in charge of the counting rooms

Master Ganyeki: another trader for House Chohu, in charge of grading pearls

Lin: a villager in Hiromura, one of the town elders, a net-mender and occasional tailor by trade

Ganai: another villager in Hiromura, one of the town elders, an herbalist and healer

Kaemusei: the Silent Change, an inhuman being comprised of magic and hunger

Ibaru and Iraku: two brothers, Untouched, the hands of the Silent Change

Rai: a villager of Hiromura, a fisherman, burly and crude

Daro Barindo: a thug and bully in Nariyari, one of the southern provinces. He has assembled a gang, the Kindichi ("kings" or "bosses").

Tatsui Tsuri: Daro Barindo's partner
Akino: a Honjofu, one of Shizumi's most trusted men
Geniji: Another Honjofu, Shizumi's self-appointed bodyguard when
    in the field
Dairamu: Another Honjofu
Isano: Another Honjofu
Masai: Another Honjofu
Nori: Another Honjofu
Reiko: Another Honjofu
Shirikin: "Forest King," a Robin Hood-type highway bandit who
    lives in the forests of Yunigiri
Riniki Yamoi: a noble and local lord in Yunigiri
Arata: an aiashe stationed as a guard along the eastern edge of
    Hochiro, bordering Yatamaro
Goro: Arata's fellow guard
Kazuo: another guard
Seiji: Another guard
Haru: a potter in Awaihinshi
Lady Shimoda: a noblewoman in Ginzai
Yanagida: Lady Shimoda's majordomo
Uemada: A farmer woman in a small village
Enatsu: Uemada's husband
Kome: Uemada and Enatsu's little girl
Futomo: a thug
Iha: Futomo's partner-in-crime
Murata: Futomo and Iha's muscle
Asa: Futomo and Iha's eyes and ears
Togo: a man in the village of Rakawa
Unori: a man in the village of Rakawa
Fujibuki Haro: Taikoro of the Honjofu. House crest: an otter wrapped
    around the sun
Ijichi: a convoy guard
Konami: a convoy guard captain
Jatira: another convoy guard
Ogura: a weaver who travels with the caravan
Coda Anjiro: one of the ruling nobles of Ginzai

Morihai Sugano: the governor of Ginzai

Jitu Kanai: a potter in Ginzai

Taki: the proprietor of the Happoa Kappua (Foamy Cup) tavern in Ginzai

Zeryai Yukiri: wife of Zeryai Ninbaru, the governor of Korito

Andou Hanuri: a trader of House Chohu

Suda: a young girl in Suranmui

Itamon: a chuisu (lieutenant) in the Honteno

Matsu: a servant in Aihiri

Amani Denbi: most senior of Hibikitsu's Imperial councilors, the Rojiri. House crest: star and crescent moon

Etsuya Kenshin: most belligerent of the Rojiri. House crest: a thundercloud, in blue and gray

Sunao Tadazi: a Rojiri who is also Dogenriku, Lord General of the armies. House crest: a black bear.

Watane Yatahei: a Rojiri who is also Dogenkaishu, Lord Admiral of the navies. House crest: an emerald wave. Madam Ushi: a weaver from the town of Enwara

Ieyuki Nagao: Another Rojiri. House crest: a golden swallow

Kuma: a washer-woman from Shakomi

Chisigi: a fisherman from near Shakomi

Isoko: an herbalist from Hochiro

Isoro: Isoko's daughter, a beginning herbalist

Sanedi: a basketeaver

Yori: a farmer

Sukame and Minawa: an old married couple

Mother Utu: the oldest person in the village of Kagiri and Noni-ki's birth

Daishin Nishoji: a taisho in the Rimbaku army

Uchimasa and Enomoto: a couple in Birabiro

Mizono: Uchimasa and Enomoto's son, who lives in Chinbiro with his wife Tamura and their daughter Mori

Reizei: one of the Honteno

Itami Kane: a Honjofu

Nobu and Uba: a husband and wife and the leaders of the town of Watamoto

The Bone Collectors: a group of Buddhist-like traveling priests who wear the skulls and bones of their revered teachers dangling from their belts

Geido Shinen: one of the legendary Gensaiba matekan (wizards' warriors)

Shito Kibi: another of the legendary Gensaiba matekan

Onyoku Jeizen: another of the legendary Gensaiba matekan

Bushiki Kenin: another of the legendary Gensaiba matekan

Komu Setsui: another of the legendary Gensaiba matekan

Nikiyu Sinchu: another of the legendary Gensaiba matekan

PROLOGUE

"Pah, does this thrice-damned hellhole not even know how to rain properly?" Ito Oicha complained as he stepped inside the sturdy village hall, tossing back the hood of his armor-plated cloak and sweeping droplets from his shoulders with quick, angry gestures. "My grandson's spit is stronger than this, and he is barely beyond a crawl!"

The others assembled at the far end of the building's single room laughed. "No doubt, o noble Taisho," one of the women there called out, "even the skies here know better than to attack you!"

"Or they are afraid to compete with his famous scowl," the man beside her added, to more merriment.

The barrel-chested general was indeed scowling as he stomped over to join them. "Yes, yes, you are all in high spirits," he retorted, "and why not? What do you know of true hardship, of deprivation, of sacrifice? Not one of you is even as old as my boots!" Those were indeed well-aged and weathered, but still as sturdy as their owner, as was the rest of his battle gear.

"Enough," the tall, broad-shouldered woman at the head of the table declared, and with that single word they all fell silent. Yanatai Lai was the dogenriku of Fyushu, the field marshal of all their armies. She was a fearsome warrior in her own right, but even moreso a talented commander, and her swift and decisive battle strategies had won many victories for their empress and several rapid promotions for Lai herself, until she had been appointed to her current rank despite barely having strands of gray poking through the black of her close-cropped hair. A tough, sometimes even harsh, but fair leader, she expected and received absolute and instant obedience from everyone who served under her, from the highest to the lowest. The fact that she had chosen to command this tadao herself spoke of the invasion's importance for their nation and its ruler.

Oicha bowed, but Lai waved it away. Clearly she was not in fact angry—if she had been, they all would have known it by now—but merely impatient. "How fares the village?" she asked instead.

"Solidly ours," the aging general replied. "The villagers all are rounded up—we have them under guard in several homes, awaiting your orders." He frowned through his thick, graying mustache. "Few of them even attempted to put up a fight." They had taken the village, the closest to the Fyushan-Rimbakan border, at first light, their scouts removing the handful of able-bodied warriors set to patrol it and their soldiers sweeping in to gather up the rest of the villagers, who were mostly shepherds, gatherers, and crafters.

The woman who had taunted him, a fellow taisho named Dendai En, laughed and shook her head, causing her long, black braid to whip about. "These people are sheep!" she cried out. "How have they stood against us for so long, if this is the extent of their resistance?" Her sharp gaze turned to another man at the table, a young, slim fellow whose breastplate and shoulderplates bore the insignia of an issa, and he reddened.

"With permission," the young commander replied, bowing, "though the commoners here are wise enough not to oppose an invading army, do not mistake that for the attitude or martial strength of the nation as a whole. Rimbaku may be failing, but its aiashe are as formidable as ever. And its Honjofu are demons in battle." As the commander of the force that had been tasked with raiding across the border into Rimbaku for the past year, Aioi Kazuko was the closest the Fyushans had to an expert on the rival nation, and Lai and Oicha both nodded, treating his words with due consideration. En and the other taisho, Taemon Ritei, both scoffed, however.

"You would say that," Ritei jeered. "After being beaten by

one of them!" Kazuko bowed again but gave no other reply. His report had already contained the details of the recent Honjofu counter to their raids, and his own defeat at the hands of the squad's leader, Misataki Shizumi. Though, given her reputation as perhaps the finest warrior in all Rimbaku, that was hardly to be seen as a stain upon Kazuko's reputation or prowess. At least, not by most.

Lai was mocking as well, but not of him. "'Foot bone,'" she said with a dismissive laugh. "'Bone warrior.' These Rimbakans are so obsessed with their bones! It is all they care about!"

"It is all they have left," Ritei added. He banged a mailed fist down upon the table they had gathered around. "And that makes them weak!"

"Perhaps," Lai agreed, though her tone and demeanor were more contemplative than gloating. "But nonetheless, we will treat them as we would any serious foe. We cannot risk losing this battle by underestimating them." The others nodded, though Oicha could tell his fellow generals thought such caution was unnecessary.

He sighed. He had served in the army all his life, clawing his way up from a common foot soldier to a junior officer and then through the ranks as much by dint of longevity as anything else, and he often despaired of his peers and their brash, arrogant ways. Lai he respected, and Kazuko he considered capable, but many of the others—including En and Ritei—had never been forced to manage a years-long campaign, had never laid siege or been forced to break one. They knew nothing of the slog that often accompanied war, only the quick victory of raids and short incursions. Why, both of them wore armor without a single scratch or dent, its lacquered surface still unmarred—had they ever even seen real battle? Without Lai here to keep them in line, he knew they would have already marched on, overreaching themselves and overextending their forces in the hopes of a decisive early conquest.

But that was not how war worked.

A soldier entered the room, dropping to one knee, head bowed, hands clasped and raised before him. "Speak," Lai commanded, and the soldier rose, though he remained where he was, his raised voice carrying across the room.

"An emissary, honored dogenriku," he called out. "Come to sue for peace."

En and Ritei sneered, and Lai's lips twisted as well, but none of that was evident in her tone as she ordered, "Show them in."

The soldier bowed, then ducked back through the door. An instant later, a different man entered in his place. It was obvious at once that this newcomer was not part of their forces. He wore formal robes and the small, flat cap of a bureaucrat instead of armor, and the sword at his side had a handsome scabbard, its lacquer perfectly glossed as if even the intermittent rain did not dare mar its sheen. If the man had ever drawn that blade except for ceremony, Oicha would have been shocked into immobility.

The stranger advanced across the room, stopping beside the table and executing a short bow. It was the gesture of an equal or even a superior, barely more than a nod of the head and a slight incline of the shoulders. He was not young but not yet old, his face rounded by prosperity, his hair pulled back in a short, ornate braid, his whiskers neatly trimmed and frosted at their tips. Clearly he was not of this village, for all the residents Oicha had seen here had worn rough-woven hemp and cotton, not brocade and embroidery. "Who leads here?" the man demanded, his eyes sweeping the five of them.

"I do," Lai replied, tipping her own head a fraction. "I am Yanatai Lai, dogenriku of Fyushu."

"Zeryai Ninbaru," the stranger replied, his eyes widening slightly at either her name or her rank but his bearing remaining arrogant despite that. "I am karo of Korito, and you have unlawfully crossed our border, violating the ages-old treaty between our two nations. I must insist that you withdraw your forces at once."

Lai frowned, studying him a second. Then she laughed. "No, I don't think so," she said. "We went to enough trouble marching through the hills to get here, I don't feel like picking up and

going back just yet." En and Ritei both chuckled, and even Oicha
allowed himself a grim smile at his commander's dark humor.

Ninbaru was not fazed by their ridicule. "I insist!" the regional
governor repeated, his hand falling to his sword pommel. Oicha
instinctively reached for his own weapon, as did Kazuko, but a
quick flick of Lai's fingers made him pause. "You cannot be here!"
their visitor was saying. "You risk all-out war!"

"Risk?" Lai rounded the table, stalking toward him like a
great hunting cat, all glittering eyes and sharp teeth and deadly
grace. "It is no risk," she informed him, stopping with only a few
feet separating her from the man. "It is our intent. We have come
to invade your precious Rimbaku, you pompous little man, and
we will not leave until this entire crumbling kingdom has bent its
knee to Rilani, Empress of All She Surveys!"

Their visitor gaped at her. "You are mad!" he cried, his face
going flush then pale. "I will—" Now he did reach for his blade,
but if he had ever been a warrior it had been long ago and he had
forgotten all his previous skill. Before he could bare even an inch
of steel Lai had lashed out, her own nihono still snug in its sheath
but her yori-toki in her hand, and the thick dagger blade flashed
in the dim lantern light as it carved an arc through the air—and
through the Rimbakan official's throat. Ninbaru gasped and
stumbled back, both hands going to the gaping wound in his neck,
the blood there spurting out to coat his fingers and palms as he
dropped to his knees and then pitched sideways into a twitching
heap upon the ricemat-covered floor. The Fyushan field marshal
gazed down impassively, waiting for the last movements to cease
before kneeling and wiping her blade upon his exquisitely patterned silk sleeve.

"See that the body is burned," she ordered, rising once more
and sheathing her weapon. "Send the bones to their emperor at
Awaihinshi, with my compliments." The smile that touched her
lips was as bloodless and cold as the body by her feet. "That is all
they care about, after all."

She turned back to the table and its maps, and her officers
gathered around her as they once more contemplated this strange

kingdom they had entered—and began making plans for how they would bring it to its knees. Ito Oicha could not help a last glance back at the dead governor behind them, and wondered if perhaps his younger counterparts were not correct after all. If this was truly the best Rimbaku had to offer, the nation was as good as theirs.

CHAPTER ONE

"A good morn to you, Noniki!" the sun-browned man in simple, sturdy clothes called out as Noniki stepped from the short dirt path and onto the richer, darker soil of the fields. "May you know the warmth of brotherhood!"

"And to you, Brother Pilaru," Noniki replied, raising a hand in greeting as he threaded his way through the waist-high rows of plants. "May your spirit rejoice in the kindred of others."

The monk smiled at that, his expression as sunny as the cloudless sky overhead, and leaned upon his hoe, waiting for the younger man to reach him. "You are very nearly one of us," he stated when Noniki finally stopped beside him. "Perhaps it is time to do something about this, eh?" One weathered hand reached out to tug at Noniki's bangs.

With a laugh, Noniki swatted him away. "I'm not quite prepared to go bald yet, thank you," he replied, indicating the monk's shaved pate. "Besides, there's little chance I could wear it as well as you do."

Brother Pilaru grinned, taking the compliment with only the slightest roll of his eyes, but let the subject drop. Instead he gestured toward a large basket just behind him. "This is ready for the kitchens. Careful, it will not be light."

"That's all right." Noniki sidled past the gardener and grasped the sturdy handles woven into the basket's frame. "I can handle it." He heaved—and the basket refused to budge.

"Are you sure?" Though the kindly monk did not laugh outright, his amusement was all too evident in the crinkling around his eyes, and in his voice.

"Yes, thank you." Noniki gritted his teeth, bent his knees, and heaved again. The basket rose a few inches before thumping back down to the ground with a decisive thud. Sweat had broken out across his forehead, and he saw the monk's expression change from amusement to concern. "I am fine," he promised, waving the other man back before he could offer to help. "Truly." This time he crouched lower, using his legs to do most of the work, and managed to hoist the basket up onto his thighs. That allowed him enough time to slide his hands underneath, cradling the basket in his arms like a newborn babe, and when he straightened he had it nestled securely against his chest. "See?" he said, ignoring the way he was gasping and puffing like a bellows. "I have this."

Brother Pilaru watched him closely a second before finally granting him a short nod. "Straight to the kitchens, then," he warned. "Do not dawdle, or your strength may desert you."

"Understood." Noniki grinned at the monk over the basket, which was filled with tubers and peppers and onions and other vegetables. "Have a good day, Brother Pilaru."

"And you, Noniki." The old monk's smile was warm again as he turned back to his tasks and Noniki focused on carrying the basket inside before he collapsed under its weight.

It had been a week since he had recovered from his fever enough to move about the monastery. A week since he had begun learning more about his hosts, the Hakara Ikibanichi, the Brothers of Many Spirits. A week since he had started taking on small chores here and there, both to repay their kindness in taking him in and to rebuild his strength. And he was getting stronger every day, whatever his struggles to carry produce might suggest. Soon he would be back to full health, Brother Yamaki judged.

The only question was, what would he do then?

Noniki knew that the Brothers hoped he would stay and become one of them, taking vows and fully joining their order. And it was tempting. They were a kindly lot, dedicated to living in harmony not just with the world around them but with its inhabitants; healing those in need, bringing food to those who had none, and educating those who had the time and inclination to learn. The Brothers cared nothing about who he had been before, what he had done, what he had lost. All they cared about was a good heart and the willingness to work together.

And the decision to cast aside the Relicant Way, ignoring the call of the ancestral bones in favor of forming bonds with the living.

That was the strongest temptation of all. The Relicant Way had brought nothing but grief for Noniki, after all. It had cost him his brother Kagiri, his best friend and only remaining relative. It had left him with no place in this world, no hope, no chance. Why not cast it aside?

Except that, sometimes, Noniki remembered what it had been like, using his aitachi to absorb the strength from those bones. As when he and Kagiri had faced down those bandits, the Kindichi. How, upon swallowing those tiny chips and flakes, he had felt power seeping into him, and strength, and knowledge. How his stance had changed, his posture, his grip on the borrowed blade. It had been like something had entered and moved through him, taking control of his limbs, settling them into a new and better position. It had made him more than himself.

And, when it had faded, he had felt empty and alone. And weak. Who was he, without the bones? What was he good for? He had no skills of his own, no knowledge. None of them did. That was the Relicant Way, to draw upon the strengths of their ancestors, rather than taking the time and making the effort to build new strengths of their own.

He had thought that was enough. Everyone had. This was Rimbaku, after all. The Relicant Empire. But after losing Kagiri, he had to wonder. Was it really?

The Brothers did not think so. They had rejected that altogether, in favor of living their lives themselves. And, though it was not easy by any stretch, there was still something to be said for that, for relying upon yourself and your companions rather than on some ancient ancestor.

His musings had distracted him from his burden, and Noniki started when the ground beneath his feet shifted from hard-packed dirt to smooth, worn flagstone. He had retraced his steps down the path and was now back in the Ikibanichari, the Castle of

Many Spirits. As always, the monastery's walls left him stunned by twinned feelings of awe and horror, for the bones mortared within them could have been worth a fortune but now rendered useless, impossible to extract and draw upon. Still, the twisted grandeur of those walls, and of the monastery in general, was easily offset by the warmth of the people who lived here, as evidenced by the warm smile gracing the face of the monk now approaching him.

"Noniki! Let me help you with that!" Brother Nagira insisted, reaching out and grasping one handle in a large, capable hand. Noniki knew better than to argue, and merely dipped his head in thanks, clutching the other handle and then sliding to the side, letting the basket sink down so that it could be carried more easily between them. "How are you feeling?" Nagira asked, studying him with a keen eye. "You look flushed."

"I am fine, just a little winded," he replied. He knew better than to lie to her—Brother Nagira was in charge of the monks' physical fitness and kept nearly as close an eye on his health as Brother Yamaki, their chief healer and the monk in charge of Noniki's recovery. "Truly."

She assessed him a second longer, then grunted and nodded down the hall. They set off toward the kitchen together. Nagira was easily as tall as Noniki, and as broad-shouldered, but her arms were thick with muscle and she hefted her half of the burden easily, whereas he found himself using both hands and huffing to keep pace. Perhaps he was not fully recovered yet, after all.

When Yamaki had first introduced them, Noniki had thought it strange to find a woman among the Brothers. She had not taken offense. "It is not what is between your legs that matters," she had told him then, "but what comes from your heart. Brotherhood is the appreciation of kindred spirits, and any who can find that within themselves are welcome." Since then Noniki had met several other female monks, and it was true that they were treated exactly the same as everyone else. That was one of many things he liked about the Brothers—they truly accepted anyone and everyone who came to them with an open heart. And cared for anyone who came to them seeking aid.

They had just reached the kitchens and set the basket down upon one of the many sturdy wood tables there when another monk, Brother Kalout, burst into the room. "Ah, there you are!" she declared upon seeing Noniki. "Brother Yamaki needs your help! Hurry!"

Hearing the urgency in her voice, Noniki nodded his thanks to Nagira and then took off at a trot. He still got lost in parts of the monastery, thanks to its sprawling nature and winding halls, but the route from the kitchens back up to the meditation rooms— which were also used for healing—was one he had mastered early on, and he was able to hurry along that path, the soles of his sandals slapping against the stones, without conscious thought. If Yamaki had summoned him, it could only mean one thing— someone had come seeking healing, and for whatever reason the fierce but kindly monk could not handle them on his own. More and more he had been using Noniki's assistance to fetch supplies, clean wounds, and hold patients still while he tended them, but this sounded more urgent than a simple scrape or break. Noniki pushed himself to move more quickly.

Climbing the stairs, Noniki finally reached the door to the meditation room and pushed it open. Sure enough, Yamaki was there, struggling to hold a large man still as the stranger thrashed against him. "Quickly!" the monk snapped, glancing back toward him. "Grab his other arm!"

Rushing over, Noniki did as instructed, wrapping both of his arms around the patient's one. Bones! His arm was thicker than Noniki's leg! The man stood easily a head above than him, higher even than Yamaki, who was the tallest of the Brothers, and his shoulders were broader than Nagira's by half again as much. This was not a man; it was an ox in human form! The heavy brow and thick, matted hair complemented that assessment, as did the man's rough, hairy flesh. Flesh that was searingly hot and slick with sweat, Noniki realized. This man was in the grips of a heavy fever, much as Noniki had been when the monks had first found him staggering about the countryside, half out of his mind with grief, pain, and deprivation.

"We need to get him cooled down," Yamaki stated, and even as he spoke two more monks hurried in, carrying a large iron-bound wooden bucket—actually half a barrel, Noniki saw, nearly large enough to serve as a tub—between them. Water sloshed onto the floor as they approached, then slowed. "Dowse him!" Yamaki ordered, sparing Noniki only a glance and a half shrug as he gave that command. The two monks did as instructed, heaving the heavy bucket toward the three of them, and the bulk of the water did indeed splash full against the stranger's head and chest, though enough spilled over to soak Noniki as well. He sputtered, then clamped his mouth shut to keep his teeth from chattering. Bones, that was cold!

If they'd hoped that the sudden chill would soothe their feverish patient, they were quickly disappointed. Instead he roared, an incoherent bellow of rage, pain, and surprise all mingled into one, and with a mighty heavy he yanked both arms free. Then he lunged forward and grabbed the bucket from the monks, who both yelped and pulled back. Now the big man was holding the heavy wooden implement, gasping and panting, glaring all about him with deep-set eyes barely visible beneath the thick, wet tangle of hair plastered to his face.

"Calm down," Yamaki urged. "We are only trying to help."

The monk's voice was soothing but his words drew the patient's attention, and the big man rounded on him. It was clear the fever had addled his brain, and the cold water had only registered as some form of attack. Which was why he now raised that heavy bucket like a boulder and loomed over Yamaki as if to smash the monk into the ground.

Noniki reacted without thought. He only knew that he could not let the healer monk get hurt. He owed the man—and all the Brothers—far too much. So he hurled himself forward, shoving Yamaki to the side just as the big man brought that bucket crashing down—directly onto Noniki's head, neck, and shoulders.

Pain burst about Noniki like the sun rising at dawn, radiating through him in an instant. He crumpled to the ground amid shards of wood, twisted bits of iron, and puddles of water, numb enough that the impact against hard stone went unnoticed. Nearby, he could hear Yamaki shouting, now joined by what sounded like Nagira and a few others, but he could not make out their words. Everything was dissolving into a red haze of agony that ate away at his thoughts, reducing them to scattered impressions and half-formed impulses.

Bones, he thought as he felt everything slipping away. *And the day had started out so well, too.*

CHAPTER TWO

"We will stop here," Kagiri declared, tapping his knees against his horse's sides. It halted at once, so quickly a lesser rider might have been thrown forward. That had not been petulance on the beast's part, though, Kagiri knew, or a mean-spirited attempt to throw him. It had merely learned, in the past week, to obey his commands the instant they were given. It was a good steed, and he tended to its needs personally, grooming it carefully and making sure it was well fed and watered. A horse was like any weapon—it worked best when it was cared for properly.

All around him, the merchants milled, slowing to a stop as well, as did Joshi and his guards. "Here? Why?" Shizu Yokori demanded. Ever with the sharp tongue, that one. "There's still an hour or more to the day, and we have a long way to travel. Or are you tired?" That last came out with a sneer, but her eyes were wider than usual. She was testing her boundaries with him.

None of the others spoke, all waiting to see how he responded to this latest petty rebellion.

"It is a good spot," he replied, ignoring her tone and keeping his own level, his voice calm and quiet, barely above a whisper. "Level, with enough space for us all and the horses. The rocks there provide cover at our backs, and the stream offers both fresh water and a barrier to that side, meaning we will only need to patrol the two remaining sides against intruders." He swung down from the saddle, keeping one hand on the saddlehorn but the other dropping to the handle of his nihono as he turned to Joshi. "Set up the camp and gather firewood and water."

The guard captain scowled, but then that was his natural expression. Finally he nodded and barked orders to Gento and the others, who scurried into motion.

It did not escape Kagiri's notice that, this time, Joshi had not glanced at Kishin Narai for permission, even though the lead merchant was still at least nominally his employer. Good. The guard was beginning to accept the new hierarchy.

Kagiri did look at Narai, who was studying him closely, as was his wont. But after a moment the broad-faced merchant nodded and dismounted. "We will do as you think best," he agreed, his voice as calm as ever.

Of course you will, Kagiri thought. *You have no other choice.*

That night, as Kagiri patrolled with the guards, Kishin Narai and his fellows sat around the fire that had been placed up against the rocks, tea and mulled wine steaming from the delicately glazed cups they each held cradled in their beringed hands. "What shall we do about him?" Shizu Yokori demanded, the fire tossing out dark shadows that leant her already-narrow features an even more vulpine cast, transforming her into a skeletal demon with angry, glowing eyes. "If I have to take orders from that peasant one more time, I'll…"

"You will what?" Eien Kawatai replied, his long, beaked nose casting a prodigious shadow that swallowed his feet and much of his lower body like an inky cloak. "Challenge him to a duel? That 'peasant,' as you call him, is Gensaiba. He would eat you alive! And then all the rest of us, too, including the guards, without even a pause for breath." As was often the case, Narai wondered about his companion then. Kawatai was a surprisingly successful merchant, given how dim-witted he seemed, but at times like this that fogginess seemed more an act than a reality. But then the other man giggled, his close-set eyes nearly crossing, and Narai frowned and told himself he was only imagining things. Again.

Still, what Kawatai had said certainly rang true, and they all knew it. Kagiri might have begun this expedition as nothing more than the poor boy they had brought along to fetch and carry and absorb aishone on their behalf. They had wanted him to enter the Tawasiri for them and loot the fabled Tower of Ghosts, retrieving the ancient and powerful bones said to litter the ancient citadel and then using those in their service. Instead he had emerged having absorbed all the aishone within—which had long since crumbled to dust from centuries of neglect, and which he had breathed in while he had been trapped inside—and had evidently taken on the skills of the legendary "Living Blades" as a permanent feature. Now he was a warrior beyond compare, capable of defeating an entire squad singlehanded.

Which meant he was truly more dangerous than all the rest of them combined.

That changed the equation somewhat, but did not completely negate it.

"Look here," Fujiko Oritano declared, gesturing with one thickset hand even as the other raised her cup to her lips. She gulped at her wine, then lowered the cup, wiping her mouth on the back of her hand. Of them all, she was perhaps the least polished, but that often meant she was more direct as well, a trait Narai sometimes found refreshing after the constant dissembling and vagaries of others in their profession. "We always intended to use the boy—and his brother, come to that—as weapons, yes?"

The others nodded. They had wanted to pit the brothers against the might of Awaihinshi, using the Tawasiri's fabled aishone to carve a path through the capital and its guards and to the emperor himself. After all, why should a spoiled, pampered young man like Hibikitsu rule just because his ancestors had? They would do a far better job overseeing the empire than he ever could!

"And a weapon is what we have gained," Oritano continued, her usually cheerful features surprisingly grim. "Nothing has changed."

To her side, Jiro Masute exploded. "Everything has changed!" he insisted, flinging that long, lustrous hair of his back out of his face and clenching his cup so tightly Narai worried it too might burst. "We brought him to fight for us, to serve us! Now he is telling us what to do! We have become the servants, not the masters!"

The others all murmured their agreement, and their

displeasure. It had escaped no one's notice that, the longer they traveled away from Tawasiri, the more Kagiri had begun to exert control. It was he who determined when they mounted up in the morning, he who called for a break in the afternoon, and he who determined when and where they should stop each evening. He had also begun to dictate which guards would take what shifts, and to patrol with them. The other morning Narai had caught the young man checking over Gento's weapons and lecturing the massive guard on how to properly maintain his sword and armor. And, despite the disparity in their sizes, Gento had accepted the rebuke without a single protest, and had immediately gone off to gather whetstone, oil, and rag, and clean and sharpen his blade.

Still, Narai did not see things as negatively as it appeared his partners did. "The boy is learning to assert himself, yes," he agreed, pitching his voice deliberately to smother some of Masute's fire and blunt Yokori's edge. "And, in matters martial and strategic, I feel it best to acquiesce. We are not warriors, after all. Why not let him tell us the best place to camp? We should make use of his newfound knowledge, should we not? If we fail to listen to his advice in such matters, why did we go to such lengths to ensure that he received it?" The others nodded. "But he is still a babe in the woods," he continued. "Take him off the battlefield and into the counting house or the courtroom and what does he know?" He paused, inviting comment, and the others did not fail to leap into that gap.

"Nothing," Oritano offered.

"Less than nothing," Masute agreed.

"They would eat him alive!" Yokori added, her eyes glittering with delight at the prospect.

Narai favored them all with his most genial smile. "Precisely. Kagiri needs us—and he knows it. He is capable in battle, yes, more than capable. Exactly as we planned. But he knows nothing of the world, nothing of commerce and trade and negotiation, nothing of diplomacy, nothing of leadership. That is where we come in."

"As what, his advisors?" Kawatai demanded. Of them all, he

seemed the least placated by Narai's words. "We could have had that with Hibikitsu! We chose this path because we wanted more!"

"And more we shall have," Narai assured him, speaking to them all. He stroked the cup in his hands, enjoying the faint, lingering warmth within it. "Servants to an emperor can only rise so high, for he will always be of the nobler blood and therefore beyond our reach. Advisors to a warrior, however—especially one common-born—can be equals. And more. The true power behind it all. He is the sword and the spear, but we are the brains and the wit."

"Only if he does as we say," Oritano said with a sniff, but by her tone she sounded at least partially mollified. For now.

"We simply need to find better ways to exert control," Narai pointed out. "Subtler ones, perhaps. He is a warrior now and will react to open challenges with his own show of force. But between us we have a great many years' experience at manipulating others to do as we wish. Let us put that to good use."

Masute twisted about to glance off toward the road, where Kagiri was barely visible stalking the border of their camp with the guard Surito at his side. Masute's sharp eyes could no doubt pick out both men's features, though they were a mere smudge in the night to Narai. "He and his brother were stunned by the silver we offered them," Masute mused aloud. "Mere pocket change, yet they acted as if it was treasures untold."

"They grew up poor and were worked ragged by that wretched tavernkeeper," Oritano reminded him. "To them, a handful of silver is practically a king's ransom."

Narai could see the way his companion's thoughts were wending. "You are suggesting we control him with wealth?" he stated, freeing one hand from the cup to stroke his chin. "Yes, that might work."

"We have more experience with money," Yokori agreed. "He knows that. It would only make sense to let us oversee any wealth he gains and guide him in its use."

The others nodded. They were merchants, after all. Money and goods were their stock in trade. And whole villages, cities, even regions could be controlled through such things—why not one headstrong young man, no matter how skilled at arms?

"Very well," Narai stated. "We will try that method of control on him and see how we fare."

"We must be ready, however," Kawatai cautioned, "to consider other options should it fail. More drastic ones, if necessary." In the shadows, his normally foolish face seemed stern and even threatening. Until he giggled again.

Still, his point was well made. "We will do what we must," Narai agreed, speaking for the group as he often did. "This way first, and if not this, another, until we find a method that works." His fingers squeezed the cup and he raised it to down the last of his wine, letting the warmth and spices slide down his throat. They had indeed come too far, risked too much, to bend the knee to some boy from the paddy fields. They would not cede control without a fight, and while Kagiri might now be a master with nihono and spear, they had weapons of their own to employ, ones against which he would be defenseless.

That thought warmed Narai more than the wine ever could.

CHAPTER THREE

Hibikitsu, the Echo of Victory, Emperor of all Rimbaku, spat some sort of small flying insect from between his teeth. Several strands of hair had pulled loose from his chonmage and kept whipping into his face, forcing him to toss his head frequently to clear his vision. He freed one gauntleted hand from his reins to reach up and—carefully, mindful of the thick yet supple leather coating each finger and the sturdy metal plates overlapping across their backs—wipe hair, bugs, grass, and dust from his eyes.

He was having the time of his life.

Oh, he had taken riding lessons since before he could walk. He and his horse, Shisino Sukudo—"Speed of thought," which was an audacious and boastful name for a beast but certainly fit the glossy black stallion—had spent many years training together and moved as one. But that had been entirely within Aihiri, the white marble walls of the Imperial compound rearing high all around like planed cliffs, smooth and unyielding and blocking all but the sky and the birds from entry. He had taken tours of Atsani a few times, and Motohiri once or twice, but that was as low as he had ever been within Awaihinshi. This trek toward distant Korito marked the first time he had ever passed through the lower levels of his own capital, much less set foot beyond its walls. In fact, he suspected it was the first time in living memory any member of the Imperial family, much less the emperor himself, had traveled beyond the borders of the City of Polished Light. He vaguely remembered, from history lessons as a child, that there had been some sort of Imperial summer palace somewhere along a lake, and that his great-grandparents or such had transferred the entire court there during the warmer weather, taking advantage of the cool breezes emanating off the waters. That had been long ago, however. He wondered if that place even still stood.

For now, he was enjoying the freedom of riding out in the countryside, of Shisi's flanks against his legs, of the wind in his face, bugs and all. He was surrounded by his Honjofu, of course, but for the moment he could pretend that he was merely one of them, another Bone Warrior riding to aid some village or protect some border or put down some bandit horde.

He could pretend that he was not the emperor but just a man like any other, armed with nihono and yori-toki, riding to battle. Not worrying about the fate of the empire, the disposition of his karo and daijin, his troops and ships, the welfare of his people. Not worrying about anything except himself, his horse, his gear, and the battle ahead.

Hibikitsu laughed and spit out another bug. Yes, this was the life!

They stopped for lunch at a small inn, his Honjofu entering first to clear out building, check that it was secured, and give instructions to the cook. By the time Hibikitsu dismounted, handing Shisi's reins to a waiting stableboy, the inn was empty save for his warriors, who stood at attention as he stalked past them. The inn was well-situated here beside the road and was a handsome, white-washed building with high, broad-beamed ceilings and large windows whose screens had been pushed up to allow in the light of such a pleasant day. The floor was not tayomi, which surprised him at first, nor was it tile; instead he found himself walking across planks of bamboo, worn smooth and glossy with age but well-maintained with only a few cracks here and there from bearing countless years of patrons tramping to and fro. It was a new experience, walking on a surface both harder than mats and more yielding than tile, and the young emperor found himself enjoying it. As he had almost everything thus far on this trip.

A single table had been left by the window, its one chair back to the wall so that the light would be pleasantly along his left side but not full in his face, with all the wide, open room's other furniture shoved to the sides. A pair of his warriors stood to either side of the chair, one a man of average height but imposing width, the other a slender woman with narrow features. They saluted, hands to chest, as he entered and slid between them, settling into the chair with a creak from both the aged wood and his own armor. Fortunately his mail had been constructed for riding and adapted well to sitting like this.

A servant hurriedly brought tea, pouring it with only the faintest tremor to his hands, and as Hibikitsu lifted the cup to his lips—it was very old and very delicate, he saw, the perfect pale milky green, with faint cracks around the rim indicating its age but its glaze still smooth and unbroken, no doubt a family heirloom—he allowed himself to relax and take in his surroundings. He imagined sitting here during the inn's normal course of business, surrounded by other patrons, men and women pausing in their day's work to sip tea and eat rice and fish and perhaps raise a cup of ale or tsekuri as well. He tried to picture what that must be like, to rub elbows with hunters and trappers and farmers and potters, to be jostled as they navigated the tight quarters between each table, to hear the steady hum of conversation all around. All his life he had eaten first with his parents and then by himself, in silence, with only servants and guards near but never close and never engaging him. They were there to see to his needs and his safety, not to interact.

His gaze wandered to his two current protectors and he swallowed the mouthful of tea, which was not as smooth as back in the palace but was refreshing, with an unusually hearty flavor and a darker color against the pale cup. "What is your name?" he asked, turning first toward the man and then to his companion. "Both of you?"

The man clasped hand over fist against his chest. "Diritan, your Majesty," he replied, and even though Hibikitsu could tell he was attempting restraint the warrior's voice boomed out across the room. If that embarrassed him, however, he gave no sign.

"Nioko, sire," the woman offered, matching her partner's salute but not his volume. Indeed, her voice was so soft Hibikitsu had to strain to make out the answer. He had heard both of those names recently, however, and after a second he recalled the circumstances.

"You were part of the shotao Misataki Shizumi took to Korito recently, to deal with the recent Fyushan raid," he stated, and was pleased to see the burly man flush slightly at the realization that his emperor knew who he was and where he had been stationed. But of course he did. They were *his* elite, after all.

"Hai, we were, sire," the warrior agreed after a moment. "Only just got back, in fact." Hibikitsu nodded. Of course Maniko Kohori would have sent them with him. They had already taken this route, had already faced Fyushu. They would know the area, the terrain, possibly even the leader of the opposing force. It was an advantage he would have been foolish to pass up, and the head of his household guard was far too canny to miss that. That was not what currently aroused his curiosity, however.

"What is she like?" he asked instead. "Your gunso?" He had reports, of course. According to her direct superior, Fujibuki Haro, Misataki Shizumi was "talented enough, for a commoner. Solid with a blade, follows orders well. I would not have promoted her to gunso, however, if I had not had a need to fill that position in a hurry. Still, she has yet to disappoint me."

Fortunately, Hibikitsu knew that the Lord Commander of his Honjofu was a pompous ass. The rumors he had heard around the Imperial compound told a different story—they painted this Misataki as a warrior's warrior, a demon with a blade, a gifted commander who inspired true loyalty in her unit. He was curious to hear what those who had served under her had to say.

The direct question clearly made at least the stocky man uncomfortable. "She is…a credit to your Honjofu, your Majesty," he answered finally, his face red. "She serves you without question. Her loyalty and dedication are without equal."

The emperor waved that off. "Yes, I am sure she is loyal," he replied drily, leaning back as the servant returned bearing a tray of food and began arranging dishes upon the table. "I am asking what she is *like*." He turned to the woman, Nioko. "I am not interested in platitudes," he warned. "Just the truth."

The warrior took a second to consider this. "Focused," she replied at last. "Fierce. Bold. But incredibly disciplined. And more willing to risk her own life than to waste those of her men." She bowed. "Your Majesty."

Some might have taken that almost as a rebuke—that a mere gunso would risk herself instead of her troops, implying that perhaps those above her, maybe even as high as the emperor himself, were less careful at husbanding lives. Hibikitsu chose to see it differently. Nothing in the woman's voice had indicated criticism, and on his other side Diritan was nodding agreement—surely he would have expressed dismay if he'd thought his companion was criticizing their emperor? An honest assessment of Misataki Shizumi, then, and an impressive one. He nodded his thanks and turned his attention toward his meal, filing that information away for a later date.

Much like the tea, the food proved to be simpler and heartier than he was used to but flavorful and well-prepared. If it lacked the ostentation of his usual meals, it made up for that in tasting fresh, for clearly the fish had been caught in the stream they had passed over to reach this inn, and the rice was not his usual uniform white but a mix of colors, shapes, and textures he found oddly refreshing. When he had eaten his fill, Hibikitsu indicated that the meal should be removed. He was beginning to rise when he heard a commotion outside.

Glancing through the window, he saw that people had gathered in a ragged line just beyond where his Honjofu stood, legs braced, arms cocked, hands on weapons, forming a human barricade around the inn. But these people did not carry weapons, that he could see, nor were they shouting or making threatening gestures. Instead they merely stood, waiting, several with their caps in their hands.

Ah.

"Shall we run them off, sire?" Diritan asked, frowning, and Hibikitsu could not tell whether that expression was directed at the crowd or at the question he had just posed. Regardless, he shook his head.

"No," he replied, standing and pulling his money pouch from his belt. "It is my sacred duty to see to the welfare of all my people. That includes giving alms to the poor." The Honjofu saluted, and perhaps it was Hibikitsu's imagination but it seemed this time the gesture was crisper somehow, as if in approval of his answer. But perhaps that was just him reading into it what he wished.

He exited the inn, idly hearing one of his men thanking the innkeeper and the clink of coins being laid upon a counter, and approached the people there. All of them were ragged indeed, their clothing worn though most were carefully clean, the fabric bearing that faded sheen of material that had been washed too often. "Behold, your emperor, Hibikitsu, Echo of Victory, ruler of all Rimbaku, may Fortune preserve him!" Diritan bellowed, his voice filling the entire courtyard and echoing from the surrounding trees, and the people bowed, several of them dropping to their knees. He had to resist the urge to shake his head to clear the ringing from his ears and resolved not to stand so close to the burly warrior next time he asked him to announce something.

"May Segei Genbinken, the First Emperor, preserve and protect you," Hibikitsu intoned as he reached the first person in line, an older woman whose face was deeply lined with wrinkles and furrows and whose back seemed permanently bowed, making her look like an old, gnarled tree brought to life. He placed a gold coin in her palm and wrapped her hands around it, feeling an unexpected pang as tears sprang to her filmy eyes. He repeated the process with each supplicant, and each one turned away, mouthing their thanks with lips barely able to form words around their shock and surprise, their eyes brimming with more gratitude than they could readily express.

When he reached the last of the line, however, Hibikitsu stopped. He frowned as he studied the man before him. He was of middle age, and looked to have been stout once, for his flesh hung from him in great folds, his face made up of loose jowls and shadowed eyes. His clothing was finer than that of the others, silk rather than cotton, with hints of thread where the cuffs had once borne embroidery, but it was all tattered now, and badly worn. His hair was pulled back in a loose tail, but something about the way it hung suggested it had once been kept in a different style. Perhaps a topknot? And the man's face… "I know you," the emperor stated. "Do I not?"

The man bowed deeply. "You did, your Majesty," he acknowledged, his voice as rough as his appearance and as haunted as his eyes. "Anitu, sire."

"Anitu? Tagami Anitu?" Now it was Hibikitsu's eyes that widened as he considered the man anew. "What happened to you?" This man had been one of his Dojo Kuge, the minor nobles who saw to the day-to-day administration of his empire! To see him in such a state was a severe shock!

Anitu bowed again. "No longer Tagami, sire," he answered, and his voice had that carefully blank quality of one who knows they must be sure their tone can give no possible offense. "That name was stripped from me, your Majesty, as punishment for my failures."

"Ah." Now Hibikitsu remembered, and it rocked him back on his heels, physically as well as metaphorically. Of course. He was the one who had taken the man's family name from him. Tagami Anitu had been tasked with making a report on the empire's finances, some months back, and it had been he who had revealed to the emperor that their great nation was nearly destitute. Hibikitsu had not taken the news well. He had blamed the Dojo Kuge, even though they did not have control over the treasury or the power to make crops grow or the ability to find new sources of revenue. And, as the man presenting this news, he had blamed Tagami Anitu most of all. Casting him out of the nobility had seemed a fair sign of his displeasure at the time, but now, with the man standing before him begging for coin, Hibikitsu felt a niggling of doubt.

"What has become of your family?" he asked, glancing about. He was sure the man had been married, with children.

"My wife returned to her family, sire," Anitu replied, bowing a third time. "The children went with her. They must bear the shame of my reduction, but at least they are well cared for." The emperor knew at once that that parting had been this man's decision, not theirs. He had sent them away, sacrificing any happiness his family might still have brought him, in order to protect them from the capricious punishment of a thoughtless and impulsive ruler.

Hibikitsu was horrified. What had he done, in a moment of pique? He had ruined a man's life, severed him from his family, and for what? Because he had not liked the news they had brought him, which they had only been faithfully conveying? What sort of man was he, to cause such wanton destruction without even realizing it?

His first impulse was to restore the man to his former title. But that would be difficult and would not change the original punishment—he would, if anything, be twice the outcast, for having been cast down and then just as summarily raised back up. What, then? How could he make it up to this man, after what he had done to him?

Taking the rest of his money pouch, Hibikitsu thrust it into the former noble's hands. "I know this cannot remedy the pain I have brought you," he whispered, forcing himself to meet Anitu's eyes, "but I hope it can, at least, ease some of your current suffering. I will think on some way to provide you with at least a position and income, enough so that your family can be with you once more."

"I—thank you, your Majesty!" Anitu fell to his knees, then, and pressed his forehead into the dirt there. "Your generosity knows no bounds!" He began to weep, and Hibikitsu found he could not stand to witness it any longer.

"Find the nearest town," he instructed Diritan after summoning the warrior to him with a flick of his wrist. "There must be an overseer position there, a governor, something we can grant him. If not, we will create one for him." The man nodded, saluted, and waved over one of the minor functionaries traveling with them. Of course, that made more sense—why would he send an elite warrior to handle such a task, when a junior administrative official was better suited?

That just drove home to Hibikitsu how little he knew about

the way the kingdom—his empire—truly worked. How could he, when he had lived his whole life sheltered deep within Aihiri, at the very peak of Awaihinshi? There was an entire land out here, an entire people, he knew nothing about!

Well, perhaps it was time for that to change.

He glanced around him. The Honjofu were nearby, all alert as always. Beyond them were a few functionaries, attendants and the like. Past them, camped along the road, was a chotao of aiashe— the foot soldiers had been preparing to march when they had been setting forth, and so had been conscripted to provide additional protection for their emperor.

Perfect.

He beckoned to Diritan again. "Find me an aiashe roughly my size," he ordered, and for a second he thought the warrior might refuse, or at least question. Instead he tightened his lips, saluted, and marched toward the waiting army. That give Hibikitsu time to think things over, to consider this sudden notion of his, in order to make sure it was not yet another of his foolish, impulsive whims. He found few faults with it, however, and by the time the warrior returned, a soldier tagging along behind like a chastened pup, he was fully resolved.

Yes, he decided, studying Diritan's choice. This man would do nicely. "Strip off your armor," Hibikitsu commanded, and the soldier started, clearly surprised to be addressed directly by his emperor and then equally startled by the strange and preemptory demand. "You are not in any trouble," Hibikitsu reassured the man. "Your commander will see to it that you are given a suitable replacement. Now remove it."

The man nodded fervently, saluted shakily, and then, quickly but with much fumbling, did as instructed. Fortunately, his gear was simple enough—a maikiro of lacquered plates, emblazoned with a faded copy of the Rimbakan Higeibara crest across the front and secured by cotton straps across the back. Smaller plates hung from the front and sides to protect the groin and thighs, a simplified version of the kazure his own armor included. The man had a conical iron hat, the jingaso also marked with the red spider lily crest, and both gauntlets and shin guards bore overlapping plates similar to his own, though unornamented, their simple glaze bearing the scuffs and scrapes of frequent handling. When the man was down to hosode, ponmei, and boots, Hibikitsu dismissed him with a wave of thanks.

Then Hibikitsu retreated to the inn, carrying the soldier's gear with him. Once inside he closed the window screens, laid his weapons on the table, and began to remove his own armor, one gilded, inlaid piece at a time.

"Sire?" Diritan asked hesitantly as Hibikitsu tugged off his heavy, gold-edged and flower-petalled hanketo, flexing his fingers once they were freed of the thick gauntlets, and set aside his gold-lacquered deo with its masterful ivory inlay of a crane taking flight, the royal tsodami clutched in its beak, that bright red flower picked out in garnets and rubies. "Might I ask, your Majesty, what you are doing?"

"You might," he allowed, not pausing as he stripped away his haidoto next, placing the beautifully shaped and decorated thigh guards, with their tracery of gold and crimson tsodami vines to match his breastplate, beside the other pieces already strewn atop the table where he had so recently eaten. By himself. In an inn made empty to accommodate him. What thoughtless privilege he wielded, and always had! Well, no more!

The stocky Honjofu cleared his throat, and Hibikitsu could not resist a smile. The man was brave, to question his emperor in such a way. Brave, and loyal. He should not treat such noble qualities so poorly. "It has occurred to me," he explained, removing his gilded suneoto and adding the shin guards to the table's collection, "that I do not truly know the way my empire works. And that I cannot, as long as I remain so isolated from it. So protected. An emperor only sees what is presented for his approval." He shrugged, standing there in only hosode, ponmei, and boots just as that soldier had, and turned to that man's armor, lifting the plain, battered shin guards that mirrored his own in function but were mere shadows, crude copies without decoration, lacking even the fine materials that went into his own gear's construction. Then he crouched to tie them to his boots. "A simple soldier, however, sees the world as it really is," he continued, straightening back up and reaching for the soldier's maikiro, which he settled across his chest. It was lighter than his own breastplate—a necessity when one was expected to march long distances while wearing it—and though it offered far less protection, it would do.

"Sire." Hibikitsu felt bad for the hefty warrior as he watched the Honjofu struggle to speak. "With the utmost respect, your Majesty, if you are planning what I think you are—" Diritan tried to continue, but his courage failed him.

That only made the emperor smile more widely. This was not his court smile but something different, something Hibikitsu had rarely allowed himself the freedom to use. It was a genuine smile, one of true amusement—not disdain, not condescension, just entertainment.

"You have surmised correctly, noble Diritan," he informed the warrior, pulling on the soldier's gauntlets and then placing the jingaso atop his head. It fit well enough. "You and the rest of my retinue will continue on toward Korito. As will I, but I shall do so alone." He held up a hand to forestall the forthcoming objection, marveling at how clumsy and rough this gauntlet felt compared to his own. How did the aiashe accomplish anything when they could barely move their fingers? "This is my will," he stated clearly and decisively. "You and the others will obey."

For a second, he thought the Honjofu would object, and he was impressed anew. To dare to contradict his emperor in order to keep him safe! What had he ever done to earn such loyalty? But in the end Diritan could not oppose a direct order and nodded, though his salute was almost violent in its anger.

Recognizing that he meant well, and that he was not wrong, Hibikitsu sighed. "You and that other, Nioko," he said. "You may follow me, though you will keep out of sight. You may post two other Honjofu to circle me as I travel. That way you may ensure my safety without preventing me from accomplishing my objective." The following salute showed relief, and Hibikitsu rejoiced at how well he was coming to understand the subtleties conveyed through that one routine gesture. It was like a whole other language he had never even known existed!

Clearly, he had much to learn.

Turning back to his armor piled atop the table, he frowned for a second. "Have this gathered up and brought to Korito," he stated, then corrected himself. "No, select someone my size, preferably a noble, to wear it in my stead. My helmet, crests, and menatu are in Shisi's saddlebags—have someone retrieve them as well." That way, anyone looking would see what they thought was the Relicant Emperor, riding with his full retinue. They would not think to inspect a lone soldier traveling well behind that force. He tied the soldier's sash—silk, yes, but rough-spun and undyed—around his waist and then lifted Kosshiki and slid the blade through it. His sword was something he would not be leaving behind, nor allowing anyone else to wear in his stead.

The only other things he chose to retain were his kanashi. The hair sticks were carved of solid jade, and with Kosshiki they were the only relics Hibikitsu retained from his illustrious ancestor, the first Relicant Emperor. He would not be parted from them in this life. Nor would he leave Shisi behind. If it struck anyone as strange that a common soldier should be astride such a noble steed, so be it. Given that he was carrying a nihono, hopefully anyone he passed would assume he was a minor noble and the horse and blade his only inheritance.

What they thought of him did not matter, however. As long as they did not recognize him for himself, he would finally see his empire properly. Faults and all.

He wondered, as he waited within the inn for Diritan to carry out his orders—for the fewer people who even knew of the emperor's deception, the better—if it was right that he should feel such excitement, such nearly overpowering glee, at the prospect?

CHAPTER FOUR

"Oh, excuse me!" Seikoku muttered as she rebounded off a couple not so much threading their way through the market as sailing serenely forward on a perfectly straight path, trusting everyone to move out of their way. When you wore fine silks and jewels, that was evidently how you saw the world, as something that you had a perfect right to and that everyone else should recognize and acknowledge.

Seikoku wouldn't know. She'd never had such things. Even if she had, though, she doubted she would have treated the rest of the people in Ginzai the way these fine folks did.

"What were you thinking?" the man was demanding of her, raising the folded fan in his hand as if to strike her with it. She'd like to see him try. "Can you not see to stay out of our way?"

The woman with him merely sighed. "Oh, it's all right, dear," she said, and for an instant Seikoku thought she would excuse the collision, perhaps even apologize for their obliviousness. But then the woman smiled, all lips and no teeth, like a cat toying with its prey, her heavily rogued eyes with their enameled lashes raking across her worn but serviceable ponmei, her short canvas coat, her favorite scarf with its colors of the sky. "Look at her—clearly she was never given proper instruction on how to behave before one's betters."

A dozen retorts sprang to mind, each one resting on the tip of her tongue and aching to be released, but Seikoku swallowed them all. "A thousand pardons," she managed to grate out instead, bowing deeply. "The fault was mine."

"Indeed it was," the man agreed, lifting his chin so that he could sight down his rather prominent nose at her. "See that it does not happen again." Offering his hand once more to his companion, and with a final sniff of disapproval, the pair sauntered off to parade their superiority before the rest of the market.

Seikoku let them go without a backward glance. Her hand slid into her jacket instead, and she smiled at the weight she felt nestled there. The man might be an arrogant fool, but his money pouch was reassuringly solid. Better still, she opened her other hand, which had been cupped tight at her side, to admire the necklace coiled within. Pearls and emeralds and a single tear-drop sapphire. Gaudy and horribly matched, both within itself and to the lady's saffron robes, but its components would fetch a pretty price. Seikoku was humming softly as she sauntered away herself, mimicking the couple's prancing steps for a turn and laughing.

That laughter fell away, however, when she reached her favorite stall, and Seikoku froze, forgetting all about her recent acquisitions as she stared, horrified. Where normally there was a neat order to the racks and baskets and barrels and trays, now there was only a jumbled mess. The air was thick with flour, the ground slick with juice and pulp, and it took her several seconds, blinking away the haze, before she spotted the body laying amid the chaos.

"Master Hintaro!" She rushed over as quickly as she could, her feet sticking as she moved, and dropped to a crouch at his side. He was splayed out, limbs every which way, blood from a dozen cuts staining various breads and cakes and other foodstuffs that were crushed beneath him, but she was relieved to see that his chest was rising and falling. Then he groaned. "Master Hintaro!" She tugged the waterskin from her belt and uncapped it to splash a little onto his face. "Can you hear me? It's Keiko."

"K-Keiko?" The merchant groaned again, shaking his head, and blinked at her, his eyes having trouble focusing. "We are...out of those dumplings you like...I am afraid."

She almost laughed but proffered the waterskin instead. "Here, sip this." He did, and after a moment he was able to sit up and look around at what had been his place of business.

"Ah, my poor shop!" he cried, holding his head in his hands. "Everything is ruined!"

"What happened?" she asked, resting a hand on his shoulder. Master Hintaro was one of the kindest, most honest merchants here, which was why she always made her purchases with him. She had never seen him get in an argument with anyone—even with the most difficult and demanding customer, he remained calm and polite. But this much destruction was clearly deliberate.

"It was those boys," he admitted, trying to stand and sinking back down with a moan and a grimace. She helped him up, and he leaned on her for support. "You know the ones I mean, the ones who trawl the market."

"The Jogoturi." She knew exactly who he meant. They called themselves that, "Lords of the Street," but they were nothing more than a band of thugs. She'd heard of them waylaying people on the streets before, saying they were collecting a toll, but attacking a merchant? Especially one as well-liked as Master Hintaro?

"I ran across them the other night, on my way home," the merchant told her. "They demanded a toll. I refused." He crossed his arms, revealing the stubbornness that normally lurked below his ready smile. "They promised to collect later." He shook his head, staring at his shattered stall again in dismay. "Perhaps I should have paid them after all."

"No," Seikoku replied firmly. "People like that, they would only take more the next time. And the time after that. As long as people keep giving in to them, they will continue." Her eyes narrowed. She had never messed with the Jogoturi, or any of the other little gangs that existed throughout the city. It was none of her affair, as long as they did not cross her or interfere with her own work. Just like that rich couple, they were an annoyance to be skirted, little more.

Now, however, they had gone too far. She liked Hintaro. She considered him a friend, or as close as she ever got.

The Jogoturi would have to be taught a lesson.

That night, Seikoku crept out of her house, moving carefully to avoid waking Mother Pidiri or any of her other neighbors. She was dressed in what she considered her working clothes: midnight silk hakami that clung more than her ponmei but not enough to restrict movement, a snug shatage of the same material, a gray canvas jacket that belted at the waist, and soft black boots. A bag slung across her body contained her tools. The outfit was daring enough to draw attention, perhaps, but only because she was eschewing a kitoro or any other traditional female garb. What it did not do was cry out "thief and graverobber," which was the intent.

She had asked around a little and learned that the Jogoturi had claimed an old closed-down fish market as their lair. It was past the market and toward the town cemetery, but not so close that the bannin would be willing to deviate from their normal patrols to investigate it. Everyone knew the town guards only cared about protecting the city's horde of aishone—or, rather, keeping it for only the wealthy to use. But Seikoku couldn't worry about that particular inequity just now. She had other matters to attend.

Reaching the block before her target, she paused and stepped into the shadows spilling out from a nearby alley. There she removed her jacket and reversed it so that its black lining was now outermost. Then from her bag she pulled black gloves and her scarf, also black, which she wound around her neck and then up over her head and finally around her nose, mouth, and chin. It was thick enough to disguise her features like that but thin enough that she could breathe through it unimpeded.

Now she felt prepared to face the Jogoturi.

The old fish market was crumbling at the edges but still sturdy, the two-story wooden building surrounded by a wide, open porch on all sides. Seikoku vaguely remembered when the place had still been open for business and the porch had been covered with row upon row of open crates, each one filled with ice upon which rested fish, shrimp, eels, and other seafood. Now the only life on display there was of the two-legged variety, as she spied several of the thugs lounging against pillars, keeping watch.

Which was fine, as she had never meant to enter through the front doors.

Past the old fish market was a small three-story building, its first floor a small tailor's shop and the two upper floors housing apartments. It was made of rough stone mortared together and proved a simple matter to scale. Seikoku climbed up the far side, crossed the roof carefully so as not to disturb or crack any of the fired pottery shingles there, and then hooked her rope around a convenient chimney pipe and lowered herself over the other side, onto the porch roof. Though old, it did not creak from her weight, and she scampered quickly across to the building itself. There were windows here, but they were all dark and cold. Evidently the Jogoturi had not considered that anyone might approach from above. Seikoku tried three before she found one that was not latched. She withdrew a small can from her bag and squirted its contents along the inside of the window frame, waited a moment for the oil to do its work, and then slid the window open. It did not make a sound. Nor did she, as she eased herself inside.

So far, so good.

Moving stealthily across the worn wood floor, she crossed the room she had entered and carefully listened at the door. She could hear the murmur of conversation, but it was muted. Gently she cracked the door open and peered out. Ahead of her was a walkway, with a railing beyond. The sounds were coming from past that, and below.

Sliding through the opening she'd made, Seikoku crouched low beside that railing and glanced down.

The entire building was essentially an empty shell, she saw at once. There were rooms around the railing up here, and rooms directly below them, but the center of the building was a single open space. And it was here that the Jogoturi had made their home. The wide room was littered with cushions of various shapes, sizes, and qualities, and sprawled across many of those were the youths themselves. She counted a good dozen of them, most within a year or three of her own age, and all attired more or less the same—gray ponmei, black hosode, and a loose open vest of scarlet silk over that to match the bands tied about their heads, keeping their hair back. Many had weapons beside them or still tucked into their belts, clubs and rods and knives and even a short chosode or two. Though from here they looked more like unruly children playing at being tough, Seikoku knew better than to discount them. Like any rat, they would be most dangerous if cornered.

Fortunately, she had not come here to fight.

Instead, she went about her task quickly and quietly, without ever disturbing or drawing the attention of those below. When she was done, she let herself out the same way she had entered, sliding the window shut again behind her.

It was not until she had clambered back down the other building and was walking away, her jacket once again gray, her scarf and gloves safely out of sight, that Seikoku let herself relax just a little.

That had been the first step. Now for the second.

"How are you today, Master Hintaro?" she asked the merchant. It had been two days since the attack, and she was glad to see that he was back on his feet, his stall all but restored. If there were one or two fewer baskets and trays for the moment, he had spaced the others farther apart to prevent any unseemly gaps. He himself looked better as well, the bruises already starting to fade, his customary smile back on his face.

"Ah, Keiko!" he called, stepping over to give her a quick, one-armed hug. "Good to see you! I am better, thank you. Much better." He leaned in and lowered his voice. "And did you hear?" When she shook her head, he continued. "The Jogoturi! They have all been tossed in prison!"

"Oh? For attacking you, I hope!"

He chuckled, though the sound was tinged with bitterness. "Would that not be nice, to know that such justice existed?" he asked her, and they shared the smile of those who knew better how the world truly worked. "No, they were arrested for stealing some wealthy woman's jewels. But no matter the reason, they are off the streets and will never harass good, honest citizens again. And that is enough for me."

"I am glad to hear it," Seikoku agreed. She was sorry to have sacrificed that necklace, but it had been worth it to remove the Jogoturi from the board. Ginzai was safer now, which meant its citizens could breathe more easily.

And, as a result, its wealthier residents might let their guard down, just a little.

In that way, planting the necklace in the old fish market and then leaving a note for the rich couple as to where they might find their missing jewels had been less a sacrifice and more an investment.

Besides, Seikoku was protective of the people she cared about. Causing them grief meant upsetting her, and she was not one to let such a slight go unpunished.

She was smiling again as she chatted with Master Hintaro and selected several items for purchase. After all, the rich man's coins could not be identified, so there had been no reason to part with them as well.

CHAPTER FIVE

By the time Chimehara slipped through the heavy bronze gates of House Chohu, gliding across the wide courtyard with its ornamental gardens, around the large brass gong used to strike the hour, and in through the broad front doors carved entirely of some lustrous golden wood, the servants were all a-twitter. She could see several of them whispering to each other as she entered, and indeed she had barely set foot into the hall when Yuni and Ritaru hurried over.

"Oh, Chimehara!" Yuni gasped, grabbing her arm with hands that had been permanently wrinkled by soapy water and linseed oil but were still fearsomely strong. "I am so happy to see you! We were so worried!"

"Worried? Whatever for?" Chimehara patted the cleaning lady's hand gently, not even minding the roughness of the other woman's skin. Upon entering House Chohu's service, she had gone out of her way to build relationships with all the household staff and had every intention of preserving their impression of her as a lovely, sweet, slightly sheltered young woman. Besides, while they could be as petty as anyone else, at least they tended to be honest about their enmities, which she found refreshing amid so many who lied and hid disdain behind a smile.

Though, of course, she did the same herself. Just with far more skill than most.

"There was a murder last night!" Ritaru whispered, clutching her other arm. "It was horrible! And, what with you living outside the compound now, we feared the worst!"

"That is sweet of you," Chimehara told the other maid, stroking her hand as well. Ritaru was old and gnarled like a tree, Yuni stout as a stump, and both of them bore the rough, reddened skin and straggly, crusty gray hair of one who worked with cleaning solutions all day long, but they were kind to her, and fiercely protective. She valued that more than all the gold and jewels in the world.

Which did not mean she did not intend to collect the latter as well.

"I was fine," she assured the two older women now. "No one disturbed me all night." And that much was true. When she had acquired her little apartment outside the compound, she had known it was essential to have privacy in which to plan. She had not realized just what a luxury it would become to have a place all to herself.

Growing up, she had lived mostly on the streets, sometimes in small hovels or huts or tents, more often in lean-tos or simply curled up among piles of cast-off rags and scraps of paper. It had been necessary to squeeze as many bodies together as possible, for warmth. Once her form had begun to mature, and she had started to attract certain types of attention, she had been forced to seek other accommodations, lest those attentions led to unwanted complications. It had proven easy enough for Chimehara to find men willing to share their bed for a night, and she had rarely slept out in the cold and the wet again, but still she had been merely a guest, and careful not to overstay her welcome, always leaving while they still wanted more. Coming to House Chohu, she had slept in the dormitories with the other staff and junior workers, and that had been lovelier than she had expected, for she had been granted a clean bed and a dresser and a chest and a chair in a tiny cubby all her own, with a curtain across the front for privacy.

Now, however, she had an entire apartment all her own, on the top floor of a three-story nahiya. It had three rooms—living room, kitchen, and bedroom—and its own private bathroom! It had a window that looked out upon the walls of Atsani, above, and a tiny garden at the center, complete with a little stream and a handsome teak bench. The entire place was more beautiful, more spacious, more peaceful than she had ever imagined, and it was all hers.

She was so pleased that she had chosen young Master Nagoi

to kill and take it from. Truly, so much luxury had been wasted on him!

Of course, Yuni and Ritaru and the others had been devastated when she'd informed them that she had found a place of her own outside the compound, though they had all been pleased for her. She had left out the details—as far as anyone in House Chohu knew, Chimehara was sharing a rented room somewhere in Bejinuri or even Mazihini, hurrying up through as many as three levels to work each morn. But that was for the best. Though the gem merchants had known Nagoi lived elsewhere, he had owned the apartment himself and so they had not thought to check on where it had been or what had happened to it after he had been found dead a week or so before, from an apparent heart attack. Nor did Chimehara wish them to connect her to the deceased junior trader. They had only gone out to dinner that one night, after all. His body had been found a few days later, while she had been back at work, sorting and counting jade beads as always.

That, at least, was now behind her.

"Shoo, you two!" A silk and carved bamboo fan, still folded, rapped first Yuni and then Ritaru upon the shoulder, not hard but with enough force to produce a sharp pop of sound. "Let the poor girl get to her work, and the two of you off to yours!"

"Yes, Madam Ponsoi!" both cleaning ladies intoned, leaping away. "At once!" They hurried off to their chores, leaving Chimehara alone with Chohu's senior housekeeper. Ponsoi was as tall as she was, and had as many curves, if not more, though hers had gone soft over the years whereas Chimehara's limbs still bore the smooth, sleek tautness of youth. The real difference was in their faces, however. Chimehara was well aware of her own beauty, the unmarred expanse of her forehead, the delicate arc of her brows, the gentle curve of her nose, the lushness of her lips, and most of all the entrancing color of her large, shimmering emerald eyes. Madam Ponsoi had perhaps been considered handsome in her youth, though perhaps not. Now she was merely imposing. Yet she ruled the compound with an iron fist, and when she barked orders even the senior merchants jumped. Only Master Eijiri himself dared to stand against her, though he did so sparingly, for he was wise enough not to cross the woman who controlled his clothes, his linens, and his meals.

For Chimehara, there had been a far easier route. Such women as Ponsoi could either envy and dislike young beauties—or take them under their wings.

"Is it true?" she asked the housekeeper now, allowing a shudder to run through her. "They said someone had died?"

"Oh, yes, you poor dear, you have not heard!" Madam Ponsoi wrapped her arms around Chimehara, her kitoro gray like the rest of the household's but made from finer silk and with a delicate pattern woven through it. "Indeed, there has been. I am afraid Mistress Oisare was found early this morning, in an alley not far from here."

"What? No! Not Mistress Oisare!" Chimehara let herself go slightly limp, so that her companion's arms tightened to support her, and wept into the older woman's shoulder, though she was careful not to let her tears stain the delicate silk. "She was always kind to me!"

"She was a kind soul," Madam Ponsoi agreed. "It is indeed a tragedy." She sighed. "If only she had stayed in the compound, where it is safe! But she insisted upon her evening walk, you know. Said it kept her healthy and strong." She shook her head. "Not so healthy now!" A little gasp followed that, as if the housekeeper was surprised at her own disrespect for the recently dead.

"How—what—do they know what happened?" Chimehara managed, straightening and brushing at her eyes, but gently, gently. She knew not to let them get too red—a little heightened color was attractive, too much was off-putting.

"A robbery, nothing more," the older woman answered. "The thief or thieves stole her aishone, of course, and her money, and her jewelry. They even took her shoes!" Mistress Oisare had been particularly vain about her shoes, silk slippers with tiny seed pearls and sapphires sewn in a pattern of flowing waves. Those shoes had been her most treasured possession.

"Oh, how horrible!" Chimehara wrung her hands. "I hope they catch whoever did this and make them pay!" Not that they would, of course.

She had been far too careful for that.

The sound of the gong just outside made them both jump and pull apart. "Off you go, do not be late!" Madam Ponsoi instructed, motioning Chimehara toward the counting room, and she did indeed quicken her step, for Mistress Limini was of the type who hated her for her beauty and was always hoping to find ways to show her up. A shame it had not been her whose throat Chimehara had slit last night, but the old hag was her direct superior and known to dislike her, which would have made her connection to such a crime far too obvious. Chimehara had only met Oisare thrice, and the woman had been several ranks above her, so there was no obvious motive.

But then, Chimehara was too good, too clever, too careful to go for the obvious.

Indeed, the gong had just struck to signal lunch, and she had been filing out of the counting room with the other junior clerks, when a man appeared in the doorway, his broad frame and fine satin robes filling much of that wide space. It was Master Eijiri himself, and he glanced around once before his small, dark eyes affixed to her.

"Ah, there you are," he declared, striding into the room as if he owned the place—which, in fact, he did. "Come along, Chimehara. You may eat after we have got you settled."

"Sir?" she asked, bowing deeply. He dipped his head to acknowledge the gesture, his short, neat beard bobbing, but then turned and waved for her to follow as he stomped from the room. She did so at once, and soon they were marching down the hall.

"You have no doubt heard of Mistress Oisare's tragic fate," he said over his shoulder as they passed doorway after doorway, some shut, some open as workers streamed toward the dining hall. "It is terrible and has required certain adjustments here." He stopped before a door, frowned at it as if the polished wood frame and clean rice-paper squares offended him by barring his path, then nodded and slid the barrier aside. Inside was a room similar to the counting room but far smaller, with only two low desks, seat cushions behind each, a wide woven basket before each one, and a row of small boxes before them, each one made of teak and cushioned with silk. A man sat at one of the desks, his face narrow and deeply lined, his scalp nearly bare, his face clean-shaven, a set of ivory spectacles perched atop his beak-like nose. He glanced up as they approached, and smiled, revealing that he had few teeth left.

"This is the girl I spoke of," Master Eijiri declared. "Chimehara. Chimehara, this is Master Ganyeki. You will work with him now." The head of House Chohu favored her with a smile that was equal parts kind and salacious. "I remember your audition, and the skill you displayed then. I told you it was wasted in the counting room. This is a far better match for your talents." He nodded and exited, leaving her alone with the old man.

Chimehara smiled at him, and he smiled back, but with none of the lust a younger man might have displayed. She was not used to such a lackluster reaction, but knew how to work around it. Desire was only one way to win someone's trust, after all. "I am honored to assist you, noble master," she intoned, bowing deeply. "I hope you will find my aid acceptable."

He bobbed his head and laughed, the sound surprisingly deep and musical to come from such a wizened figure. "I am sure you will do admirably, my dear," he assured her, his voice equally rich. "Now off you go to eat. Come back when you have had your fill, and we will begin your instruction."

Chimehara smiled, bowed, and retreated. She did not want to miss the noon meal—she was still not used to being so pampered as to have such good food, and in such quantities, with such regularity.

Besides, she already knew what this new job was, and it did make perfect sense. When she had first applied for a position here at House Chohu, Eijiri had tested her by having her sort eight pearls by order of their value. She had impressed him enough that he had offered her a place with them on the spot, though only the counting room had been available. Those baskets in the little room would contain pearls, and the boxes were to hold them once they had been sorted. It was far more delicate work than counting jade beads, and far more prestigious.

She allowed her smile to broaden as she skipped off to lunch. Yes, killing Oisare had created an opening. One she was far too junior to fill. But that had left vacant the spot Oisare's successor had occupied, and then that created one below it, and so on. Now she was out of the counting room, and working with pearls. Her rise had begun, exactly as planned.

The only shame was that Oisare's slippers had not fit her. Who knew the older woman would have such tiny feet? Still, the pearls and sapphires would fetch a handsome amount of coin to add to Chimehara's hoard, as would the rest of her jewels. The aishone she would keep for herself.

Right now, however, she hurried to the dining hall. Scheming always left her with an appetite!

CHAPTER SIX

Dawn crept over the tiny village of Hiromura, its gentle swathes of lavender and rose teasing residents into opening their eyes and stumbling from their pallets to greet the new day. The air was crisp and clear, the sky lightening steadily from dawn's touch and blemished by only a few tiny wisps of cloud, while everywhere birds sang out, chirping their delight at the fine weather and the prospect of grass, seeds, and grubs.

Villagers stretched and yawned, stumbling out to the well to splash cool water on their shoulders and heads, scrubbing the sleep from their eyes and greeting their neighbors with lazy smiles and smothered yawns as if to say, "I suppose we'd better get a start on things, then."

Hiromura was a peaceful little place, even squabbles among the residents few and far between, and though the little town did not possess anything of enough value to tempt bandits, still they grew enough food and traded enough goods to keep themselves clothed and fed, with a little left for drink and music besides. It was a good place to live, and few of the residents ever felt the urge to seek out a more fulfilling life beyond the collection of huts and cottages.

On this day, however, a pair of strangers appeared at the horizon, just as the last of night's shade fled the sky. They advanced as one, seeming too pale to be real, and those who spotted them first blinked their eyes, rubbing at them in the hopes that more natural colors might appear on the approaching duo. Color did soon follow, but not in the expected fashion, not bleeding into the two young men's features and clothing as their features sharpened with decreasing distance. Instead, the color seemed to hover above them, a thing wholly separate, like a small cloud of hues and shades that sheltered them from their own pallid nature. It was not a cloud, though, not truly, for it had no clear edges, and indeed seemed to possess little substance. Nor were its colors bright like a sun-touched cloud or a rainbow might be, or dark and heavy like a storm cloud. They were faded, worn, tired, yet they swirled and clashed and fell apart and bled together in a constant riot of motion. The dichotomy was disturbing to the eye and bewildering to the brain, and the villagers frowned and looked away, their uneasiness growing as the pair neared. The path they took seemed to have lost its brilliance as well, as their footsteps left white and gray imprints upon the very land.

Nonetheless, a man and a woman strode forth to meet the strangers. Lin was tall and slender, with equally long features, his gray-touched brown hair tugged back in a braid as tidy as the knots in the nets he made and the clothing he repaired. Beside him, Ganai was far shorter and rounder, many of her curves still enticing despite the streak of pure white running through her long, dark hair. Her fingers were stained from the herbs she found, dried, and ground for people's use and for her own healing practices. Together they were the nearest Hiromura had to town elders, and all the small community required.

"Greetings!" Lin called out, his voice thin but carrying across the distance to the approaching pair. "Welcome to Hiromura! Is there aught you require? You are welcome to the use of our well, and we are happy to provide you with a light repast, though we are simple folk and have little more to offer than rice, fish, and greens. May we know your names, and from whence you hail?"

The strangers were now close enough that Lin could make them out clearly, and he struggled to hide the shiver that ran through him. Both were young men, or so he would judge by their faces, which still bore the tautness of youth and whose lines seemed more from suffering adversity than from age. Yet their hair was gray and their flesh so white it rivaled that of a dead fish left too long in the water. Their clothing, little more than rags, was also pale, not so much bleached as somehow leeched, like the color had been stripped away all at once. And their eyes! The youths' eyes were a swirl of white and gray that danced and swam and left him dizzy to behold it. Those staggering gazes now turned his way as the newcomers considered him and his words. And, at last, one of them spoke.

"I am Ibaru," he declared, and his voice was soft and almost sibilant, less like a hiss than a hush, yet with undertones that screeched against the mind and grated upon the ear. "He is Iraku. And we hunger." Each word was like a stab in Lin's head, causing him to wince with pain, yet he kept his smile plastered to his face.

"Of course, of course," he replied, bowing slightly. "Come, sit and refresh yourself while we prepare food!" He gestured toward the center of the village, where the well's broad stone lip often served as convenient perch.

The one who had spoken—Ibaru—did step forward, but not toward the well. Rather, he closed the gap between himself and Lin. "We hunger," he repeated in that strange, eerily quiet voice of his, and stretched out a bone-white hand toward the net-mender's face. Lin wanted to shrink away, but he could not bear to be so rude, so he stood his ground.

Then his flesh and that of the stranger touched, and the village elder swooned.

To those watching, it was as if the strange, swirling cloud above had suddenly swooped down, moving fast like a hunting bird sighting its prey among the river reeds. A tendril of that odd mix of color and emptiness had tapped Lin just as the boy had made contact, and the net-mender's body jerked as if he had been struck by lightning. Only this blow did not cause light to arc over his limbs, nor did it light up the sky. Instead, it drew the color from him in a spray of hues, siphoning off the browns and reds of his hair, the pinks and salmons of his skin, the hazel of his eyes. The man it left behind to crumple to the ground was as pale as the two youths, as empty of color, and wizened as if he had endured a decade of hard summers and harder winters, his body eating itself to survive. And all of this occurred in utter silence, the sound of the strange attack seemingly stolen away as well.

Ganai quickly dropped to her knees beside her friend, rolling him over as he gasped for air. "Lin!" she cried out, shaking him, for his eyes were glazed and unfocused, a film replacing their normal warm hue. "Can you hear me?" He turned toward her, opening his mouth, but no sound emerged. "What have you done to him?" she demanded, clutching him round the shoulders as she glared up at the pale young men before her.

"We brought greetings," Iraku replied. His voice was as unnerving as that of his companion. "From Kaemusei." He smiled, though the grim expression had no warmth or humor to it, and reached for her.

She tried to pull away, still puzzling over his words—the Silent Change?—but could not evade his touch. When his hand landed upon her head, she stiffened, the whole of her hair instantly turning as white as that one streak, her skin and eyes and clothing swiftly following suit. He released her only a second later, but already she was as drab and pale and silent and sorrowful as her friend. The brothers—for so they must be, their features were so similar—on the other hand, seemed reinvigorated, and though their own color had not changed, nor their expressions lightened, they moved with fresh energy as they turned toward the other villagers who had gathered to watch in horror as their friends were struck down.

A few of the other men, led by Rai the fisherman, snarled and hefted sturdy clubs and stout sticks. "You'll pay for that!" Rai declared, charging forward, his club already sweeping down in a fierce arc aimed to intersect Ibaru where his nose rose between his cheeks. But the emaciated and decolored youth reached up with one slender hand and caught the club, arresting it in mid-swing so suddenly Rai stumbled, though the boy's hand never wavered. The club instantly lost its rich wooden hue, now as bleached and dry as old driftwood, and then crumbled away, leaving Rai holding nothing but a small stump. He tossed that aside and swung again, this time with his own meaty fists, but when he connected Ibaru merely smiled as the color fled his assailant, along with his voice and vitality. The same fate befell the other attackers, the two frail-looking strangers demonstrating strength far beyond their size, their touch causing weapons to crumble and people to wither and gray. A moment later the town had gone quiet, its elders now mute ancients, its defenders in an equal state of decay and despair.

Next the boys turned to the remaining villagers, and the village itself. The cloud above them seemed to expand, as if gorged by its recent feast of color and life, and spread out, cloaking all Hiromura beneath its shimmering veil. Then it fell upon them, its vaporous strands stroking each and every person or beast, each and every structure or building. Bodies fell without a sound, buildings collapsed noiselessly, food decayed, crops shriveled, animals dwindled.

In moments, the faded pair stood alone amid what might have been the decades-old ruins of some strange community where all color had been banned, surrounded by both bodies and artifacts of gray and white and dusty black.

Ibaru turned to Iraku. "I hunger," he intoned, and his brother nodded. Together they turned from the remains of Hiromura, picking their way across it, and continued on their trek.

Above them, the Silent Change wended and waved, swirling and puffing and dancing upon the air, leaving the world lifeless and silent in its wake.

CHAPTER SEVEN

Geniji giggled. It was a disconcerting sound to come from the big, burly warrior, and somehow even moreso now when she was wearing simple worker's clothes, hempen toritori and a padded web-sashiko hantien of faded red and black cotton.

"Will you stop that?" Misataki Shizumi muttered, but her companion merely shook her head and continued, her entire broad form vibrating as she struggled to keep the high-pitched peals from escaping.

"This is serious!" Shizumi insisted, but that did nothing to quell the larger woman's amusement.

"I...know," Geniji managed at last to gasp out in between snorts. "It's just...that!" And she waved one heavy, well-callused hand at Shizumi herself.

Or, more precisely, at her garb.

"It is not that funny!" Shizumi snapped, fighting in vain to keep the flush from her face. "It's like you've never seen a woman before!"

"Not many," Akino drawled from her other side. "And not like that." He raised an eyebrow as slender as he was, and as wiry. "And not you."

"Yes, fine, I am female," she retorted. "Satisfied? Shall I bare my bosom so you may be certain?" Despite herself, she brushed her hands down the length of her clothes, marveling at the rich feel of the embroidery there. She wore a simple but elegant kisoni, but over that was a kitoro patterned with lilacs and bamboo, tied by a thick sash stitched with a lotus motif in gold. The obe tied in back rather than in front, making it difficult to move freely, but that was the point—she was not the sort of woman who needed mobility for such mundane things as household chores. That was why she had servants, after all.

I don't understand how anyone can stand to live like this, she groused silently. *I can barely walk, this thing is wrapped so tight! And I can't lift my hands higher than my waist! Forget drawing a sword, I would be lucky to raise a cup to my lips!*

Her gocho drew her back from her dark musings by shaking his head. "Not necessary," he told her in his usual soft tones. "Already knew that much." Which was true—warriors couldn't afford modesty, not when they often had to huddle together at night for warmth or strip off sodden clothing after a sudden downpour.

Still, she knew what her two corporals meant. She was hardly the type to wear such ostentatious clothing. Nor did her face or figure lend itself to such finery—she was too lean, too flat, her mouth too wide, her nose too long, her eyes too narrow. She knew this and had long since accepted it. She had even been pleased to have an excuse not to dress in such a flashy and simpering fashion.

Except, apparently, today.

"How much longer, do you think?" Geniji whispered, having finally overcome her fits of laughter. "I feel naked without my armor!"

Shizumi glanced around them, where the trees nearly crowded the path they were taking through the woods—her and Dairamu on a litter carried by Masai and Nori, Akino beside her in the robes and cap of a merchant or a majordomo, and Geniji walking ahead of them with a stout stick to push away branches, ostensibly as a local guide and perhaps servant. The foliage swallowed up sound, allowing only the soft hiss of the breeze and the chirp of birds flying overhead to shatter its silence, but her eye caught a flash of motion up ahead, and then answering glimmers to either side. "About now, I would say," she answered softly, and schooled herself as best she could, crossing her hands primly in her lap.

Her scream when the masked men leaped out to circle them scattered the birds in a frenzy of wings and shrieks that exploded out of the treetops, drowning any other noises for a good minute. By the time that had passed and they could hear anything else again, the men had them surrounded, bows in hand and arrows nocked, though the weapons were not fully raised and only half drawn. Still, the way the men held them indicated they knew how to use the weapons.

"Good day to you, fine lady," one of the men in front called out, striding toward her. He stopped beside her litter and bowed deeply. "Welcome to the forests of Yunigiri. I am Shirikin, and I rule here." He wore sturdy pants and jacket, as Geniji did, but with a leaf-patterned kitoro of green and gold open over that. At his belt was a fine nihono, and Shizumi's eyes narrowed at the sight. The long, curved sword was certainly a better weapon than the more common chokoto but it was also a noble's weapon, and for a commoner to carry one was punishable by death. She herself was only allowed one because of her status as a Honjofu.

And this man wore his with the curve up, as was correct when bearing it in such a manner instead of hanging from straps below the belt. Which meant he most likely knew how to use it.

She realized she had been sizing him up and covered that lapse by raising her hand to her lips and feigning surprise, shock, and fear. "Oh!" she managed, pitching her voice higher than normal. "You are truly…him?" She batted her eyes, feeling ridiculous in makeup and silk robes, but he seemed to be buying it. "Please, noble thief, do not harm me! I am but a poor woman seeking passage!"

"Poor?" The so-called "Forest King" lofted an eyebrow, his brown eyes slipping from her fine robes to the sumptuous beadwork and handsome carving adorning her litter to the heavy pouch at Akino's belt. "I think not, my lady. But never fear, the Forest King is no common criminal, to mistreat such a noble woman! You will be my guest tonight, and then on the morrow we will see you safely on your way." A smile twitched at his lips, visible through the thin silk he wore across his face as a veil. "Minus a small fee for the evening's accommodations, of course."

Shizumi wanted nothing more than to rip that sword from his belt and run him through with it—even through the scarf she could see the smarminess of his expression. She resisted the urge, however, settling for sinking back down onto the silk cushions of her litter and balling her fists where he could not see.

The bandit's men gestured for the small party to follow them, and escorted the disguised Honjofu deeper into the forest, eventually stepping off the path and ducking beneath and around trees as they made their way along a route none could see but that they clearly knew well. Eventually they arrived at a small clearing, where several more men waited. All of them wore outfits similar to their leader's, but Shizumi noticed that they all carried nihono and seemed comfortable with the weapon at their side. Nor did they have the rough and tumble look she would normally have associated with such robbers—instead, to a man they seemed well-groomed, their hair neatly brushed and plaited, their hands clean, their nails short and well-filed, their teeth a healthy white. What sort of ruffians were these?

"Come sit by the fire, dear lady," Shirikin declared, offering his hand to help her descend to the ground. She did so and was pleasantly surprised to find it soft and springy, covered with pine needles that lent the air a rich fragrance to combat the stew cooking in a heavy pot over the blaze. The bandit king gestured and one of his men tossed him a cushion from the litter, which he set down just beyond the stones ringing the fire pit. Shizumi allowed him to help her settle herself there and did her best not to shrink back when he lowered himself into a cross-legged position beside her.

"I had not expected to find such hospitality here," she stated, accepting a cup of tea from one of the other men. The cup itself was little better than a rough earthenware mug, but the tea was delicate and laced with a hint of jasmine. She sipped it, eyeing her host over the fragrant steam.

He laughed, elbows resting loosely on his thighs, seeming completely relaxed though she suspected he was aware of everything around him. "These forests are my home," he answered, "and a far kinder one than any city or manse. Since I reside here, it would be ungenerous of me not to welcome any who pass."

"And the fee?" Shizumi asked, making him chuckle again.

"Nothing you cannot afford," he assured her. "Do not worry, your honor is safe with me. Neither you nor your servants shall be touched, provided you do not resist. And your jewels and coin and aishone—well, such things can be replaced, yes?"

She dipped her head in acknowledgement, not trusting herself to answer as her fingers tightened around her tea.

The meal was a fine one, the stew rich and flavorful and well-stocked with pheasant and mushrooms, accompanied by a hearty bread baked over the same coals and enriched by herbs. Shizumi did her best to eat in what she imagined to be a ladylike fashion, taking small, nibbling bites when she would rather have torn into the food, which was far better than she normally got, especially on the road. She envied Geniji, who was ripping off hunks of bread to sop up the remains in her bowl and chasing it all down with a large tankard of ale.

Shirikin continued to make small talk throughout, all his conversation directed at Shizumi herself even though Dairamu and then Akino had been placed on her other side, as befitted her lady-in-waiting and her majordomo. Nori and Masai were off to the side with Geniji and the rest of the bandits, though none of them had been mistreated—indeed, several of the men were currently roaring at some joke Geniji had just told. If not for the disparity in weapons, and the promise to strip away all their valuables on the morrow, it might have been a happy gathering of old friends.

Finally, the meal was over. Shizumi yawned, quickly covering the gesture with a hand and doing her best to appear mortified. "Oh, excuse me!" she whispered. "It is just, it is late, and I am not used to such excitement!"

"Of course." The bandit leader rose smoothly to his feet and gave her a hand rising from the cushion. "There is a stream just beyond those trees there, and my men will give you and your maid privacy to see to your washing up. The ground here is sufficiently soft, but you may sleep in your litter if you prefer. I promise, none will disturb you." He bowed deeply. "May you rest well, dear lady. Until the morrow."

She dipped into a clumsy curtsy in return, then hurried away as quick as her robes would allow, Dairamu following behind her. Sure enough, they found the stream barely a stone's throw past the curtain of branches and vines he had indicated, its waters shallow and narrow but swift and cool.

This time, when a man jumped out at her, Shizumi did not scream. Instead, she smiled—and held out her hand.

Several hours later, as the moon rose to its peak and cool silver light bathed the clearing, Shirikin awoke—to find the edge of a nihono against his throat. "Stand, slowly," Shizumi ordered. "Or your head will roll at your feet."

The Forest King's eyes, still sticky with sleep, widened at the threat, and at the sight of her standing there, for she was now in nothing more than the hosode and ponmei she had been wearing beneath those robes, and wielding her own sword, which Isano had returned to her by the stream. But then his eyes met hers, no doubt seeing the gravity there, and he judged the way her hand did not shake in the slightest, and he nodded, ever so carefully.

She stepped back to let him rise to his feet, the sword never leaving his neck. All around them, his men slept—while her own crept among them, using sturdy leather straps to tie hands and feet. A few woke to the rough treatment but were quieted by a hand over the mouth before they could cry out.

"You have been busy," Shirikin remarked, seeming oddly calm for a man in his predicament. "And your transformation is remarkable." He waved his hand in a bow, as he could not very well incline his body just now, not without disastrous consequences. "You are not, then, a lady of means?"

Shizumi chuckled, though she kept the utterance low to keep from rousing anyone. "No. I am Misataki Shizumi, of the Honjofu.

And you, Shirikin of Yunigiri, are under arrest for repeated acts of robbery, including that of many nobles. Such crimes are punishable by death."

His gaze, which had narrowed upon seeing his situation, had widened at her name, but now they returned to their normal size, and he even smiled. "It is an honor, noble Misataki," he intoned. "Truly, your reputation precedes you."

"As does yours," she replied. "Which is why I am here." It had not been particularly out of her way to detour through this forest, and she had been hearing tales of the Forest King and his crimes for months. Best to put a stop to his thievery now, while she could.

But he laughed. "And will you execute me yourself?" he asked lightly, tapping a finger against her blade. "Or turn me over to the local authorities?"

She frowned. "I am no executioner," she pointed out. "I will deliver you to the local lord and allow him to sit in judgement. I am sure justice will be swift."

That only made him laugh more, so much so that she was forced to pull her blade away lest he slit his own throat upon its edge from his body's shaking. "Why wait?" he managed at last, holding his arms wide. "For here I am!"

It took her only an instant to grasp his meaning as she put the pieces together. The blades. The neat appearance. The fine language. "You are the local lord," she stated, frowning as she considered this new wrinkle.

He brushed her sword aside again, gently, and bowed properly now, the short bow of one to an equal. "Riniki Yamoi, at your service," he declared as he straightened back up and eyed her, grinning widely. "And these fine fellows are my men, nobles all. So you see," he continued, "you have already reported me to myself, and I have already passed judgement." He seemed to find this all terribly amusing, his manner that of a man who had just told a fine joke and was waiting for the rest of the room to laugh and applaud his wit.

Shizumi's frown only deepened into a scowl. "You rob from

your own subjects," she accused, "and from those who you should, as the local lord, be protecting!"

Riniki shrugged. "What of it?" he replied. "It is my land, and I will behave upon it as I see fit." He let his grin slip, and drew himself up to his full height, which while not tall was well above her own. "Only a noble of equal or greater rank may judge me, and you are not such a one. Therefore, you will untie my men and be on your way." A ghost of the smile touched his lips. "You may leave your costly disguises behind."

Shizumi clenched her teeth, a low growl escaping her throat. But what could she do? As Shirikin, the Forest King, this man was nothing more than a thief, and deserved to be punished. But as Riniki Yamoi, he was a noble and untouchable save by orders from the emperor or one of his senior nobles, such as a karo or one of the Rojiri. She herself was only a Honjofu, and a commoner to boot. She could not touch such a man, no matter how he deserved it. And he knew it.

She glanced around, hoping for some way out of this dilemma. Fail in her duty or break the same laws she upheld? Her gaze strayed to Geniji, who shrugged, and then to Akino—who tilted his head to the side and tapped his ear, looking puzzled. Had he not heard? Riniki's words had been loud enough to carry, surely.

And then she understood.

"Shirikin," Shizumi declared loudly, "you are hereby found guilty of multiple counts of robbery and theft, including against those of noble blood. You have interfered with the emperor's peace and threatened the lives and prosperity of his subjects. The penalty for this is death." She raised her blade, twisting it so that its edge was down toward the ground, its length extending forward from her arm, its chiseled tip aligned with the man's left eye. "You may attempt to defend yourself if you wish."

Finally her host's sense of humor failed him. "Are you mad?" he demanded. "Did you not hear what I said? I am Riniki Yamoi, lord of this land! You cannot touch me!"

She only shook her head. "I am afraid I cannot hear you over the wind in the trees," she announced, though the sky was clear and the night silent save for them. "But there is no need, for words will not save you. Draw your sword, or be cut down." And she drew back her blade, her arm crossing her body as she raised the weapon over her head, her other hand rising to grip the hilt as well and hold it ready in a classic strike pose.

"You would not dare assault a noble!" Her opponent tried again. "The emperor would have your head!" But still she acted as if she had not heard. Nor did any of her warriors respond to his increasingly desperate entreaties. Finally, with a curse he spat to one side, Riniki pulled his aishone pouch from his neck, quickly extracting and downing a small shard, then drew his own sword with rapidly increasing skill and settled into a practiced fighting stance. "Very well then, mudborn whore," he snarled, all gentility and humor stricken from his face and tone, "come at me, if you can."

He was not a terrible swordsman. In fact, he was better than many—his aishone must have been from someone who had fought in true combat, a warrior of some sort and not just a noble who practiced swordplay for sport. But to Shizumi he was only slightly better than an untrained youth. His first strike was clumsy, his motions too wide, his control of the blade too loose. It was child's play to slip past the weapon, knocking it aside with her shoulder against his arms as she stepped in and slashed with all the speed and strength she possessed.

As promised, then, Shirikin the Forest King's head rolled at his feet, even as his body toppled backward to land with a muffled thud upon the needle-coated ground.

After wiping and sheathing her blade, Shizumi sought out the man among their captors she judged to be the most senior of them. "It is a shame," she said loudly, "that before his own death Shirikin killed Riniki Yamoi, your lord and master. But now the bandit is gone, and these forests are free of him and his kind. Should they ever return, merely send for me and I will clear this place of any who linger and would cause harm." She fixed the man with her sharpest glare as he quaked upon the ground, his face pale and coated in sweat. "Do you understand?" she asked, and he nodded frantically, not making a sound though he had not been gagged.

"Good. See that the others do as well," she warned. "It would be a shame if I should need to return."

Then she gathered her warriors and had Isano lead them back through the forest to the path, for he had been following them and had mastered the route to the bandits' hideout.

"Will any of them speak of this, do you think?" Geniji asked as they walked. She had shucked her hantien and was already buckling her breastplate back on.

Shizumi considered that, then shook her head. "No. They are too afraid of what could happen next." She allowed herself a grim smile. "If I am willing to overlook their lord's stature, why would I hesitate to ignore theirs?"

"He had stature?" Akino remarked, his voice as dry as ever. "I heard nothing."

"Nor I," Dairamu agreed solidly. The others all chimed in as well, and Shizumi smiled. Who needed wealth or fine clothes when you had loyalty such as this?

She would miss those cushions, however.

CHAPTER EIGHT

Arata leaned on his yanoi and sighed, both gauntleted hands clenched around the metal-wrapped shaft of the spear with his cheek against the right where it sat uppermost, the weapon's long, slim blade pressing against the edge of his jingaso but not hard enough to unsettle the iron hat from his head. At least it was peaceful here, he thought. The night was clear, the temperature pleasant, almost warm but for the mild breeze whistling through the peaks up ahead, and here in this spot the stone beneath his boots was nearly level, as if this one tiny plateau had been worn down for him so that he might stand amid the crags and cliffs that surrounded him. Standing here, staring out across the mountain range, he felt that he could be the only living creature left in all the world.

That idea left him feeling sad, but he still appreciated the quiet.

It was better than fighting, at least. He had joined the aiashe because he'd needed a job after his father had tossed him out of the house, and his aitachi was not strong enough to be of any real use. Fortunately, the emperor's army did not require that you have a strong Relicant Touch, only that you be able to hold a spear and march and follow directions.

These were all things Arata could do.

It had been four years now. He was still a common soldier, not even a gocho, but he was fine with that. Truth be told, he didn't like the idea of having to give orders, or having to be responsible for anyone but himself. This way, all he had to do was keep his armor clean and his weapons sharp, make sure he was presentable, and follow whatever instructions he was given.

Which, considering he had not fared well the two times he had been forced to actually enter combat, currently consisted of standing here, occasionally hiking along the range, and keeping an eye out for anyone trying to slip across from Yatamaro.

That much, Arata could handle.

He straightened from his slumped resting stance, lifting his spear and settling it against his right shoulder with his right hand comfortably settled on its lower haft to keep it balanced and his left dropping so that he could hook his thumb into his belt. Time to patrol again. He had no way of telling the time, of course, but he and Goro and Kazuo and Seiji took turns covering this stretch of mountain, trading off every few hours, and he considered it sufficient to get in at least two patrols during each shift, one at the start and one near the end. He judged that Goro would be here to relieve him soon, which meant it was time for that final walk.

Besides, his legs got stiff if he didn't move around from time to time.

Whistling softly to himself, Arata clambered down from his vantage point, using his free hand to catch himself against the rocks when he stumbled and shifting the yanoi back to an upright position so it could function as a walking stick. He had grown up in the flatlands, so picking his way over rocks and up steep inclines or steeper descents was new to him, but his boots had good strong soles and his sturdy gauntlets allowed him to clutch at cliff sides, so he was not overly worried. They had also selected this stretch to patrol because it was the most level spot for miles around, so it was not as if he were forced to scale the peaks like some armored goat.

Up ahead, Arata could already see a steep drop, the ridge beneath his feet ending as abruptly as if someone had sliced it away with a massive blade. A long ways below, the Zinyang River ran, its swift, cold waters having cut that deep, deep channel through the mountains themselves. He could hear the soft but furious rush of the river if he listened, though normally that sound was lost amid the general billowing of the breeze. When they had first been sent up here as guards, Arata had wondered why they did not worry more about the Zinyang, for it ran clear across Rimbaku, right along the top edge of Hochiro before angling northwest to skirt Saruto's rim and then run out to sea. A determined man in a fast boat, it seemed to him, could take that to almost within a stone's throw of Awaihinshi.

Then he had seen the river for himself. Up here, where it raged to cut through solid stone and escape the bare mountains for the richer lands below, it was impossible to even consider about venturing into, no matter how sturdy the boat. The waters churned so fast they whipped a froth nearly halfway up the channel, the spray able to fleck Arata's face if he leaned out over the edge and peered down. No, the river was not a passable zone, they had little to worry about on that score.

These mountains, on the other hand, could be traversed, given a little time and a lot of patience. And a good, sturdy pair of boots.

A strange sound made Arata freeze, shifting automatically into a high crouch as his right hand lifted the yanoi, rotating to put the spear haft across his body where his left hand also grasped it, ready to target the glittering spearhead at whatever threat presented. "Goro?" he called out, his friend's name echoing over the peaks. "That you?" No one answered, though Arata would not put it past his replacement to play such a prank upon him. Still, when there were no other sounds after another moment he straightened and, with a quick backward glance or three, resumed his inspection of this area they had been ordered to guard. But the night now remained stubbornly silent and utterly empty, even birds choosing not to venture into these lifeless heights.

After checking the Zinyang—which still raced past down below, oblivious and empty—Arata turned and retraced his steps, then continued on in the opposite direction, his eyes scanning his surroundings. There were no new sounds, however, nothing but the thump of his own boots upon the ground, the sharper *tap-tap-tap* of the spear butt's metal knob rapping against the stone, and the gentle hiss of the late-night breeze. He walked for a while, finally reaching the cliff that made going farther impossible, and pivoted on his heel to return to his perch.

Only to find himself staring at a shadow, up ahead. A shadow of a man, but upright rather than stretched out upon the ground, standing and facing him like a wrestler facing off at the start of a match.

Arata blinked—and the shadow was gone. The stone before him was as empty as before. As empty as ever.

Had he dreamed that? Moving quietly and carefully, Arata stepped back over to where that shadow had been. There was no trace of it now, no sign of scuff marks, no burns, no ancient and arcane symbols carved into the rock. Perhaps a cloud had passed before the moon, and it had been that shadow he had seen?

He shook his head. Whatever it was, figment of his imagination or misinterpreted cloud or even reflection of some dark figure lurking nearby, it seemed to have gone. He was alone out here, as always.

Retreating to his perch, Arata turned to study his surroundings once more, the spear once more resting against his cheek.

He barely had time to stiffen in surprise when a shadowy arm wrapped around his head and a dark hand clamped over his mouth, squeezing his jaws shut and preventing him from calling out.

Then the other hand rose before him, brandishing a blade that seemed carved from twilight, so dark it appeared to absorb other light. That midnight weapon flickered as it swooped in, and Arata cried out against his bonds, feeling the line of fire etch itself across his throat. But the hand held him immobile.

He let his spear fall, scrabbling at that arm, but it held him in a grip of iron and already he could feel his own strength beginning to fail. Still he tugged and scratched and slapped and pulled, desperate to free himself. All to no avail. Soon enough he felt his legs begin to give way, their sturdiness leeched out along with the blood geysering from his carved-apart throat, and he would have stumbled and sunk to his rear if that same arm had not kept him upright. His vision began to dim, his breath coming in labored gasps, and still that arm did not waver in the slightest. Arata slumped, his world dwindling, his consciousness fading, and at last the arm released him, allowing him to slump to the ground.

His last sight was of a pair of shadow-shrouded feet, standing mere inches from his head.

The dark figure waited another moment, as if to be sure Arata were truly dead and not just hoping to catch his would-be killer off guard. Then it bent, grasped the dead guard under his arms, and dragged him quietly away from the designated guardpost, around a large boulder and out of sight.

A few minutes later, Arata returned to his post, adjusting his jingaso as he did. Stooping, he retrieved his yanoi and settled back into his usual position.

"Oi, Arata," another soldier declared a few minutes after that, jogging up the incline that separated this spot from the small camp they'd set up in a tiny little valley down below. "It's Goro, come to relieve you." The other soldier, shorter and rounder than Arata but still sturdy and capable, saluted with the hand not currently holding the spear.

"Oi, Goro," Arata replied. "Welcome." He stood and waited for the other guard to arrive. "It's been a quiet eve."

His friend nodded. "What about that sound I heard as I was making my way up here? Like metal or stone scraping against stone."

Arata shook his head. "I heard nothing," he assured his fellow guard. "Nor saw anything, either." He smiled. "Enjoy the peace. I need food and then sleep." And, without waiting for a reply, he sauntered off, shortening his steps so that he could more comfortably wend his way down to their camp.

Behind him, Goro shook his head. Arata had always been a little odd, but that was not a problem. He was a decent soldier, and a good partner, always solid, always dependable.

Except that he might not have thought so if he had turned to stare toward their own kingdom instead of facing out toward the rival nation ahead.

Because then he might have seen Arata skid and skip and stumble his way down into their camp, pause to pull from the fire a stick upon which roasted a winter hare they had caught that morning—and then continue on, stick in hand, to the camp's far edge.

And keep right on walking.

Within seconds Arata was swallowed up by the night. Almost as if the guard had never been.

Goro knew nothing of this, however. He had his own shift to start, his own patrols to make.

He was just swapping places with Kazuo as the sun emerged, lending the mountains a rosy hue like a young girl blushing.

And it was then, in the new day's light, that Goro noticed something on the ground up ahead, partially hidden by a large boulder there.

It was a man, or at least he judged that it had been once. Now the body lay blackened and twisted as if roasted in a fire. Was it Arata? Goro could not be sure, what with all the features having burnt away. He could make out a vicious cut clear across the front of the neck, most likely the cause of death. But this body had been stripped naked, all of its burnt flesh exposed. It lay there, twisted in agony, its mouth open in a silent, black-toothed scream.

Only its eyes had escaped such damage, though perhaps they too were suffering some hideous torment.

For they had been plucked from the corpse's anguished face, leaving empty sockets to gape out at the world that had betrayed it.

CHAPTER NINE

Kagiri had been paying little attention to their surroundings, allowing the spirits within him to handle such mundanities as determining campsites and setting up guard rotations. He rode, lost in his head, battling for space there with the five ghosts that haunted him day and night, struggling to maintain any sense of self as their thoughts and emotions swirled inside him.

Thus it was with some surprise that, upon feeling his horse slow to a stop one day near noon, he glanced up and realized that he recognized the town that had sprung up before them like a mirage forming out of the heat haze hanging thick upon the still, dry air.

He also recognized the men who were slouched or leaned or stood waiting for them. Particularly their leader, distinctive in his lilac-shaded kitoro with its pattern of flower blossoms and curling vines and delicate leaves, the fine silk robe in sharp contrast to his dark fur vest and glossy black pants, and equally at odds with his gold brocade sash and the nihono shoved through it at a rakish angle.

"Well, well," Daro Barindo, leader of the Kindichi, called out as Kagiri and the merchants halted some distance from him, his words carrying easily across the dirt and rock and occasional scrub brush between their two groups. "Welcome back, travelers! Truly, we did not expect to meet again, and certainly not so soon!" He and his bandits had tried to rob them when they had passed through before, but Kagiri and Noniki had used warrior aishone to stand up to the men's threats, and Barindo had backed down. It seemed, however, that they might be so fortunate this time. "You have one fewer of you now, though, eh?" the bandit leader continued, stroking his thick, scraggly beard. "The youth with the loud voice. What happened to him, hm?"

Kagiri felt a pang at the thought of his younger brother, one that cut through all those other voices, silencing them with a wave of fresh grief. Where was Noniki now? he wondered. He had sacrificed himself, allowing the merchants to toss him into the Tawasiri toward what they assumed would be his death or madness, so that Niki could escape. And he had, since there had been no sign of him when Kagiri had staggered back out again, now carrying the Gensaiba like unwanted memories that would not fade away. But where had his brother gone from there? There was little out here, only a few scattered villages at best, and he had been alone, unarmed, with little coin and—in all fairness—less sense. Niki had always been the impulsive one of them, leaping to conclusions and diving into situations without stopping to consider. But, before, he'd always had Kagiri there to balance him out, and to pull him back out of trouble.

He hoped Niki had survived somehow. Otherwise, what had been the point?

Still, he suspected none of that showed on his face as he nudged his horse forward, deliberately positioning himself in front of the merchants and their guards, hands loose against his thighs, his two nihono within each reach.

"That is none of your concern," he answered—or at least, Geido Shinen did. He was the loudest of the Gensaiba, and frequently it was his words that tumbled from Kagiri's lips. "Friendly word of advice," he added now, "stand aside and let us pass once more. It would be your best course of action."

Daro Barindo seemed to consider that a second, but then he shook his head. He seemed almost sad as he replied, "We appreciate your kind offer not to cause trouble, truly we do. But I think this time we will need to insist upon proper payment for passage." He whistled, and more bandits spilled from the houses along the edge of town, all of them as rough as Barindo himself, all of them with wild hair and mismatched clothing. And all of them heavily armed, most with clubs and spears but a few with chokoto and two with bows.

Last time, the bandits had numbered an even dozen, against fifteen in Kagiri's party. It seemed Barindo had not liked being outmatched, however, and had recruited more help. Now they had twenty in all, against fourteen.

Or, more accurately, against one, for Kagiri saw no reason to let Joshi and the other guards get in his way, and the merchants would be nothing but a liability in any sort of combat that did not involve sharp words and rows of numbers.

Which was why he held up a hand, indicating that the others should hang back, as he rode forward to meet the Kindichi alone. They let him approach, their leader clearly both amused and curious as to why he would behave in such a foolhardy manner, and thus Kagiri was able to halt his horse less than a full length from the bandits assembled before him.

"I will only say this once," he stated, his voice loud and clear. Shinen, again. "Step aside, or die." He shrugged. "It is all the same to me, but believe me when I say you would prefer the former to the latter."

This close, he could see that Daro Barindo had surprisingly delicate features beneath the beard and mustache and all that hair. If shaved clean, bathed, and coiffed, the bandit king could have been striking, almost beautiful with those high, sharp cheekbones, that straight nose, the finely arched brows over delicately angled eyes, and those bow-shaped lips. None of that potential beauty was visible in his sneer, however, as he laughed in Kagiri's face.

"Your concern is touching," Barindo declared. "But I think not." He drew his nihono, which actually required him to shove the entire sash to the side first and then haul the sword forth as if it were a hatchet, yanking it upward before being able to reverse his grip and slide the blade fully clear from its scabbard. Then he leveled it at Kagiri, the chiseled tip relatively steady, at least, though his arm was extended too far for any real strength and his other hand was still clutching the sheath instead of adding to his grip. "Dismount and strip and I may still let you live." His teeth were as bad as ever, uneven and yellowed and even more unsettling given their clash with the potential allure of his other features, as he grinned. "Hesitate, and I will not be so merciful."

Kagiri frowned, then gave a short, clipped nod in return. "So be it."

Shinen took a step back, the time for blustering past, and allowed Shito Kibi to rise to the fore. She was generally quieter than him, but words no longer mattered here, and Kibi was undisputed at her mastery of the blade. It was she who guided Kagiri's hands as he yanked both nihono free in a single, fluid motion, drawing with opposite hands so that the blades slid across his waist as they emerged before flashing out, over his horse's head, to take two of the Kindichi in the throat. Daro Barindo was just out of reach, sadly, but he reeled backward, cursing, as the bandits to either side crumpled, their blood spraying outward, flecks staining his delicate robe.

Two down, Onyoku Jeizen stated. As the best Gensaiba at hand-to-hand, he often took over when in close combat, though at times he gave ground to Bushiki Kenin for his skill at wrestling. *Eighteen remaining.*

"Get him!" Daro Barindo screamed, though he took several more steps back, placing himself safely behind the bulk of his men. "Now!"

Archers, Komu Setsui warned. *Do not let them have a clear shot.* An expert with the bow herself, she kept Kagiri from stumbling into their path, using other bandits to block them from firing down into the melee. He would have to deal with them soon, as the more foes he dispatched the more of a target he became, but he could not worry about that yet.

An opportunity presented itself, however, when one Kindichi leaped forward, spear extended to impale Kagiri through the chest. The yanoi was of the standard sort, with a long, narrow blade and no crossguard, and he batted it aside easily, letting the spearhead glide through the empty air before him. The bandit had moved in too close on the attack, not trusting in her weapon's greater reach, and Kagiri granted her the fate she had chosen for him instead, his one sword taking her right between the breasts, cleaving her heart and bestowing upon her the quick release of a painless death.

She slumped forward and he left his sword there a moment, trapped in her chest, as he tugged the spear from her fading grip. A quick overhead spin of the long weapon knocked back several of her approaching friends before Kagiri let it settle into his grip, the yanoi now pointed back the way she had come. He cocked his arm and then snapped it forward, the spear flying overhead—to take one of the archers in the stomach, the long blade piercing him front to back. He let out a gasp as both air and life fled, then tumbled backward on the roof where he had perched, disappearing from view even as Kagiri retrieved his second sword from the dead Kindichi now draped against his horse, kicking her body away into the other bandits crowding to reach him.

Sixteen, and only one of them with a bow.

Do not get overconfident, Kenin warned, serious as ever. *It only takes one lucky strike to down you, just like any other man.*

And if you do not stop to consider your actions, it becomes even easier for you to misstep, Nikiyu Sinchu agreed. Ever the pessimist, his soft voice always disapproving. Yet of them all he was perhaps the most well-rounded, not the master at any one skill but talented at all. He sized up the rabble now and was forced to admit, *Provided you do not get careless, this should not prove overly challenging.*

In other words, Shinen cut in, *easy as pouring tea!* He laughed, the joyous sound escaping Kagiri's lips, and several of his foes cringed to see their sole opponent so clearly unconcerned. Which was of course why Shinen had done that. He was boisterous by nature, true, but he also knew the value of undermining an enemy's confidence.

Two more Kindichi surged forth—they could not all reach him at once while he remained mounted, especially as he nudged his horse with his calves and it responded by turning in a tight circle, knocking several of the bandits back—and swung with chokotos, the ring-pommeled straight swords less elegant than a nihono but no less deadly in the right hands.

Fortunately, theirs were not those hands, and Kagiri disarmed one—literally—with a single sweep, severing the man's arm just below the elbow before booting him away so that his screams and his blood engulfed his friends on that side. The other's blade he blocked, sending her thrust scraping across his saddle before his elbow took her in the face, smashing her nose to pulp. She fell bonelessly to the ground, only to be crushed by his horse's hooves.

Fourteen.

The remaining Kindichi were growing wary, having just seen four of their friends die in as many seconds, and backed away a step, giving him space. That was a bad sign—they were now starting to think instead of merely reacting. Kagiri knew he had to change that, and quickly.

Wiping one nihono clean against his leg, he sheathed the blade and drew a simple dagger from his boot instead. A quick flip put the blade solidly in his palm, and a flick of his wrist sent the weapon spinning end over end through the air—to plant itself point-first through the eye of the remaining archer. She had been perched on the opposite roof from the first, leaning forward as she struggled to find a clear shot, and now she pitched forward, her body slamming into the ground at her friend's feet, the impact driving the dagger even farther in until its point actually pierced the back of her skull. Several bandits cried out in fear and dismay and no little anger to see her like that, and Kagiri felt a tight, humorless grin etch itself across his face.

Good, Setsui allowed. *Rile them up so they cannot think straight.*

Which was why his next move was to charge.

His horse barreled into the assembled bandits, the stallion's broad front smashing two aside. Then he reared, his hooves cracking one's skull and another's chest. They were down to a dozen now, and that number dropped still further as Kagiri laid about him with both swords, drawing the second again so that he could strike to both sides at once. His blows lacked the power of two hands but his height advantage made up for that, and the nihono's razored edges could slice flesh as easily as paper, even when wielded one-handed. By the time he allowed his horse to stop again, huffing for breath, there were only six bandits remaining.

Including Daro Barindo, who stood a good ten paces behind the rest, eyes wide as he watched his gang of thugs be destroyed by a lone man.

"Face me!" Kagiri bellowed, unleashing Shinen again, for he was the best of them at posturing. "Spare your remaining men and face me in single combat! Let our blades alone decide their fate!"

Barindo hesitated, his cowardice even more evident now without his usual swagger to cover it, and Kagiri lashed out, slaying two more bandits as they turned to watch their boss. Four left, including their leader.

"How do I know you will fight fair, and keep to your word?" the bandit chief answered finally, swishing his blade before him in what the uninitiated might think was a display of martial prowess but Kagiri dismissed as inexperienced bravado.

"Why should I lie?" he replied, thrusting one blade through a bandit's throat and the other sweeping out to take a second's head. Now only one stood near him, and that one dropped her club and fled, screaming that she was quitting this life of bullying and banditry for good. "Besides," he added, his grin now a mean one as he nudged his horse forward in a slow walk, "it is not like you have any more bandits to hide behind."

Daro Barindo drew himself up and raised his sword before him with both hands, the tip wavering slightly from the tremor in his limbs. "Very well, climb down from that horse and face me like a man. If you dare." To his credit, the former bandit chief's voice shook only slightly more than his hands.

Kagiri laughed at this final, desperate display but nodded and slid from his steed, sheathing his second nihono as he did. He transferred his free hand to the remaining blade, advancing until he was mere steps from Barindo, then stopping and letting his sword tap against the bandit's. The two glittering lengths of steel crossed in mid-air like horses entwining their long necks in greeting.

"Very well, I am here," he told the bandit, who was beginning to quake visibly now that his death was so close. "Begin."

For an instant, Barindo only stared at him, eyes widening, color leaching from his face. Then, with a strangled cry, he raised his sword over his head and leaped forward—

—and without even having to shift his own blade, Kagiri impaled the bandit chief through the chest, the man's own momentum forcing the sword through his heart and out his back. Barindo's hands lost their strength as he died, and Kagiri freed one hand from his own sword to reach up and catch his dead foe's nihono before it could fall to the dirt and be dishonored by such treatment, twisting his other wrist so that his sword turned to the side and the dead Kindichi leader slid off it and onto the ground in a twisted heap.

It was over.

He was studying his new blade—which was longer and finer than his current second, and would be replacing it—when he heard horses' hooves behind him. Turning, Kagiri saw the others approaching openly now that the danger had past, picking their way through the corpses piled all around.

"Impressive," Kishin Narai proclaimed, and Kagiri did not miss the slight tremble to the merchant's voice. They had not witnessed his one previous battle against aiashe sent to retake the Tawasiri, so this had been their first glimpse of the Gensaiba in action. "Truly, you are a marvel to behold, Kagiri, and we are ever more delighted in our choice of you as our strong right arm."

"Absolutely," Fujiko Oritano agreed, her voice cheerful as ever though he noticed she averted her eyes from the brutal reminders of bloodshed surrounding her. "We were right to put our trust in you."

"And now, you must trust us in return," Shizu Yokori added. Her sharp eyes swept the dead bandits but she seemed unfazed by the carnage, which did not surprise Kagiri—of the merchants backing him, she had always struck him as the most coldly pragmatic.

"These Kindichi have been controlling the region for months, I suspect," the narrow, sharp-planed Yokori continued. "They must have robbed every traveler who passed this way. I would not be surprised if the houses here are bursting with all the coin and jewels and silk they have stolen. Aishone as well." A crafty look claimed her narrow features. "We could use that treasure, invest it, and grow it by leaps and bounds. You will be a rich man."

"And of course we will advise you on how to maintain that wealth," Jiro Masute stated, his long hair blowing in the breeze as he guided his own horse up beside the others. Only Eien Kawatai had not joined the little half-circle, for he was still staring and frowning at the dead bandits, as if he could not comprehend why they were not on their feet still, laughing and joking and swaggering about. "Allow us to manage your wealth and you will want for nothing," Masute concluded.

Kagiri frowned as he bent to retrieve his new weapon's sheath from the body of its former owner. "Do with the money as you will," he informed the merchants around him, straightening back up and sliding the weapon home before swapping it for the second of the two that had been at his side. That one he added to the back of his saddle, with the two other blades he had taken from the officers he had killed before.

"I have no need for wealth," he added as he remounted and wheeled his horse about, stepping it over Barindo's body and walking into town toward the well that waited there. Fresh, cool water was all he required at the moment, though he had barely broken a sweat during the fight. Then some food, some rest, and supplies for the rest of their journey. What did coin matter to him now? The ghosts inside his head had no need for it, and without his brother here he had little to spend it on himself.

"Well, that was an abject failure," Yokori snapped, though she kept her voice low so that the retreating warrior would not hear. "No need for wealth? What kind of man is he?"

"One from a different world than our own," Kawatai offered, finally joining them, "and very different from his brother, whose greed we at least understood."

"Yes, greed we could work with," Oritano agreed. "This?" She shook her head, the jeweled pins in her hair glittering in the sun-light. "What can we do with this?"

"Nothing," Narai confirmed, his eyes on Kagiri's back. He sighed. "Which means we must needs turn to other options, if we wish to retain any sort of control."

"We will have to be very, very careful," Masute warned, his sharp eyes judging the corpses heaped about them. "He is even more deadly than we had first thought."

"True, but a knife is still a knife, no matter how sharp its blade," Narai countered. "Keep a tight grip on the handle and you have nothing to fear." He frowned, stroking his short, neat beard as he considered. "Our first attempt to grip it failed," he allowed after a moment. "We will adjust, and hold more tightly the second time." The smile that touched his lips was devoid of warmth or mirth, but it had confidence to spare. "We have between us a great deal of experience, and he is still at his heart naught but a callow youth. We will prevail in this contest."

"We'd better," Kawatai muttered, but nodded along with the rest. They were all committed to this path, after all. They had little choice but to see it through.

It was that or share in the Kindichi's fate.

CHAPTER TEN

"I do not know." It was Brother Yamaki's voice, drifting into Noniki's head like a stray wind sneaking in through a cracked window, tickling at the edge of his thoughts like an itch inside his mind. "The damage is...severe." The healer monk sounded concerned, even resigned, his usual wry humor absent from his voice and replaced by sorrow and what sounded suspiciously like guilt. Who was he talking about, Noniki wondered. What had happened?

And why could he not see anything?

He glanced around—and then realized that he had not. In fact, he had not moved his head, nor had his eyes opened. He blinked, but still his eyes remained shut, their lids firmly fastened as if sealed there. What was wrong with him? He opened his mouth to ask—only to discover that none of his face was obeying his commands, and his voice remained trapped in his chest, mute as a stone.

Which was when the thought lanced through him like lightning, rendering a moment of clarity amid the strange haze he found himself fighting through:

He was the patient Brother Yamaki was speaking of! And the guilt he heard was because it had been defending the monk that had gotten Noniki injured in his place. He recalled the massive, feverish man, the bucket, the impact, all of it. And nothing between then and now, when he could not speak, could not move, could not see.

Had he died? Was he now nothing but an akatai, doomed to haunt this monastery for all eternity, plaguing its still-living tenants?

But if that was the case, would he not have more mobility? And more awareness of his surroundings? Or did those household demons all begin like this, little more than stray thoughts and the occasional burst of hearing or vision, slowly becoming more active over time? Was that what he had to look forward to, rejoicing when, a decade or more hence, he suddenly became able to leave this healing room and extend his spectral presence to the hall?

No! Noniki gritted his teeth—or at least he did so in his head. *I will not let that happen to me,* he insisted. *I will not haunt my friends, who tried to save me from myself! I will purge myself from these walls first!*

As if that had been some sort of test and he had just passed, he felt his mind leap upward. Suddenly there was light, and he could see again! But not the meditation room where he now knew his body lay in some sort of battered and broken state, not the monks no doubt clustered around his bed, not even the walls there with their bones jutting forth like people had been trapped in liquid stone which had then hardened all around them.

No, instead Noniki found himself looking down upon the monastery as he soared high above it, his view rapidly expanding to take in the entire castle and all of its grounds, then the surrounding hills, then the mountains beyond. Settlements dotted the land, and he could make out lights in homes, see smoke from fires, even pick out small flashes of color from clothing and jewelry. He felt as if he could somehow see the people within those huts and cottages and houses and tents, even, not so much through normal sight but as some sort of sense of their heat, their warmth, their very life.

Was this what being a spirit was like? Because, other than not having any sense of his own self beyond thought, and not being able to interact with anyone or anything, it was not entirely all bad!

A tall, dark shape down to the south caught his attention, and Noniki shuddered, or would have if he'd still possessed a body with which to shake. He knew that collection of carved black stone spires. The Tawasiri, the Tower of Ghosts. That was where he had lost Kagiri. Odd that, from up here, the ancient fortress did not have the same sense of dread he'd experienced upon seeing it from the ground. Or perhaps that was because he lacked a body and therefore had little left to fear?

But what was that strange, swirling patch north of there?

His attention seemed to act as a rudder, steering his consciousness, because he felt himself shifting, no longer gaining height, and now gliding northwest from the Tawasiri, toward that odd mix of colors and shadows that had caught his mind's eye. It resembled a cloud, if a cloud were to possess hues beyond gray, and for those to spin and flash and flutter within it like moths trapped in a jar. It was too low for a cloud as well, and too singular, and too purposeful, following a steady course rather than letting itself be blown hither and yon by the winds.

As Noniki descended toward it, it seemed to sense his presence, and stopped, coiling in upon itself like a snake preparing to strike. Then, when he was near enough to see separate strands of color within its billowing mass, it launched itself upward, wrapping around him and engulfing him in its flickering mix of shades.

Ah! It was like being plunged into an ice-cold bath! He felt the sense of comforting warmth that had enveloped him suddenly vanish, its protection stripped away, leaving him raw and defenseless before the biting cold of the strange cloud, which tore at the edges of his consciousness like a rabid dog gnawing at anyone foolish enough to come within reach.

Everywhere it struck, the cloud left him smarting, his entire self pinched and bruised, and his mind whirled, desperately seeking some way to defend itself. Even worse, with each passing second that cold sucked away some of his strength, some of his will to live. It was stealing the color and energy from his spirit, he knew, turning him as cloudy and gray and listless as itself—moreso, since it had attacked with such sinister purpose and clearly had a sense of purpose driving it forward. But he would not, once it was done with him—he would be little more than his own patch of mental fog, drifting here and there, unable to focus and without enough will left to care.

What would Kagiri think of him then, should his older brother still somehow survive—in this world or another—and ever hear of his fate? He would be disappointed that his little brother had not fought back, had not clung tighter to the life he had purchased for him so dearly.

That thought filled Noniki with warmth again, but it was not the soft glow of comfort and well-being. It was the fiery furnace of sheer rage. How dare this cloud seek to rob him of Kagiri's precious gift? How dare it try to steal from him the colors that gave life meaning, when his brother had sacrificed himself to make sure Noniki still had an opportunity to enjoy such things? No, he would not allow that! He had fought against becoming akatai and he would fight against this as well! He might be naught but a spirit now, but he would not be a mere film upon the world, dark and dreary and nothing more! That was not his path!

With the power of rage fueling him, Noniki thrashed against the cloud's embrace. He tore holes in its shifting strands of color, burning away its swirls of gray and black, ripping free of its shadowy tendrils. He leapt upward, taking to the sky once more, leaving his assailant far behind, for something bound it to the earth and it could travel but a short distance above, at least for now, whereas he was unencumbered and could touch the very stars, if he wished. But he did not venture that high just yet, pausing when he was well above the flight of most birds, safely out of the cloud's reach, to take stock of himself now that he was free.

There was damage around the edges of his identity, he saw at once, frayed strands to the fabric of himself where that cloud had tried to unravel his spirit so that it could swallow him up. But the longer he was free, bathing in sunlight and the cool, crisp air, the more those tears reknit, sealing back together like damage done in reverse, leaving him feeling more cohesive, more coherent, more focused and stable than he had since he had awakened to this new state of being. Somehow the mere act of fighting free had helped him remember who he was and allowed him to reclaim himself.

Suddenly, Noniki felt that he had been given a choice. By whom, he could not say. Perhaps by the elements, perhaps by the sun and the stars, perhaps by the First Emperor himself. Or perhaps it was just a personal choice, one from deep within. However it came about, he knew that it was there, and that he had only a moment to decide. But truly, even that fraction of time was more than he needed. The choice was made the instant he knew it was even there, and he felt himself winging back across the countryside, rock and dirt and foliage blurring by beneath as his spirit was drawn back toward the hills, the monastery, the room, the bed, and finally his own body. Noniki felt himself falling, but it was the fall of a dusty worker into a cool stream, of a tired man into a warm bed—welcoming, relaxing, comforting. His body was there waiting for him and he nestled back into it eagerly, happily accepting once more that sense of weight upon his self, flesh and bone and blood drawing his thoughts down and cloaking them once more in substance, giving his mind a home and an outlet for its expressions.

He opened his eyes.

The monks were indeed clustered around his bed, and several of them gasped as they saw the fluttering of his lids. Brother Yamaki was instantly by his side, resting the back of one cool hand against his forehead.

"How—?" he muttered, but cut off when he realized Noniki was watching him intently. "How do you feel?" he managed instead.

Noniki considered that question fully. "Tired," he answered after a moment's thought. "Weak. A little dizzy." He frowned. "How should I feel?"

Several of the monks were whispering, their eyes wide, but Yamaki waved them to silence. "We were worried about you," was all he said. "What do you remember?"

"I remember an ox garbed in shirt and trousers," Noniki answered, chuckling, and groaned as his ribs and chest protested being shaken in that fashion. His head throbbed in protest as well, though it was a muted complaint. "I remember a bucket on my head, and not as a hat." He winced, studying the healer monk. "It's bad, isn't it?" he asked.

Brother Yamaki was not one to beat around the bush. "It was," the tall monk agreed. "Though now I am not so sure." His hands were not idle as he spoke, but rather were poking and prodding Noniki's head, his shoulders and neck, his chest and sides. "That bucket…it broke you, I'm afraid," he admitted once his examination was through. "I worried that, even if you recovered from the new fever your injuries had produced, you might never be able to lift your arms or feel your legs again." He bowed his shaved head, his sharp features drooping, his normally bright eyes dim. "I am sorry. You took that blow for me and I am grateful, but I would have taken it myself rather than subject you to such a life."

"Perhaps we both should have given it away, and then neither of us would have been struck," Noniki suggested, laughing again. His body's complaints were less than before, and he pushed himself into a sitting position. "I feel fine, though," he argued, swinging his legs over the side and resting his bare feet on the cool stones of the floor. He stood and was pleased to find that the dizziness had also passed. "See?" He crouched and then straightened again, twisting this way and that, and was pleased to see the old monk's face crease in a smile.

"I do not understand it," Yamaki declared, and surprised him by reaching out and pulling him into a brief but fierce hug. "It is a miracle, to be sure. But just like the sun, I do not need to explain it in order to be grateful for its existence."

Noniki grinned back at him. He felt better than he had even before his encounter with the bucket, truth be told. How strange. And his head felt clearer than it had in a long time. Evidently being transformed, however briefly, into an aimless spirit and being forced to combat a strangely ravenous cloud was good for helping one rediscover not only their joy in life, but their sense of self.

Now he just had to decide what to do with all that.

CHAPTER ELEVEN

"It was an…unusual…request, to be sure," the jeweler declared, spearing Chimehara with his sharp little gaze, his eyes as hard and bright as the diamonds in a pair of silver earrings dangling from the small stand upon his counter. "How did you come by these, again?" His fingers, long and slender, were still clenched around the objects in question, as if he would not release them to her if he were not satisfied with her answer.

She knew better, of course. That was her property, by right of kill, and she would not allow anyone to withhold it from her.

But now was not the time for a show of force. Instead she wrung her hands, the act sending flakes of dried clay drifting into the air between them. The jeweler raised an eyebrow in distaste, no doubt horrified at the mess she was making of his tidy, flittering little shop.

"It was my great-aunt," she stated, roughening her voice to match her current appearance, for the clay was not just on her hands but on her face, her clothes, even her hair. Slapping the clay-filled water all about her had been loathsome, but along with some cotton stuffed into her cheeks it had done the trick—no one looking at her now would see the lovely, elegant young lady in the House Chohu kitoro.

"She left them to me." She shrugged. "I don't have any use for them, myself—can you see me wearing jewels?—but my son, he's old enough to seek a bride, and this will be enough to win some girl's affections." Scrunching up her face had forced laugh lines to appear by her eyes, and Chimehara had taken care to dab those with the silty water. When that had dried, it had fixed the lines in place, adding years to her face. And making her eyes less noticeable, too.

The jeweler seemed satisfied by her story, for his hand extended, fingers spreading to offer the object nestled against his palm. A lovely silver bracelet, each link a single brilliant sapphire the rich, deep color of the sky at dusk. The stones were perfectly matched in size and color. Mistress Oisare had had a good eye. "I'm sure it will," he agreed as Chimehara took the bracelet from him. "And I hope it brings them and you much happiness."

Chimehara smiled as best she could with her cheeks so swollen, handing him several gold coins to cover the rest of the cost of his work. Then she tucked the bracelet away in the pouch at her belt and took her leave, not rushing but not dawdling either. She could not wait to get home and soak away all this horrid, itchy clay!

The disguise had worked, however. If anyone ever asked the jeweler about that particular piece he'd created, he would only remember a middle-aged potter with a rounded face and a marriageable son. Chimehara would wait a few weeks, then sell the bracelet somewhere. There would be nothing to connect that bauble to the dead woman's gem-crusted slippers.

Once a block or two from the shop, Chimehara paused at a corner long enough to spit the cotton from her mouth. Ah, that was better! Her cheeks were sore from being stretched, but they would recover. Fortunately it was a rest day, as was tomorrow—House Chohu was too wise to overwork its members, knowing that some time to themselves would leave them all the more ready to resume their labors after. Yuni and Ritaru had invited her to go shopping and dining and drinking with them, and Madam Ponsoi had offered to take her to a spa, but Chimehara had begged off, claiming family obligations. It was the one excuse no one could take offense to. And by the time she returned, her face would be as lovely as ever.

Her face itched where the clay pulled at it, as did her hands. But she smiled nonetheless, feeling the sun on her skin and the comforting weight of that bracelet at her belt. It was a good day.

"Kotone?" a voice, gruff but high, called out. "Baby bird, is that you?"

She froze at once, her blood turning to ice and her fingers and toes going numb. Only one person had ever called her that, and she had hoped, very nearly prayed, never to see him again.

Yet when she turned, the figure stumbling toward her looked exactly as she remembered. Haru was not tall, and he was as gaunt as ever, but his shoulders were wide, his arms long, and his hands enormous. His beard was still scraggly, and still so thoroughly caked with clay as to be entirely almond in color, leaving it lighter than his fire-reddened skin. His eyes, which were startlingly pale like fresh ice, were fixed on her own as he reached her and raised one massive hand to cup her cheek. "It *is* you!" he breathed, the scent of fried onion and cheap rice wine wafting over her. "I thought it was!"

Chimehara shoved his hand away and took a step back, glancing about them in a mild panic. They were standing in the middle of the lane, right out in the open in Bejinuri. She did not know anyone here, but it was not far enough from House Chohu in Motohiri for her liking. What if someone from the merchant house were to walk by and see them together? Even with her disguise, anyone looking too long might recognize her. Haru had, and he was clearly not even remotely sober. She had to get rid of him, and quickly.

She opened her mouth to tell him that he was mistaken, that she had no idea who he was and did not care, but what came out instead was, "Go away. Please. I cannot be seen with you."

The drunken potter's face drooped, registering his hurt confusion. But then he brightened, breaking into a wide smile. "It is good to see you, baby bird! And you've grown up!" His hand, which had stayed near her, dropped to her waist, pulling her against him, and his smile turned to a leer. "You've grown up nicely."

"That is enough." She pushed against him, trying to pull free, but even in this state Haru was strong. He always had been. All those years of throwing pots and pumping bellows had given him a wiry strength that, when sober, he had been careful to contain. When he got drunk, however, he often broke things.

Or people.

"You should come drink with me," he urged, his other arm rising to encircle her as well. It was like being wrapped in bands of steel, albeit ones with coarse hair all up and down their lengths. "I have some wine. Back at my place. You remember my place, baby bird?"

She did indeed. They were the sort of memories that, in a weaker woman, might wake her in the middle of the night, alternately sobbing or screaming. Not that Haru had ever forced himself on her. He had not needed to. She had known all too well what fate awaited her on the streets, and had since she could remember. Which was why, as soon as she'd been old enough to catch a man's eye, she had let him take her away from all that.

With Haru, it had just been a little younger than most others might have admitted to.

He had not been awful to her, either. He had his wants, of course, and those had needed to be seen to, but he had given her shelter, food, and space to herself while he was working. And most of the time when he'd gotten drunk he'd only gotten louder, more demanding, but not often violent. Not as long as he got what he wanted.

She had stayed with him a full year before finally deciding she could do better. Then she had stolen what she could—he'd never had much coin about, and his wares were decent but common—and had slipped away one day while he was delivering a cartload of cups and mugs and pots.

This was the first she had seen of him since. And she would have been happy if it had been another five years.

"Come home with me." He was pleading, eyes wide, but he was also stepping back at the same time, dragging her with him by sheer strength of arms. "It will be like it was before. Only better." He licked his lips, and that was the final straw.

"Let me go," she hissed, her eyes narrowing, and something in her tone made him stop, though he still did not loosen his grip. "I will not be going anywhere with you, you disgusting, drunken, lecherous swine of man. Not now, not ever."

For a second he looked wounded, like a little boy who had just lost his favorite toy. Then his brow lowered, and he met her glare with one of his own, only far uglier. "You think you're too good for me, is that it?" he growled, his voice soft and low and for her ears alone. "Do you think I cannot see what you have become?" He lifted one hand to flick at her cheek, flaking off some of the clay there.

"Those who do not work the kiln might be fooled, but Haru is not—I can see. A true potter would not have such splotches, not so evenly placed, not so spread out, the flesh still perfectly clean in between. You are posing as a potter, perhaps, but you are not one." He frowned. "I tried. But you lacked—not the patience, no, that you had, eh, baby bird? It was the artistry that was wanting. The empathy. The sense of beauty. Your cups were as cold as you, and as empty inside."

Bones! Chimehara did not need this, not here, not now. "Yes, fine, you tried to teach me," she agreed, adopting a more concilia-tory tone. Haru had always been stubborn—best not to get him upset right now. "Thank you. And you did give me shelter—thank you for that, as well. But that was a long time ago. Please let me go now. Please."

For an instant he seemed to consider her request. But then a new gleam awoke in his eye, and it was one she knew all too well. Not lust but an equally familiar passion—greed. "You are up to something, eh?" Haru muttered in her ear. "Something clever. You were always clever. And ambitious. Whatever this is, it is valuable to you, yes?" He chuckled, making his whole body rumble against hers. "Which means it could be valuable to me, too." He adopted a sorrowful expression. "I am out of wine, baby bird, and have no coin to buy more. But you do, yes? You could buy tsekuri for your old friend Haru, couldn't you? Your old friend, who will keep your secrets for you?"

By the First Emperor! Chimehara wanted to scream. This was all she needed! Some old drunken fool trying to blackmail her! The problem was, he did know who she was and where she had come from. If he chose to talk, word could get back to the wrong people—not just House Chohu, which would expel her the instant it learned she was just some street urchin from down in Mazihini, but also some people she crossed on her way up from that lowest level and who might still be searching for her.

No, she could not afford to let him go around telling her secrets.

But she also could not stand to let him hold his knowledge over her head. Both because he might slip up and let loose something someday, and because she had decided when she'd left that she would never again allow anyone else to control her.

Something would have to be done.

She painted on a warm, tender smile. "Yes, I will buy you rice wine, Haru, dear. Come, let's go to that old wine cellar, the one you always liked, the one with the fountains. I will buy you drinks, and one for myself, and we will celebrate our unexpected reunion."

"Ha! Good!" He lowered one arm and turned, keeping the other around her waist so that she could not bolt, and steered them back the way he had come. "It is this way."

"I remember." She did. Just as she remembered that there was a narrow alleyway between here and there, one they had often used as a shortcut. Sure enough, Haru led them toward that tight passage, gesturing for her to step between the adjoining buildings first.

She did—and, as he pushed in behind her, forcing her to move ahead of him, she slid her hand up under her obi and drew her knife.

Despite being drunk, Haru was wary, and tried to fend off the blow when she twisted around to stab at him. But he was at a severe disadvantage here, where he could not face forward because his shoulders were too wide to let him pass except sideways. His one arm was extended ahead of him to keep hold of her, and so with his other hand he could only bat at her weakly, the motion jostling her forearm but not enough to throw off her aim.

The knife slid into his throat just below the thick knot there, and she yanked it to first one side and then the other, producing a grunt and a whistle of pain from him as she carved a savage tear across his neck. When she finally yanked the blade free, blood gushed forth, painting the wall before him with a wide crimson swathe.

His grip on her loosened, his arms dropping to his sides, and he stumbled back against the other house, then staggered forward again, coating his chest with his own blood as he bumped against the wall there before stepping back and then sideways as his legs gave out. He started to pitch toward Chimehara but she dodged away and kicked him back, forcing him to topple in the opposite direction. The buildings muffled the sound of him hitting the ground, and she watched as he lay there, twitching only a moment more before finally going still.

But inside, she was seething.

How dare he force her to do something like this! She liked to plan her kills, check all the details, make sure of every aspect, keep it clean and herself completely disconnected from it all. Not slash someone's throat in a dark alley! That was what other street urchins became, mere thugs and cutpurses and killers. She was better than that! She was beyond that!

Yet here she stood, bloody knife in her hand, Haru dead at her feet. Where anyone could walk by and see them both.

No. She would not let him do this to her.

Crouching quickly, she wiped the blade clean on his shirt. Then she studied their surroundings. The building before her was solid stone, its walls extending seamlessly into the ground. But the one behind her was plaster and wood, and stood on short, stout legs so that air might pass beneath the floor planks.

It would have to do.

She had to heave and thrust and kick and push, but eventually she got Haru's body rolled back under the house. Anyone who peered under there would see him, but there was little she could do about that. She'd done her best to keep his blood off her, but struggling to move him had left long, angry red streaks across her sashiko jacket. She pulled that off, wadding it up inside out and then tying it into as small a bundle as she could. She could carry that out of here and dispose of it elsewhere, where it would not be connected to Haru or to her. She still looked like a potter, only now she was in hemp trousers and a soiled hosode. That would do for a moment, but she would have to be quick—her body's curves were all too visible through the thin silk shirt, belying the image of her as a stocky and unmemorable minor craftsman.

Rising to her feet, she hurried from the alley, the bundle tucked under her arm. She knew of a pretty little fountain in Sakiriti— she could perhaps wash away the clay there, shedding years as she did. By the time she returned to her home, there would be nothing left of the potter woman, save the bracelet she had bought.

And nothing of Haru but a few flecks of blood she would quickly scrub away.

She did not glance back as she left, but her thoughts lingered upon the dead potter, the time they had been together, and her own disgust at what he had forced her to do.

She hated to kill in such an inelegant fashion.

CHAPTER TWELVE

Seikoku thought things were going well—until suddenly they weren't.

She'd found a convenient tree—why was it that all these rich people, for all their guards and locks and thick walls, never thought to trim back the trees growing alongside their homes? It was like they were *begging* to be robbed!—and had scaled it as easily as walking. Lady Shimoda's home was a stately one, with a balcony around the upper level, and it had been a simple matter for Seikoku to hop from a sturdy branch down over the teak railing and onto that balcony, where between the moonless night, the roof's overhang, and that railing she was practically invisible to anyone walking past, including the guards patrolling the grounds. That gave her ample time to carefully crouch-walk to the nearest door and try it.

It slid open with ease, and with nary a sound. This was almost too easy!

The thin rice-paper of the door had revealed dim lights within the house, and with the door open Seikoku could see that there were indeed lamps lit somewhere ahead and below. It seemed the house had both an outer balcony and an inner walkway. Odd, but that was the rich for you—they had to do things differently. She slipped through the partially open door, her feet moving soundlessly in their soft-soled boots—

—and then had to swallow a yelp as her foot came down on nothing but air and she tumbled forward, falling into the house in far too literal a fashion!

She twisted about, trying to grab hold of the doorframe, the wall, something, but there was nothing to catch—the wall was slick as glass and the doorframe that had been handsome, heavy old beams on the outside had been planed smooth and flat against the wall here.

A trap, she acknowledged, mentally kicking herself. Of course it was a trap. Lady Shimoda was known for being as eccentric and paranoid as she was wealthy. That was why Seikoku had always avoided the place, in fact—she'd always felt the uncertainties and risks involved far outweighed any potential gains, even though rumors claimed that, like the fabled Tawasiri, Lady Shimoda's manor was littered with aishone and precious gems alike, both spilled out across the floor like leaves across a forest floor.

But if that was the case, why hadn't anyone ever managed to rob her yet? Everyone knew of the place and the riches it was said to contain, but no one had ever successfully come away with any of that treasure? Clearly that was a bad sign. The only reason Seikoku had decided to go for it now was because she had needed an easy mark and one well away from anywhere she'd recently been—and maybe because she'd wanted to push herself a little. And yes, it *had* been too easy. She shouldn't have let herself get lulled by such easy early success.

She was bracing herself for a bruising impact against the floor when something brought her plummet to an abrupt and wrenching halt. What it was had some give to it, far more than a regular floor mat would, and Seikoku instinctively flung herself forward, rolling and then springing up and away as far as she could. With an interior like this one, she wouldn't be surprised if there was a pit directly below, covered only by a thin rug! Well, they weren't going to catch her so easily!

She landed in a crouch a good six feet away—and was stunned when the floor suddenly snapped shut around her, yanking her up into the air and wrapping around her at the same time. What the bones?

She thrashed and flailed, trying to break free, but her surroundings gave way easily beneath her kicks and punches, yet continued to restrain her. After a moment she realized that she was battling nothing more than a collection of tightly knotted cords.

A net. She had been caught in a net like some sort of exotic fish or colorful bird, and now she was hanging in the air like a goose waiting to be plucked.

It was a good thing Noniki was not here to see this, she thought, and then hated herself for even considering that. Still, he would never have let her hear the end of it.

Despite herself, she wished he was there to mock her now.

The dim lights burst to full brilliance, sending stabbing pains into her eyes and dark spots to dance before her face, and Seikoku struggled to shield her sight, even though it was already too late. She was still blinking away those spots when a voice rose up from below.

"And what have we caught this night, hm? Is it a pigeon, Yanagida? A turkey? Or perhaps an alley cat." The voice was old and reedy but filled with laughter and even contempt. Lady Shimoda—assuming that was her—was a lot more alert than Seikoku had heard. And, from the sound of her taunting, a lot nastier.

"I would say closest to an alley cat, milady," a deep male voice like a heavy stone plunging into the river offered. "Though perhaps trained monkey might be more accurate." Seikoku did her best to glare down at the series of dark splotches where she thought that voice originated. "Shall we find a circus to take it off our hands? Or just chop it up for stew?" The casual way he suggested that last option—and the audible glee lurking beneath that nearly bored tone—warned her with a chill that he was deadly serious about that possibility and would evidently enjoy it far too much for her liking.

She needed to get out of here. Quickly.

"Let us not be too hasty," the old noblelady replied. She was a smaller but equally dark blotch to the first one's right. "It has been many years since I possessed a decent monkey. I should like to know if this one can do any tricks for its supper before I decide whether to dispose of it." By squinting Seikoku could make out the old woman's face, though it was still blurry, and the vicious grin stretched there nearly froze her in fear. Who were these crazy old people?

She resumed her war against the net, but its strands were thick, its knots too tight for her to be able to break free. Even the knife tucked in her belt would be little help here—yes, its sharp edge could sever the knots, but then what? She might win free just in time to resume her lethal plummet toward the floor.

No, she had to be smart about this. Which meant ignoring the crazy old lady's taunts and taking stock of her situation, her surroundings, her possessions, and her skills. Surely there was something here she could turn to her advantage.

"Come down, little monkey," Lady Shimoda was calling up at her. Seikoku's vision had now cleared enough that she could easily make out the tiny, wizened old woman in the cloth-of-gold kitoro, tapping an elegant ivory and gold fan against her gnarled limbs while avidly watching Seikoku's lack of progress at her attempted escape.

That just gave Seikoku additional fuel for her efforts. Sadly, the net resisted any attempts to yank her body free of its knotty embrace. And even if she had managed to extricate herself, thanks to her reflexive leap before it was a good six feet or more back to the still-open doorway where she'd entered. And twice that distance to the ground below, which was polished wood planks rather than rice-paper mats.

So much for hoping for something to break her fall.

That sparked an idea, however. It was incredibly risky, possibly insane, and not any sort of manuever she would ever recommend to anyone.

It also might be her only chance.

Drawing her dagger, Seikoku inserted its sharp tip between two knots right by her other hand. The blade cut through the ropes with ease, and she found she could move her arms a touch more easily. Then, without sitting up, she peered all about. There were several other nets here, all spread out at the same height, their knots and strands overlapping in the shadows and casting a faint latticework across the pair below.

Each net appeared to be held open at each corner, but with stout ropes rising from those same spots to a single thicker braid that looped over a thick iron hook mounted in the ceiling high above. The rope continued past that hook, and ended in a large iron weight, roughly the size of her head and many times heavier. She had seen similar traps used by hunters outside the city to capture birds and other game. Her falling against the net had shaken it and apparently knocked the weight from wherever it had been perched. The weight had fallen, and that had yanked up on the ropes, pulling the net up and in and trapping her inside its webbed embrace. Clever.

Fortunately, she was clever, too.

"Best to reel her in now, Yanagida," Lady Shimoda was saying below. "She strikes me as the restless type."

"Indeed, milady," the man agreed. "I shall fetch the ladder." He turned and moved away out of view, and Seikoku knew that she would never have a better opportunity.

She cut away at the strands binding her, carving a large rent in the net. Then she slipped through, latching her fingers into the knots for purchase. The whole net swayed with her motion, but the weight was heavy enough to keep her from dipping down toward the ground as she instead shimmied up the rope to that hook.

"Bad monkey!" The lady of the house shrieked, waving and pointing with her fan. "Come down here at once and accept your punishment like a good little animal!"

Seikoku certainly had no intention of doing that! But she couldn't remain hanging from this hook indefinitely. And it was too far to jump back to the door from here.

There were other, closer hooks, however.

Hauling up the net that had trapped her, Seikoku hefted the mass of knots and cords in one hand. Then she flung it forward, up and toward the door. It swung upward, smashing against the roof beams with a slithering sound before sliding back down—except for one portion, which had gotten caught on the hook there.

Exactly as Seikoku had hoped.

She gave the rope a tug and felt as much as saw the hook sink deeper into that tangle, holding it firm.

Then she latched both hands on that rope and climbed hand

over hand toward that second hook.

"Yanagida!" Lady Shimoda was screaming. "Anyone! Get her! Shoot her down or something, but get her!"

Seikoku increased her speed. She was almost to the hook when a wide, curved blade narrowly missed slicing off her leg. The man-servant, Yanagida, thrust the long polearm at her again, and she knocked it away with one foot, but she was not in the best position to defend herself.

Still, she thought as she reached the hook finally and clasped it instead of the rope, there were some options. Another net trap hung from this hook, the one she must have touched down on originally, but apparently the contact had been too light and too brief to trigger it because this one was still set, which meant that the rope end with the weight was up near her head. Grabbing that, Seikoku took careful aim—then let it fall.

Clonk! It struck Yanagida in the head, driving the man to the floor in a crumpled heap. That also yanked the net trap closed, and Seikoku grabbed that net and flung it—right through the still-open door to the balcony. She quickly switched to that rope and slid down it, because it did not have anything to anchor it there and was already starting to slip back into the house. She made it far enough to leap through the doorway just before the net fell inside once more, and quickly slammed the door shut behind her, then flung herself onto the tree branch and half-ran, half-skidded down it to the tree trunk and from there to the ground just outside the estate's thick stone walls.

She did run then, not stopping to catch her breath until she was well away from the house and its crazed owner who set traps for unwary thieves. What a nightmare. No aishone to show for her efforts, no money, and she'd nearly gotten herself killed—or worse. Seikoku shuddered, thinking about that old woman. Monkey indeed!

Well, she counted herself lucky that she'd gotten out of there alive and—save for a few small rope burns—unscathed. Still, her night's work had been an utter failure. And for good reason—normally she did a far better job studying a target than that. Was it just because she was running out of coin and had mouths to feed, she wondered as she walked the rest of the way home, taking a long and circuitous route just in case anyone was following her. Or was she losing her touch?

Or maybe she was simply losing her taste for stealing from others. A boy's face appeared in her mind and she pushed it away, but it persisted, following her home like a bad dream.

CHAPTER THIRTEEN

Hibikitsu reined in when he heard the sobs.

He had been making excellent time on the road. In fact, several times he had been forced to circle around in order to stay behind the rest of his men, instead of racing on ahead of them. What a difference it made, a single horse and rider versus a long train of men and horses and foot soldiers and supplies! He had caught a few glimpses of Diritan and Nioko now and again, though he suspected that was less because he was so perceptive and more because the two Honjofu wanted to make sure he knew that they and their fellow warriors were still guarding him. Nonetheless, it had been a novel experience to be so solitary for the past two days, no one but Shisi to keep him company, nothing to occupy him but his own thoughts and the wind and rain and the road ahead.

Of course, that had its drawbacks, as well. The first night, when he'd finally realized he was drooping in the saddle so far he was in danger of sliding off and had nudged Shisi to a halt, the Honjofu had materialized out of the woods like some sort of forest demons and quickly got to work setting up camp and pitching his tent. "What are you doing?" Hibikitsu had demanded when he'd overcome his shock enough to find his voice again.

"Making camp, sire," Diritan had replied.

Hibikitsu had folded his arms across his chest. "And do you often stoop to setting up camp for a lowly aiashe?" he'd asked, tapping his foot.

That had made the burly warrior chuckle. "No, of course not, sire," he'd replied. "But you—"

"I am nothing but your average foot soldier," Hibikitsu had

cut in. "And I expect to be treated as such." He waved the warriors off. "I will set up my own camp."

Nioko had frowned. "Have you ever made camp before, your Majesty?" she'd asked softly, and he'd favored her with an arched brow. He had not bothered to make any other form of reply, and a few minutes later the Honjofu had drifted back into the shadows as quickly and quietly as they'd emerged, leaving him all alone again.

The answer had been "no," of course. When would he have ever had the opportunity—or the need—to learn how to set up a tent or light a fire or any of a dozen other things he didn't even know about? Which was why he'd spent that first night wrapped in Shisi's saddle blanket, shivering.

Last night it had rained, a thunderstorm that had slammed down so hard and so fast that he could not see more than a hand's length from his face. He hadn't been able to find proper shelter, so he'd spent the night huddled against a boulder, that blanket still clutched around him but now so waterlogged and cold it hardly helped.

At least the sun was out today. Between that and the wind he had mostly dried out, though his boots still squelched on the ground as he dismounted to seek out the source of the cries he'd just heard.

"Hello?" he called out, leading Shisi by the reins to prevent the stallion from galloping away in hopes of a stream or some oats or just a few particularly appetizing-looking blades of grass. It seemed his horse was enjoying their newfound freedom as much as he was. Though he suspected that, like him, Shisi would prefer a warm, dry place to sleep and some fresh oats and carrots rather than this foraging.

Up ahead, through the trees, Hibikitsu caught sight of a small cottage. That must be the source of the sobbing. Loosening his sword in its scabbard, he moved closer. Stealth was impossible, considering both his armor and his steed, but he did his best not to present too threatening a picture.

Despite that, the girl gathering branches near the house shrieked and ran away when he stepped into view, scattering her collection in her haste.

"It's all right, I will not harm you!" Hibikitsu called after her, but she vanished into the house without a backward glance. A moment later, a man and a woman emerged, the little girl peeping out from behind the woman's legs. The two adults both hefted sturdy clubs, though those were little more than long logs for firewood.

"What do you want?" the woman demanded, brandishing her weapon. "There is nothing for you here. Begone!" If she was frightened at seeing a soldier, fully armed and armored, at her doorstep, she gave no sign—instead her broad face was knit into a fearsome scowl.

"I am sorry," Hibikitsu replied, holding out both hands, palms out, fingers splayed. "I did not mean to frighten your daughter. I am just passing through and hoped I might water my horse and perhaps find something to eat. I can pay you." In truth there was very little in his pouch after handing all his gold to Anitu—there had been a few coppers in his saddlebags, he'd discovered that first night—but he suspected it would be enough. Besides, it was the principle of the thing. Anyone willing to pay for food was not here to rob the place.

Sure enough, the woman lowered her club slightly to study him. "We do not have much," she admitted finally, "just rice and vegetables with some fish and tea, but you are welcome to it. Come inside." She turned back toward the house. The man had not said a word this whole time, nor had he ever so much as raised his club, and now he followed meekly behind his wife, leading the little girl in with him as well.

Hibikitsu tied Shisi's reins to a heavy post near the front door, then followed his hosts inside. The house was small but clean, its wood plank floors scuffed enough that he did not pause to remove his boots, especially after seeing that the family still wore their own footgear. Thick wood beams stood in each corner, with wood outer walls and rice-paper inner ones, and thinner but still substantial beams bisected the ceiling. A sunken hearth occupied the center of the great room, and the family were already seating themselves on threadbare cushions around it. Hibikitsu took the seat opposite the mother, between the father and daughter, and bowed his head in thanks.

They ate in silence, the food plain but fresh and served from the cast-iron pot hanging from its heavy hook over the stove. He could not help noticing how worn all three of them looked, how tired, and how there was barely enough food for three, let alone four. The land had looked fertile enough, but these people's clothes were as faded and patched as their pillows. What was wrong here?

As they finished their meal and sipped their tea he opened his mouth to ask, but he was cut off by the sound of voices outside. Instantly the woman's head whipped up and the man cowered. "Why are they back?" the man whimpered. "They were just here!" His eyes were bright with tears, and Hibikitsu realized there were tracks of dirt down his cheeks. Had he been the one sobbing?

"Who is here?" he asked them, rising to his feet. "Perhaps I can help."

He was surprised when the woman whipped around to glare at him. "You'll only make things worse!" she hissed, waving him away. "Now stay here and keep quiet! I'll deal with this." She stomped toward the door, tugging it open and hurrying through before sliding it shut again behind her. Hibikitsu quickly followed, but contented himself with standing to one side by a closed but not fully shuttered window there so he could at least hear what was going on.

"Uemada," a man called out, "you've been holding out on us. You keep whining about not having any more money, but here you have this fine, fine horse instead."

Bones! Hibikitsu thought, clenching his fists. He had forgotten about Shisi! He reached for the door, but the man caught his wrist. "Don't," he whispered. "They'll kill us all!"

"We'll see about that," Hibikitsu replied, pulling loose. He was not about to lose his horse!

"It isn't mine," the woman—Uemada—was saying as he slid the door open, allowing the warm afternoon sunlight and cool, refreshing breeze to seep in as he exited.

"He is mine," he declared, eyeing the quartet arrayed before him. "I am just passing through, on my way to join up with the rest of my unit and paused here to beg some food and water." He glared at the strangers. "And who are you, exactly?"

"Who are we?" the man in front replied. He stroked his chin, which had a short, wispy beard springing from it. "Why, I am Futomo," he answered with a bow. "And this is Iha." She was tall and dangerously thin, with a long face and longer nose. "Over there are Murata and Asa." The big woman and the small man both nodded hello, trying not to grin. "And who might you be?"

"Hibio, of His Majesty's aiashe, at your service," Hibikitsu replied, offering a quick bow. "Do not worry, I will be on my way and trouble you all no further." He turned to Uemada and bowed to her. "Madam, thank you for your hospitality. May the bones grant you wisdom, strength, and peace."

She nodded back, though her eyes never left the foursome before her. Nor did she drop her club. Which seemed a wise precaution, as all four carried true weapons and Murata, at least, moved like she'd had military training.

"That's very gentlemanly of you, Hibio," Futomo told him. "Isn't it, Iha?" The tall woman nodded, her eyes sharp and her sneer unpleasant. "But perhaps Uemada didn't tell you? You see, all these woods belong to us, and there is a fee for safe passage." The man, who was Hibikitsu's height but stockier, with rough features, considered a second, head tilted to one side. "I would say that horse of yours should just about cover it." He grinned as if expecting Hibikitsu to be pleased about this news.

It was now painfully clear what was happening here, and why Uemada's husband had been crying. "I think I've had enough of your attitude," Hibikitsu declared, letting his fingers wrap comfortably around Kosshiki's hilt. "Leave now and do not trouble these good people any further."

If he'd thought that would make them back down, he proved to be sadly mistaken. Instead, the quartet began laughing. "One of you, four of us," Iha pointed out, her sneer widening until it stretched across most of her narrow face. "Not good odds for you, soldier boy."

Rather than answer directly, he tugged his aishone pouch from underneath his armor, loosening its straps and dipping his fingers into it with practiced ease. A pinch of bone dust in his mouth, swished and swallowed, and Hibikitsu straightened, his other hand adjusting to grasp Kosshiki more firmly. "I am not the one you should be worried about here," he shot back, drawing the nihono and holding it before him in an easy two-handed grip. "This is your last chance."

His show of strength did nothing to diminish their humor, but it did take a darker turn as Futomo, clearly their leader, barked, "So be it." They reached in near-perfect unison for pouches of their own, each extracting dust or chips and then swallowing them. And then each standing straighter, shifting into a better stance, their arms looser, their gaze sharper.

Bones. They all had warrior aishone. And it seemed Iha and Murata were of the type who, despite being women, had what was normally considered masculine aitachi. Meaning they absorbed muscle memory and skill rather than intellectual knowledge.

Futomo's grin turned ugly as he drew the chokoto at his side. Murata unslung a massive sword from her back, an old-fashioned nodaki, Hibikitsu's training whispered. Sturdier than a nihono and nearly as sharp, it was meant for fighting off cavalry and in strong enough hands was capable of cleaving a man in two with a single blow. The wiry little man, Asa, unsheathed a pair of long, leaf-bladed daggers, holding them with the handles angled down and the blades flat against his forearms, knife-fighter style. And Iha—Iha tossed back the front of her coat to reveal a pair of bandoliers crossing her thin chest, each bearing at least a half dozen short, wide-bladed throwing knives. She pulled three from each and held them, handles upward, splayed between her fingers, giving him a smile as sharp and deadly as those blades she held.

"Now we must teach you a lesson," their leader declared with another ugly chuckle. "Sadly, it is not one you will live long enough to appreciate." And the four of them advanced, spreading out as they did to surround Hibikitsu and force him to split his attention among them.

Deal with the biggest threat first, his training—and his ancestors—whispered. *Futomo has only a chokoto. You can deal with that later. Asa has daggers and has to get in close to use them. Iha can strike from a distance, but once you close with any of her compatriots she'll have a hard time unleashing those, for fear of hitting her friends. Murata, though—that nodaki was a significant danger.*

So rather than waiting for them to close the circle around him, Hibikitsu charged.

He saw the big woman's eyes widen in surprise, but they narrowed again almost immediately and she planted herself to repel a direct attack, raising that big blade in both hands, point facing him.

Which is why Hibikitsu slid past her to her right—she'd unsheathed with her left on the handle and her right on the scabbard, meaning she was left-handed and thus had to cross her own body or switch to only her weaker hand to defend on the right side. He did not slow down as he moved, so her retaliatory swing cleaved only the air where he had been, and he lashed out left-handed with Kosshiki as he came level with her, the nihono's razor-sharp edge sweeping out and around and taking her in the back of the neck. He did not have enough force, one-handed, to slice clean through, but she toppled anyway, eyes bulging as she struggled to breathe, that massive sword falling from hands that had suddenly gone limp. He had severed her spine, and her ability to move. Threat eliminated.

Now he was outside their trap, and the three remaining bullies were forced to turn and face him. That did give Iha an open field, unfortunately, and she raised her knives, readying herself to throw. Hibikitsu crouched in response, presenting the smallest possible target, his sword returning to guard position. He could perhaps bat aside one or two of those knives, but it was unlikely he could deflect them all.

A scream of rage distracted them all. Uemada had been standing there, watching those opening seconds of conflict, and had evidently realized the danger Hibikitsu had put himself in. Now she barreled toward Iha, club raised, a wordless cry of defiance bursting from her lips.

The thin woman pivoted away from the clumsy attack, back-pedaled three steps, then unleashed all the knives in her right hand. One took the poor farmwoman in the throat, one between her breasts, and the third between her eyes. Brave, foolish Uemada was dead before she hit the ground.

No! Hibikitsu felt a wash of rage at seeing the woman fall. She had only been trying to save him from his own stupidity, challenging these four without thinking it through. And now she was dead? They would pay for that!

All three were still distracted, though that would not last long. Asa was closest, so he was the one Hibikitsu lunged toward. The wiry little man turned, raising a dagger to block, but it was a purely reflexive action—Hibikitsu twisted his sword to come in under the man's rising arm and took him through the side, piercing his heart and lungs like roasting a bird on a spit. He retrieved Kosshiki as the man crumpled, turning back toward Futomo and Iha, whose slack jaws and flushed faces showed that they were only now realizing their little quartet had just become a duo. Of course, they were far enough away that he could not strike at them both, which meant he would have to go after Iha first, lest she unleash her knives on him.

And that was when Uemada's husband—whose name Hibikitsu realized he did not even know—threw himself at the woman who had just murdered his wife.

He stood no chance, of course. Not at all. The poor fool hadn't even paused to grab a weapon, he just charged forward, arms spread wide as if to smother Iha into submission. She didn't even bother to throw anything at him—her right hand dipped into her bandolier and drew only a single blade, holding it by the leather-wrapped handle as she slashed once in a wide arc.

The man stumbled and fell to his knees, blood spraying from his cut throat. He reached for Iha with one hand, the other clutching at his wound, before gurgling and pitching forward to lay, face-down, mere feet from his wife.

Hibikitsu saw red. These people had taken him in. They had offered him food they could ill afford to share, and now they were dead—because he had not had the foresight to hide his horse, or the wisdom to stand down when the bullies had approached. This was all his fault.

He turned to face Iha, determined to kill her or die trying—and froze as she staggered back, staring down with a look of dazed confusion at the red-feathered shaft suddenly protruding from her chest right where the bandoliers crossed. She managed to keep her feet for a few steps before losing her balance and dropping to her rear on the ground, a cloud of dust billowing up from the impact. Her strength was clearly failing already, and she soon slumped, the arrow propping her up as she tilted forward, so that even in death she still sat upright, the knives from her hands clattering to the dirt beside her.

Futomo stared at his dead friends, then at Hibikitsu. He began to back away, but an arrow took him through the throat even as he turned, and he managed only a single strangled gasp before he hit the ground as well, leaving Hibikitsu surrounded by dead bodies and an overwhelming sense of guilt.

He watched, numb, as Diritan and Nioko emerged from the bushes, a longbow still in her hands while he held nihono and yori-toki. Seeing them was no surprise, since only the Honjofu fletched their arrows with crimson feathers to match the royal crest. Hibikitsu realized, as they approached, that they must have circled around when he'd stopped. They had stayed out of sight as long as they thought he could handle the threat himself, and had only stepped in when they felt he was at risk. Which was good strategy but had left poor Uemada and her unnamed husband to the band's not-so-tender mercies.

"Are you harmed, sire?" Diritan asked as he crossed the clearing, weapons still at the ready, eyes scanning the area, entire body alert to any other dangers.

"I'm fine," Hibikitsu managed. He wiped Kosshiki clean and then sheathed the blade, his hands moving entirely by rote, his eyes and thoughts still filled with the corpses all around him. "This is my fault," he said aloud, because he felt it was important to voice such a truth where others might hear. The two warriors frowned at that. "My horse is what led them here," he explained wearily, the rush of battle draining away and leaving only bone-deep fatigue and numbing guilt behind. "And I refused to give him up. Bones, I goaded them into fighting me. These people would still be alive if I had not blundered in and started giving orders."

Diritan frowned, opened his mouth, then closed it again with a snap as Nioko shook her head at him.

"What?" Hibikitsu demanded, but his two bodyguards remained silent. "Tell me," he insisted, though it came out as less of an order than a plea.

Finally Nioko relented. "You ordered them like an emperor," she answered in that soft, clear voice of hers. "But they saw only a common foot soldier. Why should they obey?"

Which made sense. Of course he had expected the thugs to obey—he was the emperor, after all. And if they had known that, they might have, more from fear of retribution than because they respected him. But as just some wandering aiashe? They'd out-numbered him, and their kind was quick to take advantage of superior numbers. They had deserved their fate, no question, and he was glad he could at least rid this region of their taint. But the farmer and her husband, that was a guilt he would carry for many years to come.

Something else occurred to him, and he straightened with a gasp, glancing toward the farmhouse. Immediately the two Hon-jofu stiffened, and he quickly gestured for them to stand down. "It's not a threat," he whispered, his heart breaking as he saw a shadow shift through the open doorway. "It's...their daughter."

The pair exchanged a glance. Then Diritan sheathed his blades and stalked toward the farmhouse, his steps quick but soft. "Come out, little one," he called, his loud voice surprisingly gentle. "We will not hurt you." Behind him, Nioko had pulled a kerchief from her belt and was laying it over Uemada's face. "I promise you, by the emperor himself, you are safe." That made Hibikitsu bite back a laugh that threatened to become a sob instead. Because the emperor had brought such safety and security to her family already!

Still speaking softly, Diritan stopped at the doorway and crouched down. "Come out," he urged again, holding his arms wide. There was more trembling in the dark, and then a small, dirty form leapt into his arms, which he wrapped around her in a massive embrace. "There, there," he soothed, patting her back as she sobbed into his shoulder. He let her cry as he glanced back toward Hibikitsu, the question plain on his broad face.

"We will bring her with us," Hibikitsu answered. "We will find her a good home. If necessary, I will bring her back to Aihiri with me and raise her as my ward. But I will not abandon her."

He was surprised how much the gratitude and respect of his Honjofu's gaze warmed him. It pushed back the grief and guilt, at least for a moment. Long enough for him to cross to where Shisi waited. But as he set one foot in the stirrups, he thought to look back at the bodies all around, and stopped. "We will bury them," he declared, stepping back away from his horse. "Find me a shovel," he told Nioko, who bowed and hurried to the farmhouse to look inside. "See if there is anything she would bring with her," he instructed Diritan, who nodded. Then he began to pull off his armor. By the time Nioko returned, a shovel in hand, Hibikitsu was down to hosode and ponmei. Diritan started to protest, to offer, but was cut off by a raised hand.

Then Hibikitsu, the Echo of Victory, Emperor of all Rimbaku, thrust the shovel's dull point into the hard dirt and began to dig. The thugs could rot, or be picked apart by wolves and buzzards, but Uemada and her husband would be buried properly, and by his hand alone.

He owed them that and far, far more.

CHAPTER FOURTEEN

"Where will you go?" Brother Yamaki demanded, his scowl far fiercer than usual, his arms crossed over his chest as if to restrain himself from doing something foolish. "Not back to the life you had before, I hope! When the brothers found you, you were little better than an animal, howling at the moon!"

Noniki laughed to cover the stab of bitter, bilious grief that threatened to creep back up his throat. "I'd just lost my brother," he reminded the healer monk as he packed his few belongings into a sturdy shoulder bag. The brothers had gifted him with two sets of sturdy cotton trousers, two silk hosode, a second pair of hemp sandals, underclothes, and a padded hemp jacket. He was wearing one set of the clothing, and the bag would hold the other along with a waterskin, some bread, some dried fruit and dried meat, and flint and tinder. It was not much but it was more than he had arrived with, and he was exceedingly grateful for all their generosity and their affection. And none moreso than the man glaring at him now. "I think I can be forgiven for being a little out of mind with grief at the time."

The tall monk grunted but did not argue the point. Instead he simply asked again, "Where will you go?"

For this, at least, Noniki found he had an answer. "Awaihinshi," he replied. "I've always wanted to see the fabled City of Polished Light. Giri…Giri and I used to talk about it, about going there someday, once we had enough coin and enough aishone." He sighed. "Now I'll have to see it for both of us." Speaking of Kagiri hurt, of course, but it was no longer the jagged, raw pain that had brutalized him so badly he'd stopped thinking, stopped caring. Was that what healing felt like, he wondered. The pain was still there but it was…dulled, muted. Tinted with fond memories. Most importantly, it was no longer the only thing in his head or his heart. He could still think and plan and feel, even around that pain. It might never fully go away, but at least it was no longer controlling his life.

He thought Giri would be pleased about that. "You're finally starting to grow up," he could almost hear his big brother say, complete with an eye roll and a slap to the back of his head. "About time!"

"And what will you do when you get there?" Yamaki was demanding. "Just wander around, staring with wide eyes and slack jaw at the wonders of the capital city? Is that your marvelous plan? You recover from not one but two deadly fevers, and miraculously from being near crushed to death, and now you wish to gape at the scenery?"

Noniki did his best to ignore the old monk's anger. He knew that it was not entirely aimed at him, and even if it was, it was with the best of intentions. "No," he admitted, "that is not what I had in mind." He sighed and turned to face the man who had nursed him back to health not once but twice. "I mean to see the emperor. I feel that he and I have a few things to discuss."

That received a snort in reply. "Oh, you're just going to drop by for a chat?" Yamaki retorted. "Old friends, are you?" He studied Noniki carefully. "And what is it you want to say to him that's so urgent?"

"I think you know," Noniki replied seriously. "You, better than anyone." He gestured toward the window, and the lands beyond. "This realm is in a terrible state," he said, measuring out his words carefully. That was new as well, and he thought Kagiri would be even more pleased about it. Before, his words had always just tumbled from his mouth as fast as they popped into his head. "It cannot continue the way it has been going, relying upon old bones to get anything done, or soon there will be nothing left *but* bones. You and your brothers have shown me that there is another way, but"—he paused, for he did not wish to give offense—"you are content to live here in the mountains and maintain this monastery and aid those who come to you. That's noble and good, but if

Rimbaku itself is to be saved we need to think bigger. We need to take your teachings to every corner of the empire." He shrugged. "That starts with the emperor. If I can get him to listen and to agree, he can issue orders or decrees or whatever it is emperors do. He can change our way of life."

He had been pacing as he talked, and now stopped to gauge Yamaki's response. He was startled and a little worried to see the fierce old man blinking back tears. At first he thought he'd upset the monk, but then Yamaki broke into a smile filled with something Noniki had rarely seen before and certainly had never expected to see again:

Pride.

"You may not have shaved your head, or torn your pouch," Yamaki said, coming forward and clasping Noniki's forearm, "but you are truly one of us in spirit. You have learned the lesson of forging your own path, standing on your own feet, perhaps better than any of us, and so it seems only right that you should do so now, forging a path that is not ours but leads toward the same goal." He caught Noniki in a fierce embrace. "May you know the warmth of brotherhood, Noniki. Always."

"May your spirit rejoice in the kindred of others," Noniki returned, tears trickling down his cheeks as he returned the hug. "Thank you. For everything."

"I fully expect you to repay us," Yamaki replied, pulling free and stepping back to regard Noniki at arm's length. "By coming back some day and telling us all about your adventures." He smiled again before releasing his grip and retreating to the doorway. "Do not forget," he warned before ducking out and disappearing down the steps. "Or I will come and find you myself."

Noniki laughed, listening to the healer's footfalls retreating. Then he slung the bag over his shoulder, settling the sturdy leather strap across his chest, and picked up the last two items the brothers had gifted him: a plain but sturdy knife with a sharp, straight blade and a smooth wooden handle, and a stout walking stick with leather wrapped around the middle for a firmer grip. Now, at last, he was ready.

None of the monks saw him off. At first he felt a stab of sorrow at that, even anger, and wondered why they would snub him in that way. But then he understood. Leaving was difficult, and sometimes saying good-bye only made it worse. The monks had all bid their farewells already, and now they were giving him the space to depart without hindering him. It was yet another in a long line of gifts, and one that showed that, far from snubbing him, they were trying to do what was best for him. Even if meant depriving themselves of a few last minutes together.

As he descended the steps and paced down the halls and finally stepped out of the monastery and began navigating the paths and trails that led down from it into the hills beyond, Noniki wondered if he would ever know this sort of perfect peace and harmony again. He hoped so. Perhaps someday he would return, and not just for a visit. He knew the monks would welcome him if he did. For now, however, his path led elsewhere, and it was a long way away.

So he had better start walking.

It was three days later when he encountered the first people along his path—and they were old acquaintances, though Noniki would hesitate to call them friends.

"Who goes there?" a woman's voice demanded, his first hint that he was not alone as he followed a narrow trail through trees and scrub brush to the top of a small hill.

"I hear nothing," a different woman replied. "Are you certain someone is there at all? Perhaps it is merely the wind."

"Yes, it could be the wind," a third agreed. "Nothing but the leaves in the trees."

"Perhaps," the first voice answered. "I thought I heard—but no. You may be right."

Reaching the hill's peak, Noniki emerged from the foliage to find a quartet of women clustered around a small fire. Their thin robes fluttered in the breeze, as did the unbleached cloths that wrapped their faces like shrouds, so that their features were merely smudges behind the fabric.

It was the burahone, the Bone Blind. He had met them before, shortly before being found by the Brothers of Many Spirits. He had been half out of his mind at the time, and the encounter had frightened him badly, for the strange aitachi-mad women had muttered many strange and terrifying things, about him and about his brother. It had been as much to flee from them as to escape his grief that Noniki had stumbled away and wandered mindlessly for so long, nearly killing himself in the process.

Now here they were again. Not the same women, necessarily—he did not have clear recollections of the group he'd met before, but vaguely remembered one being stout and one being lean and one being old and wizened, whereas he thought one of these was barely more than a girl and another was tiny but had the curves of a grown woman, while a third was tall and angular like a female Yamaki. But still they were burahone.

Yet, whereas on their last encounter the women had all turned unerringly toward him, scenting him somehow and sensing the lingering mark of aishone on his very soul, now they did not even turn in his direction. Instead they continued to speak together in low voices, not whispering but simply not needing to talk louder than to be heard by each other, and none of them tilted her head in his direction.

Strange. He marched more slowly than usual, taking care where to place his feet so as not to make too much noise. The wind was sharper up here than it had been on the climb up, and its keening masked the sound of his own footsteps. Still, he passed within a handful of feet of the women, holding his breath as he did—and not one of them so much as looked up.

Interesting, Noniki thought as he passed them by and continued down the hill's far side. The burahone's aitachi was so strong, so extreme, that they could detect the aishone in others, and simply being around the relic bones was enough to drive them mad.

What did it mean, then, that they did not seem to notice him at all? Before, they had told him that the past would claim him rather than the bones, and that it would rise up from within. Of course, they had also told him that Giri was still alive but being torn apart by five spirits, so clearly their madness was in full effect.

Still, he found himself both pleased and a trifle unsettled as he slipped away, leaving the burahone blissfully ignorant behind him. What did that mean, that they could not see him?

It meant that he truly was weaning himself from this whole nation's fixation on relicant bones, he thought. He had chosen a different path. And while he had no idea where exactly it would take him, he found that he was already enjoying the journey, and becoming curious to see where it led next.

CHAPTER FIFTEEN

Kagiri was alone—except, of course, that he wasn't.

To all outward appearances, he was. He had taken his horse and ridden away from the town, not stopping until he had come across a small outpost the villagers—for there had still been a few of those, mainly so that Daro Barindo and the rest of his Kindichi would have someone to cook and clean and fetch for them—had claimed was here. The single small hut stood out on the flat, dusty plain, as did the single small, stunted tree beside it. But even more important was what stood inside the hut, at its center where a firepit might be expected: a well. That was why the hut had been built in the first place, the villagers had explained, to protect and conceal the well. Water was hard to come by out here, after all.

The Kindichi knew about its existence, of course. They had claimed it at the same time they had taken possession of the village, dragging back with them the poor man whose turn it had been to keep watch here and sound the alarm on the old horn if anyone approached. Kagiri was surprised to find the place empty when he arrived, expecting a few of the bandits to still be quartered here, but he did not object. Riding out here to inspect the outpost had only been an excuse to get away for some desperately needed solitude.

As much as he could ever manage anymore, anyway.

"This is pointless," Nikiyu Sinchu groused, kicking at the dirt after he'd dismounted and looped his horse's reins through the iron ring set into the outpost's wall a few paces from the door. The building was solidly constructed, with sturdy beams and a thick door, in order to withstand the dust storms that most likely plagued this region. "We should head back at once. What if more of those bandits show themselves while we're gone? We have cleared out the surrounding villages, but there could still be others, and Joshi and the rest cannot possibly stand a concerted attack, not even by that rabble."

"Perhaps that would be for the best," Bushiki Kenin replied, raising a hand to shade his eyes as he peered out over the landscape. No sign of horses or men anywhere, no clouds of dust to indicate movement. Good. At least it would be easy to spot anyone approaching them here.

"What are you saying?" Shito Kibi demanded. "You'd let them die?"

"He is saying," Komu Setsui answered, "that the best thing that could happen for us is for those merchants to no longer be a concern. And the easiest way for that to happen, short of eliminating them ourselves, is to absent ourselves long enough for some other threat to end them." She nodded, tapping a forefinger against her lower lip. "Our hands are clean, and suddenly untied. An ideal outcome."

"Provided you don't mind letting people you've promised to protect die," Geido Shinen retorted with a scowl. "I, for one, do not approve such behavior. Like them or not, we agreed to serve their interests, and letting them die most certainly does not fulfill that duty."

"We never agreed to such a thing," Onyoku Jeizen argued. "He did. That was before our time, and we shouldn't be bound by those terms." He laughed. "Perhaps it's time to renegotiate."

"Shut up," Kagiri whispered, though the words grew into a moan as he clutched both hands to his head. "All of you, shut up!" He turned in a circle, staring out at the dust, the rocks and dirt, the rare brush, the clear blue sky with its smattering of clouds that did nothing to block the glare of the sun, the outpost behind him with his horse standing patiently beside it. What he did not see, of course, were the Gensaiba, the "living blades," the legendary warriors from the earliest days of the Empire.

But of course he wouldn't since they were within him. It was his body they had been moving about, like small children wrestling over a single length of rope, tugging it first this way and then that, shouting and screaming and laughing as it changed hands. He had engaged in such contests himself as a youth, with Noniki and others from their village.

He had never imagined that he might someday be forced into the role of the rope.

His shouting had at least quieted the Gensaiba for a moment, and he took advantage of that. "You are driving me mad," he warned, closing his eyes because it was distracting talking to people who were not really there, or at least not there physically. "If you all keep talking and taking control all the time, I will go insane. And then where will you be? Trapped inside the body of a raving lunatic. Some good that will do you!" He took a deep breath, trying to slow his racing heart as he waited for their reply.

In his mind's eye he could see them, as if the five warriors and himself were standing in a darkened room, only the six of them visible. Which was why he could make out Shinen's frown as the big man rumbled, "I'd have expected a little more gratitude from you, Kagiri. We saved your life, don't forget. More than once, in fact, but first from the Tawasiri. Your bones would be decorating its floor right now if we hadn't convinced you to get up."

"He's right," Sinchu agreed, his narrow features as disapproving as ever. "A little time enjoying the ability to touch and feel and interact again isn't too much to ask, all things considered."

"I think we've been quite fair, and quite patient thus far," Setsui added. Though she was stunning, she always reminded Kagiri of a sculpted flower, beautiful to look at but cold inside. "We could be a good deal more demanding, you know."

"Enough," Kenin stated, twisting his stocky body about to glare at the others. "Perhaps the boy is right. We are tenants and he is our host—we all need to learn to live together, and that means being considerate of one another." He bowed to Kagiri.

"Thank you," Kagiri told him, returning the gesture. "That's all I ask." He gulped air again. "I do appreciate all that you've done for me, all of you. And I know our situation is...unique. We're all adjusting. But I do need some space to myself from time to time. I need to be able to control my body and not have to constantly worry that someone else is going to take over—especially without warning."

That had become more and more of an issue, of late. During battle was one thing—when facing the Kindichi, Kagiri had been only too happy to let the Gensaiba take over, watching as a mere spectator as his body did things he could never have managed on his own. When they were not fighting for their life, however, he had originally had full control again. That had been changing. The Gensaiba had been getting more comfortable in his head and in his skin, and had started exerting themselves more often, and often without asking first. This morning, for instance, he had woken at dawn, risen from his bed, and begun performing a series of exercises to limber up after sleep. He had not objected to that, even though it had been Jeizen taking the lead, since he himself did not know how to do those exercises. But later when he had sat down to a simple breakfast, Kagiri had been surprised to realize that it was not him but Shinen who was wolfing down flatbread and eggs and sausage, and when he had ridden here it had been Setsui who had enjoyed the feel of the wind on her face and in her hair. If he was the landlord, his tenants were abusing their privileges and using the rooms without his permission.

"That is not an unfair comparison," Kibi admitted, her voice unusually subdued and her face oddly serious. "Perhaps if we were to ask first, then?" That was one advantage to having them in his head—he did not need to speak for them to hear him.

"That would certainly help," he agreed now. "Thank you." He was about to say more when Sinchu whispered, "You may want to open your eyes now."

Kagiri did so—and found that he was not in fact alone any longer.

Five men surrounded him, and he could tell at once from their beards and their hair and their garb that they were Kindichi. Where had they come from? But the sight of the outpost's door still slightly ajar behind them answered that question, and he kicked himself for letting his internal dispute blind him from certain necessities of the real world.

When you rode out to a place to inspect it and make sure there were no enemies still lurking about, it was generally a good idea to actually go inside and check before allowing yourself to be distracted. Clearly they had been in the outpost and had hidden when they'd heard his horse. Then he had been considerate enough to stand here with his eyes closed, allowing them ample time to ease the door open and sneak outside to ring him, as they had done.

"You came from the direction of the village," stated one of them, a barrel-chested man with a completely shaved head and small, serious eyes. His thick hands clenched a long, sturdy stick, narrower than a club but probably more agile and capped in iron on both ends. "What has transpired there?" the man continued. "Why did Barindo send you to us?"

In a flash Kagiri realized that these men did not know the Kindichi had fallen, nor that he was the one responsible for their friends' demise. "He sent me to check on you," he replied. "To see if you needed anything." The Gensaiba were strangely silent, the abrupt quiet in his head oddly disturbing.

A few of the bandits relaxed—but not the bald man. "I don't know you," he said, his eyes narrowing. "And you are not garbed like one of us." He tapped the end of his stick against Kagiri's shoulder, and the armor there. "Who are you, and what are you doing here?" At his tone the others hefted their weapons again, and Kagiri cursed inside.

And, again, his imprecations fell into a deep, dark well, echoing within him where he had moments ago been surrounded by other voices.

"A little help here?" he muttered into that void, and felt a hint of dark amusement.

"You were just complaining that we were around too much," Shinen pointed out. "You should make up your mind!"

Kagiri didn't have time for this, not with the bandits clearly waiting on a reply. "I told you," he started, but the man tapped again, this time harder and against his chest, putting enough force behind the gesture to send Kagiri stumbling back a step.

"No lies," the man insisted. "Tell me the truth or it will go badly for you." His manner was quiet, but his eyes were cold and hard.

"I—" Kagiri cast about for an answer, an excuse, anything. He was not good at this sort of thing! Niki had always been the one to spin tall tales, he thought fast on his feet—Giri was the slower, more solid one, the one who backed up his wild excuses. How was he supposed to come up with something on his own?

The Gensaiba could have answered for him, but it seemed all of them were taking a certain perverse pleasure in respecting his stated wishes at this particular moment, and he could barely even sense them in his head.

Or elsewhere, he discovered, as that iron-shod rod poked him in the chest again. He had gotten used to the Gensaiba's reflexes, which would have batted the weapon aside or caught it or shoved it back into the man or something. All he could do was gasp and retreat, until he bumped up against someone and a pair of hands shoved him roughly forward again.

"No matter," the bald man announced, hefting that rod and stepping up to loom over Kagiri as the shove forced him to his knees in the dirt. "We'll ask Barindo ourselves—after we've dealt with you." And that rod raised up over his head, its shadow landing across his face.

"Please!" he cried out in his head. "Help me!"

"Are you sure?" Sinchu asked. "You said you didn't want us taking control all the time," he pointed out. "We're just trying to respect your wishes."

"You're going to get us all killed!" Kagiri wailed, his mental image quailing from attack to mirror his physical self.

"So now you want us to take control?" Setsui asked, sounding perfectly calm considering that their skull was about to be bashed in.

"Yes!" Kagiri screamed. "Do it!"

"Very well," the Gensaiba answered together. And Kagiri sighed in relief as he felt his body leave his control and pass to someone else.

Jeizen lashed out with one fist, catching the bald man square in the stomach and doubling him over with the force of the blow. His other hand caught the rod and yanked it free, twirling it like a baton before settling it into a firm grip.

Sinchu hammered the weapon backward, catching a woman behind him full in the face. The iron cap shattered teeth and nose and she stumbled away, hands going to her ruined features, a pained moan escaping her bloodied lips. He flung the weapon at the bald man, taking him in the throat and knocking him backward as well, and just like that the circle dissolved.

Kenin took advantage of that brief respite to surge to his feet and lock arms around the nearest Kindichi, binding the man's arms to his side and preventing him from swinging the chokoto he held. A quick lift and a wrench and the man's whimpers of pain nearly drowned out the snap as his spine gave way. The sword fell from his grip and, as Kenin released him, he crumpled to the dirt, still conscious but completely limp.

That left two standing and uninjured. Kibi whipped his nihono from its scabbard in a lightning strike, pulling it out and across so that its edge cut through one woman's stomach, slicing the leather vest and silk shirt there as easily as flesh. Then he continued the motion, flicking the blade forward at an upward angle even as he twisted to avoid the remaining bandit's attack, letting the man's club slide past his shoulder as the sword tip took the man under the chin and laid open his throat.

The woman with the broken nose was still up and now charged him, screaming in rage as blood streamed down her face, heavy club held high. It was child's play to step into her approach, preventing her from bringing that weapon down on him, and thrust forward so that her own momentum impaled her on the blade.

The bald man had recovered from the blows to middle and throat and was staggering forward, so Sinchu dispatched him, then knelt and finished off the man with the broken spine. Now all was silent again, as they wiped the sword blade clean and resheathed it.

In his head, though, Kagiri was sobbing as he found himself

surrounded by five men and women once again. This time, however, the figures did not carry weapons, nor did they threaten him.
In fact, they ignored him and his weeping, facing outward instead,
though he thought he saw Kibi and Kenin both toss him sympa-
thetic glances. Still, the message was clear. They were not there
to harm but rather to sequester, to trap him within his own head.
And it was all his own doing. In his fear and his haste, he had
ceded complete control to the Gensaiba, at least for now.

Whether he would ever gain it back again, in part or in whole,
was something only the future could reveal.

CHAPTER SIXTEEN

Ibaru and Iraku paused at the top of the hill, gazing down. Below them, a river sparkled like a silver ribbon in the sharp noon sunlight, the sounds of the rushing water reaching them even here. And there, along the nearer bank, sat a small village, its buildings running right up against the water's edge.

"I hunger," Ibaru stated, but there was a question to his voice, moreso than before. Beside him, his brother cocked his head to the side, considering both that declaration and the cloud that hovered above them, giving them purpose and power even as it drained them of color and emotion. The part of him that still held conscious thought completely understood the change in his brother's tone. Before, the Silent Change had been a mindless, ravening force, intent only upon gorging itself on the vitality of the world around it. And the two of them had been its chosen servants, speaking on its behalf but also tethering it to the ground, giving it a focal point so that it did not lose itself entirely to its appetites but instead retained enough coherence to feed.

Somehow, that had changed. They did not know why, exactly, but they knew when. It had been mere days ago—they had been walking, and suddenly Kaemusei was not there, floating above them so that its shadow constantly darkened their sight. It was gone somewhere, not far but far enough that the sun touched their faces again for the first time in a long while, and the brothers became frightened of its heat and warmth. Then, almost before they could register their fear or the fact that they could feel it, their master returned, plunging them back into the cool depths of a numb mind and a muted spirit.

But all was not as it was. Their master was different now.

Whatever had drawn it away, whatever had transpired during its brief absence, the Silent Change had itself been changed. It was more restless now, but also more aware, more...cunning. Its simple desires had grown more complicated, more sophisticated in their needs and demands. It now hungered for more than just life and color and energy.

And, as its avatars, its messengers, the brothers hungered for something different as well.

The town, they saw as they neared, was not a simple hovel the way Hiromura had been. The homes here were larger and more elaborate, covered in handsome wooden shingles, sturdy posts extending beneath them to support the buildings' backsides over the water, where a lower level offered shelter for a boat. These people clearly made their living on the water, fishing and gathering, and were happy and prosperous as a result.

Several of the villagers emerged from their homes and gathered to watch and wait as the brothers approached. "A good day to you," one of them called at last, when the brothers were no more than a dozen feet away. The speaker was a short, solid man who might have been thought fat if his breadth of arm, leg, head, and chest had not matched that of his stomach. His hair was thinning in front but still long enough in back to be knotted into a simple braid, and his clothing, though simple enough in design and made from hemp and cotton rather than silk, had beautiful patterns sewn around the cuffs and collar.

"Welcome to Rakawa," he continued, his voice thin but strong enough to bridge the gap between them. "I am Togo, the mayor of this town. Who might you be, and what is your business here?" He did not say the latter in a suspicious way, and his general tone and posture were welcoming, if also curious.

"I am Ibaru and he is Iraku," the older brother stated, his voice continuing to be as flat and lifeless as his appearance. "We hunger."

Togo fidgeted with the cuffs of his jacket. "We are certainly happy to provide you with a meal," he replied, "but are you here to buy or sell or trade goods, or to arrange passage across the river, or simply passing by?" It was clear that he thought the latter option preposterous, for who could come to Rakawa without a purpose in mind?

Ibaru stepped closer, and one of the men at Togo's side tensed, his hand tightening on the sturdy walking staff he carried, but the mayor gestured for him to relax his guard. He waited patiently as the brother approached, though he became more nervous when he saw the strange young man's eyes, with their swirls of black and white dancing within. He started to glance about, as if seeking a way to escape, but by then it was too late. Ibaru reached out and laid a hand on the man's shoulder, and Togo stiffened.

The color drained from the mayor's face, and from his clothes as well, leaving him white as snow. Yet he did not age the way the previous village's inhabitants had. Nor did he die. He simply paled.

"Leave him alone!" That was the man with the walking staff, recognizing too late that not all dangers came from swords and clubs and moving to his friend's aid. But Iraku was there, gripping the man's stick with one hand and his shoulder with the other, and that man froze as well as everything about him darkened, the colors all bleeding together into a deep shadow that rapidly turned to a flat, lifeless black.

The other villagers gasped, seeing their two neighbors transformed thus—one palest yet dulled white, one bottomless and lifeless black. There was a hushed silence as the two turned to each other.

"You never appreciate the value of openness and generosity, Unori," Togo said, his voice flat like the brothers'. Even his eyes had turned a milky white, yet clearly he could still see or sense his friend as he berated the man. "Your mind and heart are closed to the possibility of compassion."

"You are a fool, Togo," Unori replied, his eyes a featureless black like the rest of him, as if he had become a walking silhouette of a man. "You are too eager to open your heart to others, and do not stop to think about the dangers, or to take proper precautions. You are a danger to yourself and to everyone around you." He raised his stick, which had also become black, as if to strike down his former friend.

As the two men squared off, still trading insults in emotionless tones, Ibaru and Iraku turned their attention to the other villagers. Each brother reached out to touch another local, then another, and with each touch those people transformed. Some become white. Some became black. All lost their color, and with it their passion. They possessed no warmth any longer, their skin as cool to the touch as their voices were to the ear. Yet they still walked and spoke and acted, and still remembered themselves and their neighbors—and all the petty jealousies and quarrels between them.

The brothers moved through the fishing village, trailing ghost-white hands along buildings as they went, leaving each dwelling as gray and lifeless as cold stone. But the people become white or black and began to argue over trivial matters. Every ounce of compassion seemed to have fled with those colors, every inkling of consideration, every iota of willingness to compromise. These people were no longer interested in being pleasant or meeting halfway or striving to avoid conflict. Instead they had become monolithic in their focus. They were either black or white, and so were all topics. There could be no middle ground, no understanding, no concession or flexibility.

Behind them, Unori struck Togo with his stick. Togo reeled beneath the blow but did not fall. He grabbed the stick in both hands, attempting to wrest it from his former friend. They struggled back and forth, fighting for control. All around them, their neighbors also squared off, white against black, battling within the gray and crumbling village, fighting with grim determination and an inability to conceive of being wrong or even uncertain.

The brothers felt refreshed from the turmoil they had caused. And above them, the Silent Change buzzed and hummed, its energies seemingly restored for the first time since its strange disappearance. It guided them toward the river, and there the boys stopped and stared.

It was tremendous, easily as far across as a strong bow might shoot, and a village very similar to Rakawa nestled on the far side, the balconies of its buildings seeming like eyes that watched the brother's approach without concern. But how would they cross the water, when all the villagers behind them were locked in conflict?

The answer came as Kaemusei descended, drifting ever downward until its lower edge touched the highest peaks of the lively, fast-moving river.

At its swirling gray touch, the river lost its color in that spot, turning perfectly clear—

—and it froze, as if this small patch of it had turned to time-worn and age-dulled ice.

The Silent Change floated forward, then paused as if beckoning the boys to follow. Unafraid as long as their master stole their emotions away, the boys stepped out onto the water—and did not fall, its frozen surface seemingly as solid as hard-packed dirt.

Kaemusei surged forward, freezing a steady path across the rapid waters. The brothers followed in its wake, the river staying solid beneath their feet like a gray carpet unrolling ahead of them. Fish caught within its influence faded, aging and growing dull and lifeless as it passed. Their bodies floated upward but could not pierce the surface of the frozen water and so remained trapped underneath, once-silvery scales shaking beneath the boy's footsteps.

By the time they reached the other side, and the building there, the brothers could feel the hunger gnawing away at their insides once more.

And above them the Silent Change hovered, equally demanding, ready to siphon color and warmth from the villagers on this side as well.

CHAPTER SEVENTEEN

Misataki Shizumi found her commanding officer, Fujibuki Haro, Lord Commander of the Honjofu, one of the most senior and influential military officers in all Rimbaku, in a tea house. *At least it is not a brothel*, she thought as she stepped into the small thatch-roofed building, pausing just inside the sliding doors to shed her boots and then padding in socks across the mats of the main room to one of the small alcoves, where he waited. He was seated cross-legged upon a cushion, as was proper, an unadorned porcelain cup cradled in his hands, a thin ribbon of steam wafting upward to tickle at his nose—but she could not help but notice that he was dressed in a handsome kitoro emblazoned with his house's otter-around-the-sun crest rather than his armor and that his nihono, an ancient and honorable blade, leaned against the far corner, well outside his reach. She said nothing about that, however, as she paused inside the alcove and bowed low.

"Hai, Taikoro," she stated, her hands coming together in the traditional cupped-palm-over-fist salute. "I am here, as instructed."

Haro glanced up, looking mildly surprised to see his sergeant standing beside his table, despite the fact that it was his orders that had brought her from the Fyushan border. Or perhaps he had not expected her to locate him so readily, but there was only one tea house of any size or substance in this vicinity, and Shizumi had resolved to try there first before moving on to the more unsavory options. Not that Haro had told her to seek him out at a place of recreation, and with a different commander she might have expected him to already be about the work of ridding this district of its bandit infestation, but with Haro she knew better.

"Ah, Shizumi," he said, dipping his head in the merest nod, his mustache barely fluttering with the motion. "Good. Now we can get started." Setting the tea back upon the small table before him, he rose to his feet—not gracefully, but with more ease than some men his age, at least—and reclaimed his sword, sliding it back into his sash as he gestured for her to precede him out the door. She did so, waiting as he handed the proprietor a few coins and then slid on his boots, before stuffing her feet back into her own footgear and joining him on the teahouse's shaded front porch. The rest of her unit had been lounging on the benches set up out here, for the teahouse opened onto the village's central square, as did the winehouse, the brothel, and the inn, but they straightened to attention as their commander appeared. He executed a lazy bow in their general direction, but did not otherwise acknowledge them or Shizumi, instead turning his eyes toward the horizon. Just beyond the town she could see dark shapes, and knew those to be the tents of the chotao he had brought—this village did not have the capacity to house sixty or more warriors, not without expelling most of the residents from their own beds, and she was glad that at least Haro had chosen to have his men quarter themselves and not inconvenience the locals, though perhaps that was simply a matter of his not considering where his troops would bed down and one of the gochos making the decision instead.

"We must find where the Kindichi are headquartered," Haro stated, as if this were a remarkable suggestion. "Any group must have its leader, and any leader must have a place from which to issue commands. Find him, deal with him, and the rest will fall in line soon enough." He stroked his mustache, his lips pursed in a smug little smile, clearly well pleased with his own deductive powers.

Shizumi nodded. "Hai, Taikoro," she agreed. But now she was faced with a dilemma. The next step, logically, was to send scouts to the surrounding villages searching for any sign of these Kindichi. If they found any of the bandits, they could trail them back to their headquarters, or simply interrogate them to learn its location. If they did not find any, they could speak to the villagers, who would presumably know something about the bandits who claimed to have taken control of this entire region, and who had enough strength to have vanquished a full shotao before and to send the heads of those warriors back to the emperor. That was, of course, assuming no one here knew anything, since tea houses were a common stop for travelers and thus a useful place to seek information.

But these were all things any decent military leader would already have thought of. Therefore, if she were giving her commander the benefit of the doubt, she could assume that he had already issued these orders and had already gathered whatever intelligence was to be had. But could she safely assume that? Or should she suggest this course of action to him? If he had already put these plans into effect, he might take offense at her implication that he would not have thought of this on his own. But if he had not, and she did not suggest it, he would be angry at their lack of progress, and no doubt blame her for not mentioning what they should do next. Either way, she risked giving offense. But was it better to err on the side of caution in terms of wounding his pride, or better to err on the side of ensuring they were pursuing their objective?

Considering it carefully, she finally opted for as near a middle ground as she could find. "My apologies, Taikoro," she stated, keeping her tone deferential, "but as I am only just arrived, I do not know what we have learned thus far about these Kindichi, if anything. Might I request the honor of a briefing, so that I might better serve you?"

Haro frowned, sending a sidelong glance her way, as if trying to determine if she was mocking or insulting him somehow. Finally, apparently seeing no cause for offense in her question, he nodded. "Of course, gunso. I have ascertained that there are no Kindichi here in this village," he informed her, adding, "no doubt they heard of our impending arrival and vacated the immediate area with all due haste."

"No doubt," she agreed. "With your permission, then, I will dispatch scouts to the neighboring villages, in the hopes of locating some of these bandits or at least learning of their current whereabouts."

"Yes, that is our next step," he agreed as if he had proposed it himself. "See to it." And, with a short nod and a wave, he dismissed her and pivoted on his heel, heading back into the tea house. She heard him calling for a fresh pot as he re-entered.

"So?" Genji asked as Shizumi rejoined them. "What's the plan from our illustrious leader?" Although Shizumi was careful not to denigrate Haro in front of the other Honjofu, or indeed anywhere except in her own head, she knew her bantao was aware of her opinion of him and shared it. After all, a true warrior could tell another warrior at a glance.

That was not relevant to their current activities, however. "We will canvass the area," Shizumi replied. "Paired scouts to each village within two days' ride. Avoid notice if possible—the Kindichi are said to have as many as fifty in their band. If you find any of them, send word and then follow at a distance, unless it is only one or two, in which case capture and bring back for questioning."

"Hai!" her team responded, and immediately dispersed. Shizumi stood and watched them go for a moment, admiring the way they sprang into action without question but also with a clear head and an obvious understanding of what needed to be done. This was what a true warrior was like—decisive but not impulsive, motivated and focused but still alert to all possibilities, and especially to potential dangers.

Then she marched across the square, making for the wine-house on its far side. She would find out what the proprietor could tell her, after buying a moderately expensive bottle of rice wine—which she would then gift to Haro, lest he think she was drinking on duty.

Two days later, Shizumi presented herself at the tea house again. Haro had more or less taken up residence there, which made sense given that the wine house was darker and had rougher furnishings, and the brothel was not of the highest order and was of dubious cleanliness, as were the men and women in its employ. The tea house, however, was scrupulously clean, and with the doors and windows slid back a pleasant breeze drifted through, carrying the scent of pine and water to offset the region's ever-present dust and rock.

"You have the information we require?" her superior asked. He sat in the same chamber as before, and indeed had the same teapot and teacup. Shizumi suspected it was the only set here that was glazed rather than left rough, and that the proprietor had guessed a nobleman like Haro would prefer simple elegance over rough beauty. In that, he had chosen wisely.

"I do, Taikoro, though it is...odd," Shizumi replied, saluting. She took a breath before plunging straight to the heart of the matter. "We did discover the name of the Kindichi's leader, Daro Barindo, and where he had headquartered, a town called Yudishu, a few days' ride south of here." She paused. "But he is no longer there."

"Oh?" Haro set down his cup to give her his full attention, which always made her repress a shiver, his gaze as oily as his mustache. "And where has he gone, this Daro Barindo? I am eager to make his acquaintance."

"I regret that this will not be possible, sir, as he has been dispatched from this life," Shizumi reported. "As have all his Kindichi."

"What?" Now her superior rose from his seat and stepped closer to her. "What do you mean? The aiashe had failed to defeat him! That is why the emperor dispatched me, to see to this man's capture personally!"

And why you called me here, to handle that for you, Shizumi added, but was careful to keep that addendum from her face or her tone. "It was not the army, sir," was all she said. "Apparently it was the work of one man."

"What?" Haro pounded his hands together. "That is not possible! One man against, how many, fifty bandits? Preposterous!"

"Not all at once, no," she agreed. "Evidently he hit Yudishu first. Barindo had perhaps a score of men with him there, and this stranger dispatched them all in one decisive battle." She recalled what a basketweaver had told her, a woman who had actually come from Yudishu and claimed to have witnessed the combat first hand. "They say he was like a demon, sir, moving faster than the eye could follow, wielding two nihono at once, carving his way through the bandits like a sharp wind through the reeds."

"And we believe these old wives' tales?" her commander demanded, a sneer ready on his lips.

She bowed. "I have received firsthand reports of this, sir, from multiple sources. All agree that it is so."

Haro stroked his mustache. "He must be a Jubanichi," he mused, pacing the tiny room, "and possessed of powerful aishone, to have defeated so many at once. Where is this warrior with the perfect touch now?"

"No one knows," she was forced to admit. "He left Yudishu a few days ago. Reports indicate that he was headed northwest—he is accompanied by several merchants and their guards." She'd found that part strange, for what use did a warrior of such skill have for merchants, and if he were traveling with them why would they need other guards? One of many questions to ask the man, if they should be so fortunate as to find him.

"Hm." Haro considered the matter. "The Kindichi are no longer a threat to this region?" he asked, and Shizumi nodded. Difficult to be a threat when you were all dead, unless it was as akatai haunting the places they were killed! "Then our task here is done," he declared happily. "But"—he held up one hand as if to forestall any premature celebration on her part—"we now have a new task. This man, this Jubanichi, is clearly immensely dangerous, to have slaughtered so many fierce bandits on his own. And he is not part of the Honjofu—or the aiashe," he added, almost as an afterthought, "which means his sword is not sworn to the service of the empire. That makes him a criminal, and a deadly one." He nodded sharply. "We must pursue him and capture him. Either he will swear allegiance to the emperor, or he will be executed for his crimes." He grabbed up his sword and swept from the little room and out of the tea house, where Shizumi could hear him calling for the chotao to assemble.

For once, she found herself agreeing with her commander as

she hurried after him. This man could pose a significant threat if he chose—who was to say that, having dispatched bandits, he might not shift to targeting nobles, or merchants, or the emperor himself? They would need to apprehend him and question him as to his motives and his future intentions.

But Shizumi found another reason quickening her heartbeat and her step. From the tales she had heard, this stranger was indeed a virtuoso with the blade, his skill far beyond that of anyone else she had yet encountered.

She had long hoped for a worthy adversary, one against she could truly test her own prowess.

Now, at long last, it appeared she may have found one.

CHAPTER EIGHTEEN

"Ash and bone!" Maniko Kohori cursed, ducking back quickly and putting her back against the wall, the delicately inlaid tiles there cool even through the lacquered panels of her armor. "I count at least a dozen."

Beside her, her chuisu, Itamon, nodded. He had crouched low in order to peek around the corner at the same time. "Agreed," was all he said, his broad face grim as he glanced her way, one hand already resting on the hilt of his nihono. "What are your orders, sir?"

Kohori considered that, cursing again under her breath. Besides Itamon she had four Honteno here with her in this side corridor, and she trusted each of them to be able to hold their own, but six against twelve or more? Hardly good odds. Especially when she had no idea who these strangers were. Their armor, in the one glimpse she'd had, appeared to be edged in crimson, which made no sense. But clearly they were neither her Honteno nor their brothers-in-arms the Honjofu. Which meant they did not belong here.

She was just opening her mouth to respond when they all heard a new rhythm pounding through the floorboards just ahead.

"What now?" she muttered. That rhythm was one of marching feet—a beat she knew all too well—and if she strained she could also make out the scrape of metal studs on wood, meaning who-ever was approaching was wearing heavy boots made for combat, just as the dozen warriors around the corner were. Was it a second unit moving to join up with the first? Or were they rivals? Or completely unconnected?

One thing she did know about the men and women whose feet

were producing such a noise—they were not hers. And here inside Aihiri, that was a bad thing indeed.

The heavy footfalls grew closer, then suddenly stopped, as did all noise from the troop she had already sighted. For an instant, all was silent. Then the halls erupted with curses, shouts, and the hiss of metal sliding against wood. The sound of nihono being drawn for battle.

So, not two halves of a whole, then.

Itamon had clearly noticed the same thing. "Is it too much to hope they all kill each other?" he whispered with a grin. Behind him, one of the others chuckled.

"I doubt we are that lucky," Kohori replied. "But it does mean both of them will be busy, at least for the moment. We can take the long way 'round."

There were a few good-natured groans, all kept to a whisper, but no one objected as she pushed off from the wall and led her guards back the way they had come, until they reached a small corridor branching off this one. Though intended for servants so that they might move about the imperial compound unseen, Kohori had long ago made it her job to know every route in and out of this massive structure, and she was not above using these narrow passages when necessary.

Right now, she deemed it highly necessary.

Leading her team at a fast sprint, Kohori kept her sword hilt pressed up against her belly so that the blade would not jut out and catch against the walls they were already brushing and scraping past. She had this terrible feeling that there was no time to waste.

Why, oh why, had her emperor decided to leave the capital? If not for that bold but rash decision, none of this would be happening.

At least, she admitted as she veered around a corner and down a different passage, everything had been quiet for the first week.

Then she had caught one of the servants about to enter the throne room.

"What are you doing here?" she'd demanded, catching him by the arm. His name was Matsu and he was not a bad man, or a disloyal one. He was, however, easily cowed, and had all but curled in upon himself at her tone.

"Rojiri Amani sent me to open the throne room for her," he'd replied, his voice quavering so that each word trembled like a tiny bird before a stiff wind. "So they can address those seeking audience."

"Go back to your chores," Kohori had told him, trying to keep her irritation from spilling over onto this poor, terrified little man. "I will deal with the Rojiri." He had been only too happy to make himself scarce as Kohori had circled back around—first summoning one of her Honteno to stand guard at the door she'd just left, which led from the emperor's private quarters to the throne room—to the beautifully carved and inlaid double doors that marked the proper entrance to the seat of the Relicant Empire. She had found the imperial councilor waiting impatiently there, arms folded over her narrow chest beneath her purple kisoni of office, foot tapping in its elegant silk slipper, lips pursed in their customary disapproval. She had ceased the tapping upon seeing Kohori.

"Where is the servant I sent?" Amani Denbi, most senior of the emperor's Rojiri, had demanded. "He should have completed his task by now! The other Rojiri will be here soon, and we have a great deal to discuss—some young fool in Nariyari has been preaching nonsense and stirring up trouble, and we must address the situation at once!"

"There is no task," Kohori had replied, "and any discussions can be held in your usual council chambers. The throne room remains closed, by order of the emperor himself." She had bowed, though only as to an equal, for as a Lord Commander she was more or less on par with even the highest nobles.

Also, because she knew perfectly well that it irritated Denbi to no end.

The lead Rojiri had glared at her then. "I ordered him to open the room," she had stated, her snow-white brows drawn in close. "And I speak for the emperor."

"In matters of the nation, yes," Kohori had agreed. "But not when it comes to the safety and function of Aihiri. And your representation of him does not supersede orders from his own lips." She had bowed again, and then turned and walked away, leaving the councilor to stare after her, speechless.

But she should have known that would not be the end of it.

A few days later, her guards had intercepted an unfamiliar servant attempting to sneak into the throne room. She had been unusually haughty for someone of her occupation, though that been explained once she had stated that she was "the personal aide of none other than Rojiri Amani, who speaks with the emperor's own voice and whose commands must be obeyed as if from His Imperial Majesty's own lips."

That was when Kohori had decided to not just latch but bar the throne room's doors, both the double doors with their massive, heavily carved teak beam that a dozen men could not hope to break and the smaller side door with its single bar on the outside to prevent anyone who did manage to breach the throne room from then reaching the emperor's private study and bedchamber. She had stationed guards at each entrance as well, and rotated them on standard shifts.

She and Itamon and the others had been on their way to relieve the guards outside the main doors when they had sighted the unfamiliar warriors invading their halls.

Now, as they emerged from the servants' corridor, passing through a small and well-concealed door only a single turn from the throne room itself, she was both horrified and relieved to still hear the sounds of battle somewhere behind her. Evidently those two groups were keeping one another occupied. Perhaps Itamon's hope would come true, after all.

Then she had stepped out into the hall—and almost walked into another pack of warriors who were in the act of striding past. Also wearing unfamiliar armor. Heading toward that same corner.

With a sigh, Kohori adjusted her sword, took a deep breath, and shouted, "Stop!"

They did, almost as one, which spoke well to their training and poorly to her chances, for again she was outnumbered, though at least here it was only ten to six. Now she could see them more clearly, and as with the others this group's armor was rimmed in scarlet, a color reserved exclusively for the emperor and his household. Her own armor was entirely crimson, with the higeibara stamped in relief across every panel, and edged in gold to indicate her rank. But these strangers bore the thundercloud of the Etsuya family, only that house's colors were blue and gray, not silver and red as these were attired. Still, she was able to single out their leader, a short, stout man whose open faceplate revealed a strong, square jaw bare of any whiskers, and she had to stifle her surprise. Despite his wearing armor instead of his customary robes, she knew him at once. It was Rojiri Etsuya Kenshin himself!

He clearly recognized her as well and dipped his head in a slight bow. "Taikoro Maniko," he called out, striding forward as his men parted to make way, though she noticed they also slid to the side so that, in battle, they would still be able to draw and fight unencumbered. "I understand you have kept that traitor Denbi from taking the throne. You have our thanks. We will not forget your loyal service."

Kohori towered over the stocky noble as she closed the gap between them. "I serve the emperor, Hibikitsu, ruler over all Rimbaku," she replied, firing each word at him like arrows from a bow, straight and sharp and hard enough to bowl a man from his feet. "He has ordered me to bar the throne room from all comers, and I will do so."

Kenshin's eyes narrowed. "The emperor has gone to war," he pointed out coldly. "And, in war, men die. We will guard the throne until his return, and rule in his stead until such time."

She shook her head, and gripped her scabbard with her right hand, her left falling to her hilt. "This will not come to pass," she warned. "Return to your own chambers at once, or I will be forced to remove you by force."

He sneered at that, backing away to a safe distance and making a show of drawing his own blade with one hand and his aishone pouch with the other. As soon as he had gulped down a bone chip, his grip on the weapon steadied, as did his footing. "You are outnumbered and outmanned," he retorted. "Stand aside or perish."

Her only reply was to draw her sword and settle into her preferred stance. She was pleased to see his eyes widen at that, as his own newly bestowed skill informed him that she was not a foe to be trifled with. True, she might only absorb the knowledge of her forebears, not their actual muscle memory, but she had put that wealth of information to good use for many long years and had honed her own body according to its precepts. She had no doubt she could defeat Kenshin, who had rarely bothered to use his aishone before.

It was the fact that they were outnumbered nearly two to one that concerned her. But she could not let that prevent her from doing her duty.

The stout Rojiri had just taken a step forward, his sword raised, when a shout came from behind them: "Stop, in the name of the emperor!" And there, as Kohori shifted to glance back without allowing Kenshin to attack her unawares, was Amani Denbi— with a group of warriors at her back. These must have been one of the two groups Kohori had seen earlier, for there were only six of them, and all bore dents and scrapes and wounds, but of course the senior councilor carried herself as if she had already been crowned and had a thousand Honjofu trailing in her wake.

"You will both stand down at once," Denbi continued, stopping just beyond the reach of Itamon, who had taken the position of rear guard. "We command it." She too had cast aside her purple robes, Kohori noted, and her kitoro was Imperial red beneath her house's stars and moons.

"I will not bend the knee to you, traitor!" Kenshin bellowed, holding his sword high. "I will split you in half first!" His warriors shifted their attention from the Honteno to this new rival, who all wore the Amani star and crescent moon but were, like them, limned in crimson.

Kohori quietly readied herself to step aside and let these two kill each other. Perhaps then this madness would stop.

Denbi appeared to realize, at last, that she did not hold the upper hand here. "Perhaps we can discuss this amongst ourselves," she stated, frowning at her fellow Rojiri before turning a sharp, venomous gaze toward Kohori. "After we have eliminated certain obstacles."

"A temporary alliance?" Kenshin replied. He lowered his blade, clearly considering. Then nodded. "Very well." And his men once more pivoted to focus on the Honteno.

But now it was Kohori who straightened and smiled. "Allow me to respond appropriately," she declared, putting two fingers to her lips and releasing a piercing series of sharp tones. At once there came a responding shout from around the corner, followed by the clatter of feet in quick march.

She nearly wept with relief when the six guards she had been coming to relieve rounded the bend and gave a resounding cry, raising their spears and swords high.

"You are still outnumbered," Kenshin pointed out, though he looked far less confident now, for he and his warriors were caught in between the two guard units.

"Perhaps so," she agreed, "but I do not have to worry about a supposed ally turning on me, nor about not striking that ally by mistake. And my warriors have not already been bloodied," she added, directing that last to Denbi. She shrugged. "Besides which, if I fall, my Honteno will continue to fight. If either of you do—what will your men do?" And she raised her blade before her, a sliver of silver between her eyes, light and sure in her hands.

Both councilors gave this serious thought. It was Denbi, ever the realist, who acknowledged the stalemate first. "This conversation is far from over," she warned, then turned and strode off, every bit as fierce in her robes and finery as the armored warriors who hastened after her. Left on his own, Kenshin quickly withdrew as well, sidling past Kohori with a growl and a snarling show of teeth like a hungry beast deprived of a tasty morsel.

"That was close," Itamon commented as they watched the councilors and their pet soldiers depart.

"It was," she acknowledged, sheathing her blade with a sigh.

"And when they return, there will be more of them." She shook her head. Even with all the Honteno turned out at once she had only twenty. If even two of the Rojiri marched against her, she was done for. Which meant she had only one course of action left.

"Get word to the Honjofu," she instructed her lieutenant. "Tell Fujibuki Haro that Aihiri is under attack, the Rojiri have turned traitor, and the Honteno request the Honjofu's aid at once."

She only hoped they lived long enough for her to face the consequences of making that request.

CHAPTER NINETEEN

Ijichi chuckled to himself, adjusting the angle of the yanoi slung across his shoulder. "Did you hear the one about the girl, her grandmother, and the tanakia?" he asked his companion as they trudged along behind the rearmost wagon. The other man grunted and shook his head, but it was clear that he was barely listening. Ijichi frowned. Strange fellow, far too focused and humorless to part of a caravan like this one. "What'd you say your name was, again?" he asked, sidling a little closer. The other man was about his height and build, neither tall nor short, fat nor starved, and had wide, plain features Ijichi could barely make out beneath his broad iron jingaso.

"Arata," the other man replied, though it seemed the answer came grudgingly, for he scowled as he admitted to it.

"Right, right, Arata," Ijichi agreed. He had asked this morning as well, when the newcomer had taken up position beside him here. "I'm Ijichi." He shook his head. "Sorry, memory like a sieve—where'd you sign on, again?"

"Matoyan," his erstwhile partner answered.

"Matoyan! For serious?" Ijichi laughed outright. "They even have guards up there? For what, to keep the bears from drinking all the rice wine and not paying?" He'd heard of the tiny hunting village only because a trapper from there had once traveled with them, bringing her furs to a larger settlement for trade. She'd described the place as barely more than a collection of a few rough huts, only half a step up from lean-tos, that was just a convenient meeting place and storage site for the hunters who roamed those mountains seeking bear and fox and marten pelts.

Arata shrugged. "Not really," he agreed. "That's why I left.

Needed to do something more with my life." He gave a brief smile but there was no humor to it, merely a stretch of the lips and a flash of teeth, before turning his attention back to the rear of the wagon they were marching behind.

"Not sure this qualifies as more," Ijichi told him with another chuckle. "But hey, I guess it gets you out of the mountains, at least, right?" Which was certainly true. The caravan had first gathered up in Obanari and then wended its way down, across the Zinyang at the Doh Bridge, and was now traveling along the eastern edge of Hochiro just below the mountains. They'd cross into Nariyari before eventually turning west and making their way across, into Bezenkai and ultimately back up into Hochiro again.

It was a steady, predictable route, and a steady, predictable job guarding the wagons and the merchants who owned them and the wares they stored within. Ijichi liked it when they reached actual towns and the wagons stopped so the merchants could unload their goods and try to sell or trade them to the locals, because then he and the others actually got to stand guard, looking fierce in their chain shirts with their yanoi in front of them and their chokotos at their side. And Konami always gave them some of their pay on the spot so they could spend coin buying sweets or rice wine or fresh bread or whatever else they wanted. Those were good times.

The long stretches in between, like this one, were just slogs that had to be got through to reach the next destination, the guards ostensibly serving to scare off potential bandits and looters but mostly just trudging along in front of, beside, and behind the wagons to keep the caravan together and on track.

Which made it even stranger that this new fellow, Arata, would have joined them on the road rather than at one of the towns, and that he would claim to be enjoying this mindless, monotonous marching. Still, if he'd come from Matoyan, maybe this was a step up, at least for now until the boredom set in.

That didn't explain his attire, however. Most of the guards had something similar to Ijichi, a chain shirt or jacket and a leather cap dotted with small metal studs or scales. The caravan provided yanoi but expected each guard to outfit themselves otherwise, out of their own pocket, so most started their career with nothing more than a sturdy hantien and passable sandals or boots and maybe a stout branch for a club.

Not so this newcomer. He wore a full kit, maikiro, hanketo, suneoto, and jingaso. The armor was plated rather than studded, as were the gloves and shin guards, and the hat looked to be iron rather than wood or woven reeds. All of them were scuffed and smeared with dirt, which also struck Ijichi as strange, since Arata's boots and pants and face were relatively clean and his yanoi and chokoto looked positively spotless. Everything about the man struck him as odd, and the next time they paused to water the horses and let the traders stretch their legs Ijichi sidled over to Konami.

"No, I'm not letting you walk beside Ogura's wagon again," the guard captain stated before he'd even had a chance to open his mouth, wiping her own lips from the waterskin she'd just held there. "You'll just make inappropriate advances toward her again, she'll complain again, and I'll have to move you again. Easier for everyone if you just keep to the rear where you belong." She looked more resigned than truly upset, but her tone was firm and her heavy features set, so Ijichi knew there was no talking her into changing her mind.

He laughed, though. "They're only inappropriate if she says no," he insisted, waggling his eyebrows at his superior. "And one of these days she'll say yes, you'll see. I'm wearing her down." The weaver Ogura was the most attractive woman in the caravan, as far as Ijichi was concerned, with her long hair and round face and tiny, almost delicate features. She lived in her wagon by herself, and he knew she was secretly longing for some company. One of these days she'd see that he was everything she needed—strong, loyal, dependable. They'd get there in the end.

That was not what he'd wanted to speak to his captain about, however, so he forced his mind back on track. "That new fella, Arata," he started. "He's a little odd, no?"

Konami scowled, pursing her lips. "What new fellow?" She

followed Ijichi's gaze to where Arata stood at the rear, then shrugged. "Huh. He isn't one of ours." She didn't seem overly concerned, however. The caravan picked up strays from time to time, people who saw the safety in traveling with a large, well-armed group instead of setting out alone. The caravan itself shrank and grew along its route, only a few of the merchants traveling the entire way with them—most had homes somewhere along the path and detached themselves when they were close, or joined as the caravan passed nearby. Anyone was welcome to join them, provided they checked with the caravan master first and paid the appropriate fees, which went to paying the guards and providing food and water for the horses. Individuals could join without paying, as long as they were able to feed themselves and potentially lend a hand defending the caravan in case of an attack. Some of those wound up being hired on as proper guards at some point, once they'd proven themselves. It was an easy way to audition for the job.

Ijichi didn't like it, though. "Where's Jatira?" he demanded. "He usually walks with me." Short, stout Jatira was always willing to laugh at Ijichi's jokes and to swap stories with him, though his stories did tend to become more lavish and unbelievable the longer they ran on. Still, he was fun to have alongside, not like this Arata, with his silence and his scowls and his terse replies.

"Twisted his ankle," Konami replied. "I put him in the wagon to rest it for now. Don't worry, you'll have him back in a few days." The caravan master had the lead wagon, which contained the guards' food and bedrolls and other supplies and served as a place for them to heal if they got injured. The procession could hardly slow down to accommodate a guard who walked with a limp.

Konami stoppered her waterskin, slinging it back at her side, and lifted her brass horn to produce a loud wail. That was the signal to get everyone moving again. Still annoyed, Ijichi stomped back to his place behind the last wagon. Arata was already there, waiting.

"You've got a few minutes before we're on the road again," Ijichi warned. "Might want to take advantage of it while you can." They could always wander away to relieve themselves, of course, since the caravan only moved at a brisk walk, and then jog to catch up, but it was easier to go now. That was the kind of thing you learned when you'd been at this job for a while, like he had.

Arata nodded and stepped away, toward some of the bushes a little ways distant. There was definitely something strange about the man, Ijichi thought, watching him go. He didn't trust him. Fortunately, there wasn't much one man could do to an entire armed caravan, but he still figured he'd best keep a close eye on his new traveling partner.

That night, Ijichi brought Arata a plate of stew where he sat a short distance from the others. Most of the guards and merchants mingled together at meal times, all circling a single fire, and often they shared their food as well, the traders contributing meats and noodles and spices to the stew the caravan master prepared for himself and his employees. "Here," Ijichi said, offering the new-comer the plate.

"Thanks." Arata accepted it and immediately began eating, using the thick-crusted bread that had been perched on the lip to scoop the stew into his mouth. He made no invitation to join him, but Ijichi lowered himself to the ground a few feet away with his own food, anyway. He could hear the others talking and laughing around the fire, and desperately wanted to join them, maybe squeeze in beside Ogura and tease her about the brightly colored shawl she was wearing, but stayed here instead, in the chill of the shadows, beside his silent companion.

"So, you grow up in Matoyan?" Ijichi asked finally around a mouthful of stew and bread. His dinnermate just grunted. "Do a lot of hunting?" No reply. "You don't like to talk about yourself, do you?" There, that had been direct, and at least it made Arata pause and glance up at him. Something in the other man's eyes made Ijichi shiver.

For a second, he thought he had finally cracked the stranger's shell, as Arata licked his lips and set his plate down beside him. Then he levered himself to his feet. "I need to pee," he announced, striding quickly away, deeper into the dark, past the row of trees that edged the clearing the caravan had chosen. But just before disappearing from view, Arata turned back—and Ijichi could swear he saw the man's eyes glow like those of an owl, luminous disks more visible because of the shadows surrounding them, but reddened like the dusk instead of silvery like the moon.

"What?" That had Ijichi on his feet in an instant, stumbling after the other man. "Hey, what was that?" he demanded, stomping toward the trees. "Come back here!" He shoved branches aside, feeling the prickle of pine needles against his skin, and then he was in the forest, the stars above vanishing behind that dark canopy. He paused to let his eyes adjust to the dark—

—and started as an arm clamped across his chest, just below his neck. It was dark as well, and seemed to bleed shadows like it had been woven from them, but darker still was the blade that rose from the other hand and slashed his throat, its bite numbing his flesh so that Ijichi barely felt the cut until his own grasping hands probed the gaping rent in his neck and became slick with the blood jetting forth from it.

His last thought was that now Ogura would never know the pleasure of his company. *I could have been good to her*, he thought fervently as the darkness claimed him once and for all.

A few minutes later, Ijichi rejoined the rest of the caravan, setting his empty plate atop the others waiting to be washed and lowering himself to the ground in an empty spot by the fire. He held out his hands to warm them, for with the sun gone the night air was still crisp here in the hills.

"No luck with Arata?" Jatira asked from a few seats over. He had his bad ankle propped up before him, the bandages around it making it as wide around as his head, but otherwise seemed to be in good humor. And why not, when he had been able to ride in comfort all day?

Ijichi shrugged. "He'll come around—or he won't," he answered, accepting a cup of rice wine from one of the others and tossing it back. "Either way, I won't let it bother me."

His friends nodded. That was the way of caravan life—if you let one of your traveling companions get under your skin, you'd spend the entire trip miserable. Better to just ignore anything that didn't suit you, and focus on the things that did, and on the journey itself.

The next morning, Konami stomped over as they were getting ready to roll out. "Where's your friend?" she asked Ijichi, gesturing toward the empty space Arata had occupied the past few days.

He shrugged. "No idea. Haven't seen him since last night."

The guard captain frowned. "Better check for him," she instructed. "Make sure he didn't break his neck tripping over a branch or something." As someone who wasn't in her employ and wasn't paying for protection, Arata's well-being was not truly their concern, but he had fallen in with them and so was at least nominally someone they should worry about. That was one of the good things about Konami—a lot of other guard captains, in her position, would have shrugged and left a man to his fate.

Ijichi nodded and began checking the campsite. A few of the others joined in. It was Jatira, limping in among the trees, who called out, "Over here!" His normally cheery voice sounded oddly strained.

In minutes, Ijichi, Konami, and several others had converged on his location. And there, splayed out on the pine-strewn ground, was Arata.

At least, they assumed it was him.

He wore the same uniform as the newcomer, though his jingaso had fallen beside him, turned upward so that morning dew had gathered in its basin. But the man himself looked as if he had been burned, his skin blackened and cracked, his mouth open in a silent scream. A deep, ugly wound split his throat from side to side, and his eyes—

His eyes were missing entirely.

Jatira shuddered. "What did this to him?" he asked, his voice hushed.

"No idea," Konami admitted. She shook herself. "But we're leaving. Now."

"What about him?" one of the others asked.

Their captain sighed. "Not our problem," she said slowly, her voice and face grim. "We need to look to the caravan, and that means getting as far as we can from whatever did this to him." She nudged the jingaso with the tip of her boot, turning it over. The dewdrops spilled across it, sluicing away some of the mud—and revealing a symbol beneath. A red spider lily.

"An aiashe," Ijichi pointed out. "He was a deserter—no wonder he had all that mud on him!" He shook his head. "I knew there was something off about him."

"You were right," his superior agreed. "And it looks like he got what he deserved." She glanced at the body once more before resolutely turning her back on it. "Get everyone moving. The sooner we leave this site, the better."

The others nodded and followed her lead, Ijichi taking up the rear. No one else saw as he turned to give the body a parting look—and smiled, raising one hand in mocking salute before following the other guards back to the caravan.

CHAPTER TWENTY

Kagiri reined in with a frown. "Who are they?" he demanded, glancing behind him. Kishin Narai and the other merchants rode a handful of paces to the rear, trailed by Joshi and the other guards—but behind them were a dozen or so others, all on foot although one man dragged a cart in which nestled a woman and a little girl. The people all wore simple clothes, farmers or laborers or craftsmen of some sort, he would guess, and all of them stopped respectfully when he did, their eyes fixed on him as he wheeled his horse about to stare at them all arrayed before him in attentive audience.

"They are villagers," Shizu Yokori answered, her tongue as ready as ever, though he noted she did not seem to test its sharpness on him as often anymore. Which was definitely for the best. "Many are from Yudishu, but a few are from other villages we've passed since." She sniffed as if noting an unpleasant smell in the air, and her smile was clearly forced. "You saved them from the Kindichi, and they have decided to follow wherever you go, in the hopes that your strong arm will somehow lend them prosperity as well."

"Or at least protection," Eien Kawatai suggested from Kagiri's other side. "Which does make sense—as long as they stay near you, they certainly won't have to worry about any bandits!" The merchant laughed at his own joke, but as was often the case there was some wisdom to his words beneath the frivolity.

Kagiri considered this. He had no desire to attract followers, any more than he had any interest in money. What did he want with such things? True, the old Kagiri might have liked fame and fortune, wealth and attention, but that seemed a lifetime ago. He was a different person now—or persons, more accurately. And none of them cared for sycophants.

Still, there was their duty to consider. They owed it to the people of this land, who they had failed once before, to protect them as best they could. If that meant allowing those people to travel with them, they could hardly say no, could they? And yes, at least that way they could be sure the people would not succumb to physical attacks. Beyond that, though, these people were on their own.

"Very well," he stated, nudging his horse back around and tapping him into a steady walk once more. "They may accompany us."

"And are we expected to feed them, then?" Jiro Masute muttered, no doubt to his fellow merchants rather than to Kagiri. Especially since Fujiko Oritano shushed him almost immediately.

Kagiri allowed himself a short smile at that. Let them worry about whether these followers were costing them money. It would keep them from bothering him about such details. He had more important things to worry about, after all.

Like the question of their final destination—and what they would do when they reached it.

A few nights later, they came to a river. It was not wide like the Zinyang but its water still glided past with deceptive speed, all silvery motion slipping by with a faint, almost musical rush. "We will camp here along the banks tonight," Kagiri decided, admiring the view. "In the morning we will locate a bridge, or a shallow where we might ford."

No one argued. Good. Slowly, the merchants were learning not to dispute his decisions. Besides which, anyone with any sense could clearly see the wisdom to stopping here. The river moved far too quickly for anyone to simply swim across, and a boat would not only require great skill to handle but would also be too loud to go unnoticed. Thus the river provided an excellent defensive barrier. With it at their backs, they need only patrol ahead and to the sides, and the land here was wide and flat and green, with little to hide behind.

Besides which, after so much time traipsing through the deserts of Nariyari, Kagiri was eager to enjoy fresh water and greenery for as long as he could.

Which was why, later that night, he found himself strolling along the riverbank well after everyone but the posted guard had fallen asleep. It was peaceful like this. The moon was high and full overhead, a brilliant disc casting its cool silver light down upon the landscape and rendering all the world into shades of blue and white and palest gray. The air was warm, but the breeze was cool, gentle enough to tickle the skin and strong enough to ruffle hair, whisking away sweat and leaving a pleasant near-chill in its place. The smell of cooking lingered over the camp, faint traces of grilled fish, fresh greens, and strong tea, and mixed with the sounds of slumbering humans and horses to create a quilt of warmth, familiarity, and comfort. *It feels like home*, Kagiri realized, like the tiny village where he and Noniki had been raised.

It was perhaps the first thought since the Kindichi's final ambush that was his and his alone, and that only made him clutch to it that much more tightly.

A splash made him whirl about, hands going to the hilts of his nihono as his eyes tracked the sound to its source out on the river—and then he froze. And stared, swords forgotten, at the sight unfolding before him.

His first thought was that some sort of long, silvery otter had burst from the water, for the figure arcing up into the night air was long, sleek and sinuous. Then he thought it must be an eel, for it twisted like a ribbon in the air, and he could see the glimmer of scales all along its length. But its head was more like that of a horse, with a long, tapering snout and large, liquid eyes to either side, flaring nostrils up front, a crest atop its head like the fins of a noble fish—and similar streamers all along the lower edge of its jaw and draping down beneath its mouth, like the whiskers of a wise old man. It had feet too, he saw, four of them, each one tipped with claws like ice, shimmering in the moonlight, and the fins along its back flared out as it rose, as if it were a bird about to take flight. And it was larger than any animal he had ever seen, its head twice the size of his horse's, its body several times that steed's length, its claws large enough to encircle a big man's chest without strain.

He had never seen anything so majestic, so beautiful. So magical.

As he watched, unable to think or speak or turn away, it twisted in the air, performing a loop that left a shining after-image even after it plunged back down, entering the water in a smooth dive that barely rippled the surface but caused a glow to rise up from below. That glow intensified until the magnificent creature sprang upward once more, soaring at least a man's height out of the water and writhing this way and that, circling in on itself in a complicated, ever-moving ribbon of gleaming light as if it were dancing in the air, with the stars in the sky as its backdrop, before returning to the water a second time.

It did this twice more before the submerged glow faded and it did not reappear.

"That was...amazing!" he whispered, still staring at the spot where it had vanished in the vain hopes that it might show itself just once more.

"It was," Bushiki Kenin agreed, his tone for once filled with the same awe and wonder Kagiri was feeling. Evidently even the Gensaiba's unflappable wrestler had been moved by what they had just seen.

"What was it?" Kagiri asked and felt confusion and hesitation among the spirits sharing his body. But just as he sensed one of them was about to answer, Komu Setsui gasped.

"Look!" she demanded, forcing his gaze to the river's far side, some distance ahead.

A woman was emerging from the water there, stepping up onto the bank as casually as crossing one's own room. Even from here Kagiri could see that she was gorgeous, her limbs long and lithe, her body shapely, her skin glistening with a hundred droplets clearly as reluctant to part from her as he was to let her escape his sight. Long hair hung down her back in gleaming strands turned silver and glowing white by the moon, ending just above her rear—which he could tell because she was utterly unclothed. A part of him wanted to look away, embarrassed to have caught anyone in such an unguarded moment, especially such a beauty, but he could not. Nor did he feel as ashamed as he might, since she strode onto the grass with the confidence of one who was fully comfortable in herself exactly as she was—and if being nude did not leave her feeling awkward, why should he feel distress at witnessing her that way?

He shook his head, confused by these thoughts and feelings—and when the motion ended, he stared, for the beautiful woman was gone. There were no trees on that side of the bank either, no nearby bushes, nowhere for her to have gone in the instant he had looked away, and yet there was no sign of her. Nothing but the memory, which he knew he would cherish for as long as he could remember it.

It was Shito Kibi who broke the silence. "Nizukai," she breathed, the word emerging with wonder wrapped in reverence almost like an old prayer. "It has to be."

"Who?" Kagiri asked.

"Nizukai is a water dragon," Nikiyu Sinchu answered, his voice at least as soft and critical as ever. "Stories are unclear whether that is a proper name or a species, whether there is one being named Nizukai or several all fitting that description."

"It is a name," Kibi insisted. "And she is not an it, she is a she. The daughter of Satumasu, the king of all waters. She swims in the rivers and lakes under the full moon, emerging as a beautiful, silver-haired woman after, and to see her is to have extreme good fortune." Kagiri's arms wrapped around his torso, hugging himself excitedly. "This is an amazing stroke of luck!"

"I think Kibi is right," Onyoku Jeizen agreed, far more seriously than was his wont. "It matches all the old tales of Nizukai."

"That's not possible," Kagiri protested, unhanding himself only to fold his arms obstinately across his chest. "This is Rimbaku—we don't have mythic creatures splashing about in the water here!" The only magic in all the empire was that of the aishone. Everyone knew that.

Everyone except the Gensaiba, apparently—and the glorious dragon who was also a princess and who he had just happened to see out for a midnight swim.

His head spinning, Kagiri walked back to his tent, barely noticing his surroundings. His dinner had been set out some time ago but he had ignored it earlier, not feeling any pangs of hunger. Now he left the food still untouched but did lift his glass. The merchants always set out both water and wine for him—most of the Gensaiba except Sinchu and Kenin enjoyed the rice wine, though of course they were always careful not to imbibe so much as to let it impair their judgement or their reflexes.

Now, however, it was Kagiri who raised the glass to his lips, needing something to help overcome the shock that visitation had caused. But the glass froze just shy of touching his mouth.

"Something is wrong." It was Sinchu, so that statement was not out of character, but the words were even sharper than usual, and more urgent. "Do not drink that."

Kagiri frowned, staring into his wineglass. Something was wrong—with the wine? He didn't see anything odd about it, or smell anything unusual, though admittedly his experience was not the widest—old Taki back at the inn where he and Noniki had worked in Ginzai had only kept a handful of vintages, most of them barely a step above vinegar in odor and flavor. He was inclined to ignore Sinchu's paranoia, especially since for once he actually had control over his own body again, but then Setsui chimed in.

"I agree," their master archer declared. "There is something off about this wine."

"Fine." Kagiri started to tilt the cup, intending to pour it out onto the ground, letting the grass and dirt soak up the offending liquid, but then paused. The wine did not smell spoiled, which meant that, if Sinchu and Setsui were right, this was not simply a matter of the beverage going bad. It was a deliberate alteration, and presumably aimed specifically at him. Spilling it out would save him from whatever were the intended effects, but that would not tell him what it had been meant to do, or who had altered it.

Instead he moved to the tent flap and peered out, his eyes seeking any sign of movement. There!

"Surito!" he called, shaping his voice so the words would carry to the guard without being so loud as to wake anyone else. "Come here!"

The guard hurried over. "Yes, sir?" he asked respectfully once he'd reached the tent. He was an older man, grizzled but still hale, with a stocky build and slightly bowed legs.

"Do you have any wine on you?" Kagiri asked. He almost laughed at the older man's downtrodden expression. "I am not angry," he promised quickly. "Entirely the opposite." He held up his cup. "Look, this stuff is good, or so I'm told, but to be honest, it's wasted on me. So I thought perhaps you'd be willing to trade. Your skin for my cup."

Surito regarded him suspiciously, though his hand had already gone to the wineskin at his belt. "Are you certain?" he asked. "What I've got is barely drinkable."

"I'm certain," Kagiri insisted. "Here." He thrust the full cup at the guard, forcing him to raise a hand and take it before it slopped against his broad chest.

"Okay, okay," Surito said, laughing as he offered the wineskin in return. "Thanks." He raised the glass in salute. "Your health."

"And yours." Kagiri took a tentative sip and nearly choked. Bones, this stuff was foul! Surito, on the other hand, gaped and then grinned as he drank deep. Evidently it was *very* good wine!

"That was well done," Kenin said as the happy guard left, still clutching his prize. "An excellent stratagem."

"Thank you." It was rare for any of the Gensaiba to praise him, Kagiri knew. So why, then, did he feel so awful about having given Surito his wine? He hoped he had not just made a terrible mistake.

It was with those doubts and concerns swirling in his head that Kagiri went to sleep—but his dreams, when they came, were of a silvery creature dancing in mid-air, and a beautiful woman rising from the water.

CHAPTER TWENTY-ONE

It is a good thing, Seikoku thought to herself as she took short, shallow breaths, easing each bit of air gently into her lungs, *that I do not mind tight spaces.*

Her thoughts went to another time, not all that long ago, when she had been forced to lay flat and still. Then it had been beneath old bones in a crypt, as she and Noniki—why did that boy keep haunting her thoughts so?—had struggled to hide from the banning in the town cemetery.

At least now she was surrounded by clean linen instead of moldy flesh and rotting cloth. That was a definite improvement.

The cart rolled to a stop and she held her breath. This was the moment of truth. Or at least the first of many. She heard voices, though they were muffled, and felt pressure shift somewhere above her, almost like a storm front rolling into an area. Then that passed and the cart began moving once more, creaking and rattling as it bumped its way over a tiled path. Seikoku wanted to sigh in relief but knew she didn't dare, both because she could not afford to be discovered and because she didn't dare waste any of the air she had left.

After a few minutes there was a bump as the front wheels rolled over some sort of low barrier, then another as the back wheels followed. Suddenly the cart's gait smoothed out, and the rumble and crack of its wheels lessened.

They were inside.

She waited until the cart had stopped completely, then another minute, before starting to shift. It was not a quick process. The frame she was laying beneath had to be deconstructed carefully, each crosspiece and brace removed in turn. As the first corner was

disassembled, a heavy weight crashed down in that spot, obliter-
ating the pocket of space Seikoku had built there. She had been
prepared for that, fortunately. Leaving the rest of the frame intact
for now, she wriggled forward until her head and shoulders were
in that same corner, pressed against the woven rattan of the
cart itself. Then she heaved steadily upward, her hands grasping the edges there and shoving them aside as she moved. Slowly
the weight slid to the side, until finally a patch of light appeared
above her, accompanied by fresh, sweet air. There it was!

Now she could work more quickly, and needed to, before she
was noticed. She tugged the rest of the frame free, collapsing it
and sliding the pieces into an unbleached bag she then knotted
shut. A quick peek out showed that she was in a large, high-ceil-
inged space with handsome wood floors below and clean white-
paneled walls on either side. The downstairs hall. Hearing voices,
she quickly clambered out of the cart and scooped up both her bag
and a pile of the linens that had been mounded above and below
her. Then she turned and hurried away, heading for the stairs she
could see at the hall's far end. There was a guard stationed there,
but he merely nodded as she scooted on past.

After all, in her plain, worn torito, shatage, and hantien, her
hair bound up in a faded floral kerchief, she was just one more
laundry woman delivering fresh sheets to the bedrooms above.

It took only two tries to locate the room she wanted, and as soon
as she did Seikoku ducked inside, sliding the door shut again
behind her.

The room was beautiful. Its walls were paneled but not in the
standard square-on-square pattern, instead with a single enormous central pane flanked by long panels on all sides and then
squares in the corners. The floor was patterned as well, the normal
dark wood inlaid with squares of bleached wood in neat rows. A
skylight above let in light but could be closed against rain, and
right now several sunbeams were drifting lazily down toward the

massive bed that dominated the space with its low, carved wooden frame turned to jut from the corner and the long, angular headboard and footboard matching the style of the small bedside table, low dresser, and stepped tanu placed against the other walls.

And there, sitting atop the bedside table, was what she sought. A handsome kune mato, the sturdy merchant's safe displaying sturdy metal plates at each corner and spaced around every edge, including those of its door, which was held in place by no fewer than four hinges on the right and two large, heavy lockplates on the left. Between all that burnished metal the wood gleamed, its handsome grains showing the signs of frequent polish.

This was the sort of strongbox a cautious noble might use to protect his aishone and other valuables.

And Coda Anjiro was certainly cautious.

That was one of several reasons why Seikoku had never attempted to steal from him before—that and the fact that he was perhaps the most powerful noble in Ginzai, many said more influential than even Morihai Sugano, their lord mayor. Coda Anjiro was certainly wealthier.

Fortunately for her, he was also more vain, and his favorite way to show off his wealth and importance was to hold a sumptuous dinner each month for the top tier of Ginzai society. Only the elite were invited, and the party was said to be magnificent.

Seikoku would soon be able to judge that for herself.

She set the linens down and started across the floor, eyes intent upon her prize—and stopped, her right foot hovering over the first step. Something was wrong. She could feel it in her bones and in her blood. Coda Anjiro was cautious—there were no trees within bowshot of his home, guards were placed at every corner with clear sightlines, more patrolled the grounds, it was said that his staff were searched on their departure every evening—and yet his treasures sat here in the open, for anyone who entered to approach and possibly steal?

That made little sense.

Was it a trick, she wondered. Was the box empty, just a lure to draw would-be thieves to their doom? Yet he was fabulously wealthy, and like most was likely to keep his greatest treasures close at hand.

The locks looked solid, even from here, but would a man like Coda Anjiro trust his wealth to that alone? Or would there be something else?

It might not be a trick but it is certainly a trap, Seikoku decided. Only, of what sort?

She began to inch forward again, even more cautious now—and as her toe tapped the floor, grazing one of the bleached panels, it let out a soft, musical sigh. She froze at once. Of course! The pattern was not just decorative—he had Nightingale Floorboards! She had heard of such things but never encountered them, and she was both alarmed and fascinated. A part of her desperately wanted to hear them perform, for it was said that rather than squeaks and moans true Nightingale Floorboards sounded like a chorus of birds in full song. But of course for now she merely needed to figure out which boards would not elicit such noises—for there was always a safe, silent path through, otherwise the staff and residents would be treated to a symphony every time anyone rose to relieve themselves.

Or, she thought with a smile, admiring that fine, wide bed again, find another way around.

She retreated until her back was brushing the door, then, taking a deep breath, launched herself forward. And just before her feet would have reached the start of those inlaid tiles, she crouched and sprang. Her leap took Seikoku sailing out over the floor, and she flung her arms out ahead of her, hands open wide—and latched onto the bed's footboard, using her momentum to swing herself up and over. She landed gracefully atop the firm mattress, barely creasing the orange silks stretched there, and then slid into a seated position, cross-legged, near the bed's edge.

Facing the small table with its kune mato within easy reach.

Reaching out, she caressed the front panel with her forefinger. The wood was smooth enough that she could barely feel the grain, the metal cool to the touch and marred by tiny scratches and dents that spoke of genuine use. This was no mere prop.

At least, so she hoped.

Reaching for the hidden pocket sewn into her coat, she pulled out her lockpicks. These locks were more sophisticated than most, but Seikoku had once had the aishone of a master lockmaker, and had used that knowledge to teach herself how to assemble—and defeat—almost any lock. After only a few minutes of careful probing she felt the first lock's tumblers glide into place and twisted, the motion accompanied by a faint click.

That was one.

The second lock was much the same and took far less time now that she'd found the right tension for them. That was the real trick—just enough pressure to move the tumblers, not enough to knock them out of alignment or jam them together. When the second lock clicked, Seikoku supressed a giggle of delight, settling for a broad smile instead as she grasped the sturdy iron ring set between them and tugged the door open to reveal a row of three drawers nestled within—

—each with a lock of its own.

"For serious?" she muttered, but turned her attention to the lowest and largest drawer's lock immediately. She was too invested to walk away now, and the longer this took, the bigger the chance of getting caught.

Fortunately, that lock opened as easily as the pair on the door. She pulled the drawer out, and was rewarded by the clink of heavy coins and the yellow gleam of metal. Aha!

Reaching in, she selected a handful of coins and slid them out of their resting place, settling them into a pocket of her coat instead. She would relocate them later, when she had more time. She was careful not to take too many—no doubt Coda Anjiro knew exactly how many coins were in here, but if the drawer did not look noticeably emptier it might take him some time before he realized any were missing.

She closed that drawer again, carefully so the coins would not rattle too loudly, and moved to the next one. This proved to contain small silk drawstring bags, each tucked into a wooden lattice and each carefully labeled: "Warrior," "Jeweler," "Diplomat," "Orator," and so on.

She had found his aishone.

Seikoku knew she did not have a lot of time, so she pulled only one bag from its place, opening that one and shaking out a pair of small chips, each smaller than the nail on her pinky. They were still large enough, and more valuable than the coins she had already claimed, she knew as she carefully wrapped them in a piece of silk and pocketed them.

Now for the final drawer. It certainly had her curious—it was shallower than the other two, and yet it seemed the drawers must be increasing in value as they ascended. What could this one have, then, that would be more valuable than aishone? Finer bones, perhaps from a past emperor?

But when she got the drawer unlocked and slid it out to peek inside, Seikoku was surprised to find, resting on a black velvet lining, only a single ring. It was large, its circumference too wide even for her thumb, and its surface was a pale, milky green. There had been symbols carved there, she saw, but evidently they had worn away. Odd. Jade was beautiful, and precious, but surely not worth more than the aishone in the drawer below?

Still, something drew her to the strange old ring. Even though she knew its absence would be noticed at once, Seikoku snatched it up and slid it onto her thumb, where it rattled about. She had to clench the finger across her hand to keep the jewelry still as she relocked all three drawers, then the outer locks, and rolled backward, twisting as she did so she came up on her feet again facing the door once more. A quick flip forward and she was standing by that door, the room untouched by all appearances. A few seconds later, linens once more safely in hand, she slipped back into the hall and continued down it, keeping her head down as she passed another woman bearing a fine kitoro back toward the master's bedroom.

It appeared Coda Anjiro would soon be dressing for dinner.

Seikoku knew she did not have a great deal of time. She quickened her step down the hall before stopping at another door, perhaps three removed from her previous location. That should be far enough.

Her luck held as the door revealed another bedroom, neither as expansive nor as luxurious as the master's but still beautiful. And, just as importantly, empty.

Sliding the door shut behind her, Seikoku glided across the floor—which was plain teak without a single breath of song. She set the linens on the bed and checked the tanu. As she'd hoped, Coda Anjiro was a considerate host—he kept his guest rooms well-stocked for the needs of any guests. Including spare clothing should they require it. Seikoku held up the kitoro, which was crimson with white and pink roses falling from one sleeve, across the bodice, and to the hem. It was paired with a snowy white underrobe of finest silk and a girdle of black and yellow, with the same roses stitched in relief.

This would do quite nicely.

Now she just had to wait, and then dress, and wait some more.

Several hours later, as the last of the sumptuous dinner was cleared away, Coda Anjiro's guests began to depart, drifting away singly and in pairs and in small groups. One of the latter included a slightly heavyset young woman in a fine crimson kitoro, her hair done up in a beautifully worked knot atop her head and secured with a pair of handsome ivory kanashi. She walked with small, mincing steps, her legs bound by the elegant robe, and nodded along with her companions' conversation, though she did not speak herself. The guards paid her no mind, as just another of their lord's dinner guests—the staff were searched as they left, certainly, but to attempt that of a guest would be the height of rudeness. Besides which, guests like the young lady were only allowed in the entry hall, the dining room, the salon, and of course the facilities, so there was little reason to worry about them. The guards did not see this particular guest slow after leaving the house and its grounds, falling farther and farther behind the rest of her little group until she had drifted away from them completely.

Then Seikoku allowed herself to slip back into the comfort of the shadows, and finally to relax. Everything had worked exactly as planned. It was a shame she had not been able to actually attend the dinner, of course, but she had always known that would be too great a risk—most of the guests would already know each other, and she lacked the training to pass as one of them. Slipping into the crowd as they were leaving, however, had been child's play, and although the guards had carefully checked each guest against a list as they entered, they had not bothered to go back through that list as they exited. Invisible servant in, anonymous guest out.

She quickly tugged off the kitoro, its girdle, and its underrobe, revealing her launderer's clothes beneath—and the unbleached bag, its cord looped around one shoulder, the bag and its contents pressed against her side. As she'd made certain through careful practice beforehand, the robes had concealed both the bag and her other clothing. Now she quickly folded the robes and added them to the bag, then walked away at a more comfortable pace, by all appearances a working woman heading home after a long day and night. She could feel the coins within her jacket, and the ring in a different pocket, and laughed in sheer delight. She had just robbed the richest man in town and gotten away with it. Evidently she still had the touch!

Then she cursed, because her next thought had been, *I wonder what Noniki would say to that!*

CHAPTER TWENTY-TWO

G inzai seemed smaller than Noniki remembered.

No, that was unfair and untrue. The town was still the largest collection of buildings he had ever seen in one place, far bigger than the towns and villages he had passed through along the way. The river still bisected the town, and Ginzai was big enough and sprawling enough that it had a sizeable amount of ground on either side of that deep, cold waterflow and the wide wooden bridge surmounting it.

Bones, the graveyard in the town's center was larger all on its own than any of those other settlements he'd visited! There were more people here than he had seen in all the rest of his travels put together, with more colors, more vibrancy, more life than anywhere, either.

But somehow it still felt different. Or maybe it was just that he was different. For all the grandeur of some of these homes and businesses, with their polished wood beams and carved stone lintels and gleaming tile roofs, compared to the awesome, brooding majesty of the Tawasiri they were like crude little huts cowering from that ancient tower's far-reaching shade. And for all the hustle and bustle on the streets and in the shops and along the open-air markets, they could not compete with the quiet, cheerful industry of the Brothers of Many Spirits, all working enthusiastically and all handling different chores but sharing a common goal, the prosperity of their brotherhood and the care of those who came to them in need.

When he had left here, Noniki had still stared wide-eyed at every warehouse and workshop and inn, stunned by the sheer number of people filling this village's borders—and feeling insignificant against them, in his worn, drab work clothes, with no money and no aishone to his name.

Now he was back and his clothes were better than before but he was still penniless, still boneless. Yet he found he could study the crowd before him without dismay, no longer intimidated by their numbers or their sense of purpose. He no longer hungered to be one of them, plumped up with self-importance, distracted by the constant need for more money, more relic bones, more everything.

Now he only saw Ginzai as a place to pause for a night or two, find a way to gather some supplies, and then pass on through. Once, his dreams had been filled with this place, and his nightmares, too. Now his nightmares were populated by ravening clouds and screaming brothers and crumbling nations, and his dreams... he could not remember what he dreamed about. Only that it was filled with light and life and hope.

He would not find any of that here.

While he had been pondering his changed feelings about this, his former home, his feet had continued to carry him along, and Noniki became aware of his surroundings again as he finally slowed to a stop, staring at the place that had in fact been his home as well as his place of work and his prison, all rolled into one:

Happoa Kappua. The Foamy Cup. The cut-rate tavern where he and Kagiri had worked while they had been here in Ginzai. There were not many fond memories to be had from this place, with its rough walls and crude, heavy shutters concealing the equally unfinished furniture within, the tables and benches, the big heavy fireplace with its massive cast-iron stewpot, the long blocky bar with the shelves of rice wine on the wall behind it. The tavern's owner, Taki, had taken them in not out of generosity but out of cunning, knowing the two poor, half-starved brothers would work themselves to exhaustion for little more than enough food to survive and a place to sleep out of the rain and a single bronze coin each week. She had also known that would never be enough for them to escape such a fate, and so they would continue to slave for her forever.

Kishin Narai and his fellow merchants had changed all that.

Yet, despite how the merchants had treated him and Kagiri in the end, despite the fact that they had cost him his brother, Noniki found he could not hate them. If they had not come along, he and Kagiri would have rotted away here, just like one of the rats Taki's traps caught behind the wine barrels where no one could reach to dispose of them. At least the merchants had taken them away from here, out into the world. A world Noniki was seeing more and more of. That was something he could thank them for, despite the heavy price he had paid for such freedom.

So lost in thought was he that Noniki barely noticed he was not alone. Not until a heavy hand landed on his shoulder.

"Ha!" The loud voice so close to his ear, coupled with that hand, made him jump and twist sideways, to stare at the man standing there. He was barely taller than Noniki himself, and about the same girth, but with a heavier brow and lighter hair pulled back into a thick bun that wobbled atop his head as he grinned. "I thought it was you!"

Noniki stared. "Kanai?" he managed after a moment. "Is it you?"

"One and the same!" the potter laughed, pounding him on the back. "And you are Noniki! It has been a while, yes?"

"It has," Noniki agreed, laughing as well, for the man's good humor was as contagious as ever. "How are you?" Jitu Kanai had been one of their regular customers at the tavern and had always been kind to Noniki and his brother. Though far from the sharpest blade, Kanai was a good man, as solid and dependable as the cups and bowls he cast.

"Eh, much the same as ever," Kanai replied. He chuckled, shaking his head, and waggled a thick, clay-caked finger at Noniki. "Though, thanks to you and your brother pulling that disappearing act, Taki went back to shorting her mugs!" When they'd first started working for her the brothers had been told never to fill a mug all the way to the brim, but they had refused to follow that rule, trying to give customers at least what they paid for, even if that was just a mug full of the land's cheapest, meanest rice wine.

Evidently once they'd gone their former employer had decided to discontinue that practice.

"I am sorry about that," he told his friend. He glanced about, half expecting to see Taki herself emerge from the tavern, though it was only mid-day and she was most likely still bustling about inside, readying the stew and lifting the benches down from the tabletops. Which was for the best, as he had no desire to run into her again, or to feel the acid bite of her sharp tongue. Instead he asked Kanai, "Do you know of a place I might stay for a night or two? I don't have any money, unfortunately, but I could do chores in exchange for a spot on the floor."

Kanai frowned. "Nonsense!" he declared. "You'll stay with me while you're here!" Another thump on the back, and then he was turning away, waving for Noniki to follow. "Come, I know a nice little teahouse with the best buns in Ginzai. My treat! We will eat, and you will tell me all about your travels!"

That was an offer Noniki could hardly refuse. Besides which, he had been mostly alone ever since leaving the monastery, other than brief encounters with people in villages and on the road, and the last of those had been several days ago. It would be pleasant to speak with someone again, especially someone as familiar as Jitu Kanai.

The next morning, Noniki did something he had not done since the first time he had arrived in this town—he walked all the way round it. Back then he and Kagiri, fresh from their tiny fishing village and flush with their vast wealth of eight whole bronze coins, had gaped and stared like country bumpkins, gawking and pointing at everything and ostensibly searching for a good place to try for a job and some aishone but just being perpetually stunned by the sheer size and activity and complexity and noise of Ginzai, which they'd been convinced must be the most amazing and fantastic settlement to ever exist in all recorded history.

Now he walked to stretch his legs, to get a sense of the city again, and to see whether he ran across any situation where he might be able to work in exchange for a few coins to buy fresh supplies for the road. His night had been pleasant enough—Kanai was a kind and considerate host, and though hardly wealthy the potter had done well enough to own a small building that functioned as home, pottery studio, and store, and to be to serve a meal that was as honest and unfancy yet warm and palatable as the potter himself. But Noniki had no intention of imposing upon his friend for more than a few nights at most. Once he had enough food to see him safely to Awaihinshi, he could be off again. The City of Polished Light awaited.

He was just skirting the edge of a large, open-air market, his eyes open for any signs indicating a need for help, when a voice called out from his left. "Noniki?"

He turned—and found himself staring at a lovely young woman in simple but attractive clothing that flowed and fluttered about her lithe frame. Her silky black hair was up in a tight, tidy bun, her large, dark eyes focused on his face, a faint, disbelieving smile on her delicate lips as she practically glided across the ground between them. She was as graceful now as she had been when they had met, though at least they were not sneaking into a graveyard this time.

"Seikoku." Noniki smiled to see her and saw her eyes crinkle and her lips turn up more in response. "It is good to see you again." He had been all but tongue-tied during their first encounter, stunned by both her beauty and their circumstances. She was as lovely as ever, but at least here in daylight by the market he felt more sure of his footing.

"You too." She was smiling fully now, though she bit her lip and glanced away before looking back again. "I haven't seen you around since—" *Since you messed up my own plans to loot the graveyard with your botched attempt, and I told you to go away and never bother me again,* Noniki remembered, but kindly chose not to say. It seemed she was willing to let the past fade away, and he was happy to do the same.

"I have been away," he admitted instead, and did not miss the way her quick gaze took in his sturdy travel clothes, the bag slung at his side, the knife at his belt, and the staff in his hand. "I am only back long enough to equip myself again."

"Oh." She frowned for a second, then banished the expression, though it left her cheeks lightly flushed. "Where are you going?" She turned to walk along the market edge and something about her stance and her tone invited him to join her, so he did.

"To Awaihinshi," he answered. Should he have told her that? A voice in the back of his head—possibly Kagiri's—pointed out that he barely knew this girl, that she was a graverobber, and that he had no reason to trust her or confide in her. Yet something else told Noniki he could trust her, and he chose to believe that intuition, which is why he continued, "I am hoping to speak with the emperor."

"The emperor?" She laughed, the same delighted, unselfconscious little peals he remembered, and despite the fact that it was aimed at him Noniki found himself laughing as well, for there was no guile nor meanness in her response. "Why, do you hope to interest him in a business venture?" Her smile turned mischievous. "I seem to recall you were a great one for…creative redistribution of wealth."

That made him laugh even more, once he worked out what she meant. "Ah! Yes, well, I've given that up, it seems." He tugged at the collar of his hosode, pulling it down to reveal his neck and collarbone—and the complete lack of an aishone pouch. "I've found a different path."

She studied him seriously now. "Really?" She frowned, her delicate brows furrowing. "That's quite a change in attitude, then. You seemed…determined, before."

"I was. But the price was too high." He sighed and forced his grief back down to where it usually sat, providing a grim, gray base for the rest of his life. "I don't suppose you know of any place that could use a hand for a day or two, do you?" He smiled at her. "I don't need much, just some dried fruit and dried meat, perhaps some flatbread, and I'm more than happy to work for it."

He was happy to see that she was taking his question seriously, and even happier when she nodded. "Actually, I do," she answered. "I've a friend here in the market, and he was saying yesterday that he had a large shipment coming in. I think he might be happy for another strong set of arms. Come on." She favored him with a quick smile that warmed him through to the core, then turned and slipped away, darting into the crowd and threading her way through it as easily as a fish darting about in the river.

Noniki shook his head, but he was laughing as he did his best to follow.

Sure enough, Seikoku's friend Hintaro was only too happy to hire Noniki for a few days, and even happier when Noniki offered to work for goods rather than coin. "I like your friend, Keiko," he said, draping an arm around Noniki's shoulders, the grocer having several inches on him in height. "He seems solid."

Noniki cocked an eyebrow at the name but didn't say anything. After all, she had just found him a job—what she chose to have people call her was her business. Still, he filed the information away as something to ask her about later. He hoped they would *have* a later.

The rest of the day was spent working. Hintaro proved to be a decent man. Though he did expect Noniki to work hard, the merchant labored just as heavily himself, if not more, and was always quick to call for a break or offer food or water if either of them seemed winded.

Helping him tote bales and boxes and baskets and unpack them and organize items reminded Noniki of the Brothers, with their warm spirits and their love for both physical activity and clear organization. Before he knew it the sky was dimming and the market emptying as people concluded their business and returned to their homes. "Good work," Hintaro told him. "Thank you." He glanced around his wide stall with a satisfied eye. "Another two days should see us done, I'm thinking."

"Perfect," Noniki agreed. "First light, then? Or before?" He had no qualms about rising before the dawn, and knew the man might wish to get as much done as possible before the market officially opened again for business. As it was, today he'd had to pause every time a customer entered.

"Before would be better," Hintaro replied, and Noniki nodded. They parted ways then, the merchant presumably back to his own home and Noniki struggling to remember how to retrace his steps back to Kanai's. Only he never got that far, because at the market's edge he found Seikoku waiting for him.

"All done for the day?" she asked, stepping forward and pivoting to fall in beside him, her arm looping with his. "You must be hungry. Come on."

"I don't have any money," Noniki protested as she dragged him along, though in truth he was more than willing to follow wherever she led.

"That's all right, I'll buy," she answered. Then she poked him in the chest, but playfully. "You can pay me back by telling me where you've been and what you've been up to." She cocked her head, studying him for a second. "You're not the same boy I met, are you? Not entirely."

"No," he agreed. "Not entirely." He left it at that for now, but already knew that he would tell her everything. Even if he wasn't sure why.

"That's amazing," Seikoku said, nibbling the last bit of meat off her stick with sharp, even white teeth. She had taken them to a small corner stall and bought them both several sticks of chargrilled chicken and fish and vegetables served over shallow paper cones of steaming white rice, which they'd washed down with fresh juice from a different stall a few blocks away, walking as they ate and drank until they'd reached a tiny park that held a single wooden bench beneath its one mature tree.

Then they'd sat and finished their meal—which was better fare than he'd had since leaving the monastery, and possibly better than that as well—and Noniki had told her about what had happened to him since they'd met: the merchants, the Tawasiri, Kagiri's sacrifice, his wanderings, the monks. He'd even told her about his strange dream or vision or whatever it had been, and his battle with the cloud he'd encountered there.

"Do you think it was real?" she asked him now, her eyes wide, her tone completely serious. For someone who could turn so impish, she was capable of listening like your every word mattered more than life itself, Noniki noticed. It made him feel important, that someone would give him such attention and show such respect for what he said.

What's more, it made him want to be worthy of that respect.

"I think it was," he answered slowly, reliving that strange aerial conflict. "I think my spirit was loosed from my body, and whatever that cloud was, it could sense me in that state. And it wanted me." He shuddered, remembering the way it had attacked him and tried to swallow him whole.

Seikoku rested her slim hand over his. "But you fought it off," she reminded him, admiration clear in her gaze. "You found your way back to yourself." She smirked just a little. "And then back here, too."

"I did." He smiled and fought to keep his hand still, enjoying the warmth of hers against it. "And I am glad I did."

Her mood shifted and she withdrew her hand and tossed the stick away with the other before wrapping both arms around herself, her expression changing to somewhere between a frown and a pout and making her look younger and more vulnerable than before, if only for an instant. "But now you're leaving again."

He sighed. "I am. I—I feel like this is something I have to do. I don't know if that makes any sense or not, and I have no idea if I can even manage it, or if it'll do any good, but I need to try."

She nodded and rose to her feet, as graceful as a swallow in flight. "You have changed," she told him. "But in a good way." Then she held out her hand.

Noniki took it and let her pull him to his feet and lead him back the way they'd come. She seemed not to realize her hand was still in his as they walked, and with every fiber of his being he willed her to continue to not notice. The wind rose as if in agreement, and its gentle touch tickled their faces with the cool, fresh first breath of night.

The next two days fell into the same pattern as that first one. Noniki rose before dawn, washed, dressed, and headed to market to meet Hintaro. They worked until dusk. Seikoku appeared as if conjured by the twilight and took Noniki out to dinner. They walked and talked and ate and laughed. Then he went back to Kanai's and spoke with the potter for a while before falling into a deep and dreamless sleep.

All too soon, it was over.

"You have been a tremendous help," Hintaro told Noniki the morning of the fourth day. "Thank you." The merchant proffered a small sack stuffed full and tied shut. "Everything you asked for, plus a little extra," he said, handing it to Noniki. "And take this as well." He pressed a small pouch into the younger man's hand, and it jingled as Noniki took it. "For those times when you need a little coin in your pocket." Then he offered his hand. "Good luck with whatever you do next. If you are ever back this way again, I would be happy to see you."

"Thank you," Noniki told him. "If I am ever here again, I will make a point of stopping by." He had already packed his clothes into his bag and brought it with him, bidding farewell to his host as he left. Now there was nothing to stop him from leaving at once.

Nothing except a certain young woman he very much wished to say good-bye to.

He found her standing near the edge of the market, as usual. Only this time she was carrying a shoulder bag of her own, and another bag across her back. "Going somewhere?" Noniki asked.

"I am," she agreed. "I'm going with you." He started to protest, and she stopped him by inclining her head behind her. "And I'm not the only one."

Noniki looked past her, then, and was surprised to see Jitu Kanai standing there, a large pack at his feet. "What is this?" he asked, and the potter shrugged.

"You are a man with great purpose," he answered, the slow way he chose his words lending that sentence even greater weight. "I wish for purpose as well, something more than casting cups and bowls. So, if you do not object, I will follow you, and let your purpose become my own."

Noniki turned to Seikoku, who shrugged. "I don't feel like I fit in here any longer," she admitted. "Maybe I never truly did, and I was only fooling myself. But now I want something more. I want to go places, see things, do things. You are doing that." She gave him a shy smile. "I'd like to do that with you."

He considered a moment. "I have little money," he pointed out. "And it is still a long way to Awaihinshi."

"That's all right," she replied with an airy little wave as if his concerns were no more than a trifling breeze. "If we need something, I'll just steal it." For an instant, he thought she was serious. Then she laughed, making him chuckle as well. "Seriously, we'll manage somehow." She smiled. "If that's all right with you."

"It is," he agreed. And it truly was. In fact, for the first time since leaving the Brothers of Many Spirits, he felt like he was not alone, and not just physically. The three of them set out together, all in high spirits, their steps light as the rising sun cast their shadows out ahead of them as if guiding the way. He held out his hand after a moment and Seikoku took it—and when she did, a strange thrill shot through him, almost like he had banged his elbow against a wall, but without the pain, only the shock.

"What's wrong?" she asked, feeling him tense up.

"I don't know," he told her. "I felt...something." He tilted his head to study her. "Are you...is there something different about you? No, on you? Something odd?"

She started to shake her head, then paused. "Actually..." Rummaging in her coat, she pulled out a small bundle of silk and unwrapped it, revealing a thick jade band. Symbols were still faintly visible in its milky surface, as if they had worn away over time. "Maybe this?" she proffered it, and Noniki carefully took it from her. The second his fingers touched the cool stone he felt that same thrill, even stronger.

"Keep it," she told him when he tried to return it to her. "I... found it recently, but I had no idea what to do with it." She smiled. "Now I do."

"Thank you." It fit onto his thumb as if it had been made for that digit, and Noniki thought he could sense a faint but welcome chill from it against his flesh, far more than mere stone would produce. Strange, but not unpleasant. After a few steps, he barely noticed.

That night, they camped well past town, laying out bedrolls by the side of the river, their backs to a small jumble of rocks. The walking had tired them all out, and they each dropped off to sleep quickly, lulled by the day's exertions, the cool night air, and the merry jangling of the river racing past.

And Noniki dreamed.

He was on the banks of the river, though it felt different than the spot where they camped. He couldn't see Seikoku or Jitu Kanai, but felt that he was not alone.

And out over the water, a stunning, sinuous creature of silver and blue and light danced, cavorting in the air with a grace that took his breath away.

When he awoke the next morning, Noniki was smiling.

CHAPTER TWENTY-THREE

"Welcome to Furukotai, sire," Diritan stated as the four of them reined in atop the hill overlooking the town. Hibikitsu nodded and edged his horse forward past the Honjofu so that he could study this, the largest town in Korito and the home of its regional governor.

Before they had started this journey, he would have said that the place was small and mean, its streets meandering and mere dirt rather than neat cobblestones and enameled bricks, its buildings low and rough, their roofs thatched instead of tiled, their walls plain whitewash without color or ornamentation, their porches crude and made of plain pine rather than teak and other more noble woods.

The past week had taught him an immeasurable amount. Now he admired the size of the town, which was indeed the largest settlement he had seen since leaving Awaihinshi. He admired the way the streets were laid out, wide and as straight as could be hoped when there was not an entire society of royal architects to assist. The buildings all looked clean and well-maintained, and enough people still bustled about even this late in the day for the entire town to have a prosperous, busy feel to it. Yes, if all the villages and towns and cities in his empire were like this one, he would have been pleased indeed.

"Rider," one of the others announced, directing their attention to a lone horseman picking his way up the hill toward them from the town. Her way, Hibikitsu corrected as she drew nearer, the shortening distance allowing him to see the black-enameled armor she wore, with its higeibara crest and a single tsodami petal overlapping the edge. It was one of his Honjofu, and as the elite warrior continued toward them he saw at last that it was none other than Nioko, who had ridden on ahead after they'd broken camp at dawn, to alert the town of his impending arrival.

Pulling up before them, she saluted, hand over fist to chest, and then lifted a tied bundle that had been cradled in her lap. "Your armor, sire," she announced in her soft voice. "I felt it might be best for you to arrive in more familiar attire."

"Thank you." He accepted the bundle gravely, for it meant a return to his normal life, and to his full responsibilities and duties. He had enjoyed these last few days, riding with Diritan and Nioko and the others, camping with them at night, sharing the same stew and hardbread, passing around the same skins of rice wine, sleeping on the same ground. For that brief time, he had been able to lie to himself and pretend he was just another man, just another soldier.

Now that temporary escape was over. It was time for Hibikitsu, Emperor of Rimbaku, to return.

Dismounting and handing Shisi's reins to Diritan, he retreated to a nearby rock and, setting the bundle down upon that rough natural table, untied it. Within were deo and kazure, haidoto and hanketo and suneoto, karute and menatu and modato. Everything that declared him to be the ruler of this land.

And who was I while someone else wore this? he couldn't help wondering as he began removing the simple aiashe's gear he had grown accustomed to. *If this is all that is required to distinguish an emperor from a foot soldier, was the man who wore this at my behest truly the emperor for that time? Is it so easy to trade roles that a simple change in garb can suffice?*

He hoped that was not the case. His ancestry had entitled him to the throne but he liked to believe he was slowly proving himself worthy of sitting it, worthy of being responsible for this great nation and all its peoples.

Though, as he glanced back at his guards and at the little girl who sat before Diritan on his massive charger, clutching a simple rag doll in one hand and sucking the thumb of the other, Hibikitsu had to admit that he still had a long way to go in that regard.

Once he was back in his own armor, all crimson and gold and gems, Hibikitsu mounted Shisi again and allowed his Honjofu to lead the way down to the village. The largest building in town, a handsome three-story edifice facing the central square, was the home and offices of the regional governor, and that was where they found people waiting to greet them. As they stopped their horses a woman stepped forward from the rest, her fine kitoro, elaborate hairstyle, and expensive jewelry proclaiming her to be a lady of great wealth and importance, especially this far from the capital.

"Your Majesty," she declared, sweeping into a deep bow. "Welcome. You do us and our humble town great honor with your presence. I am Zeryai Yukiri, wife of your duly appointed governor and representative Zeryai Ninbaru, and on his behalf I bid you welcome, and lay ourselves at your feet to await your bidding." She was a sturdy, well-fleshed woman with a pleasant face but narrow eyes, and it was clear from her ringing tones that she was not accustomed to being anyone's social inferior but at the same time gloried in being able to directly address the emperor himself.

For his part, Hibikitsu nodded back but frowned. "And where is your husband, noble lady?" he asked, trying to mask any irritation in his tone. But why was the governor himself not here to greet them, as was proper?

Lady Zeryai bowed again. "I regret to say that he is deceased, Your Majesty," she replied without any overt traces of sorrow. "He insisted upon confronting the Fyushans himself after they had the audacity to not only cross the border but also seize the town of Birabiro." Her eyes widened and her lower lip trembled, which the emperor took for mere artistry as she continued, her voice shaky, "They killed him for fulfilling his duty. We were told that his bones were shipped to the capital, to you, with the Fyushans' compliments."

Hibikitsu glared down at her, but his fierce gaze was not for her but for those who had done this. "I see," he stated, his words clipped, his mouth drawn into a tight line. "Thank you for informing me of this, my lady, and you have my deepest condolences. The Rimbakan Empire will never forget your husband's dedication or his sacrifice, and neither will I." She seemed pleased with that, as well she should be—by stating that he was in her dead husband's debt, Hibikitsu had just agreed to grant her the man's salary until the end of her days. Still, she had been right to tell him, and he was angry indeed that these Fyushans should dare to harm his appointed representative. Who did they think they were? Clearly, they needed to be taught a lesson.

"Is there a town between here and Birabiro?" he asked. Lady Zeryai's brows knit, but a man behind her leaned forward to whisper quickly in her ear and she nodded.

"There is, Your Majesty," she stated, acting as if she had known this all along. "Chinbiro is perhaps half a day's ride from here, and roughly the same distance from Birabiro." Which meant that they were only two days from the border, Hibikitsu calculated. It felt as if the entire nation of Fyushu was suddenly pressing in on him, the stares of thousands of their warriors beating down upon his forehead, and a part of him wished to cower and hide from such hateful scrutiny, but the rest of him straightened in the saddle, daring them to intimidate them. He was the Echo of Victory! He would not allow anyone to overwhelm him!

Instead he gestured to his Honjofu, spread out behind him. "Send a messenger to Birabiro," he instructed. "Find whoever is in charge there and inform them that Hibikitsu, Echo of Victory, Emperor of Rimbaku, will meet with them in Chinbiro at noon the day past tomorrow to discuss their violation of our treaty and the consequences thereof." He sighed and dismounted, turning back to Lady Zeryai. "Now, if you will, I am weary, as are my warriors."

"Of course, Your Majesty," she replied with another deep bow. "We have prepared rooms for you and your escort." Her gaze rose to Diritan, and the little girl perched before him, whose simple clothing proclaimed her to be neither noble nor a warrior, but careful training allowed the lady to not react to this surprising addition and Hibikitsu knew she would find a way to accommodate the child's presence as if she had known about her all along. That was what the nobility excelled at, after all—never letting irritation or surprise show, and above all else, never letting anyone so much as hint that you were not fully prepared to provide the most gracious welcome imaginable to any and all who deserved it.

Hibikitsu knew that at some point soon he would have to decide the girl, Kome's, fate. For now, however, all he could only think of a warm bath, a meal not prepared over a fire, and a proper bed. Everything else would keep until the morrow.

The following day passed in a blur of meetings and strategy sessions, poring over the maps of this region with his Honjofu and the local soldiers, including Taisho Daishin, who had arrived a few days before them and had his aiashe camped all around Furukotai, ready to march at a moment's notice. The sun was only just beginning to show hints of emerging the following morning when Hibikitsu set out surrounded by Honjofu. The aiashe had already begun their march, and he and the others on horseback passed the foot soldiers an hour or two before the thatched reed roofs of Chinbiro began poking up over the hills ahead.

This was a mere village, perhaps a tenth the size of Furukotai, he saw as they rode closer. And even that might have been overstating. There was only a single road cutting through the small community, widening at its center to form a town square around a wide, squared stone well. None of the buildings here had more than a second story, and most were only a single level. That and the fact that they were bunched so closely together there was barely a hairsbreadth between them gave the entire settlement a feeling of fearful concern, as if even its homes huddled together for warmth and safety. Which, given how near they were to the border, and how the wind whistled down over the mountains at night and set teeth to rattling and limbs to shivering, was not entirely unreasonable.

Hibikitsu deployed his Honjofu around the edges of the town, placing archers on rooftops to protect the tiny village from being overrun. Daishin's aiashe, when they arrived, would surround the southern border, ensuring that he and his guards could retreat safely should the Fyushans be so foolish as to attack. For himself, he rode into the center of the small settlement, Diritan and Nioko at his back, and dismounted by the well, tying Shisi to an iron post nearby. Then he leaned back against the rough stone wall and waited.

Almost immediately, it seemed, one of the archers whistled and pointed to the north, then gave three quick bursts of a single note. "Three riders approaching," Diritan reported. He frowned and loosened his sword in its sheath but then returned his arms to their previous position across his chest, as if unconcerned. He had proven a stout traveling companion, cheerful and optimistic but also loyal and oddly gentle, and Hibikitsu realized he had begun to think of the man and his partner, the quiet but perceptive and surprisingly dry-witted Nioko, as almost friends.

He hoped he would not get them killed, even though he knew they would accept that fate as part of their duty.

A few moments later, three riders rode into the town from the north end, making straight for the well where Hibikitsu waited. In the lead was a tall, broad-shouldered woman with dark, close-cropped hair and the stars and swirls of a full Fyushan dogenriku upon the shoulders of her emerald green deo and on the karute that was slung from her saddlehorn. To her right was a stocky gray-haired man, an old veteran by the looks of him, with the marks of a taisho. On her left was a far younger man, slender and fine-featured, with the bars of an issa and the grim look of someone who has fought a long, hard campaign and knows that the worst may be yet to come.

Hibikitsu nodded for his men to let them approach and waited as the three halted their horses only a few yards away and dismounted to join him. All three carried nihono and yori-toki but none reached for the weapons as they approached on foot, though the old general clearly had to struggle not to reflexively rest his hands upon those hilts. Hibikitsu bit back a smile, keeping his features carefully stern, and deliberately did not rise, forcing them to stop and stand before him while he still reclined, apparently at his ease. The fact that he had them massively outnumbered in this particular encounter certainly made that pose easier to maintain, but he would have fought to do so even if it had been him alone against the entire Fyushan army. This was *his* empire, after all.

The woman spoke first, as was her right, since she was the ranking member of the trio. "Greetings to the Relicant Emperor from the Empress of Fyushu, the glorious and noble Rilani, Mistress of All She Surveys," she intoned, her voice deep and strong, husky but smooth like an aged wine. "I am Yanatai Lai, dogenriku of Fyushu. My companions are Ito Oicha, taisho, and Aioi Kazuko, issa." She bowed, showing the proper respect of a high-ranking official or officer before the ruler of a rival nation.

Hibikitsu acknowledged her presentation with a nod. "Greetings to my fellow ruler, and to you, her representatives," he announced. "I cannot, however, bid you welcome, as you have crossed our border in violation of the treaty between our two nations, have taken hostage one of our villages, and have murdered my regional governor. These are serious offences, Dogenriku Yanatai, and demand suitable recompense, lest we are forced to retaliate in kind."

The Fyushan field marshal bowed again. "With all due respect, Your Majesty," she replied, "there will be no recompense, nor any apologies. In war, one does not request permission before claiming territory, nor does one hesitate before dispatching leaders from an enemy force."

He made a show of examining the jointed, gilded fingers of his right hanketo. "Are we enemies, then?" he asked as if surprised and puzzled to hear such a thing. "And are we at war? Truly, this is the first I have heard of this. Did Rilani pen me a missive that went astray?" He lowered his gauntleted hand to fix the dogenriku with a hard glare. "The last I knew, we were merely neighbors—contentious ones, perhaps, but hardly enemies."

She chuckled, clearly not intimidated by his look or confused by his manner. "We have many mouths to feed in Fyushu," she replied, "but little usable farmland with which to grow crops. You have land aplenty, but your people sit about all day, mooning over their dead ancestors, swallowing bone dust and reliving past glories rather than farming." She shrugged. "We need the land and will put it to good use. Therefore, we will take it. If that means we are at war, so be it. We are prepared for that. Are you?" Her stare was as hard as his and backed not by a crown but by thousands of able warriors.

But he was not without warriors of his own. Still, he hated to commit to bloodshed if there was another way. "If what you need is food, we may be able to assist," he told her now. "We are not unsympathetic to your nation's plight. We will sell you food at a reasonable price."

She shook her head. "Why buy when we can produce for ourselves?" she countered. Then she paused, seeming to consider. "But if you are so determined to shirk from a fight," she continued, "cede us the regions you name Korito and Obanari. Perhaps Tabichi and Yunigiri as well, just for good measure. I am sure I can convince my empress to accept that in exchange for not slaughtering your people."

Hibikitsu did not have to feign his anger. "That is all the land north of the Zinyang!" he retorted. "You would halve my empire! Shall I just hand it all over instead and retreat to Tatsuma, to spend the rest of my days ruling over a few small villages and pruning vines? I think not!" He clenched his hands into fists. "My offer was not out of fear or cowardice but out of compassion for those of your people who would lay dead upon our lands, their blood leaking into foreign soil, their spirits trapped forever on this side of the mountains far from their ancestors, if you persist in this folly. If you choose to spurn such generosity, their fate is on your head and yours alone."

The dogenriku bowed that head, though only slightly—an acknowledgement of his statement rather than a mark of respect. "I always accept responsibility for the deaths that occur under my command," she replied matter-of-factly, her tone and gaze level and more than a little cold. "It is the price one pays for maintaining and expanding our great nation." A thin smile touched her lips. "As there seems little else to discuss, may I have your permission for myself and my two officers to withdraw safely?"

He rose to his feet, his hand going to Kosshiki's hilt at his side. "And what is to stop me from refusing, and having the three of you shot?" he demanded. "If I display your heads to your soldiers, will that perhaps deter them and prevent this war you seem determined to incite? Three deaths for thousands spared seems a worthwhile trade."

She laughed at that, though it was as cold as her tone had been, like ice cracking in the dead of winter. "I might think so, but you do not," she answered. "It would stain your precious honor to violate the precepts of noble behavior. Why do you think I came here with only my two officers beside me? I knew you would never allow us to come to any harm." She bowed again and then turned and walked away, casting yet another subtle insult in his face by showing him her back. He itched to give the signal and watch that back sprout feathered shafts but did not, for she had been correct. He would not lower himself by behaving in such a fashion. Still, he cursed her in his head, for her confidence and arrogance and blatant derision of Rimbaku and its ways.

Alas, such insults could only be answered in blood.

None of his Honjofu lifted a finger as Yanatai Lai and her two subordinates returned to their horses, mounted, wheeled the steeds about, and rode back the way they had come, moving at a steady walk. His elite were too well trained to question, and most of them were of noble blood as well. They understood how circumscribed his responses were in a situation like this. As soon as the trio had vanished from view between the farthest buildings, however, Diritan turned to him.

"My emperor, allow me to take a band and pursue them," he asked all in a rush, bowing deeply. "For the insult to you, we would happily release them from this mortal plane, to perhaps learn wisdom and respect in the next life." Several of the other warriors nodded, hands going to weapons, though none were so undisciplined as to bare steel in his presence.

"My thanks, noble Diritan," Hibikitsu replied. "For your loyalty, and your willingness to avenge that slight to my honor. However, we will allow them to retreat, for to do otherwise would show us to be as barbaric as them." He knew, of course, that they were counting on that. "What is the disposition of their officers in Birabiro?"

One of the other Honjofu, a short, slender woman with a long face, stepped forward and bowed. She was one of the unit's advance scouts, he remembered. "They have quartered within the village proper, Your Majesty," she reported in clipped, nasal tones. "Each officer has taken over a local residence, but rather than turn the families out they are sequestering them within their own homes. We do not know precisely which houses have been occupied in this manner."

The emperor ground his teeth together, a low growl escaping between them. Those cold, calculating fiends! They were using his people as human shields, knowing he would never deliberately endanger his own subjects with an all-out assault upon the otherwise innocent village!

"We will return to Furukotai," he announced at last. "There we will gather and discuss our options. Perhaps we will find a way to cut short this war they seem so determined to inflict upon us and upon themselves." He moved to step away from the well, but as he did something within its shaded surface caught his eye. Was that a glimmer of something silvery below the surface?

For a second, peering in, he thought he saw a shape gliding through the water there, long and sleek and serpentine. It carried with it an impression of age and grace and also of a size that belied the space it now occupied. As he watched, entranced, it pivoted and rose, bursting from the water to spring up beneath his very nose, something like a horse and an eel and an otter all melded together in a sculpture formed from water and silver and moonlight. Then it was gone as if it had never been, the well's surface as still as stone and as dark as the bottom of a cave. Had he imagined it? What did it mean?

Still puzzling that, he mounted Shisi by reflex, turning him and following the Honjofu that formed up around him as they headed back to the regional capital. As they rode, however, his thoughts drifted from that strange vision and returned to the conundrum of the Fyushans. This Yanatai Lai was clearly formidable, and just as clearly willing to sacrifice as many warriors—and as much personal honor—as necessary to conquer all Rimbaku. How did he combat someone like that? Her words kept coming back to him, along with his own, and he felt a terrible weight begin to settle upon his shoulders, one far greater even than what he had experienced at Uemada's farm.

Yet, for the good of his people, it seemed the only way.

By the time they returned to Lady Zeryai's, dinner had been prepared. Hibikitsu ignored it, however, striding past the dining room and heading for what had been his governor's office and was now their temporary war room. "Summon my generals," he instructed as he passed the lady and her servants, nodding to acknowledge their bows but not slowing. "I have decided upon our answer to the Fyushan problem." The scent of the food tickled at his nostrils and elicited a rumble of response from his stomach, but Hibikitsu refused to acknowledge them.

Once his orders had been acknowledged and carried out, he suspected he would no longer have an appetite, anyway.

CHAPTER TWENTY-FOUR

The previous day had been strange and unsettling. That was why, on this rest day, Chimehara found herself returning to a place she had once sworn she would never set foot in again—Suranmui.

The shanty town was as she remembered, a wash of humanity untainted by soap or virtue, compressed by space and spiced by desperation. She had not missed this place, with its narrow, twisting alleys that were little more than patches of ground left uncovered between the various lean-tos and tents that comprised the area's homes and businesses alike. The ground was wet and slick in many places, the puddles of questionable nature, and the overall stench was strong enough to turn the stomach of many a fine gentleman or noble lady. For Chimehara it was, if not sweet, at least familiar, and within moments of passing through the city's outermost gates she had stopped noticing the smell at all.

She had dressed appropriately for this little excursion, wearing a simple wrap of rough, unbleached hemp and an equally poor scarf of badly dyed green cotton. Simple hemp sandals, worn and stained, protected her feet from the worst of the effluvia coating the ground, and the hand that held her scarf closed around her face also bore her knife, unsheathed and hidden within the scarf's folds but ready to be wielded in an instant. She carried no more than two bronze coins in the sash at her waist but had stuffed a small pillow beneath that crude belt to alter her shape into one of less winsome proportions. In this way she hoped to escape notice, for many here might still know her, and more would find her face and figure too tempting to ignore.

As she walked, sliding past tiny, makeshift stalls offering

weapons and fruits and other goods normally not available below the second tier, Chimehara let her body operate on its own, her mind drifting back to the events of the day before.

It had started when she arrived at House Chohu. She had meant to head straight for the pearl room to begin the day's work, but Madam Ponsoi intercepted her just inside the gates. "Time enough for work later, my dear," the housekeeper said, settling one silk-sleeved arm over Chimehara's shoulders. "Master Eijiri has summoned everyone to the main hall. Come now, we must not be late." It was clear that she had been waiting there for Chimehara to make sure she was not tardy for this convocation, yet another way the older woman was kind to her, and Chimehara allowed herself a satisfied little smile as she let herself be shepherded along. Ingratiating herself with the household staff was a simple labor that continued to pay handsome dividends.

She wondered what this was all about, and did not have to wait long to find out. The entirety of the house was assembled in the great hall, and at their head stood Master Eijiri himself. At his side was the rotund little Master Hanuri, one of the oldest and most senior of House Chohu's gem traders, and the other senior members all stood behind them, including her own mentor, Master Ganyeki. Once they were all assembled, Eijiri tapped a fingernail against a small gong standing upon a delicate table beside him, and as the clear note resonated throughout the room, the murmurs and rustlings fell silent.

"Good morning to you all," the master of the house declared. "I have convened this assembly to give you tidings that are bittersweet. Master Hanuri has served House Chohu loyally for over fifty years, working first for my own father and then for me and starting as a mere jade counter before working his way up through the ranks to trader and ultimately senior trader. He is one of our most experienced members, renowned for his knowledge and expertise not just here in Awaihinshi but abroad, and so it is with great regret that I tell you that he has chosen to retire."

This was no great surprise, truly. For all his knowledge, Master Hanuri's eyes had begun to cloud recently, their surfaces turning dull and hazy and obscuring the once-bright blue of his irises. And a gem merchant with poor sight was akin to an expert swimmer who had been paralyzed—the knowledge might remain, but it could no longer be put to proper use.

"I would like to extend our deepest gratitude and appreciation to Master Hanuri for his many long years of expert service," Eijiri continued, "and to present him with this small token of our appreciation." He produced from his sleeve a magnificent iniro, the small segmented case fashioned from mother of pearl with a woodpecker in flight picked out in jade, a single black pearl for its eye and gold for its beak. A blue silk cord held the iniro together, tied in a bow at the bottom and tightened with a gold-dipped ivory bead at the top. A carved ivory brooch depicting the same bird held the top of the cord so that it could be hung from a belt. It was beautiful work and spoke highly of both the house's craftsmanship and the quality of their gems in general.

"I hope that you will wear this with pride," the master stated, offering the gift to Hanuri, who was practically in tears as his chubby hands accepted it, "and as you walk these grounds, for they remain your home now and forevermore." That, too, was traditional, at least for such an honorable establishment—far from turning its former employees out on their ears, House Chohu provided them with fine rooms and the usual meals for the rest of their lives. It was one of the advantages of working for a good employer, that you never had to worry about what you would do once you were too old to work any longer.

Of course, the fact that upon your death your bones would become part of that house's treasury meant they would ultimately regain those costs and then some.

Servants appeared and threaded their way through the crowd carrying trays of cups filled with rice wine, and a far better vintage than most. Everyone took a cup and toasted Master Hanuri's retirement. Then it was back to work.

Only the day's irregularities had not ended there.

It was after lunch, and Chimehara was just settling back onto the cushion at her desk when the paneled door slid open to reveal none other than Master Eijiri himself. "And how has your time in the pearl room been thus far?" he asked as he entered, his robes as neat and elegant as ever, his hair and mustache perfectly oiled.

"It has been wonderful," Chimehara replied, bowing until her forehead nearly brushed the table. That was not even a lie. She enjoyed working with Master Ganyeki. He was evidently too old to be interested in matters of the flesh, if he ever had been, and so she was able to work with him without worrying about fending off his advances or having to debate the merits of accepting them. Though old and frail, his eyes behind those spectacles were as sharp as an owl's in flight, and though he was a kind man he was also a demanding master, expecting excellence and accepting nothing less. That was fine with her, however. She preferred to be challenged, and had risen to the occasion.

Indeed, when Eijiri turned to Ganyeki, the old man nodded. "She has proven herself, and more," he agreed, his deep, rich voice as always a startling contrast to his slender frame and sunken features. "She is an excellent student and has a fine eye and exceedingly good judgement."

"I am happy to hear that," the head of House Chohu replied, bowing to them both, "and it nearly makes me regret the news I bear." His eyes sparkled, however, and his lips turned up slightly beneath his mustache, indicating that he was only jesting, and that it was not bad news, either. "Chimehara, with Master Hanuri retiring I find we have a vacancy now for a junior trader. I am hoping you will consider that position. I believe you would be an asset to House Chohu in such a role." He turned back toward the door. "Consider it," he said as he exited, "and inform me of your decision within the next few days."

And that was why Chimehara now found herself retracing the steps of her youth, for she was truly torn. On the one hand, becoming a trader, however junior, was exactly the path she had chosen, the very reason she had applied at House Chohu. This was even sooner than she had dared hope, but now that time was at hand, and it was being offered to her freely, without coercion or bloodshed. On the other hand, she did enjoy her current position, and it was both high enough to earn her respect and low enough to allow her to escape notice when she wished. That could still be useful.

Perhaps the part that confused her the most, however, was that she had not needed to murder anyone to receive this new opportunity. Nor would she need to again, in order to advance in this career. A few years would see her rising through the ranks from junior to seasoned and then to senior, using both her wits and her beauty to win the merchant house lucrative contracts and seal impressive deals. She had little doubt she could accomplish all that without ever wetting her blade again. She could lead a good life, with money and influence and respect, and even surround herself with friends and peers. Perhaps even a family, if she chose. All without ever killing again.

The question was, would that satisfy her?

She was not sure, and that worried her. She had always had a singular focus—survival. But more than just that, advancement, improvement of her place in life, and, mixed in with that, the need to advance aggressively, ruthlessly. She was honest enough to admit to herself that she enjoyed killing. It was not just something she was good at, it was something she truly *excelled* at—the painstaking planning, the attention to detail, and of course the final consummation of the act. Particularly since it involved turning the tables on someone who felt they had power over her, taking that power away from them and then taking their life as well. That was more intoxicating than any wine could ever be, more delicious than any lover's embrace, more invigorating than the smiles and laughter of any child.

How could she give all that up?

Deciding that returning here had been a mistake and determined not to make it a costly one, Chimehara turned and made for the nearest city gate. This was a smaller gate than the main ones but still led back into the city proper, depositing her in the lowest level, Mazihini, home of laborers and menials. Even this level, within its protective water-blue walls, was finer than Suranmui by far, its homes and shops actual buildings, however rough, its streets cobbled like all of Awaihinshi, gutters draining water and refuse and leaving the path clean and dry. Her current attire did not draw any looks on this level, but she knew she would get many stares if she ventured up to Bejinuri dressed in this manner and would most likely not be allowed up to Sakiriti at all, let alone Motohiri where her apartment was. She had prepared for that, of course, and headed now for a small alley where she had stashed a bundle containing a simple but tidy kitoro and several pieces of amber and jade jewelry of good enough quality to mark her as a servant in a fine household.

She had not yet reached that alley when she noticed she was being followed.

Whoever it was, they were light on their feet, and knew to time their steps to her own so that she would not hear their footfalls. They stayed well enough back that their shadow did not creep into hers, and that any scent would also be lost in the general mix of spices and sweat and oils and foods that filed the streets. But many of the shops here had polished signs hung from their awnings to declare their name and the nature of their business, and in one of these Chimehara caught a flicker of movement behind her, as if someone were ducking out of view. She paused at another shop a few buildings later and admired the hand mirrors for sale on racks outside there, holding one up to study her features—and had caught dark hair fluttering as it vanished behind a corner.

Very well, then.

She did not bother to look back again, or to pause, but continued straight to the alley she had chosen. It was narrow and dark, blocked by bundles of trash at the front but clean past that, and she slipped into the gap and then pressed her back up against the building there, her hand releasing the scarf and dropping to her side, knife now unencumbered.

She nearly took the child's head off before she could arrest her own swing. As it was, the knife blade wound up pressing against that little neck hard enough to leave a thin line, and for a drop of blood to well up at one end.

The girl—for she was such—froze instantly. Large, dark eyes

flicked up to meet Chimehara's, seeming enormous in such a pinched face, but the child did not plead or beg. In her gaze Chimehara read grudging acceptance of this price she was about to pay for her carelessness, and disappointment that she would not have the opportunity to do better.

Chimehara was as surprised as the girl when she lowered the blade and took a careful step back.

"How did you know?" she asked. Not "why were you following me?" because that part was clear—the girl held a knife of her own, little more than a jagged metal shard wrapped in cloth for a grip. But given her rags the girl had come from Suranmui, which meant she had recognized that Chimehara was not what she appeared and therefore might be a worthy mark. That meant she had slipped up somewhere, and Chimehara wanted to know where.

"Your toes," the girl answered, her voice raspy but clear, her gaze wary but still not afraid. "They're too nice."

Bones. The girl was right, of course, and Chimehara cursed herself for not catching that. She had allowed Yuni and Ritaru to talk her into going with them for a manicure and a pedicure the previous rest day, and her toenails were still trimmed and coated in an elegant purplish-blue polish, faintly iridescent like the wings of a dragonfly. Now those lady-like nails, and the rest of her clean and well-tended feet, poked out from under her robe, looking utterly out of place against her stained sandals.

She considered the situation, and this girl who had noticed what no one else apparently had. The girl was small and slight, though some of that could have been from lack of proper food. Her face was not particularly pretty but her eyes made up for that, looking like twinned black pearls, perfectly smooth and infinitely deep. Her voice was unusual, but that could be worked around and in some situations would be an asset—men often liked it when women's voices went husky with apparent desire. She was bright, observant, and quick. Those were the key traits. She was also fearless—and hungry.

The same sort of hungry as Chimehara herself.

"What is your name?" she asked, crouching and retrieving her bundle from its place under an old crate. The knife she kept in hand, just to be safe.

"Suda," the girl replied. Her knife disappeared into her sleeve and she stood carefully, clearly curious about this strange conversation.

"Suda," Chimehara repeated. "I am Chimehara. I came from Suranmui, just like you. I got out. Would you like to get out?" She held up a hand to stop the girl from answering right away. "I have a home, and a good job," she continued. "I can take you in, feed you, and more importantly, train you. You will work for me and with me. Make no mistake, when I feel you are ready you will steal, you will seduce—and you will kill. But I will keep you safe, and together we will teach this city that girls like us are not to be underestimated and never to be discounted. Or you can return to the shanties and try your luck with some other victim." She smiled. "What do you say?"

The girl—Suda—considered the question for a moment, head tilted to the side, eyes never leaving this strange young woman who had somehow gone from target to potential mentor in a matter of seconds. Finally she smiled, an expression that transformed her face like the sun peeking out after a stormy morn. "Okay," she agreed.

"Good. Drop that knife—we'll get you a better one. And we'll find you some clothes to get you past the gates for now, then look for a more permanent solution later." Chimehara rose to her feet and began to strip off her clothes, not caring that the girl was watching her closely. She had dealt with far more invasive stares, and if she was going to share her home they would have no secrets from each other, anyway.

She was surprised, as she changed, to find that she was still smiling, and to realize that her head felt clearer and her heart lighter than it had the past two days. This was her path, she recognized. This was her family. She would take the promotion, yes, and use it. But she would not stop killing.

And now, she would no longer have to do it alone.

CHAPTER TWENTY-FIVE

Kagiri woke to a flash of color, like a sunset bursting instantly through clouds. Or a bonfire erupting on a still night. Leaping from his bed, the nearer of his two swords already in hand, he burst from his room, not by way of the hall but from the balcony his still-open windows looked out upon, leaping up onto the low wooden rail and then vaulting off it, flipping over in mid-air and landing in a light crouch on the ground, blade drawn and held out before him, his other hand with the scabbard thrust behind for counter-balance.

His mind was still registering what his eyes had seen, so it took him a second to realize that the brilliant oranges that had somehow drawn him from slumber were...the robes worn by a group of men who now stood a short distance away, staring, their hands clutching at those same robes, at the bracelets of worn, carved wood and stone and shell beads around their wrists, at each other. They all had shorn scalps and shaved cheeks and chins, and their only adornments were those beads and the bones dangling from their belts.

Monks. He had thrown himself out of a second-story window and crashed to earth, blade in hand like an avenging demon, because of a pack of wandering monks.

Straightening, he sheathed his sword and bowed. "My apologies if I startled you," he told them. "I was clearly dreaming."

The men bowed back, and one of them stepped forward, a bemused smile touching his wide, fleshy face and lighting his deep-set eyes. "A potent dream, to be sure," the monk offered, his tone light, "for it to grant you wings."

Kagiri laughed and rubbed at his head, mussing his hair even further than sleep had done. "A good thing it did, or I might have needed your prayers more than your forgiveness!" he replied, and the monks all laughed with him, any fear they'd had at his sudden and precipitous arrival now evidently forgotten. "Again, my apologies." He eyed their belts, tilting his head. "You are…"

"Brother Miuri," the man answered. "And these are my brethren. We are the Aisho Hasume."

The Bone Collectors. Of course. Kagiri had heard of them, from one of the patrons back at Taki's inn in Ginzai, a trader who often traveled along the river and liked to tell the boys stories about the strange places he'd been. These monks carried the bones of their most revered teachers but did not consume them—instead, somehow they absorbed the essence of the long-dead men through closeness and contact, as a man might gain heat by being near a fire without ever touching it directly.

In a way, they were similar to the Burahone, the Bone Blind, for surely the monks' aitachi must be strong if they could access their dead mentors' skills and experience by mere proximity. But they were completely focused, whereas the Burahone often went mad because they could not shut out the resonances from any of bones around them, including those of people still living.

For an instant, Kagiri considered asking these men if they might have any insights into his own predicament, but just as quickly dismissed it. He had the Gensaiba within him because he had literally taken them in by breathing in their dissolved bones as dust for several days, to the point that his very being was saturated with their spirits. He doubted there was anyone in the world who could help him learn how to deal with that.

Still, it was not all bad. Since seeing that vision on the river, the Nizukai, he had felt more of a balance with his internal companions. They had not forced him aside since, though at times they did take over reflexively, as Onyoku Jeizen had when he had flung himself off the balcony. Even that had felt less like an invasion or an imposition, however. More like an offer or an invitation to put those talents to best use.

Bowing once more to the monks, who were already gathering

their bedrolls and begging bowls and walking sticks from beside the town well, Kagiri turned back toward the inn. He and his growing entourage had reached Himsu the day before, and the merchants had immediately insisted they take rooms for the night. Kagiri had chosen not to argue—in all honesty, he had welcomed the thought of sleeping in a real bed, with a proper mattress, and having solid walls around him instead of the taut hemp sides of a tent. Now he thought he might as well return to that room and attempt a few more hours of sleep since the sun was not yet up, and it was unlikely he'd be able to stir Kishin Narai and the others before it was fully dawn.

As he returned to the inn, however, Kagiri noticed a man slumped on one of the benches set outside. He sat with both arms stretched out beside him, head lolling back, seemingly asleep save that his eyes were half-open. Kagiri knew him at once and quickened his pace until he could stop and crouch beside the bench.

"Surito," he called, resting a hand on the stocky guard's leg. "Can you hear me?"

The older man's eyes twitched and swam in Kagiri's direction, but otherwise he did not move.

"Surito!" Kagiri shook him, and that at least caused the guard to glance his way, though blearily, his eyes unfocused.

"Sir?" Surito whispered, his whole mouth slack. "I am here, sir." The words were barely intelligible, as if his jaw had forgotten how to shape the sounds.

Kagiri frowned. All the merchants' guards drank some, of course, but Surito no more than most, and less than some. However, he was the one Kagiri had traded his wine with that night by the river—and every night since, including earlier this evening. The guard had certainly not complained about exchanging cheap rice wine for a far finer vintage, but could that have something to do with his state now? If so, the Gensaiba had been right to warn him not to drink.

Coming to a decision, Kagiri grabbed the guard's arms and draped them over his own shoulders, then clasped his arms under Surito's, linking his hands behind the man's back. Then he heaved upward, hefting the guard as if he were a particularly large and unresponsive baby. Fortunately Surito was short and Kagiri was tall, so the guard's feet dangled well above the ground as Kagiri carried his burden into the inn and up to his own room.

Once there, he let Nikiyu Sinchu take over. The Gensaiba was the most knowledgeable of them when it came to healing. But Komu Setsui quickly muscled her fellow warrior aside. "He has been drugged," she stated with absolute certainty, peeling back the guard's eyelid, opening his mouth to tap his tongue, and feeling the swollen glands under his chin. "Without a doubt."

Sinchu agreed, though his displeasure at being moved out of the way was plainly evident. "It must have been the wine," he confirmed. "No doubt whatever it was laced with is meant to have a cumulative effect so that it would be unnoticed at first. Then, when you did become aware, it would already be too late."

They all stared down at poor Surito, who lay passed out on the bed, drool dribbling down his cheek, his eyelids fluttering, his limbs twitching from time to time. He had not known, when he'd so eagerly accepted Kagiri's wine, that he had been dooming himself to this.

The only question was, who was responsible?

It was Onyoku Jeizen who suggested a way to find out.

The next morning at breakfast, Kagiri waved Joshi over. "Do not expect Surito this morning," he informed the merchants' chief guard. "He is in my room, waiting to answer some questions. I will send him back when I am done."

Joshi bowed and then retreated, not asking any questions. The merchants had trained him well. His employers, however, could not contain their own curiosity. As soon as their man at arms was out of earshot, Kishin Narai turned to Kagiri.

"Questions?" the senior merchant asked, his wide face as calm and composed as ever. "Did the man do something wrong?"

"Entirely the opposite," Kagiri replied, selecting a piece of fish with his chopsticks and settling that onto his bowl of rice before adding sauce and consuming the whole together. "He came to me just before dawn with news about a plot against me. I was too hungry to wait, however, so I told him to stay there and I would learn the details when I returned."

"A plot!" Shizu Yokori exclaimed. "How dreadful! It is good you learned of it in time!"

"I have learned nothing yet," Kagiri pointed out. "But I certainly shall." He leaned back and patted his belly. "Once I have eaten my fill." Then he gestured toward the table with his chopsticks. "Would someone pass the eel?"

It was Fujiko Oritano who excused herself from the table first, claiming she still had to tally the last of the coin they had taken from the Kindichi. Jiro Masute rose to his feet a few minutes later, stating that he needed to brush his hair once more, a claim that would have sounded ridiculous save for the luxuriousness of that same hair and the obvious care he lavished on it. Shizu Yokori announced that she had some correspondence to see to, and Kishin Narai took his leave by saying he would confer with Joshi about the best route when they departed this town. Eien Kawatai merely giggled and wandered away, singing softly to himself as he headed toward the back of the inn and the stairs leading to the rooms above.

Once the last merchant had gone, Kagiri unfolded himself and rose to his feet. He had been careful to take only a little rice with each morsel, so that he was not overfull and unable to move now, and his stride was still strong and sure as he strode to the inn's front door and quickly exited. The balcony to his room was just above and to the right, and from it currently hung a knotted white silk rope he had tied there this morning, dangling against the white-washed inn walls so that it could barely be seen. It was the work of a moment to haul himself up onto the balcony, coiling the rope and dropping it to the floor. He had left the window open a crack and stepped to that narrow gap, twisting so that he could peer into his own room.

There was Surito, still groggy but at least upright. And massed around him were the five merchants who had hired Kagiri and Noniki, dragged them to the Tawasiri, threatened to kill Kagiri if he didn't emerge from the tower with anything of value—and since claimed to be his closest friends and most trusted advisors.

"What did you tell him?" Yokori was demanding, shaking poor Surito by his collar, causing his head to whip this way and that. "What do you know?"

"Enough," Narai declared, pulling her off the hapless guard. "He can tell us nothing if you scramble his brains so that he cannot speak."

"But if he found out about the wine…" Oritano started, trailing off with a look of utter terror dominating her normally cheerful features.

"How could he know?" Masute asked. "We've been careful!"

"Perhaps not enough," Kawatai commented. "Certainly he has shown no effects from it yet."

"He will," Yokori snapped. "It's just a matter of time. And once he does, and he learns there is no cure, only a counteragent—"

"He will be ours to control," Narai finished, nodding. "But not if he finds out before the poison has a chance to seat itself fully in his blood." He glanced at Surito and shook his head. "We will have to do away with this."

Kagiri decided he had heard enough. "I think not," he declared shoving the window open and stepping into the room. Most of the merchants froze at the sound of his voice, turning slowly like startled birds suddenly faced with a hungry cat—all except Kawatai, who instantly flung himself toward the door.

The long-nosed merchant, who had often seemed so dim but at other times had been strangely perceptive, made it only two paces before he stiffened, his entire body jerking upright, his arms flung up toward the heavens, his head thrown back. He hit the floor a second later, landing in a graceless heap, the hilt of Kagiri's yori-toki protruding from between his shoulder blades.

"You killed him!" Masute shrieked, hands going to his face.

"I did," Kagiri agreed. "He tried to poison me. It is a fit punishment." Slowly, deliberately, he drew his nihono, lazily swinging it to and fro so that its blade flashed in the sunlight as he steadily advanced upon the other merchants. "But it seems all of you were equally to blame," he stated. "Therefore, you all must share in the repercussions."

His sword licked out like a ribbon of light, and Oritano screamed and dropped to her knees, clutching her hand as blood spurted from the place where her index finger had been. Another thrust and Masute's shrieks rose to girlish heights, his hands going to the side of his head, now minus one ear. Yokori refused to scream, cursing Kagiri instead as he stabbed her in the knee and dropped her to the floor. That left only Narai himself, who gazed up at Kagiri with resigned eyes.

"What shall I take from you, then?" Kagiri whispered, stepping in close enough for his breath to flutter the merchant's eyelashes. "Your nose? An eye? Perhaps that silver tongue?" In the end, he chose to pierce the other man through the hip. Kishin Narai would never be able to sit without pain again, be it on a horse, on a cushion, or even in the bath. That, too, seemed fitting.

"You work for me," Kagiri reminded the merchants, his voice low and cold as he wiped and sheathed his blade. "Never forget that, or I will remove far larger pieces of you than I have just done." He stalked past them to the door and let himself out, leaving them behind to recover as best they could.

Nicely done, Setsui murmured in his mind.

Very, Jeizen agreed.

The other Gensaiba all chimed in with their approval. Which was when Kagiri realized something that sent a shiver through him—if they were all congratulating him on how he had handled that situation, it meant none of them had. And, indeed, now that he thought upon it, he could see that they had never once tried to take control.

Which meant killing Kawatai and mutilating Narai and the rest?

That had all been Kagiri, and Kagiri alone.

In many ways, that struck him as far worse than losing control to the spirits. At least, when that happened, he could blame them for his excesses, his cruelties.

This time, there was no one to blame but himself.

CHAPTER TWENTY-SIX

Misataki Shizumi had to admit, in retrospect, that the message may have been the only thing that wound up saving her superior's life. And that her intense relief at seeing him go might have been the reason why she had accepted his latest order, ridiculous as it had been.

Having risen through the ranks of the aiashe and then through the Honjofu, Shizumi was no stranger to hardship. She had marched for miles and miles, until it felt as if the sun were broiling her brains inside her jingaso and steaming the rest of her within her makiro, until her legs had felt like limp noodles and any threat would have found her unable to even move, let alone fight back. She had slept in ditches half-filled with rainwater, and once or twice, in bogs where the water had sat for longer than she had been alive, gathering mold and decay and insects the way a miser gathered gold, pulling it in close and holding on with a deathgrip. She had been so hungry she had sawn off her armor's straps and chewed on those, worrying the tough leather between her teeth as if it were the finest meal imaginable, scanning the ground hungrily for grubs or worms or bugs as an added treat. She had been so thirsty she had considered cutting herself to get at what little blood remained, to at least ease the burning in her throat and reduce its swelling enough for her to breathe again.

She had never before, however, been forced to endure traveling with Fujibuki Haro.

Her superior was a noble, of course, and took great pride in his appearance. That much she had known. She had not realized, however, that he traveled with both a personal dresser and a pair of groomsmen, the latter being employed not to brush and comb the Taikoro's horse but his person, to assist him in bathing and washing his hair and braiding it and oiling and combing his mustache.

She had not known that her Lord Commander's servants led a pair of heavily laden mules upon which resided his personal tent, constructed of beautifully stitched silk panels over layers of finely woven rugs and piles of satin pillows. She had not guessed that he might bring along his personal chef, who prepared meals for him and him alone and who claimed first right of any game the men might flush out during the day's travels but who also had an overly burdened beast whose saddlebags bulged with dried meat, dried fish, dried fruit, vegetables, rice, and various spices.

And of course one could not forget the animal whose only encumbrance was a full tea set and several boxes of fine tea, for the leader of the most elite fighting force in Rimbaku could not possibly go more than half a day before stopping for an elaborate tea.

"This is insanity," Shizumi fumed to Geniji as they stopped yet again. "It has been four days and we have barely traveled a day's ride! At this pace, this stranger will circle Rimbaku and come upon us from behind. While riding a tortoise. With only three legs."

The burly corporal snorted. "What I want to know," she asked, lifting her waterskin for a quick swallow, "is how many outfits he brought, and why? Who does he expect to see him out here? Is he that afraid that someone might spy him wearing the same thing twice? Oh, the horror!"

Shizumi laughed, as did Dairamu on her other side. It seemed all the Honjofu held their esteemed leader in the same high regard. But he was a noble, and a high-ranking one, while they were either lower ranks or the children of merchants or, in Shizumi's case, an actual commoner. Which was why Haro led and they followed.

If only he wasn't leading them at a snail's pace.

It was two days later that they reached a river, and the small army outpost beside it. Rimbaku was dotted with them, typically at crossroads and bridges and other significant intersections and stopping points. Each one was much the same: sturdy walls thick enough and high enough to be defensible; a wide flat roof with a good vantage of the surroundings; a broad, covered porch; and a large yard out back, with the stables at the far end. These outposts were always the largest and strongest buildings in their immediate area, and they often served as way stations, makeshift trading posts, and information centers.

Shizumi and her bantao rode up—for Haro had appointed them the forward guard—as a soldier stepped out. He had his yanoi at the ready but lowered it once he saw the crest on their armor. "Is Taikoro Fujibuki with you?" the soldier called out.

"He is," Shizumi replied. The soldier saluted and stepped up beside her horse—carefully, for the animal was high-spirited and showed its teeth at his approach, warning that it might bite—to offer her a rolled-up scrap of paper. She accepted the message with a nod, and with a kick of her heels sent her steed wheeling about, away from the frightened soldier and back toward the rest of their forces.

She stood and waited silently as Haro scanned the message. He studied it then, scowling, but smoothed at his mustache as he walked and read and eventually began to smile, or more accurately smirk, an oily expression that made Shizumi's skin crawl.

"It seems," he declared finally, crumpling the paper and tossing it into the fire over which his tea brewed, "that there is trouble back at Awaihinshi. Taikoro Maniko has personally requested my help." Which explained his glee, Shizumi knew. For the head of the imperial household guard to ask him, her equal, for help must have been excruciating—but not nearly as painful as when he did arrive, all the Honjofu in tow, and rescued her and her warriors. Kohori would owe Haro a massive favor, and Shizumi knew her superior well enough to know that he would squeeze his fellow commander for everything he could get. Kohori was old enough and wise enough to know that, too, which meant she must be in genuine trouble.

Well, at least it would be good to be home once more.

Haro took himself to the water's edge and there spoke with a number of fishermen and boat captains. When he returned, he called Shizumi to his tent.

"I will be returning to Awaihinshi with all due speed," he explained, reclining upon a pile of cushions and nibbling from a bowl of candied lotus root. "The majority of the Honjofu will be accompanying me." He popped a piece of candied lotus into his mouth, jaw working beneath his mustache. "You, however, will continue our original mission." He took a delicate sip of tea, afterward daubing at the corners of his lips with a silk cloth embroidered with his family crest, an otter wrapped around the sun. "You and your bantao," he explained slowly as if chewing each word before releasing it into the air, "will track down this mysterious bandit-killer. You will ascertain his allegiances, assess his threat level, and then either enlist, apprehend, or execute him." His smile was slow and pleased. "I trust you can handle this simple task?"

"Hai, Taikoro," Shizumi replied, hand over fist to chest in salute. "It will be done."

It was only afterward that she realized what she had promised, but by then it was too late.

"Explain this to me again," Geniji asked a day later. She, Shizumi, and the others sat their horses and watched from the hill as, down below on the opposite side of the river, Haro supervised the loading of men, women, horses, and supplies onto all the boats the outpost had had available, as well as any they had been able to entice or bribe into use in the past day. "Our Taikoro is taking almost all our warriors and returning home by boat. Meanwhile, the"—she made a show of counting—"eight of us are to pursue a man who singlehandedly slaughtered an entire well-armed bandit force—one that had already defeated a full shotao—and, once we find him, we're supposed to bring him back with us? Or kill him, but it's clear they'd rather have him alive if at all possible." She shook her head. "That about it?"

"Those would be all the principal elements, yes," Shizumi agreed. She sat and watched the rest of the Honjofu march onto that array of mismatched vessels, then resolutely tugged her horse's head around to point north. At least her superior had consented to have them ferried across before he took all the boats with him. "We might as well get moving," she pointed out, nudging her steed into motion. The sooner they found this stranger, the better.

Akino pulled his horse alongside hers as they broke into a canter, his slim features as inscrutable as ever. Shizumi knew there had been occasional bets and dares to try getting a rise out of the slender warrior—and that none of them had succeeded. "I should mention," he stated now, his voice barely above a whisper but still clearly audible as they rode, "that we may have even more difficulty than expected."

She eyed him sidelong, not slowing. It was good to finally be moving at a proper pace again. No more mid-day tea breaks for her. "Explain."

He nodded. "I spoke with some of the aiashe on duty at the outpost," he answered. "Only one group of any size has passed through here in the past month. This one was a small caravan, they said, perhaps three dozen people in all. It was led by a group of wealthy merchants, but they all deferred to a tall, serious-looking young man in well-worn armor. He carried a pair of nihono at his belt and moved like he knew how to use them."

Shizumi reluctantly halted her horse while she considered this new information. She had no doubt the party in question were the ones they sought, and that this young man was the scourge of the Kindichi. She had never seen anyone wield two nihono at once, but if one were to master such a trick—they would be truly deadly.

The numbers also worried her. She had thought they might have to face as many as a dozen merchant guards, and such men could be formidable in their own crude way, but none were a match for any of her Honjofu. That would have left her to face this bandit-killer while her unit dealt with his men. If he now had three dozen traveling with him, however, that changed matters considerably. Even if half of them were not warriors, her soldiers would be outnumbered two to one or worse. This situation was rapidly becoming untenable, and she grimaced as she realized she would have to come to a decision, and now rather than later.

Did they continue after this man of unknown loyalties and intentions but demonstrable prowess, most likely throwing their lives away if he proved anything but amiable, or did they halt this chase before it saw them all dead for nothing?

Added to that was whatever was going on back in Awaihinshi. It must be bad, for Kohori to beg Haro's help. He would have the sheer numbers to help her, certainly, but with her gone there was no one but the Taikoro himself to command the Honjofu and Shizumi knew firsthand that he was hopeless at that. Kohori was a wily old woman, a fierce warrior and a sharp strategist—Shizumi respected her immensely and had every confidence the woman could direct the Honjofu to best effect. Provided she was given freedom to do so. But Haro would no doubt interfere—he could not stand to not be in control—and make a mess of things.

If Shizumi headed back now, she might be able to intervene, to serve as intermediary between the two Taikoro, smooth over any differences, and keep the two groups working together properly, at least until the current threat was ended.

True, she would be disciplined for disobeying a direct order. But if she helped save the capital, surely that would mitigate any punishment? Even if she were reduced back to corporal, or worse, she would still be a Honjofu, and still alive, which seemed far less likely on their present path.

"Ash it," she spat, glancing up at her unit, who had also stopped and gathered protectively around her as she thought this through. "We're going back. They're going to need us."

Geniji, Dairamu, Masai, and Nori all cheered. Akino and Reiko merely nodded, though the latter was grinning. Only Isano remained silent.

"You disagree?" she asked him. She was not challenging him, however. She knew he would follow her lead, and she made a point of allowing her warriors to voice their own opinions, provided they did not let any disagreements get in the way of their orders.

He considered a moment, head tilted in thought, but finally shrugged. "It is the wiser choice," he agreed in that infuriatingly slow way of his. "And if it makes you feel any better, our stranger is also headed to Awaihinshi. Provided his course does not deviate."

That made her sit up straighter in her saddle. How long had he known that? Why had he not mentioned it earlier? But of course if they were merely following the stranger it made little difference where he was headed, so long as they could catch up to him before he got there. That was Isano in a nutshell—he might notice everything but he only shared what he thought was relevant, and only at his own pace. If he weren't so reliable and such a deadly shot she'd have a harder time putting up with him.

In this case, however, his revelation only cemented her decision. If this dual-bladed mystery man was headed for the capital, she wanted to be there when he arrived, not trail behind him. Better to face someone like that with the whole of the Honjofu at her back. Also, the last thing they needed was this random element reaching the city just as they were in the throes of dealing with the trouble Kohori's message had mentioned. She knew it was not false pride to think that she could help the Honteno regain control far more effectively than her own commander ever could, and more quickly. And, with the stranger already on his way, it seemed time was more of a factor than anyone had expected.

"Right," was all she said, however. "Back to the river. We'll ride along it until we find someone with a boat, then sail to Awaihinshi. With any luck, we will reach home only a day or two behind our brothers and sisters."

She hoped Haro could manage to not doom the city in the interim.

CHAPTER TWENTY-SEVEN

They had just reached the Tonawa when Madam Ushi took ill.

It had been over a week since they had left Ginzai, and Seikoku had never felt more alive. No longer did she spend her days worrying about how much money she had saved and how much she would need to spend to feed everyone and where she could steal more money once that ran out. No longer did she stay up nights sneaking through the city, studying homes and businesses, assessing strengths and weaknesses, searching for flaws and cracks and gaps she could exploit to break in and then escape again. No longer did she worry that every night might be the one when her luck ran out, when she slipped and fell from a roof or got caught in a trap or simply was too slow and was apprehended and executed for her crimes.

Now she simply walked and talked and listened and laughed, ate and drank and slept and bathed as needed, and enjoyed the feel of the sun on her face, the wind in her hair, and the ground beneath her feet.

In many ways, traveling with Noniki was like a dream.

There was the fact that it was almost always sunny. Even when thunderclouds massed in the distance, the most that reached them was a gentle rainfall, more refreshing than anything. The sky tended to remain a clear, perfect blue, dusted with wisps of white cloud. The air was sweet and clean and cool, and there seemed to be flowers and fruit everywhere.

Then there were the others. Initially it had just been her and Noniki and slow, solid, dependable Jitu Kanai, and if the potter had quashed her idle thoughts of a romantic quest he had proven good company and become a dear friend. But when they reached the next village, Shakomi, they had received a surprise, for a woman had been waiting for them.

"Madam Ushi?" Noniki exclaimed upon seeing her sitting on a stool under the awning of the building closest to the road. She was an older woman, stout, with silvery hair and a long, thin pipe that produced a ribbon of aromatic smoke, but her eyes were bright little beads within a web of laugh lines, and her smile was warm as she rose to her feet and walked out to greet them.

"Thought you were rid of me, did you?" she asked, giving Noniki a hug. "Not likely!" she smiled at Seikoku, who instantly liked the older woman, and then at Jitu Kanai as well. "And I see you have found a few friends. Very good—so have I." She waved and another woman emerged from the building, taller and broader than Madam Ushi and dressed in the garb of a washer woman— the same as Seikoku herself had worn not long ago, though that had been only as a disguise, whereas this woman had the reddened eyes and rough skin and callused hands to prove herself authentic.

"This is Kuma," Madam Ushi explained, setting the stool atop a heavy pack beside it, securing it there with hemp cords, and then hefting the entire ungainly bundle onto her stooped back as if it weighed nothing. "Shall we?"

Seikoku had learned, as they had stopped at the town well to refill their skins and then continued on through, that Madam Ushi was a weaver. She had met Noniki just outside Enwara, a small town a few days south of Ginzai, and had been impressed upon speaking with him. Much like Kanai, the woman decided that, for all his youth, Noniki already walked a clearer path than she could see, but one she felt might benefit her as well. Madam Ushi had no love of Ginzai—she disliked large crowds, she'd explained, and concentrated smells—and so upon deciding to accompany Noniki she had, rather than travel with him to and through Ginzai, gone around the city and settled here in Shakomi to wait for him to catch up. It was here that she met Kuma, who was interested enough in what she heard about Noniki to cast aside her previous life and travel with them as well.

They had been only the first. At each town or village, Noniki stopped to speak with people. He was young and handsome and had a warm, friendly matter about him, which had been true when he and Seikoku first met. Now, however, there was a great more to him than just a clumsy, overly enthusiastic would-be graverobber. Now he exuded an aura of calm, of wisdom—of peace. He was a calming influence, and people wanted to be near that.

Also, people noticed his lack of an aishone pouch, and wished to know why he traveled without one, for it was clear from his bearing that he could not possibly be Mukanichi—none of the Untouched would ever dare to stand so straight or walk so tall or speak so directly. Noniki was always willing to explain his stance on aitachi and aishone, how he believed reliance upon the relic bones was holding the people of Rimbaku back, how such dependence upon the past prevented there from being any future, and how only by setting aside such obsession with ancient history could people rediscover their own passions and talents.

It was a compelling argument, and in each town there was at least one person for whom that message resonated. Those people wound up joining them and now they were a small caravan, twenty or more in all. A few had money, many were poor, and the rest had been able to support themselves but would never have been called wealthy. Some were young, some old, some in between. But all of them believed in Noniki and his message, and all of them chose to follow in his footsteps.

Those footsteps halted that morning, when Madam Ushi did not emerge from her tent.

"She is ill," Kuma reported, stepping out from within the brightly dyed, fancifully woven silk panels, for she shared Madam Ushi's tent, having none of her own. "Her skin is burning hot, she is covered in sweat, she cannot keep her breakfast down, and her limbs shake and twitch of their own accord."

Noniki made to go to the old woman, but Kanai stopped him, his large hands as strong as ever. "You cannot risk catching whatever she may have," the potter explained. "We will tend to her." Noniki began to protest, and Seikoku laid a hand on his arm.

"He's right," she said softly. "Everyone here needs you. You cannot risk it." She led him away as Kuma, Kanai, and a few others slipped into the tent to check on the kindly old weaver.

Hours later, Kanai emerged, his face ashen and drawn, his steps unsteady, tears streaming down his face. Noniki was on his feet in an instant. "What is it?" he demanded. "What is wrong? Where is Madam Ushi?"

"Gone," Kuma answered from just past Kanai's shoulder, her face also wet with tears. "She has left us and journeyed on to the next realm, under the First Emperor's care." And she bowed deeply toward the sun as it began its nightly descent.

Noniki sagged, clearly devastated, and Seikoku and Kanai rushed to prop him up. Between them they were able to steer him back toward his bedroll—for he refused a tent, saying he preferred to have the stars as his canopy and the horizon as his wall—and convince him to lower himself onto it in a cross-legged position. Seikoku fetched a waterskin and he drank deeply, but she was not entirely sure he knew what he was doing.

"It is not your fault," she told him gently, sitting beside him, wrapping an arm around his waist, and laying her head upon his shoulder. "People get sick from time to time."

He only shook his head. "This is still my fault somehow," he answered in a whisper. "I can feel it."

There was little she could say to that, and so she stayed silent instead, just letting him know she was there for him. They sat that way until the sun finally vanished and the day plummeted into night as if embarrassed to be seen out and about.

The next day a fisherman named Chisigi collapsed as they walked, simply toppling to the ground with a truncated gasp as if someone had caught the full sound unawares. When they rolled him over he was awash in sweat, his skin clammy to the touch, and his eyes stared unseeing straight through to the heavens.

A few days later it was an herbalist named Isoko, one of the newest members of their expanding family. She had joined them after they had finally found a place shallow enough to cross the Tonawa, a tall, slender, quiet woman with a shy smile and long, lovely hands; she complained of an ache in her throat and belly and a chill in her bones one night, and was found stiff and lifeless the next morning.

Noniki was beside himself. "What is happening?" he demanded, running both hands through his hair and leaving it a thick tangle like night come alive to catch the unwary in its inky tendrils. "Why are people dying?"

"People die," Seikoku replied, brushing his hair back from his face. "It is sad, but it happens."

She had to agree with his sentiment, however. This was all simply too unbelievable. Yes, people died. But three of their friends in the space of five days? That made little sense—if you assumed the deaths were natural.

Seikoku was hardly the trusting sort. Her line of work had taught her to question everything, including goals and motives. Thus she considered the question, "What would it mean if they were *not* natural?" Then someone or something would have to be responsible. But who and why, and what did they want? Were these deaths the actual goal, or simply a means to end, or just some sort of unfortunate side effect of their real plans?

She had no idea but intended to find out.

The first person she asked was Isoro, who like her mother was an herbalist. "I am so sorry to intrude upon your time of grief," Seikoku told the young woman, barely older than she was, who had inherited her mother's quiet ways and beautiful fingers. "But can you think of anything that could cause people to experience the symptoms your mother possessed, and Madam Ushi and Chisigi as well?"

Isoro considered that calmly, despite the fact that her eyes were red and swollen from weeping. "Fevers, sweats, nausea, and death?" she asked, frowning as her finger ticked through possibilities. "There

are many herbs that could cause such symptoms. Even some medi-
cines, if taken in too large a dose."

Seikoku thought about all three of those they had lost thus far.
"What about convulsions?" she asked. "Kuma said Madam Ushi
was twitching uncontrollably."

The young herbalist thought about that, then nodded. "Itoyako,"
she answered. "Lily of the valley. Its flowers are deadly to eat, its
seeds even moreso. They can cause convulsions, nausea, vomiting,
fever, sweating, and ultimately death."

"What does it look like?" Seikoku was not particularly enam-
ored of flowers and only knew the basic types. She had heard the
name Itoyako once or twice, but never seen one.

"The plant itself is short and stout," the herbalist explained.
"Its leaves are plain and tough and its stalks are smooth and dry
to the touch, as if it were made of leather and wood. Its flowers
are large and have long, soft, drooping petals that shade from
white to pink, often with darker streaks from within." She caught
Seikoku by the wrist, those long fingers wrapping around in a firm
grip. "You think someone gave such a thing to my mother." It was
not a question.

Seikoku sighed. "I hope not," she replied. "But I will find out."

Isoro nodded and released her, turning away. "If it is so, please
inform me," was all she said, her voice tight with grief still too
fresh to assuage. Seikoku could only nod and take her leave.

Now that she knew what to look for, it was time for Seikoku
to put her particular skills to use. *Odd how I thought I was setting
aside my thieving ways,* she mused as she crept silently into one
of their group's tents, which belonged to a basketmaker named
Sanedi. *Only to discover I still need them, but now instead of breaking into homes I am sneaking into tents, and instead of stealing aishone I am searching for poison plants. Still, who better to investigate
the others without their knowing than a thief?*

She had worked her way through half the group's belongings, checking everything but being careful to leave it all looking
undisturbed afterward, when she finally found what she had been
dreading to discover all along. It was in the rough, oft-patched

tent belonging to a simple farmer named Yori, a quiet man who kept to himself but listened closely. His tent contained little, as did most of the others, for none of them had brought much on this journey, carrying only the necessities, as Noniki did, and perhaps one or two keepsakes of their families and their past. Yori's held a bedroll and pillow, a tiny blown-glass vase holding a single dried rose, a worn leather wallet, and a small fishing net. But tucked inside the bedroll she found a small but well-crafted writing case of waterproof tooled leather, which was far too fine a thing for a poor farmer to even own. And inside the wallet, folded inside a square of raw silk, were several plant seeds and a few dried flower petals. The petals were white shading to pink, with darker streaks at the center.

Yori had joined them just after Madam Ushi and Kuma, Seikoku recalled. Why had he been traveling all that time with them and then suddenly decided to start killing the people around him? What was the point? Especially since he seemed so intent upon Noniki's words whenever he spoke?

Well, that was not for her to discover. She had done her part, she thought, returning both writing case and wallet to their hiding places. It was up to Noniki to handle the rest.

That was a strange thought for her, and a new experience. Ever since she could remember, Seikoku had only been able to rely upon herself, and so all of the important decisions in her life had been hers and hers alone. To now not have to deal with all of that—not to answer to someone else, for that she would never do, but to be able to rely upon someone, to share the weight and at times even trust them to cover certain responsibilities entirely—would have been a foreign concept just a few weeks ago. Even now, it felt odd, but she knew it was the right thing to do here. Noniki was not in charge of this expedition, since he never gave orders to anyone and treated everyone as an equal, but he was the guiding force, and it was to him that everyone turned for advice and support.

Now, for the first time, Seikoku decided that she would do the same.

CHAPTER TWENTY-EIGHT

"Turn to the right here."

Kagiri frowned. "Why would I wish to do that?" he asked, though only in his head, for that was where the instructions had been voiced. "Awaihinshi is directly ahead." Not that it was close yet—they still had to cross the Tonawa, as that river curved up along the western edge of Hochiro, separating it from the Imperial region of Saruto beyond. But the river was now in sight, a broad, gleaming sheet of silver just below the horizon and directly in their path.

"Bah!" Geido Shinen scoffed, for it had been he who had ordered the course correction. "Your little 'city of polished light' will no doubt still be there when we return. For now, turn right."

Curious, Kagiri complied, signaling for the caravan to turn. "Why do you say 'your'?" he asked as he steered his horse in the suggested direction. "As if you have no part in the capital?"

"Because it is your capital, not ours," Nikiyu Sinchu whispered. "We knew no such consolidation of political power. The Matekai saw to the well-being of the land's magic and various regions and provinces elected their own leaders, as they saw fit, to deal with the minutiae of daily life."

"Matekai? Wizards?" Now it was his turn to scoff. "They truly existed?" He had heard of them, certainly, but only as shadowy figures designed to frighten small children into obeying their parents—"Finish your dinner or the Matekai will come for you!"

"Of course they existed," Bushiki Kenin answered. "And we were their warriors. One Matekai, one Gensaiba. Thus it had always been."

Their inner conversation quieted as someone coughed softly,

drawing Kagiri's attention back to the real world. It was Kishin Narai, the merchant having guided his horse alongside but leaving several feet between them out of respect—and fear. The merchants had been careful not to overstep their bounds after Himsu, and the few times they had dared question any of Kagiri's orders, as now, they had done so with all the timidity of a servant dealing with a violent and impetuous master. Kagiri still felt uncomfortable at the way the four of them flinched when he even glanced in their direction, and oddly guilty whenever he spied the riderless horse that had belonged to Eien Kawatai. At the same time, they had earned that punishment and more. At least he was comforted to know that the merchants had finally learned their place and no longer made any attempt to control him. The balance of power had begun to shift when he had emerged from the Tawasiri and now it had settled for good, with him firmly at the top and them clearly well beneath him.

"A thousand pardons, noble Kagiri," Narai began, wincing as he adjusted his seat in the saddle to take pressure off the still-healing wound in his hip. "But we were curious as to the reason for the change in direction. Surely the quickest path to Awaihinshi was to continue straight to the Tonawa, secure boats, and sail up the Edishu directly to the city's docks?"

"I have decided to make a small detour," Kagiri replied, straightening in his saddle and peering down at the other man, who cowered reflexively. "Do not worry, it will not delay us long."

"As you say," Narai stated, slowing his steed and letting Kagiri pass him by so that the merchant fell in with his fellows once more. Clearly, he had learned his place.

Kagiri wanted to question the Gensaiba more about the Matekai, about their connection, about everything, but he did not, for he could feel their growing sense of expectation. Something was about to happen. Sure enough, as they topped a small hill Shinen declared, "Behold, for I give you—Horohaba, the fabled City of Beasts!"

"Indeed?" Kagiri replied, tugging on the reins and scanning the terrain ahead as his horse came to a halt. "And is it also invisible to the naked eye?" For before him he saw nothing but an empty plain, flat as a still pond. Off in the distance was a silvery line he thought might be the Zinyang, and the Tonawa ran up toward it like an eager child racing to greet an absent parent.

"What? No!" It was an odd sensation to feel the Gensaiba peering out through his eyes like a cluster of children all pushing and shoving to see through a small crack in a high wall. "That is not possible!"

"You have been dead for a very long time," Kagiri reminded them, though gently, for he could feel their disappointment—and that, oddly, it was somehow aimed at him. Not as if they were disappointed with *him*, however. More like they were disappointed... *for* him? "I am guessing that most of the cities you remember have long since turned to dust."

"Not Horohaba," Shinen stated stubbornly. "It was built to last."

"What is that, there?" Komu Setsui asked, directing their attention to a dark streak. "Some sort of hollow, perhaps?"

"Let us find out," Shito Kibi replied, and kneed their steed into a full gallop down the hill. "Wait here!" she called back over their shoulder but did not slow or glance back to see if the merchants and their guards and all the others now following them had listened. It did not matter, apparently. The Gensaiba's only concern at this moment was in reaching that strange shadow marring the ground ahead.

As they neared, they saw that it was indeed a hollow, but not a gentle one. Instead the ground ahead was cracked as if it had been an eggshell shattered against the lip of a table, a long, jagged edge that sheared off and disappeared below. The opposite side was equally sharp, and by the time they slowed a few lengths from this side Kagiri could see that the gap between was more than a horse could leap across, at least as wide as two large buildings end-to-end.

"That explains it," Onyoku Jeizen announced as they dismounted and stepped carefully over to the edge, leaning out to peer down into the depths, past layers or dirt and rock. "Evidently the City of Beasts decided to move underground."

"This is where it stood," Kenin agreed. "Though I doubt the change in elevation was voluntary." His voice was as matter-of-fact as always, but Kagiri did not miss the wry twist to his words. He had learned during their time together that Kenin did have a sharp wit, he merely chose to wield it with a subtlety that slid past many of his fellows' notice.

"We must go and look," Shinen insisted, already studying the chasm for the best entrance point. "There," he suggested, pointing toward a small spire jutting out over the void. "We could anchor the rope around that."

"Why bother?" Kagiri asked, though he did allow them to take the coil of rope from his horse's saddle and stomp over to the spire. "Even if that place was here once, it's long since gone. Anything down there is going to be nothing but dust." *Much like you*, he thought but did not say, even in his mind. For, despite their occasional presumptions, he did like the Gensaiba, and to remind them of their own physical state served no purpose except to be deliberately hurtful. He hoped he was not and never would be someone who acted in such a way.

"You will see," was all Shinen answered, but it was with all the boyish enthusiasm of a child delivering a present to a friend, full of gleeful excitement and hope, and Kagiri found he could not deny the man whatever he and the others had planned.

The way down turned out to be tedious but not overly difficult— the spire had indeed been narrow enough to tie the rope around and sturdy enough to support Kagiri's weight, and Sinchu proved an expert at lowering himself by rope, keeping a length of it looped around one thigh and a coil wrapped about one hand while his feet pressed together around the rope below to slow his descent. The chasm was deep, but they had knotted a second coil to the first; when Kagiri's feet finally touched rock below, there was still enough rope to bunch on the ground between his boots. It was dark down here, of course, the sunlight up above a mere sliver glimpsed only when the rock walls towering up on all sides allowed it, and he fought down the sensation of being buried alive, for the air was stale but breathable and the rope provided reassurance of a way back to light and life and freedom once more. As soon as the Gensaiba were satisfied.

He took a step and something beneath his boot. Crouching down, Kagiri felt about carefully, his fingers brushing up against a long, rough object, bits of it flaking off at his touch. The overall shape of it seemed squared, and it pricked his fingers, biting at his flesh with sharp edges that peeled away in long, fibrous strips. "It's a wooden plank or beam," he stated, closing his hand around it carefully. "Or what's left of one."

"An excellent find," Kibi agreed. She drew the flint and steel from his belt and struck them together, producing a spark atop the object, which obediently caught fire with that particular whoosh of sound only old, dry wood can produce. It was indeed a beam, and they hefted it aloft, its end now burning merrily and shedding a crackling, shifting yellow light upon their surroundings.

"This would be the docks," Setsui commented. "Horohaba bordered on the Tonawa back then, and had a single long pier leading from the water to the city itself." She gestured deeper into the chasm. "Which would be this way."

They walked for a ways, time being difficult to tell down here where the sun sent only the boldest of beams to filter down in broken bursts of light. As they ventured deeper along, the chasm widened, as if it had begun at the river's edge and expanded as it moved inland, until the torch's light could no longer reach the walls and it felt like Kagiri was walking through an empty void, the golden circle of light he carried the only reality in a surrounding haze.

Then his foot bumped against something else, something larger than the bits of wood they had stepped over, and he glance down. Before him was a set of stone steps, still almost intact, and ahead of them ran a long, wide stone causeway made up of tightly fitted hexagonal blocks in alternating shades. Past that he could just make out tall shapes looming to either side.

"Behold," Shinen tried again, with the same enthusiasm as before, "for I give you—Horohaba, the fabled City of Beasts!"

And a beautiful city materialized from the shadows, as if it had been summoned by his words, light seeping into the walls and balconies and roofs, sunlight sparkling down upon the surfaces and awakening gleams of light in response. The whole of it felt as if it had been cast from blown glass, each structure delicately shaded and pleasingly angled, every inch a testament to grace and elegance and charm, yet somehow all seeming natural and organic, almost as if it had grown rather than been built. It was the most beautiful place Kagiri had ever seen, and he felt his breath catch as he gazed about him in wonder.

"Now you see," Shinen told him, the massive man's voice soft for once. "This is the beauty that was Ritakhou."

Ritakhou—Kagiri had never heard that name before, but thanks to the Gensaiba he knew it at once. "Land rich with blessed magic," it meant, and so this empire had been called, back before the Schism. After, it had been renamed Rimbaku, "land made barren from cursed magic," though that meaning had been lost to the ages. Until now.

"You haven't even seen the best part yet!" Shinen was like a little child, dragging Kagiri by the hand to lead him to his own favorites, and Kagiri found himself laughing at the big man's obvious glee and letting himself be directed down the walkway toward the city's far end.

As he walked, he noticed that, from the corner of his eye, the structures he passed were not the same. Only a few shards still remained of these noble towers, jagged edges worn smooth from the years, the rest crumbled to tiny bits that crackled under his steps. The walkway was in better repair, but it bore many cracks from its strange descent, and its surface had faded over the long years until the torch evoked only the occasional sparkle from somewhere beneath the dust.

"How—?" he started to ask, but Sinchu cut him off, the sharp-tongued warrior's voice gentle for once and pitched for Kagiri's thoughts alone.

"He is showing you how it was," he explained quietly. "Through sheer force of will, you are seeing what we saw, long ago. It is our gift to you."

"Thank you," Kagiri replied just as privately. "But why?"

"Because," the dour Gensaiba answered, "you have been troubled since Himsu. We wished to give you joy to ease your mind."

That was oddly touching, that these fierce warriors would worry so over him, and Kagiri determined to honor that offer by unabashedly treating this vision with all the wonder it deserved. That was hardly a chore, and even less so when they reached the city's edge and found a wide walkway running perpendicular to the one upon which they stood, lined with massive cages on the far side, a tall wall rising up behind them to shield the city from that direction.

"It's the Avenue of Beasts," Shinen announced, almost giggling in his excitement, and Kagiri smiled in response. "It's what makes Horohaba so famous!"

They turned and strolled along that avenue, peering into each cage in turn, and through the lens of their memories Kagiri saw wonders he had never even dreamed possible. One held a creature made entirely of flames that put his torch to shame, burning a white-blue at its heart and head and shading to yellows and reds along its extremities, hovering over the ground like a flame flickering on the end of a waxed wick, swaying to and fro with the breeze. In another was something similar to the water dragon they had seen but far broader and with scales of black and red and gold, its eyes alight from within, its massive claws scratching deep furrows in the floor as it paced, wings furling and unfurling from its back in a steady rhythm.

There were strange tree-people, like bamboo stalks but with little black eyes and cleft mouths and fronds for hair. Another cage held a creature shaped like a man but with skin red as rubies and rough as stone and over a hundred eyes blinking from all around its oversized head. In another was a large chicken, a simple, ordinary chicken save for its size, and Kagiri almost laughed to see it there amid all these strange creature—until it bawked and fire shot from its beak. The avenue seemed to stretch on and on, and after a time the displays began to blur in his mind, melding one into the other until he could no longer keep them straight, his entire body awash in wonder.

"I had no idea such things existed," he murmured. "Now or ever. Rimbaku has no such creatures. All our magic is gone, save for the bones."

"Perhaps," Kibi replied. "But what about the Nizukai? You thought that was gone as well."

Kagiri pondered that as they turned and retraced their steps, careful to walk only along the causeways rather than cutting through what were still buildings in his shared vision even if they were merely ruins now. He was still mulling this over, and what it could mean, as they scaled the cliff, clambering back up the rope and into the sunlight. As he reclaimed his horse and turned it back toward the hills where, indeed, the rest of the caravan had stopped to wait, he wondered if perhaps this kingdom was not quite so barren as it seemed.

And that flicker of hope, he realized, was an even greater gift than the wondrous vision the Gensaiba had presented to him.

CHAPTER TWENTY-NINE

Noniki lifted his head from where it had been cradled in his hands and stared up at Seikoku, who had placed herself directly before him, feet apart, arms crossed, a look of grim determination somehow only accentuating her lovely features. "What is it?" he asked with a groan. "More deaths?"

She shook her head and offered him a hand up. "No, but this does directly relate to that. I think you need to see it for yourself."

He allowed her to haul him to his feet, as always impressed and perhaps a little frightened by the strength in those slender limbs. As she guided him through the collection of tents and carts and bedrolls, he was surprised to see that night was falling, the colors all around him already deepening to their evening cast of purples and blues. Had it not just been evening a moment ago? Or was that yesterday? Ever since Isoko's death he had lost track of such things.

Indeed, he had allowed himself to fall apart, he admitted as they walked. Everyone they passed said hello, raised a hand in greeting, and typically approached for a handshake or a pat on the back or a quick embrace, and he was appalled and ashamed to see the relief in their eyes. Did he truly look so awful? Glancing down he saw that there were splotches of dried food on his shirt and pants, and reaching up he discovered that his hair was a greasy mess and his chin was prickly with unshaven whiskers. Yes, evidently he did.

"Why did no one tell me I was a walking disaster?" he asked Seikoku as she led the way, and she glanced back over her shoulder, one eyebrow arcing up.

"We tried," she admitted. "You wouldn't listen." Her lips quirked to match her brow. "If you were still moping tomorrow, Kanai and I had already agreed to toss you into the river."

"Ha!" It felt good to laugh, and Noniki knew then that he would recover from this. He had gone through something similar when he and Kagiri had been separated: guilt at bringing that fate upon his brother, shame for not doing more to save him, grief at what he could only assume had been insanity followed by an awful death. But the monks, and then his strange spiritual journey, had reminded him that his brother would not have wanted him to throw his life away as well, and Noniki knew Isoko and Chisigi and Madam Ushi would have said the same. Bones, that old lady would have been right there with Seikoku, shoving him into the water! And he would have deserved it.

"I'm sorry," he told Seikoku now. "I let it overwhelm me. That won't happen again."

This time the former thief stopped so that she could turn and place a comforting hand on his shoulder. "Don't promise that," she urged. "You don't know what will happen. No one does. And you shouldn't say that, anyway." Her eyes and face were serious as she told him, "It is one of the things that makes you who you are. You feel things deeply. That's a good thing, not a bad one." Then she wrinkled her nose. "But next time, do it while continuing to bathe, eh?"

"I'll try," he told her, laughing again, and the air between them was back to its usual companionable warmth as they continued on. Only a few moments later they reached an old, battered tent that showed signs of frequent wear and repair. "This is Yori's, isn't it?" he asked as she tugged open the flap and ushered him inside.

She nodded but beckoned, and after hesitating a moment more he followed her in.

The tent was small and plain, holding only a bedroll and pillow, a fishing net, a worn leather wallet, and a small vase with a dried flower rising from it. "The wallet," Seikoku said, and reluctantly Noniki lifted it from the bedroll, hefting the simple container. "Look inside."

"Now, I—" he started to protest, but her look—not of outrage or annoyance but of concern and even sorrow—stopped him. She was serious about this. He untied it and flipped it open, peering inside. There were a few small coins, their edges worn smooth from years of handling. A dried, pressed flower similar to the one adorning the vase. A sketch of a young woman, perhaps his dead wife? And a folded square of raw silk. Extracting that last item, Noniki lifted its layers to see seeds and flower petals. The petals were a strikingly vibrant pink at their lower ends, fading to white toward the tips, with a few darker streaks along their length. "And?" he asked, turning to face her, the square still in hand.

"It's called itoyako," Seikoku explained. "Lily of the valley. It's extremely poisonous. Ingesting it causes fevers, sweats, nausea, vomiting, convulsions—and death."

He stared at the innocent-seeming bundle in his hand. "This is what killed them?"

"I believe so, yes." She scowled. "I thought you might want to speak with Yori yourself." She reached down and pulled a slender leather cylinder from within the bedroll. "There is also this. It's a writing case."

Noniki nodded—he had seen Kishin Narai and the other merchants carrying such items. But it was out of place with a poor farmer. Did Yori even know how to write? More questions to ask.

"Do we know where he is?" he glanced toward the flap, trying to see through it to the camp beyond.

"Most likely by the fire," Seikoku guessed. It was evening, and everyone did tend to gather around a single fire to eat as a group. Neither of them spoke as they exited the tent and headed in that direction, Noniki still clutching the flowers and Seikoku carrying the case.

Sure enough, as the fire came into view, its blaze a welcome glow against the deepening night, Noniki picked a shaggy head out from the rest. It was Yori, a bowl of stew clutched in his hands. He was listening to Jitin Kanai, who sat beside him, and to Sukame and Minawa, an older couple who had joined them a few days earlier, as they debated something with vigorous gestures and broad smiles.

As Noniki approached, Yori glanced up and saw him. The farmer nodded in greeting—then his eyes fell to Noniki's hand and the unfolded parcel there.

Suddenly the man was on his feet, his usual lethargy entirely absent as he snarled and charged Noniki, thrusting with a knife that had appeared in his grip as if deposited by the night itself.

Noniki growled back, a childhood of fending off other children causing him to reflexively plant his feet to meet that lunge, both hands moving up to defend himself.

The wind picked up as Yori closed the distance, the gentle breeze sharpening to a fierce, stiff wind—and the fire blazed higher, urged on by that gust, and licked out past its ring of stones, directly into Yori's path. He was moving too quickly to stop and let out a yelp as he passed through the flames, his skin reddening from the contact.

Evidently the knife had also received a touch of fire, for he dropped that as if it had burned him and tried for a punch instead. But Noniki was no stranger to brawling, and blocked the blow, unleashing a fist of his own that sent the farmer sprawling.

Yori was up again an instant later, rolling to his feet in a manner that reminded Noniki of the way Seikoku had moved, that night in the graveyard. Clearly, there was more to the quiet farmer than he had let on.

All around them, others were standing and closing in, voicing questions and concerns. Yori glanced about him, eyes widening before narrowing. Then, apparently making a decision, he turned—and ran, the night swallowing him up as soon as he passed beyond the fire's light and became just one more shadow on the grass.

"What was that all about?" Kanai asked, stepping up beside Noniki. "And what is that?"

It was young Isoro who answered. "Itoyako," she said softly, reaching out and carefully taking the bundle from Noniki. Then she looked to Seikoku. "So your fears were correct. My mother was murdered."

That sent a gasp through the assemblage, followed by a barrage of questions which continued until Noniki held his hand up for quiet. "It appears that Yori was not who he claimed," he explained, struggling to keep his voice calm though his heart was hammering in his chest. "We found these in his tent." He chose not to mention that Seikoku had discovered them first—he doubted many would be happy at the thought of her riffling through all their belongings! "And, as you saw, he attacked me when he saw that we had them."

"He had an acrobat's aishone," Seikoku offered. "The way he rolled to his feet, that takes years of practice." No one needed to be told that there was no reason a farmer would have such relic bones on him.

Minawa had taken the case from Seikoku and opened it. "There are letters here," she reported, her voice thin and reedy but her eyes still sharp. "They are in some sort of cipher, however. I cannot read them."

"Someone sent him to keep watch on you," Kuma suggested. "Like my old overseer came to watch whenever he thought anyone was not working fast enough or hard enough or was taking jobs on the side."

"Watching me?" Noniki shook his head. "Why? I am not harming anyone."

"You are asking questions, and making others do the same," Kanai countered. "There are some who would consider that dangerous." As usual, the potter's words were slow but wise.

"Perhaps," Noniki allowed, pacing before the fire. "But if he were here to watch, why kill Madam Ushi? Chisigi? Isoko? They did nothing wrong!"

It was Seikoku who answered that one. "They followed you," she said. "As we all do." The others murmured agreement. "Perhaps they were afraid at how many were following you now and thought to scare some off. If we began to worry that we might die if we stayed, that might send people away." There was a round of protests, but Noniki knew she was right. Nor would he have blamed anyone for leaving, if it meant staying alive. What good was questioning the Relicant Way if it meant you wound up dead?

But what good was following it if it meant never truly living, he answered himself.

One truth rose from this as well: "They are afraid of us," he agreed slowly, looking around at these, his friends, who had chosen to listen to him and had felt, as he did, that there was a better path than the one this nation currently walked.

"And how did they deal with that fear? Did they try to understand it better? Did they ask what it was we wanted, to see if we might find common ground?" He clenched his fists. "No. They sent an assassin to slip in among us, kill us off one by one, and try to drive us back to the old ways they take such comfort in. Well, if that is how the empire deals with the mere possibility of change, the very idea that someone out there might have a thought as to how to make this life better, then perhaps it is time for a change. A significant one! And since they seem so afraid of what we have to say, perhaps we will march to the capital and force them to listen to us!"

The others cheered, and Noniki basked in the glow of their respect and support as much as he did the heat from the fire, which danced merrily as if it too agreed with this plan. But as he met Seikoku's worried gaze he knew she understood as well as he that it would not be nearly so easy as he had just suggested. Still, he had set himself on this course, and he was determined to see it through—and to protect as best he could all those who chose to travel it alongside him.

That night, Noniki found himself within a strange dream. In it, he walked through a city of glass that, when he turned his head one way, was all shattered and broken, but another way was tall and gleaming and filled with a soft glow of color like a sunrise. The city ended in a high wall, but set just before it was a long, wide road, and between the road and the wall were a series of large cages.

The dream carried him along, drifting him past the cages, and in each he saw wondrous beings such as the demons and imps and spirits and dragons of ancient tales, like the stories he had always begged from ancient Mother Utu, the oldest person in their village, while Kagiri yawned and wandered away to fish or whittle sticks. These beings were even grander than any she had told of, and his heart ached from their beauty.

But another ache rose within him as well, one of sorrow and even outrage. Why were such fantastical creatures trapped in this way? They growled and snarled and whined and raged, they scraped at the floors of their cages and tugged at the bars and rose up in the air to batter the bars up above. Why should they be restrained like this, merely for others' amusement? In many ways, Noniki felt a kinship to them. Were not the powers of the empire determined to cage him and everyone else within the Relicant Way, to keep them enslaved to their aitachi and the need for aishone that only the wealthy controlled? He thought of Ginzai, and how the town owned the relic bones and even a direct relative had to pay for the privilege of accessing an ancestor. How was that just? How was that fair? Like these creatures, he yearned to be free, to rise to the heights of his own potential, not feed of that of someone else.

Noniki struggled to change the course of the dream. He pushed himself forward, against the tug to keep moving, and though it felt like battling a stiff wind he forced himself, one step at a time, to approach the nearest cage. The creatures within looked like slender trees cast as puppets and brought to life, and they turned slowly to regard him as he reached out and grasped the bars. He tugged on them, but they were too solid for him to move.

"I am sorry," he told them, his words sluggish and somehow muted, as if heard through water. "I would free you if I could."

The wind that had pushed against him reversed suddenly and grew in strength, becoming a tempest, and now Noniki clung to the bars to keep from being tossed away like a leaf in a storm. Lightning flashed overhead, thunder rumbled, and with a mighty wrench and a horrendous shriek the winds yanked the bars free— Noniki released his grip and threw himself to the ground just in time to avoid being crushed as the heavy iron went tumbling away, crashing into a building beyond with the sound of a thousand glasses shattering upon a stone floor.

A three-fingered hand, slim and smooth and green as fresh grass, appeared before him. He lifted his head to find the treemen standing there, offering to help him up. And though their mouths were little more than slits in the stalks that were both body and head, he could see that they were smiling at him.

CHAPTER THIRTY

Taisho Daishin fidgeted in his saddle, his thick-fingered hands flexing within their hanketo, his square, bluff-featured face visible below his karute while his menatu still hung open—as commander of the aiashe he was entitled to the full armor of a noble, instead of the basic maikiro and jingaso his soldiers wore. "Are you certain this is the course you wish to take, Your Imperial Majesty?" he asked, and it was a mark of his extreme disquiet that such a man, who had made his career upon his ability to follow orders without question, should gather the courage to voice such a concern to the emperor himself.

Nor could Hibikitsu fault him on that. Yet his voice was steady as he replied, "It is, noble Taisho. Ready your men." He refused to allow even a hint of hesitation in his own voice or demeanor, but held himself steady, back straight, eyes forward, chin up, as the blocky general saluted and wheeled his horse about, turning his back on Birabiro to return to his army.

Behind him, the young emperor heard a horse shuffling its feet, and only many years of training allowed him to avoid cracking a smile. "What is it, Diritan?" he asked instead, his amusement doubling as the Honjofu coughed, clearly embarrassed to have been caught out.

Yet the man did not let that deter him. "I understand your reasoning, sire," he answered instead, "and certainly it is sound. Still..." The rest of his hesitant inquiry, though unspoken, hung in the air between them, heavy as a raincloud and grim as a funeral.

"I know." Hibikitsu pivoted to regard this elite warrior he had come to know and admire and rely upon. "But it is the only way.

What matter my honor, if our empire falls? What matter a handful of lives, if thousands more die? This choice is mine and mine alone, and I will bear the weight of it, but it must be done."

Diritan nodded, as did Nioko beside him. Both Honjofu saluted, then, and the rest of the Bone Warriors followed suit. Hibikitsu acknowledged their loyalty with a nod, then echoed their salute to show the depth of his appreciation.

Then it was time. Turning back around, he stared down the hill at the small village before them. What appeared to be a miniature shooting star rose in the distance, the fire arrow the signal that the aiashe were ready. Hibikitsu sighed and extracted his aishone pouch. Then, after swallowing bones that stuck in his throat nearly as badly as this plan he had conceived, he held out both hands. His umi was placed in one, the long bow's leather grip fitting comfortably against his palm, and a long arrow in the other. The arrow's sharpened metal head had a wad of wine-soaked cloth wrapped around it, and a servant held a candle to that, lighting the entire mass until Hibikitsu held a long, slender torch. Setting this to his bow, he drew back the string and sighted along the arrow's shaft, aiming slightly upward. All around him, the Honjofu matched his motions, until it seemed a row of candles burned and bobbed in the gray pre-dawn light.

Hibikitsu took a deep breath, released it, breathed in again, and committed himself and his nation with a single word: "Fire!"

The arrows launched into the air, arcing upward before reaching their peak and racing down upon the still-slumbering village below. As soon as they were in flight, Hibikitsu handed his umi back off and clapped his heels to Shisi, sending the horse charging down the hill as he drew Kosshiki and held the ancient blade aloft, its chiseled tip pointing the way. "For Rimbaku!" he bellowed, and his warriors echoed his battle cry as they thundered after him.

Yanatai Lai was just beginning to stir when she heard something like rain outside, the hiss and spit of droplets falling fast and hard. The sky had been clear when she had finally gone to bed, however, with no clouds on the horizon, so she was surprised that a storm should rise so suddenly. Then something thunked against the thatched roof of the hut she had chosen to occupy, that dull report echoed elsewhere nearby, and all went silent, save for a sudden whoosh she knew all too well from years of hard campaigning and many hours of struggling to light campfires while on the march.

"Fire!" she shouted, snatching up her deo and settling it in place, not bothering with the straps as she grabbed her nihono and yori-toki and settled her karute on her head. The couple who lived here, Uchimasa and Enomoto, were still abed, and Lai kicked the sturdy frame, jolting the pair awake. "Get up!" she ordered, and they leaped to their feet, both in loose nightshirts of rough hemp worn smooth and thin over the years. "We need to get out of here!" She laid a hand on Enomoto, pulling the frightened woman close, and motioned Uchimasa toward the door. "You first."

He trembled but hurried to obey. They had learned right away that Yanatai Lai, dogenriku of Fyushu, did not like to repeat herself.

She had to admire the Rimbakan emperor's daring, even as the three of them made for the door and the roof crashed down behind them, spreading burning reeds throughout and filling the tiny hut with smoke and flame. She had never thought he would dare risk the villagers this way. Still, it would avail him naught, not while she and her officers could still use them as human shields. Spotting Aioi Kazuko emerging from a hut nearby, Lai motioned him over. "Send word to our warriors," she ordered. "Attack at once." The young issa saluted and took off at a run, his slender features composed and focused. He was a good officer and would go far in the service of the empress.

Assuming he survived the night.

Hibikitsu and his Honjofu swept into the village, blades raised high. All around them, Birabiro burned, brightening the sky with dozens of blazes, and the air was warm and smoky and itched at his throat. People were spilling from the burning huts, stumbling out as their homes ignited, and mixed among the simple, innocent villagers were Fyushan officers, but in the dimness before dawn and the shadows of so many fires and the confusion and chaos it was difficult to distinguish one from another.

Steeling himself, Hibikitsu trampled the first person to cross his path. Kosshiki lashed out and beheaded another. He had a yanoi lashed to his horse's side, its handle shortened for throwing, and he tugged that free of its sheath and hurled it, impaling both a woman and the man huddling behind her. All around him, his warriors did the same, cutting down anyone not on horseback. That was the only criterion for safety here, because all of them were mounted and their scouts had already secured the Fyushans' horses before the attack. Therefore, anyone on foot was considered fair game.

Even those who were clearly unarmed.

A man stepped in front of him, and Hibikitsu yanked on Shisi's reins, causing the horse to rear. One flailing hoof struck the man in the chest, another in the temple, and he reeled away, collapsing in a heap upon the ground. Just behind him were two women, the first one stocky and middle-aged, with long graying hair coming loose from her braid. But behind her, one arm clamped across her neck and upper chest, was a taller, leaner woman with short dark hair all but hidden beneath an unfastened emerald-green karute.

Yanatai Lai.

Hibikitsu leveled his blade at the enemy field marshal. "Release her and face me, one warrior to another," he demanded, tapping Shisi's sides to keep the horse dancing in place.

Lai let loose a deep, grim laugh. "And let you cut me down as well?" she replied. "I think not." Her eyes flicked to the man who had fallen before them, and to the other bodies nearby. "I am impressed," she admitted slowly. "I did not think you had this in you."

"As you said, this is war," he replied with a sharp nod. "We do what we must."

"Perhaps. But how far will you go?" Lai asked. She nudged the woman she held, who let out a whimper. "Have you met Enomoto, here? That is her husband Uchimasa your horse just trampled. They have a son, Mizono—he and his wife live in Chinbiro with their daughter Mori. She turns five in a week's time. Will you deprive her of her grandmother, so close to that happy occasion?"

Hibikitsu felt his eyes narrow. He knew exactly what this woman was trying to do and felt a sudden surge of hatred for her. But for now his gaze went to the frightened woman she was holding hostage. "Greetings, Enomoto," he told her now, doing his best to forget the battle raging about him for one instant and gentle his voice to a tone more suited to conversation. "I am Hibikitsu, your emperor. And I salute you."

Then he drove Kosshiki through her chest, piercing her heart. The old woman died instantly, her face barely registering her shock before her eyes glazed and her features went slack. The sword's tip clanged against Lai's deo with enough force to make her take a step back as her former shield dropped, leaving her exposed. She raised her own blade, drawing her yori-toki with her other hand, but Hibikitsu urged Shisi forward and the horse slammed his chest into the Fyushan commander, causing her to stumble and drop the dagger. Hibikitsu swung in a downward arc and she barely raised her sword in time to block the blow. Not giving her a second to recover, he kicked out with one foot, catching her in the ribs, and as she staggered he struck again, this time looping his arm around to come at her from the opposite side. She was not able to reverse her own blade in time, and Kosshiki's edge caught her full in the throat, where her hastily set helmet's sides had not fallen correctly, leaving only bare flesh to take the blow. The sword sliced through flesh and bone as if through rice paper, and Yanatai Lai, supreme commander of the armies of Fyushu, could not even utter a final curse upon her foes, her breath and words emerging only as gurgles of blood as her head toppled from her shoulders and rolled away while her body slumped in a growing pool of its own blood.

All around him, the battle was beginning to slow as Honjofu

rode down the last of those still standing. Hibikitsu pulled a cloth from his sash and wiped Kosshiki before sheathing it, then leaned against Shisi's saddlehorn and peered about. The fires were dwindling as well, having consumed every bit of fuel available, and their diminishing flames paled against the sunrise just starting to lighten the sky overhead. By the time Diritan and Nioko settled in on other side of him, Hibikitsu could clearly see the ruins they had made of this village and the slaughter they had inflicted upon its people.

"Did we find Ito Oicha and Aioi Kazuko?" he asked. Those were the only two other Fyushans he knew by name, thanks to Lai's having brought them to Chinbiro with her.

"Hai, your Majesty," Nioko replied. She bore streaks of soot and blood upon her face and armor, and Hibikitsu suspected he had been similarly marked. "Both have been dispatched. Kazuko was attempting to reach the horses."

That brought a bitter smile to the young emperor's face. No doubt Lai had realized what was happening once the arrows struck and had sent the commander to launch a counterattack. Instead the rest of the Fyushan army would still be awaiting orders—and Daishin's aiashe would fall upon them and catch them unawares. Their orders were to kill any Fyushan commanders they found but to accept surrender from the common soldiers.

"We found two others with the mark of taisho," Diritan offered. "A force this size, I think it is safe to say those were all their leaders." There was nothing in his tone, no disrespect or disappointment or disgust, but he kept his gaze resolutely upon the emperor himself, staring past the carnage all about them.

Hibikitsu understood that but refused to do the same. Instead he forced himself to look at every one of the dead. He would learn their names as well. He owed them that. "Gather Lai and the rest," he ordered wearily. "We will deliver her remains and her effects back to the Fyushan Empress, with our compliments—and our warning. Any who attempt to breach our borders again will suffer the same fate."

Both Honjofu nodded, though he could see that he had

surprised them a second time. It was customary to claim the bones of the dead if they had been proficient warriors, and to take their swords, helms, and other gear as trophies. Hibikitsu wanted no part of that. "Send word to Chinbiro and the other villages nearby," he continued. "We will require a roll of the deceased. Once we separate our own from the Fyushans, any surviving kin will be permitted to claim their dead." The warriors' eyes widened at that, for again he was deviating from custom. In many parts of Rimbaku the government would take possession of any bones and dole them out or sell them as it saw fit. But he would not do that here. These people's families deserved to have them back, if they so desired.

Finally, he added, "Have Lady Zeryai gather the leaders of each village. I will address them all together." It was not a conversation he was looking forward to, but it was one he would not allow himself to shirk from, just as he refused to turn away from the sight of these innocents he had ordered killed. As Lai herself had said, he would take responsibility for each and every death that occurred under his command, as the price for protecting the rest of his people. If he wished to be worthy of remaining their emperor, he could do no less.

The following day, he met with those village leaders and elders. Lady Zeryai was also present, as were Taisho Daishin and several of the Honjofu. Hibikitsu saw them in the governor's audience chambers, where chairs had been set out for each of them. He himself stood before them, hands clasped behind his back—he had set aside his armor in favor of crimson robes decorated with the higeibara shaped in ruby and edged in gold thread.

"You have no doubt heard by now what occurred in Birabiro," he began, his voice clear and firm and carrying throughout the room, even to the rafters high above. "And you have perhaps been told that the people there were slaughtered by the Fyushans in an attempt to demoralize us." He paused before forcing himself to continue. "This is not so." A murmur rippled through those assembled. "The Fyushans did invade Birabiro, and they did occupy that village, taking its residents hostage. But they did not kill them. Instead, they hid behind them, trusting that we would not dare endanger our own citizens to get at them." He stopped and faced these people full on. "I personally led our forces into Birabiro. I personally gave the order to kill everyone in sight, to prevent the Fyushans from gaining a foothold here and leading their armies deeper into our lands. I and I alone am responsible for the deaths of your friends and neighbors and loved ones." He bowed his head. "And I beg your forgiveness for that."

Then he glanced up and met the collective gaze of his audience. "But I did this to protect our nation, all of you and your families and every other family, and I do not regret that. It was a necessity, so while I will grieve for the dead of Birabiro to the end of my days, their deaths saved countless others, and that is a price I consider acceptable."

Hibikitsu held out a hand, and Diritan set a single sheet of paper in it. "These are the dead of Birabiro," the emperor announced, "and their names will be entered into the rolls of the heroes of Rimbaku, for their unwitting sacrifice has saved our nation. I will name each of them in my prayers every night for the rest of my life, on my honor and that of the First Emperor." He paused to wipe at his eyes, dashing away the tears that had begun to form there, and then began:

"Uchimasa and Enomoto. Toda and Hino. Sakuri. Ogura. Nijo…"

That night, their last before beginning the trek back across Korito and Tabichi to the shore, where they could then set sail for Awaihinshi, Hibikitsu had difficulty sleeping. On the one hand, he felt elation. The Fyushan armies had indeed surrendered and had retreated in disgrace. Not a single soldier above the rank of chuisu remained, and even of the lieutenants there were only three left to shepherd thousands of men back over the mountains. The common soldiers had been petrified at the news that their great dogenriku had been killed; as he'd watched them march away Hibikitsu had seen them slumped and despondent and had known that they had truly broken Fyushu's spirit as well as its military structure.

There was another reason for joy, though it was more personal. For the decision to attack the village had not come from any ancestor. It had been Hibikitsu's alone. True, he had swallowed aishone before the fight, and his skill with umi and nihono could be attributed to that, but otherwise this victory was due to his own decisions, his own actions, his own abilities. Was this what it meant to rely upon yourself rather than the relic bones? To know that anything you did, good or bad, success or failure, was yours and yours alone?

The consequences were also his, however, and those were what muted his satisfaction, turning it to ash in his mouth. Those villagers had died because of him. True, it had been the logical thing to do, killing a few dozen to save thousands upon thousands. But they had been innocents and they had been under his protection. Instead he had not only let them die, he had cut them down himself. That might make him a more effective ruler—certainly Yanatai Lai would have agreed—but he could not help but feel that it made him a lesser man as well.

When he did finally succumb to slumber, Hibikitsu thought he would dream about Birabiro, and see the faces of those he had killed. Instead he dreamt of strange and wondrous creatures trapped in cages along a long road beside a strange city. He did not know what that meant, but he thanked the First Emperor for sparing him the sight of the recent dead, at least for that one night. He knew he would see them again soon enough.

CHAPTER THIRTY-ONE

"**H**old the line!" Maniko Kohori bellowed, raising her umi over her head with one hand, her bundle of arrows with the other, and banging them together. Beside her, Itamon and Reizei and the rest of her Honteno followed suit, creating a fearsome din that filled the wide hall with sound from carved panel wall to carved panel wall, from polished tile floor to soaring gilded rafters, and from the massive double doors at their back all the way to the palace's arched entryway some two hundred paces ahead, washing over the small army packed in between so tightly the warriors assembled there could barely raise their arms to adjust the angle of their spears. It was a chaotic cluster, filled with a riot of colors and patterns, but all of the men and women gathered there had two things in common: their armor was all edged in crimson, denoting their leaders' pretensions to the throne, and they were all eyeing the Honteno with hatred, contempt, and rage.

There would be no negotiating here. These soldiers were out for blood.

Even as she thought that, however, a man bulled his way to the front, shoving warriors aside to clear a path. Etsuya Kenshin still looked like a born warrior, with his solid frame and squared jaw, until one noticed that his hair was too neat, his beard too carefully plaited, and his crimson-hued, thundercloud-emblazoned armor too pristine. He was a showpiece who had never seen true battle but he certainly carried himself like a warrior as he stopped before the assembled forces and glared at Kohori across the hundred paces separating them.

"It does not have to end like this," he called, his voice clear and firm. "You are a noble warrior, Maniko Kohori, and we could make good use of your talents. All we require is your loyalty and that you accept this first command: stand aside."

"I answer to the emperor," she replied, her own words ringing. "He has commanded me to bar all who seek entry to his throne room, and so I will do."

"Then you are a fool," another voice, sharp as a knife, warned, and Amani Denbi joined Kenshin at the edge of their assembled forces. It seemed that the two had formed an alliance after all. "And you are a spendthrift, to waste the lives of your Honteno in such a way. Even if you are too proud to stand down, at least allow them to walk away from this, while they still can."

Kohori glanced at Itamon on one side of her, and Reizei on the other, her two chuisu, for the Honteno lacked the numbers to need more than a Lord Commander and two lieutenants. Itamon responded first, clanging bow and arrows overhead again and shouting, "Maniko! Maniko!" Reizei was right behind, her longer arms raising her weapons even higher, her voice higher as well but just as firm, and all the rest of the household guard joined in. Every last one of them were here now, having assembled in haste when they received word that the warriors were on the march. There would be no shift changes, no relief, and no attempt to spring a trap on these massed warriors. Either they would win out against terrible odds or they would fall but they would do so as a single unit, and Kohori hoped they all understood just how much that meant to her.

"So be it," Denbi replied, and turned away, signaling the end to discussion. A warrior quickly stepped forward, holding a shield to protect his mistress as the Rojiri retreated back behind her wall of flesh and armor and weapons. Kenshin glared a moment longer before following her, also under cover. Then there were only two armed forces facing one another across a narrow space, tense and ready as dogs straining against the leash, poised for the signal to attack.

Someone near the back—perhaps Kenshin himself—roared, and that was all it took. It was as if a dam had broken and the warriors were the water, suddenly charging forward in a single wave of limbs and steel. Then Kohori stopped thinking as she lowered her bow, set an arrow to the string and released, driving the long shaft clean through the first man in the pack. He fell at once and was trampled by his fellows, as were the next two she shot. By the time she had exhausted her arrows the hallway was littered with corpses, and the gap had shrunk to half. Dropping the bow, Kohori grabbed her yanoi from where she had leaned it against the door and braced herself.

In another moment, the warriors were upon them, and she could not think, could barely see or breathe, as she stabbed and bashed and blocked and kicked, driving back anyone who came too close.

After what seemed an eternity of battle, the first wave fell back to nurse their wounds. Kohori leaned on her spear and took stock. She had started this engagement with twenty Honteno. Three crimson-clad bodies now lay on the ground before the throne room doors, and three more leaned against those same barriers, clutching at wounds. That left her with fourteen. True, they had all acquitted themselves well, leaving at least a score of foes dead or dying on the floor, but the Rojiri could call for reinforcements. She could not.

Still, there was no other option here but to fight as long as was necessary, until they had won or were dead or help arrived in some form or another.

She only hoped that either the first or third option happened soon, because otherwise the middle was inevitable.

House Amani and House Etsuya attacked twice more, and both times the Honteno rebuffed them, though not without injury and loss. Still, there was something to be said for fighting with your back to a wall. You did not have to worry about anyone striking from behind, or about the question of whether to retreat. Too, their foes' numbers worked against them in such close quarters, making it difficult for them to strike effectively, while all Kohori had to do was stab with her spear and she was almost certain to hit someone. Nonetheless, it was with some relief that she saw the warriors retreat a third time and then back away farther, setting guards at the hall's end while the rest abandoned the building. A few moments later a group of men and women appeared, unarmed and clad in only rough pants and shirts and sandals.

"We are here for the dead," one of them, a stout older woman with a thick gray braid, announced, bowing low. Kohori nodded wearily and watched as the servants approached and began the unpleasant task of grabbing each corpse under the arms and dragging the body, heavy with armor and slick with blood, back down the hall toward the door. By the time they had finished there was a swirl of crimson coating large swathes of the floor like some abstract image of a flower shedding its petals amidst a monsoon, and only the Honteno, living and dead, remained.

"They will return," Itamon commented, setting his spear aside to wrap a bandage around his upper arm, where a sword stroke had caught him just below his armor. "On the morrow, fresh and rested." Reizei nodded agreement. She alone among the Honteno had held back from emptying her quiver, setting aside two arrows in case anyone should attempt to shoot them down from the front entrance. As perhaps the finest archer in the guard, it was a wise move, and Kohori reminded herself to compliment her lieutenant on such an astute tactical decision—provided they both survived.

"They will," Kohori agreed. "We'll rotate a watch and do our best to sleep as well." She turned to smile at her guards. "Well done, one and all. They thought to brush aside, but now they see that the Honteno are not to be trifled with." Her warriors raised a ragged cheer at that, but she knew what they were thinking. Honor and loyalty were all well and good, but they had only whatever water and rations were at their belts, and it would be cramped and uncomfortable sleeping against the doorframe and the walls.

They would make do, however. And the next night, and the night after that, if necessary.

As long as it took.

The next day, Kohori woke to the sound of heavy footsteps approaching. She had fallen asleep sitting with her legs straight out in front of her and now drew them in and levered herself up, snatching up her spear as she rose. Sure enough, warriors were collecting along the hall again. She saw the blue and gray of the Etsuya thundercloud, and mingled with it the gold swallow of House Ieyuki. But where was Amani's silver star and moon? Or the black bear of House Sunao and the emerald wave of House Watane? All three had been present yesterday. Something must have changed.

"You seem to have lost some friends along the way," she called out, and could tell by Kenshin's face that her barb had struck true, for his expression matched the symbol of his house. "Has there been a falling out? Pity." Something else occurred to her, and she could not hold back a bark of laughter. "They removed the bodies of their warriors last night," she stated aloud. "Which means there is no longer any proof that your fellow councilors were engaged in the same treasonous actions you are here to continue." She set her spear and grinned at the Rojiri. "That leaves only you to face me. If you still feel this contest is one you can win."

"Oh, we will win," the councilor snarled at her, hefting his nihono. "I will personally remove your head. Perhaps I'll pack it in a fine chest and send it off to Hibikitsu, to show him what happens to those who cling to foolish hopes."

A noise rose from somewhere behind him, escalating rapidly. It seemed to originate from around the corner, down the corridor leading this way. Ieyuki Nagao stepped up and whispered something to Kenshin, who nodded sharply. Then the other Rojiri quickly moved away, taking his warriors with him. They vanished around that same corner, and a moment later Kohori heard the unmistakable clang of sword against sword.

"It seems your attention is divided," she taunted Kenshin. "And so are your forces." All around her, her Honteno raised their weapons, every one of them ready. "Now it is down to just your men and mine. Shall we see whose are better?"

The stocky Rojiri did not reply with words, but instead charged forward, an angry bellow like the grunt of a wild boar escaping his lips. And so the battle was joined once more.

CHAPTER THIRTY-TWO

Fujibuki Haro, Lord Commander of the Honjofu, marched into Aihiri with his Bone Warriors arrayed at his back. They had sailed up the Edishu and disembarked on the royal docks just outside the city, a smaller pier past the larger ones intended for public use. From there they had taken the imperial gates through the walls—normally traveling from one tier of the city was circuitous, as the main gates were staggered around the circle specifically to prevent an invading force from marching through, but the smaller imperial gates allowed a direct path up through the city's hindquarters, all the way from the outer walls to the imperial compound that crowned the whole. It was heavily guarded and well secured, of course, but the Haro had the authority to demand passage in times of need. And judging by Kohori's message, this was one such time.

As they entered the compound he could hear fighting coming from within the palace itself. "We are here to give aid to the Honteno," he announced to his warriors, pulling his aishone pouch free and drawing his sword with his other hand. "All others are suspect. Proceed with caution but do not kill unless ordered or to defend yourself." All around him, his Honjofu were downing aishone, and he quickly did the same, feeling his fears melt away to be replaced by confidence and skill. "Onward!"

They had just reached the palace doors when a small force burst from it and spilled toward him. Haro quickly took up a defensive posture, sword clasped in both hands before him, but a shout sounded from behind the approaching warriors and the new arrivals skidded to a halt some twenty feet away. Then they parted—to reveal a familiar white-haired figure in outer robes of purple and inner ones of blue and silver.

"Haro! Thank the First Emperor!" Amani Denbi rushed forward, and for an instant Haro thought the fierce old woman might hug him, but she stopped just in time and composed herself, clenching her elegant if wizened hands in seeming agitation. "It's Kenshin and Nagao, they've gone mad! Tadazi, Yatahei, and I came to the Honteno's aid, but Kohori and her guards are pinned against the throne room doors and we cannot reach them!"

If it had been anyone else, Haro might have believed this. But he knew the senior Rojiri far too well to fall for her falsehoods. That, and his eyes had noted the crimson tips of her own troops' armor.

Nonetheless, he had his part to play. "The emperor thanks you for your aid, noble Rojiri," he stated, bowing to her. "My Honjofu will take it from here."

"Of course." Denbi motioned her men to stand aside and they did so, carrying one of their own who hung limp between two warriors, an arrow jutting from his eye socket, and backing away as Haro led his warriors into the palace. There, just before the throne room doors, he found Etsuya Kenshin and his warriors being barred entry by Maniko Kohori and a dozen Honteno. All of them bore cuts and slashes and scrapes, and one was slumped against the door with an arrow through her belly, but the head of the household guard still presented a formidable figure with her crimson armor and her long, glittering yanoi. She raised that weapon in salute when she spied Haro, and he nodded in return. They might not always see eye to eye, but he did respect his fellow Taikoro. And they were both loyal to the emperor.

Kenshin glanced back to see what had distracted his foe, and the councilor's eyes widened upon seeing the Honjofu there. His warriors were heavily outnumbered and looked to be already weary and wounded, whereas Haro's forces were still fresh and spoiling for a fight. A wiser man would have surrendered and accepted any punishment in order to survive another day, but Kenshin was too stubborn to know when to quit. Instead he howled in rage and threw himself toward Kohori, clearly hoping to take her with him if he had to fall.

Haro nodded to one of his warriors, an eagle-eyed archer named Itami Kane. She already had her bow out and ready, and an instant later the air rippled past Haro as an arrow sprouted from Kenshin's left leg, passing clean through armor and flesh. The Rojiri stumbled forward and, howling in pain, dropped to one knee, the arrow's tip poking through his enameled suneoto.

Kohori stepped forward, spear up and murder in her eye, but Haro glided forward as well, and he had not been fighting nonstop for hours or more. Kenshin raised his nihono but his strength was failing and it was a simple matter to knock the blade aside, sending it clattering to the floor. "For the crime of treason against our emperor," Haro intoned, his sword rising to catch the light seeping in through the latticed windows high up along the hall, "you are hereby sentenced to death, Etsuya Kenshin!" He brought the blade down, swift and hard, and the councilor's head tumbled to the ground, rolling to a stop against one of the side walls.

The Honteno's commander glared at Haro, but when he met her gaze she nodded after only a moment's pause. That was one of the things he had always appreciated about Kohori, that she was an eminently practical woman. Yes, he had just claimed credit for defeating the attempted coup and executing its leader. But he had also spared her and she knew it. Her house was too minor for her to risk killing someone of Kenshin's status without potential repercussions. They did not even dwell in Atsani but another level down in Motohiri with the merchants. The Fujibuki, however, were one of the oldest and highest houses in Rimbaku, with a stately home in Atsani a stone's throw from Aihiri itself. As the scion of that house, as well as the Taikoro of the Honjofu, Haro could carry out such a sentence against even Denbi herself and suffer no ill consequences.

Not that he would be able to lay any such accusations against the lead Rojiri. She was far too clever for that. No doubt she'd had spies watching the walls, and they had seen him sail up the Edishu. Hence the display of loyal support.

Well, regardless of how it had begun, the attempted overthrow was now at an end. Haro stepped over to Kohori, careful to place his feet carefully, for the tiles here were awash in blood, and offered her the dipped head of an equal. "Your loyalty and prowess do you credit, as always, noble Taikoro Maniko," he told her. "The emperor will be well pleased with you."

"Thank you, Taikoro Fujibuki," she replied, nodding back. "I am grateful you answered my call for aid." Her gaze told him she knew exactly what she was saying and Haro hoped he would have the good grace to not take *too* much pleasure in extracting every last drop of benefit he could from that public acknowledgement of debt.

He knew himself well enough to know that he would not be able to match that hope.

It was late the following day, and Haro was in his office, sitting back and sipping tea. The hall before the throne room was being scoured clean, the dead returned to their respective houses, and his Honjofu were providing support for the Honteno, who had ultimately lost almost half their number. Ieyuki Nagao had surrendered and pleaded for mercy—he was being held until the emperor's return, for Hibikitsu himself to decide what to do with the traitor. And Denbi, Tadazi, and Yatahei were all pretending to be the perfect loyal councilors, at least now that the Bone Warriors had returned with enough force to put down any other attempted insurrections. Haro was well pleased with how everything had turned out and was just pondering what form his emperor's gratitude might ultimately take when his reveries were interrupted by a knock upon his study's door.

"Enter," he called, knowing his warriors would have questioned and disarmed anyone approaching. The man who slid the door open was not one of his but rather a guard or fighter of some sort, garbed in a simple chain shirt and a studded leather cap.

"Begging your pardon, lord," the man said, stepping forward hesitantly. "My name is Ijichi. I'm a caravan guard. And I—there's something I think you need to see."

"Oh? What is that?" Haro studied this stranger. He was of average height and build, and his weathered skin spoke to many long hours outdoors. His armor looked well-worn, and no doubt he had left a club or mace or even a sword with the Honjofu outside.

"It's—well, you have to see it to believe it," the guard insisted. "I'm sorry, I didn't know who else to tell. I think it's dangerous, very dangerous, maybe to everyone in Awaihinshi."

That piqued Haro's interest. What could pose a danger to the entire city? Reluctantly he set his teacup aside and rose to his feet, retrieving his nihono from its stand in the corner. "All right," he stated. "Show me this dangerous thing."

"Thank you, sir!" The guard bowed so low he nearly toppled over. "It's this way!" He rushed back out, and Haro had to quicken his stride to catch up. The man was already accepting a worn cho-koto back from the men stationed outside the building when Haro joined him. Both of them started to fall into step beside him, but he motioned them back. If whatever this man had found truly was dangerous, he would send for help. In the meantime, it pleased him to attend to the matter himself.

"We just got in," the man—Ijichi—was explaining as he led the way through Aihiri toward one of the side gates out of the compound. "And that's when I saw it. I'm not really sure what it is, which is why I knew I needed to find someone proper to figure it out. Someone like you."

They were nearly to the gate, which lay in the shadow of the compound's walls, when Ijichi stopped short. "What was that?" he demanded, glancing off to the side, where tall, well-pruned hedges lined the path. "Over there!" and he leaped forward, disappearing into the darkness beyond the path's swaying lanterns on their long, arcing metal supports.

"Wait!" Haro shouted, then, with a curse, he charged after the man. A single long step carried him from the well-lit path to utter darkness, and in another that dark had closed in around him, the lanterns seeming like a distant oasis of light in a deep abyss. A sudden chill shot through him, and he drew his sword, fumbling for his pouch—

—and a hand clamped down on his wrist, preventing him from pulling the aishone out of his collar. A hand black as pitch and somehow smoky along its edges, which bled off into the shadows all about.

"Bones!" Haro raised his sword, but without the aishone his grip was clumsy and the blade was knocked aside with such force it fell from his numbed hand. Then an inky dagger rose up, its long, sharp blade a silhouette cut from the night. It sliced downward, seeming to cleave the air itself, and Haro felt his neck go numb even before he realized he had been cut. He reached up to grasp at the wound, feeling the blood pouring forth but unable to feel the gash itself. Feeling was rapidly fleeing his hands and feet, the lack of sensation traveling quickly up his limbs and into his chest and then his head.

His last thought was that, against all reason, he wished Misataki Shizumi had been here. Woman and commoner she might be, a stain upon the honor of the Honjofu, but he had no doubt she could have stopped the shadowy terror that had just claimed his life and even now was reaching with long taloned fingers of pure dark, groping hungrily for his eyes.

CHAPTER THIRTY-THREE

Misataki Shizumi growled low in her throat as she ran, naritaba slung over her shoulder, long metal shaft leading the way forward and sheathed blade jutting out behind her. Why would these bone-blinded people not move out of the way?

She counted herself lucky yet again to have Geniji and Akino in her unit, for the two of them were at the forefront as the bantao raced through Awaihinshi, Geniji clearing a path with a loud voice and broad shoulders and Akino darting around her to shove aside obstacles, including people who stopped to stare at the Honjofu charging through them. Was it not clear from their pace and their close-lipped glares that they were in an ash-burnt hurry?

It had taken a full day of riding before they had spotted a boat gliding along the Tonawa. The boat's master had done his best to ignore their shouts and cries and gestures, but once Isano had put an arrow quivering into the mast an inch above the man's head he had remembered both loyalty and manners and quickly put ashore. Then it was a simple matter to have him take them to Awaihinshi as quickly as the wind would fill his sails. They had put in at the navy's dock, and fortunately the guards stationed there had recognized Shizumi, for they had opened the gate at once. "Your Taikoro has beaten you home," one of them had laughed as she shoved past. "What, did you stop for tea along the way?" She'd had no time to stop and teach him respect but had made a note to return and deal with that later. She was a gunso of the Honjofu and expected to be treated accordingly.

Now, however, all she wanted was to reach Aihiri as quickly as possible. Haro and the rest could have had as much as two days' head start, and she shuddered to think how her command-ing officer might have handled the situation here during that time.

Thus it was with utter shock that she and her unit burst through the final gate into the Imperial compound—and found their fellow Honjofu drilling upon the lawn before the palace. But Shizumi was sure she had fallen asleep on her feet somehow and was merely dreaming when she saw none other than Fujibuki Haro himself leading the exercises!

His form was decent—not exceptional, but certainly compe-tent—yet Shizumi knew her commander would never waste pre-cious aishone for something as commonplace as practice. Had he not chided her on such excesses often enough? There was no mis-taking, however, that either he had squandered aishone for this purpose or he had finally learned the rudiments of swordsman-ship and martial combat.

A ripple of sound rose through the warriors as they spotted Shizumi and her team off to the side. When the noise reached Haro's ears he paused and glanced over. For an instant his eyes narrowed. Then he was beckoning one of his sergeants forward to take over and sheathing his nihono as he strode toward them.

"Misataki Shizumi," Haro called out as he approached. "Wel-come home!"

"Thank you, Taikoro," she replied, settling her naritaba into the crook of her arm so that she could bow and salute. "I apolo-gize for arriving too late to assist you, but it appears you have everything well in hand." Certainly there were no signs nor sounds of fighting, and the other Honjofu all seemed relaxed, as did Haro himself.

"Quite all right," he stated, waving off her concerns. He stee-pled his fingers before him. "Tell me, did you apprehend that man, the bandit-killer of Nariyari?" His tone and demeanor seemed genuinely curious rather than disdainful or dismissive, which was unusual for him.

"I did not, sir," she answered honestly, deciding as usual not to hide behind pretty words. "In truth, I felt we would be more useful here with you, so we hurried back. Besides, at last report the man and his followers were headed in this direction, and I prefer to be waiting for him rather than running after, desperately attempting to catch up."

She waited, holding her breath, as her superior considered this. She had disobeyed a direct order, and he would be well within his rights to demote her or even cast her out of the Honjofu altogether. Especially since it appeared she had done so for nothing. There was no battle here needing her skills, no enemy holding off the other Honjofu until she could arrive and settle the matter. She could have continued on her fool's quest and Awaihinshi would never have noticed her absence.

Haro studied her, his dark eyes serious—and then he smiled. "Fair enough," he stated, sending an almost palpable flush of relief through Shizumi. "Your loyalty and dedication are to be commended, as always, and though I did not need you to handle this matter, I am grateful that you raced here in case I did. If, as you say, this man is approaching, I agree that it is far better to be here to welcome him, rather than giving him the high ground advantage."

Shizumi bowed again, more deeply than before, as gratitude threatened to leave her knees too weak to support her. "Thank you, Taikoro," she said, and meant it. "I live to serve the Honjofu and the Empire."

"As do we all," he agreed, nodding to acknowledge her show of respect. "You may go rest and refresh yourself, good gunso. We will speak again when you are ready. There is still a great deal to do to protect our city and our nation."

She saluted once more as Haro turned away and could not help noticing that he even bore his sword at the correct height and angle now. What had happened, during the mad dash back here and whatever fighting had followed, that had finally transformed her lord commander from a pretentious noble to a seasoned warrior?

Whatever it was, she thanked the First Emperor. Perhaps now she finally had a superior she could respect, and one who would grant her a modicum of respect in return.

An hour or so later, Shizumi stepped out of the palace, into the practice yards, and spied a lone figure practicing with nihono, her steps light and graceful as she moved across the fine gravel. For a moment, she paused, leaning against a column to watch Maniko Kohori go through her paces. Though the tall Honteno commander had at least a decade on Shizumi her motions were still smooth and swift, her handling of the blade precise and sure, every action perfectly poised. She was a skilled warrior, and age had barely begun to slow her down yet had already seasoned her with years of knowledge and expertise.

"You are welcome to join me, if you wish," Kohori called out, not turning her head, and Shizumi smiled. Of course the other woman had noted her presence. She would have, had their situations been reversed. Since she had been spotted, she hopped down from the low plank walkway onto the yard and circled around until the Honteno could see her easily.

"Thank you, Taikoro," Shizumi replied, saluting. "I would be honored."

The other woman halted her exercises to return the salute, a smile adding lines to her already worn but still handsome face. "The honor is mine, Misataki Shizumi," she countered. "It is a privilege to practice alongside the finest sword in all Rimbaku." She must have made a face at that, for Kohori laughed. "Not fond of that title?" the older woman teased. "I'd have thought you'd be pleased. It's a difficult legend to obtain, and even moreso for one of our sex."

"True, and I am glad to be acknowledged as skilled," Shizumi agreed, dropping into an easy cross-legged position on the gravel, angling her sword handle down so the scabbard did not scrape on the ground. "I do not know that I am the best, however." She dipped her head. "You are extremely talented as well."

Kohori dropped to the ground across from her, pulling her empty scabbard from her sash as she did and sheathing her blade before resting it across her lap. "Perhaps, but from what I have seen, you are better. And you will only improve with age." She smiled, one woman warrior to another, confiding secrets in an otherwise empty practice yard amid the late afternoon shade. "That is what men do not understand. They rely upon strength, which wanes with the years. We prefer speed and skill, and the one can remain steady far longer, while the other continues to grow."

Shizumi nodded. Not for the first time, she wondered if she should have chosen the Honteno instead of the Honjofu. Certainly she and Kohori seemed kindred spirits, and she had always admired the older woman for her skill, her poise, and the firm but kind way she managed the household guard. What had stopped her was simply the difference in missions. The Honteno were bound to Aihiri, maintaining the safety of the imperial compound and of the emperor. They never left this top level of the city except when off shift, and even then they rarely ventured below Atsani. The Honjofu roamed the land, going wherever they were sent, battling whomever posed a threat to the nation too great for the regular army to handle. And that freedom, that variety, was what Shizumi craved.

Still, if she could have had the Honjofu but with Kohori commanding, she would have considered it the best of all possible worlds.

She opened her mouth, about to say something, but was cut short by the sharp blare of a horn blowing nearby. The Honteno's leader was on her feet in an instant, and Shizumi scrambled to do likewise. "That's the alarm!" Kohori explained, already bolting for the practice yard's front entrance. "Someone has breached the compound!"

She ran out, Shizumi right behind her, and together the two women raced out of the palace and onto the same grounds where the Honjofu had been exercising earlier. Now a single pair of guards stood near the bushes planted along the path to the main gate. As they neared, Shizumi was surprised to see that one wore the full crimson of the Honteno but the other had the black of the Honjofu. Still, she had heard from the others that the household guard had lost more than half their number turning back attacks from soldiers of the two traitorous Rojiri. Clearly Haro had loaned Kohori some of his warriors until she could recruit replacements of her own.

"What is wrong?" the Taikoro was demanding before she had even slowed to a stop, eyes darting between the two guards and then scanning their surroundings. "Why did you sound the alarm?"

The Honteno, a tall, slender man Shizumi thought looked vaguely familiar from around the compound, pointed toward one of the bushes. His hand was shaking, she noticed, and his skin was pale, his eyes wide and glassy. Whatever it was, it had scared him badly.

"There's a dead man there," the Honjofu, a broad-shouldered, level-headed warrior named Itami Kane reported. As always, she had her bow in hand, an arrow half-nocked but kept pointed downward, which suggested they were in no immediate danger. Still, Shizumi stayed ready, hand on her nihono, as she trailed Kohori to where the pair had indicated.

Sure enough, they could just make out a figure curled up on the grass, though the shadows did their best to hide him. The Honteno returned carrying a lantern plucked from the path and Shizumi bit back a hiss, fighting not to turn away or empty her stomach at the sight now exposed before her.

It was indeed a man, and he was most certainly dead. He looked as if he had been caught in a fire, his skin blackened, his limbs twisted, his mouth open in a silent scream that showed charred and cracked teeth. He wore a mail shirt and a studded leather cap and a simple chokoto was at his side but still in its sheath, suggesting that whatever had sliced his throat open and nearly severed his head had done so before he could raise a hand in defense. Worst of all, however, was the sheer terror evident on his face—and the empty eye sockets that stared accusingly up at them, as if they were somehow responsible for his death and the theft of his eyes.

Shizumi turned toward Kohori, and the two shared a look filled with a dread understanding. Clearly someone or something had killed this man, in a strange and terrible fashion, here on these grounds, in what was believed to be the most secure place in all Rimbaku. And there was a good chance whoever had done this was still here.

Which meant they had their work cut out for them.

CHAPTER THIRTY-FOUR

"I hate you," the man named Nobu shouted, his meaty hand sweeping out in an arc to slap the cheek of the woman he faced. "I have always hated you. I hate your apathy, your laziness, your unwillingness to lift even a finger for anyone but yourself." All of this was delivered in a near monotone as he struck her again and again, the blows landing about her head and neck and shoulders with great force but no evident emotion, his face as blank as the white marble slab it resembled.

The woman, his wife Uba, bore the blows without flinching, her obsidian-dark features set in a mask of seeming indifference. "I hate you as well," she intoned, striking back with thinner limbs but nearly equal strength. "Your greed, your gluttony, your lust most of all. You disgust me with your blubber and your waddling like some sort of hog, and your belief that masking all that in fine robes somehow makes it acceptable."

They continued to hit each other, all the while ranting about each other's faults in cruel, merciless words that were nonetheless delivered without inflection. It was like watching a pair of matched statues, one white and one black, set to swivel and strike and rebound in a constant ribbon of motion.

Nor were the couple alone in their oddly stilted battle. All around them, others fought—some were husband and wife, some were parent and child, some were friends or partners or merely neighbors. But all of them insulted each other, revealing the deepest and darkest of their thoughts without a hint of emotion. And all of them were as colorless as their voices and their gazes, either bleached a dull white or darkened to a flat black.

Two figures stood out in this strange conflict that gripped the town of Watamoto, as much because they were not engaged in quarrelling as for anything else. For certainly this pair shared the pallid skin of half the villagers, their ragged clothing equally bleached, their hair gray despite their apparent youth. Only their eyes carried darkness, which swirled in their gaze as if tiny thunderstorms constantly danced and blew apart and reformed within their sockets.

Ibaru glanced at Iraku, and the brothers nodded, their arms folded across their narrow chests, just a hint of satisfaction upon their otherwise slack faces. They had entered this town less than an hour before, and as had been the case all throughout their travels they had been met by the town leaders, here the man Nobu and his wife Uba. When asked what their purpose was here, and whether they would take tea and food, the brothers answered with their usual litany: "I am Ibaru," the elder stated. "He is Iraku. And we hunger."

Then they had laid hands upon the townsfolk, and the chaos had begun.

As always, the brothers' master, Kaemusei, lurked overhead, its shifting swirl of faded colors casting a disquieting shadow across the entire town. It had grown larger and stronger with each settlement the brothers had disturbed and driven to madness, and as that had happened it had begun to lengthen the tether binding the boys to it. Before, they had only existed in its shadow, both literally and figuratively, for the light of the sun had burned their eyes and itched at their skin and caused them to cower in fear. Only beneath the Silent Change had they felt safe and cool and numb. Now, however, it had begun ranging ahead once it had sated its hunger on color and emotion and vitality, but the brothers had been able to withstand the light unaided.

They had felt a tug within whenever the Silent moved on, and the farther it drifted ahead the stronger and more painful that pull became, causing their hearts to skip and race and sweat to bead on their pale skin until finally they would break and scamper after it, sighing in relief once they were safely in its shade once more. But for longer and longer periods they were able to stay behind, to watch the destruction they had set into motion.

And, as they gained that endurance, they also began to draw out these conflicts they spawned. The townsfolk they stripped of compassion and kindness and all good thoughts and emotions along with their hues and shades began to take longer to become violent, and more eloquent in their accusations. What had initially been a rapid onset of physical combat, followed by an equally quick fall into decay, was now a slow, drawn-out increase in antagonism and animosity leading to a peak of vicious attack that then tapered off as despair and infirmity set in. Now it could take an entire day for a town to fall apart and crumble into dust and ruin.

The brothers loved every second of it.

When they first encountered the Silent, and it had stripped them not only of color and passion but also of fear and uncertainty, Ibaru and Iraku had existed in a state of calm, their senses sharp but their minds dull and all their emotions gone, leaving only a hollow behind that ached to be filled somehow. That was what they hungered for, the same life and brilliance their master fed upon, and for moments they would feel sated and whole again, only to have that sensation slip away as the stolen emotions passed through them and were gone once more.

After Kaemusei changed, so had their own appetites. They were no longer satisfied with just color and vitality, but those forms of sustenance now required the added ingredient of violence and bloodshed to bind them together and render them digestible. At the same time, the brothers had begun to awaken again mentally, their minds slowly regaining faculty, their thoughts sluggish at first but moving more quickly with each passing day.

And then had come the emotions.

Not all of them had returned, and still there were gaps that left an ache deep inside. But the darker feelings—hatred, rage, jealousy, perverse pleasure at the pain of others—those had welled back up, leaving the brothers still pale as corpses on the outside but dark and twisted rotted fruit within. Feeding those emotions had become what sustained them, what powered them, and so they lingered longer and longer with each town, drinking their fill of their victims' sufferings before finally putting them out of their misery and moving on, the dead strewn in their wake.

So it was now, as Ibaru and Iraku stood and observed how Nobu had just shattered his wife's jaw, while Uba had just raked her long nails across her husband's forehead, eye, and cheek. The Silent Change had drunk its fill of Watamoto's destruction and floated away, but at this moment the brothers felt only the twinge of its presence as an absent limb, rather than the tug of its demand for their return. If they concentrated, they could sense it swirling and shifting in the air well enough to pinpoint its location, even though they could no longer see it on the horizon.

Until it suddenly stopped.

It was as if a windy day had just stilled, the breeze vanishing like an old memory. One second, Kaemusei was as restive as ever, its faded hues cascading within it. The next it went utterly still, as if somehow frozen.

Then it churned into motion once more. Now, however, its inner revolutions were no longer lazy and aimless. Instead they whirled frantically, almost as if those captured colors were attempting to break free.

The Silent began to move again, but now it was not drifting. Instead it coursed forward, gathering speed as it went, the shape of a cloud but the speed and focus of an arrow fired from a heavy bow, arcing high and fast over the plains.

And the brothers felt that tug churn to live within them, building rapidly to an uncomfortable ache, then a sharp stab of agony right through their middles. Their master called, and they had little choice but to obey.

Turning away from the carnage they had instigated, Ibaru and Iraku strode from town, leaving gray-hued Watamoto to battle and eventually crumble behind them. Faster than a horse could run, they loped across the ground, pursuing Kaemusei as it forged on ahead with a startling intensity. Almost as if it had a specific destination in mind.

After several hours at that rapid pace, the brothers finally caught up to their master. It hovered atop a hill, and standing there they could make out the land stretching away below and before them in a gentle, rolling plain. That expanse was first bordered and then bisected by a broad, sparkling river cutting across it from southeast to northwest. The cheerful rush of its fast-moving waters was audible even up here.

On either side of that river the land continued—and there to the left, near the edge of their vision, past a smaller second river, Ibaru and Iraku could just make out a structure rising up from the ground in what appeared to be tiers tinged with the gentle shades of a sunrise.

Seeing it, they knew a sudden, near-crippling burst of hunger the likes of which they had never felt before. And this, they knew, was not their appetites alone, but rather that of the master hanging above them, nearly vibrating in its intensity.

Whatever was in that city, Kaemusei hungered for it.

And the brothers knew they would see the Silent Change fed.

＝PILOGUＥ

Noniki gazed across the Wagata and, beyond that, the Edishu, to where a fabulous tiered city stood in the distance. "Awaihinshi," he whispered. "We made it."

Beside him, Seikoku punched him in the arm. "We are not there yet," she pointed out as he rubbed his sore limb. "Do not tempt the fates by assuming all will go smoothly."

"Fair enough," he admitted with a wince and a laugh. "Still, it is not far from here. We should be there in a few days, if all goes well. A week at most." True, there were two rivers to cross, but neither of them was as massive as the Tonawa, and both saw frequent boat traffic. They would find a way across.

"And then what?" the former thief asked him as the rest of their companions caught up to them and gathered all around. "You still intend to speak to the emperor?"

"I do," Noniki confirmed. "This land is sick, as are our people. He needs to see that, and to find ways to make things better."

"And if he will not?" one of the others asked. "What then?"

Noniki stared at the fabled City of Polished Light, his hands clenching into fists. "Then we will make sure he does."

Kagiri reined in beside the edge of the Tonawa. From here the river was like a massive plain, stretching forward so far that the land beyond was only a thin strip between water and horizon. Still, he was pleased. Awaihinshi sat before them, the colors if its tiered walls clearly distinguishable even from this distance.

To his side and a few paces behind, Kishin Narai stirred and coughed to announce himself. "We will find a boat to ferry us across," the merchant stated, though there was deference and a question even in that announcement. "Or perhaps several boats." Their caravan had continued to grow as they traveled to the edge of Hochiro, and they were now some twenty wagons strong.

Kagiri nodded, not bothering to glance around, and after a moment he sensed that Narai had retreated. Good. He continued to stare out across the water, at the city the First Emperor had built and that every Emperor had ruled from since.

"A fine city," Geido Shinen commented. "I look forward to exploring it."

"You look forward to drinking it dry," Onyoku Jeizen corrected, though with a laugh in his voice.

"It is a fitting residence for an emperor," Nikiyu Sinchu opined, not negative for once.

"It is," the rest of the Gensaiba agreed.

So did Kagiri. And he knew what they were thinking beyond that—and agreed with that as well.

It would make him an excellent home, once he had conquered it.

Almost, he pitied anyone foolish enough to stand in his way.

END OF BOOK TWO

GLOSSARY

Adai: a kind of soup broth, made from seaweed, dried fish flakes, mushrooms, and water

Ahaiinko: a formal stamp of office used to sign official documents

Aiashe: "foot bone," a foot soldier in Rimbaku's army, typically garbed in maikiro, hanketo, suneoto, and jingaso and armed with yanoi and chokoto

Aikaye: "sea bone," a sailor-warrior in Rimbaku's navy

Aio-akeo: a riverboat that runs the channel between Tabichi and Iwikaru

Aishone: relic bones

Aisho Hasume: Bone Collectors, a group of Buddhist-like traveling priests who wear the skulls and bones of their revered teachers dangling from their belts.

Aitachi: The Relicant Touch, the ability to absorb ancestral memories, skills, and knowledge by touching or consuming objects or people from the past

Akatai: family or household demons; malevolent ancestral spirits

Aragei: chicken that has been chopped into chunks and fried

Atorido: a traditional hanging lantern with four or six sides

Atuma-yio: sweet potato

Awaihinshi: The City of Polished Light, the marble capital of Rimbaku. Divided into six tiers (one for each level of the soul), with a shanty town/slum (Suranmui) at the bottom outside the walls and the emperor's palace at the top. Each tier has an outer wall of a different shade of marble, growing lighter in shade witch each height, from black to white. The tiers are:
One: Aihiri, the Imperial compound at the very top. Walls of purest white marble.

Two: Atsani, where the Daijin and other important nobles live—and home to Sorainasei, the first "town" in Awaihinshi. Walls of palest yellow.

Three: Motohiri, where the most influential merchants and the minor nobles live. Walls of peach.

Four: Sakiriti, mid- to lesser merchants and the most important artisans. Walls of the hue of cherry blossoms (a pale rose).

Five: Bejinuri. Other artisans and craftsmen. Walls of pale violet (red wisteria).

Six: Mazihini, laborers and other menials. The walls surrounding this level are pale blue like water, and the outer walls of the city as a whole.

Bakiro: a bag, typically a large bag used for carrying one's personal items and equipment

Banezhan: a cylindrical ring worn on the thumb when using a bow, most often made of bone, ivory, horn, or jade.

Bannin: guards, watchmen

Baraken: a wooden practice sword, typically made of either teak or bamboo

Bezenkai: a southern province

Birabiro: a town in Korito, closest to the Fyushan-Rimbakan border

Botetsu: a little village in Yunigiri

Buhiyo: a mayor, responsible for a town or small city

Burahone: the Bone Blind. These women's aitachi is so strong they are constantly overwhelmed by memories and knowledge, drawing it from the very elements around them.

Chahito: the pommel or endcap of a sword

Chasai: symbolic baton, typically of lacquered wood with metal caps at both ends and a tassel at one.

Chayaburi: a small, fast sailboat

Chinbiro: a town in Korito, near Birabiro

Chituju: a house steward

Chohu: a prosperous merchant house specializing in gemstones

Chokoto: a straight-edged sword with a ring pommel

Chonmage: a hair bun, particularly favored by warriors

Chosinichi: A "reservoir," someone who can hold absorbed skills for a long time

Chunsin-inori: a full feast, served in three courses, each on its own tray

Cuioburi: the smallest class of military boat, most often used for patrols and search missions

Darakada: "body thief," a sorcerer whose magic allows him to steal another's face and form

Dayabei: the seventh and final day of a sihu, often a rest day

Deo: a breastplate or cuirass, part of a suit of armor

Dobuichi: "animal-touched," those who use their aitachi on animal bones instead of human ones

Dojo Kuge: artistocratic bureaucrats

Doh Bridge: a wide bridge spanning the Zinyang River and connecting Obanari to Hochiro

Edishu River: a small river running from the Tonawa west to the ocean. Awaihinshi sits beside it.

Essa: a doctor.

Esuge: the Rimbakan cedar, the most commonly used wood in the land

Eioha: a form of dumpling

Eikono: a formal outer robe with a round collar, wide sleeves, a long tail, and sewn sides

Enwara: a small town in Bezenkai, south of Ginzai

Eto-riantzu: a large wheeled cart with sliding front doors

Ferume: an inkbrush, used for writing

Fumisoni: a style of kisoni, the most elaborate and formal, with long, wide sleeves

Furotingawa: "floating tower", a legendary tower, long since in ruins, at the southern edge of Rimbaku, near the mouth of a river

Furukotai: the largest town in Korito, home to the regional governor

Fyushu: a rival nation to Rimbaku's north, constantly testing the borders. Symbol: a black gauntlet clenched in a fist.

Ganabo: a massive two-handed war club, usually spiked or studded

Gensaiba: "Living blades," legendary warriors of mythic ability

Ginzai: the nearest large town to the brothers' home

Goji: a folding stool most often used by men in full armor

Gotaiburi: a large, multi-masted boat designed to carry troops

Guisuke bitte: a chest for holding one's armor

Guisuke kai: a stylized stand for displaying armor, usually set atop a guisuke bitte

Haidoto: thigh guards, part of a suit of armor

Hakami: close-fitting pants, often worn under armor

Hakara Ikibanichi: the Brothers of Many Spirits, a monastic order

Hanketo: armored gauntlets

Hantien: a short, padded winter coat

Happoa Kappua: "The Foamy Cup." A tavern in Ginzai

Hakichuekai: a small, brightly colored bird, known for its trilling and its sociability

Heioki: fried octopus balls

Higeibara: the red spider lily, the official crest of Rimbaku

Higinasi: a nation bordering Rimbaku to the southwest. Symbol: a stylized blue wave

Himsu: a town in Hochiro

Hiromura: a small village in Bezenkai

Honjofu: "Bone warrior," Rimbaku's elite military unit. Clad all in black armor.

Honteno: "Emperor's bones," the Rimbaku Imperial Guard. Clad all in red armor.

Horohaba: a lost city of Ritakhou, known as the "City of Beasts" for its renowned menagerie

Hosode: an undershirt, usually plain and unbleached and typically of silk.

Hozaiburi: a large, heavy warship.

Iematsu: the red pine tree, often used for beams and posts

Ikibanichari: Castle of Many Spirits, the mountain monastery of the Hakara Ikibanichi

Iniro: a small, segmented box worn at the belt to hold small items, often beautifully carved and detailed

Irogaso: a circular bamboo hat

Irohito: a small town strategically located at the intersection of the Tonawa and Edishu rivers, guarding the way to Awaihinshi

Ishtaya: a tailor or seamstress

Itoyako: the lily of the valley, known for its soft, drooping petals that shade from white to pink

Ittei: a blunt iron rod with a wrapped handle and a hooked tine just above that, used by guards when they were not allowed to carry swords

Jagimato: a town in Saruto, between the Wagata and Edishu rivers

Jigekugi: lesser bureaucrats, the lowest rank of nobility

Jingaso: a conical iron helm, worn by the aiashe

Jogoturi: "Lords of the Street," a gang in Ginzai

Jubanichi: The "perfect touch"—someone who absorbs quickly and holds for a long time

Kaemusei: "the Silent Change" or "The Silent," a magical being of limitless hunger

Kanashi: a hair stick

Kaoni: a hip- or mid-thigh-length open coat with long, wide sleeves, worn over a kitoro

Karo: a regional governor, who reports to the Emperor

Karute: a helmet, usually with a menatu attached in front and one or more modato above

Kazure: iron plates hanging from the front and back of the deo to protect the pelvis and upper leg

Kenroichi: A solid touch, someone who can absorb decently and hold it decently

Kibango: small sweet dumplings made from rice flour

Kindichi: bosses or kings

Kisoni: A loose robe, wider and looser than a kitoro, that can be worn as either an undergarment or an outer layer.

Kitoro: a silk outer garment, like a wide-sleeved robe, usually decorated.

Koshitsu: a graverobber

Kosshiki: "the Bone Spirit," sword of the Relicant Emperor

Kogotano: a small utility knife, often found in a small channel carved out of a sword scabbard, or in a writing set

Kotone: baby bird

Kune mato: a merchant's safe, usually made of metal or thick wood and with several locks.

Magojifu: a small town in Bezenkai, between Ginzai and the Rumiri river.

Maikiro: a war vest of lacquered plates on a cotton backing, secured by cotton straps, worn by aiashe. Smaller plates hang from the front and sides to protect the groin and thighs.

Mamusha: a large, deadly snake, very aggressive

Matoyan: a small hunting village up in the mountains between Rimbaku and Yatamoro

Matekai: a wizard or wizards.

Megaita: a green tea made with roasted brown rice

Menatu: a warrior's face mask, made of metal and hooked onto or tied to a karute

Modato: a crest affixed to the top of a karute

Mosi: an inkstick, made of soot and animal glue, ground down and mixed with water to create ink

Mukanichi: An "untouched," someone who can't really absorb at all, the lowest of all people

Muraito: A larger town or small city not far above Ginzai, on the southern edge of a mid-sized lake

Nahiya: a townhouse, usually two or three stories tall, with separate apartments on each floor

Naritaba: a pole weapon, a wooden or metal shaft with a curved single-edge blade at the end. The blades were forged in the same way as nihono. Often used by mounted warriors, and by women warriors.

Nafti: a fruit, round and juicy, with mottled green and gold skin and crisp white flesh.

Nigasi: a dry, pressed sweet made of sugar and rice flour.

Nihono: a long sword with a curved, single-edged blade, carried by nobles and elite warriors in Rimbaku

Nizukai: a mythic water dragon, daughter of the sea god Satumasu, "king of all waters"

Nodaki: a "field sword," a longer, heavier nihono typically used against cavalry

Okube: a traditional sash-style belt worn around the waist, particularly with a kitoro

Onokura: a small village in Miniri, near the south end of the river that separates Nariyari and Bezenkai

Otainui: housekeeper or household manager

Otomi: a small fishing village on the shores of the Wagata

Pokanu: a type of bird, tall and ostentatious, with bright and luxurious tail feathers

Ponmei: loose cotton pants with a drawstring tie and tapered ankles.

Quisuin: a poisonous snake

Raeteru: the common tree frog

Rajo: purple yams

Rakawa: a small village in Bezenkai

Riantzu: a traditional portable storage chest, usually made with no nails, screws, or adhesive

Rimbaku: "land made barren from cursed magic," the land after the Schism

Ritakhou: "land rich with blessed magic," the land before the Schism

Rojiri: counselors to the emperor

Rumiri River: the wide river that runs north-south through Miniri, connecting the Tonawa to Rimbaku's southern coastline. It is the dividing line between Bezenkai and Nariyari.

Saisaihyu: a ten-day period of purification and contemplation. During this time, everyone is expected to not allow any outside influence—including the use of aishone.

Sashiko: a style of patching clothing, often in a pattern

Sehiro: a steaming basket, usually woven out of bamboo

Senkuniki: ancestral spirits—typically akatai are considered the darker, more malevolent ancestral spirits, while senkuniki are those more inclined toward benevolence

Senkousa: a Bone Reader. These women have strong aitachi and can actually "read" aishone, telling what memories and knowledge and skills each bones possesses.

Senoha-a: a plant, whose name means "Mother of Thousands." Often seen in gardens and homes but highly poisonous, particularly the flowers.

Shakomi: a town in Bezenkai, a little north of Ginzai

Shatage: a shirt, generally thicker than a hosode and dyed or lightly embroidered or both.

Shugiri daimyo: grand nobles, closest to the emperor in status and power

Shugodiri: lesser nobles

Sihu: week

Sokuichi: A "crude touch" or "rough touch," someone who doesn't absorb easily and needs a lot of material to absorb anything

Sorhu: a wide scarf or shawl, either silk (for milder weather) or wool (for cooler weather)

Subayaki: a species of flower, also called the common camellia, related to the tea plant and to the tsodami but less vibrant in color. Its seeds are pressed to produce Subayaki oil, which can be used for skin care and hair care.

Suneoto: armored shin guards

Suponichi: A "sponge," someone who absorbs quickly

Suzeri: an inkstone, used like a small mortar to grind mosi so that it could be mixed with water to create ink

Suzeri kabo: "inkstone box" or writing box, which held the implements and utensils needed for writing.

Taikamage: a vertical hair bun, clean and elegant, with the hair piled up on top of the head and secured by a front comb and, if necessary, several kanashi

Takaneburi: a long, narrow, flat-bottomed boat mostly used on rivers to ferry freight.

Takotsu Hakara: Home of Brotherhood, the mountain monastery of the Hakara Ikibanichi

Tanakia: a wild animal, essentially a racoon dog, rumored to be able to shape-change to human form

Tanu: a modular set of trunks and cabinets, usually arranged in a stepped pattern.

Tawasiri: the Tower of Ghosts, an ancient tower at the southeast tip of Rimbaku, long since abandoned and believed to be haunted. Originally the meeting place of the matekai of Ritakhou.

Tayomi: a traditional flooring made from compressed rice straws tightly bound together and covered with woven straw

Tehuya: the guard on a nihono, roughly disc-shaped

Tienbao: a rice paddy, typically one tien in size (approximately 3200 square feet)

Tokimichi: A "flutter touch," someone who can't hold the absorbed skills for long

Tonawa River: a major river that branches off from the Zinyang and runs south along the eastern edge of Saruto before turning southeast and then east and separating Hochiro above from Bezenkai and Nariyari below.

Torito: rough hemp work trousers with a drawstring tie and tapered ankles, often paired with a hantien

Tsao: a boat hook

Tsekuri: rice wine

Tsodami: the red camellia, the royal flower

Tsukifuko: the Moon of Lawlessness, a month during which no rules or laws apply

Tsurogo: a double-edged nihono

Tukaiono: pickled vegetables and tubers, such as radish

Ujiro: A favorite dessert in Awaihinshi, a steamed cake made from rice, water, and sugar, done in a variety of flavors.

Umi: a long bow, made of laminated wood, bamboo, and leather and typically taller than a grown man, with the upper half twice as long as the lower.

Uridon: a thick rice noodle, often used in soup

Urigani: the art of folding paper into shapes, particularly animals

Utume: the art of packaging, particularly by wrapping an object in carefully chosen layers of paper

Uzumoya: A covered pavilion.

Wagata River: a tributary of the Tonawa that splits off to the west as the Tonawa continues north past Awaihinshi. The Wagata forms the southern border of Saruto.

Wara: a sturdy straw bag traditionally used to hold rice. A full wara provides enough rice to feed two people for one year.

Watamato: a small town in northern Bezenkai, not far below the Wagata River.

Yanoi: straight-bladed spear.

Yanokai: Rimbakan cypress, very durable and water-resistant

Yatamoro: the kingdom neighboring Rimbaku to the east, across the mountains. Symbol: a winged serpent reared back, ready to strike. Ruled by a High Council.

Yori-toki: a dagger with a thick blade made for armor-piercing. Often worn in conjunction with a nihono.

Yoto: the small river that runs through Ginzai

Yudishu: a small town in Nariyari, headquarters of the Kindichi

Yue Judei: "Good Times," a zaihaya in Bejinuri, in Awaihinshi

Zaihaya: a tavern or pub, a casual place where people can go to drink together

Zinyang River: the "Central River," the large river that runs east-west across Rimbaku right through the center of Chibiri, separating Hochiro and Saruto to the south from Obanari and Yunigiri to the north.

Rimbaku is divided into four regions: Kitini (north), (Chibiri) central, Miniri (south), and (Shitimi) island. Within each region are two or more provinces. They are:

Kitini:

- Tabichi (northwest region, bordering Fyushu above and the ocean to the west)
- Korito (northeast region, bordering Fyushu above and Yatamaro to the east)

Chibiri:

- Yunigiri (northwest, bordering the ocean)
- Obanari (northeast, bordering Yatamaro to the east)
- Hochiro (southern band, bordering Yatamaro to the east)
- Saruto (the capital region, with the ocean on one side and the southern band on the other)

Miniri:

- Bezenkai (southwest, bordering the ocean)
- Nariyari (southeast, bordering Higinasi to the west)

Shitimi:

- Iwikaru (the northern island)
- Tatsuma (the southern island)

Rimbaku is roughly 1200 miles wide by 2000 miles long, or 2,400,000 square miles total area.

Military groupings, smallest to largest:

Bantao -> Squad (4-10)

Shotao -> Platoon or troop (2-4 squads, 16-40)

Chotao -> Company (2-4 platoons, 60-160)

Dantao -> Battalion (4-6 companies, 300-900)

Reitao -> Regiment (2-4 battalions, 600-2000)

Tyodao -> Brigade (3-6 battalions, 1000-3000)

Sudao -> Division (3 or more brigades or regiments, 3k-6k)

Gaodao -> Corps (2 or more divisions, 25-50k)

Gyunao -> Army (2 or more corps, 100k-150k)

Gyunshadao -> Army Group (2 or more armies)

Chukogao -> Regional Theater (the entire military force in a region)

Sanseidao -> Front (the entire military force in a war)

Military ranks:

Sotaisho: commander-in-chief, usually the Emperor himself

[Karo: military governor]

Dogenriku: Lord General, the field marshal (in charge of tactics, fills in for the Emperor on the battlefield if he is not present)

Taisho: general

Issa: colonel

Chusa: lieutenant colonel

Shosa: major

Taisu: captain

Chuisu: lieutenant

Shosu: junior lieutenant

Gunso: Sergeant

Gocho: Corporal

Naval ranks:
    Dogenkaishu: Lord Admiral
    Kagono: admiral
    Kagusho: vice-admiral
    Daiso: captain
    Kumigashi: commander
    Kogashiri: lieutenant commander
    Chudai: lieutenant

Special units:
    Taikoro: Lord Commander, in charge of an entire elite force (like the Honjofu or the Honteno)
    Chuisu: lieutenant, can command a chotao
    Gunso: sergeant, can command a shotao
    Gocho: corporal, can command a bantao

ABOUT THE AUTHOR

AARON ROSENBERG is the best-selling, award-winning author of over 50 novels, including the Twin Cities Cryptids urban fantasy/cozy series, the DuckBob SF comedy series, the Relicant Chronicles epic fantasy series, the Areyat Islands fantasy pirate mystery series, the upcoming BEO Reports urban fantasy series, and, with David Niall Wilson, the O.C.L.T. occult thriller series. His tie-in work contains novels for *Star Trek*, *Warhammer*, *World of WarCraft*, *Stargate: Atlantis*, *Shadowrun*, *Mutants & Masterminds*, and *Eureka* and short stories for *The X-Files*, World of Darkness, *Crusader Kings II*, *Deadlands*, *Master of Orion*, and *Europa Universalis IV*. He has written children's books (including the original series STEM Squad and Pete and Penny's Pizza Puzzles, the award-winning *Bandslam: The Junior Novel* and the #1 best-selling *42: The Jackie Robinson Story*), educational books, and role-playing games (including the original games *Asylum*, *Spookshow*, and *Chosen*; work for White Wolf, Wizards of the Coast, Fantasy Flight, Pinnacle, and many others; the Origins Award-winning *Gamemastering Secrets*; and the Gold ENnie-winning *Lure of the Lich Lord*). He is a founding member of Crazy 8 Press. Aaron lives in New York with his family. You can follow him online at gryphonrose.com, on Facebook at facebook.com/gryphonrose, on BSky at @gryphonrose.bsky.social, on Instagram at the_gryphonrose, and on X (formerly known as Twitter) @gryphonrose.

PIRACY, MYSTERY, & ADVENTURE

awaits a pair of...brothers?

ELDROS LEGACY
DEADLY FORTUNE
THE AREYAT ISLES
AARON R...

ELDROS LEGACY
STEALING THE STORM
THE AREYAT ISLES, Book
AARON ROSE...

ELDROS LEGACY
THE FATED BLADE
THE AREYAT ISLES, BOOK 3
AARON ROSENBERG

Sundra is a prince running for his life.
Ruhi is a young woman disguised
in order to seek her freedom.
When they are captured by pirates,
they claim to be brothers.
Now the pair has to navigate cruel masters,
mysterious murders, missing mages,
vicious feuds, and violent storms.
But at least they have each other.